Chasing Bliss

Other Books by Lexi Blake

Lost in You
Long Lost
No Love Lost, Coming September 29, 2020

Butterfly Bayou
Butterfly Bayou, Coming May 5, 2020
Bayou Baby, Coming August 25, 2020

Lawless
Ruthless
Satisfaction
Revenge

Courting Justice
Order of Protection
Evidence of Desire

Masters Of Ménage (by Shayla Black and Lexi Blake)
Their Virgin Captive
Their Virgin's Secret
Their Virgin Concubine
Their Virgin Princess
Their Virgin Hostage
Their Virgin Secretary
Their Virgin Mistress

The Perfect Gentlemen (by Shayla Black and Lexi Blake)
Scandal Never Sleeps
Seduction in Session
Big Easy Temptation
Smoke and Sin
At the Pleasure of the President

URBAN FANTASY
Thieves
Steal the Light
Steal the Day
Steal the Moon
Steal the Sun
Steal the Night

Ripper
Addict
Sleeper
Outcast
Stealing Summer, Coming soon

LEXI BLAKE WRITING AS SOPHIE OAK
Texas Sirens
Small Town Siren
Siren in the City
Siren Enslaved
Siren Beloved
Siren in Waiting
Siren in Bloom
Siren Unleashed
Siren Reborn

Nights in Bliss, Colorado
Three to Ride
Two to Love
One to Keep
Lost in Bliss
Found in Bliss
Pure Bliss
Chasing Bliss
Once Upon a Time in Bliss
Back in Bliss
Sirens in Bliss

A Faery Story
Bound
Beast
Beauty

Standalone
Away From Me
Snowed In

Chasing Bliss

Nights in Bliss, Colorado Book 7

Lexi Blake
writing as
Sophie Oak

Chasing Bliss
Nights in Bliss, Colorado Book 7

Published by DLZ Entertainment LLC

Copyright 2019 DLZ Entertainment LLC
Edited by Chloe Vale
ISBN: 978-1-942297-14-7

Sign up for Lexi Blake's newsletter
and be entered to win a $25 gift certificate
to the bookseller of your choice.

Join us for news, fun, and exclusive content
including free short stories.

There's a new contest every month!

Go to www.LexiBlake.net to subscribe.

Dedication 2012

For new friends, old friends, and friends we have yet to meet.

Dedication 2019

The dedication above holds true in any year, but I feel like I find something new each time I revisit these books. Bliss has always been a town for misfits and no one is more of a misfit than Gemma Wells. I don't always see until years later, but each of these books holds a piece of me. Gemma is the me who wore a business suit to high school. It was one I found at a deep-discount store, the type where they sell clothes with defects. I remember it was a vivid blue and I wore it because I didn't want anyone to see me as that kid who didn't have a dime, the one who was homeless for a while. I wanted to be the smartest of the smart, the one with a future, and at the time I thought that meant getting everyone to take me seriously. What I was really trying to do was rise above my beginnings. It's funny now. We're so very rigid and judgmental in our youth. We see things in black and white, never understanding the beautiful potential in the grays. So this is dedicated to my sixteen-year-old self. You will not become the journalist you think you want to be. You will not conquer the world. You will not be rich beyond your wildest dreams. What you will find is so much more. You will find love. You will have three beautiful and complicated children. You will be afraid and anxious at times, but you will not be alone. You will find people who fill your soul.

You will find bliss.

Prologue

New York City

Gemma took a deep breath as she slid the key into the door. It had taken way less time to get the motions done and filed than she'd originally thought. They were now up to date on the case, and Patrick would be able to dazzle the partners. She'd told Patrick she would be gone all night. Now she could surprise him with both a brilliant presentation—guaranteed to get her the promotion she'd deserved for the last two years—and her own dark desires. She was going to talk to him, make him understand what she wanted to try.

Hey, a guy should like a little kink in his future bride, right?

She, Gemma Wells, was freaky, and she was tired of hiding it. She needed to walk up to Patrick and find out if this thing would honestly work.

"Pat?" She set down her briefcase, a Chanel bag she'd scrimped and saved for. It was big enough to carry everything. Her laptop. The files she needed. The two thumb drives she kept on her at all times because she had to download Patrick's work or he lost it. That bag was a gateway to her future, which was bright, so bright. It had to be. She was trying to follow the old "look successful, be successful" law. "I'm home, babe."

She turned on the light, illuminating the tiny, perfectly decorated living room. For Manhattan it was livable, but she'd been raised by hippies who spent way too much time at outdoor concerts. She was pretty sure she'd been conceived to a Phish song. The place felt cramped. Sometimes she felt like she couldn't breathe, but this was the place to be, so she was here.

Gemma stretched and thought about taking off the silk shirt she was wearing. It was confining and she was always worried she would wrinkle it, but it was designer and appearances were everything. Patrick had taught her that.

She sighed. Was he already asleep? He tended to be a night owl. Maybe she should have gone back to her place, but Patrick's was damn near perfect. She should know. She'd been the one to work with the designer. She'd hitched her wagon to Patrick's three years before, and she hadn't let up. Not when he'd been promoted over her. Not when he'd taken credit for her work. They were a team. She would get her reward in the end.

The only trouble was she was starting to wonder if she should marry him.

She kicked off her Jimmy Choos. The shoes were gorgeous, but god, they hurt after twelve hours. Even as tired as she was, her heart was pounding a bit. She needed to know.

Patrick would either be in or she would have some serious thinking to do.

She walked to his bedroom door, building her courage. Up until now, their sex life had been harried and a bit circumspect. She wasn't entirely sure what he would say when she told him what she wanted.

There was a large mirror on the wall outside the bedroom door. She caught a glimpse of herself. She wasn't unattractive. She was fashionably slender, with a chic blonde bob she'd paid a fortune for. Sure, she'd always preferred her hair longer and less platinum, but this was truly professional looking. And her makeup was flawless. She was a designer version of the girl who had grown up eating tofu and listening to lectures on being cruelty free. There was no such thing. The world was cruel, and it paid to understand that fact of life.

Smoothing down her hair, she made sure she looked cosmetically perfect. It was hard to forget that Patrick had mentioned only two days ago that a lot of women her age were already getting Botox. It wasn't bad. Not yet. Just a few lines. *Shit*. Maybe she should get a bit. Just in between her eyes.

Deep breath. She would walk in and wake him up in a very sexy way, and then she would say... *Fuck*. What would she say?

"Patrick, I want you to see a sex therapist with me. I've been reading a lot about the power exchange in the bedroom, and I think we should explore it. I found a therapist who is kink friendly, and I'm going to make an appointment for us." There. That was perfectly reasonable. And when he asked what she meant? "I would like for you to take command of me in the bedroom."

Since everyone thinks you have command of me professionally, when we both know I tell you what to do, say, and wear. Since we both damn well know that you couldn't get your head out of your own hot ass long enough to have an actual professional thought, it might be nice for you to take charge somewhere.

Yeah. She wasn't going to say that last part. She wouldn't say it out loud, but it was definitely implied.

She unbuttoned the top two buttons of her Marc Jacobs blouse. If this worked out, maybe she could move in. He'd said he wanted to wait for the wedding, but that was old fashioned. And impractical. It was time they behaved like the two-income, upwardly mobile couple they were. And she wouldn't mind leaving her craptastic, roach motel studio behind.

She was going to be successful. She was going to get what she wanted because she had worked her ass off and gone to the right schools and made all the right moves. She'd picked the right man to marry because he had a plan, too. Eventually, after their careers were fully set, they would have perfectly planned children. Yes. Willpower was all that was needed.

She put a hand on the door and then heard a squeak.

And a moan. And that huffing noise Patrick made when he was either working out or having sex. And Patrick didn't like to work out. She had to force him to get on the high-tech treadmill they'd bought together but kept at his place, as they did with almost every expensive purchase.

So if he wasn't exercising, he better be masturbating.

Gemma opened the door and felt her blood pressure go straight through the roof. The hallway was dark enough that neither of the two figures on the bed seemed to notice they were no longer alone. Patrick groaned and his naked ass clenched as he came and then immediately rolled off his partner.

"That was nice." He was using his sex voice, a low growl that reminded her of a house cat with a head cold. "You're quite good, Christina."

Christina? Christina Schiller? The dumbass, just-out-of-law-school brunette with the overblown fake tits and the faker brain? She'd graduated from some Podunk college on the West Coast more known for churning out film editors than lawyers. She'd gotten hired because the partners thought she was hot and her dad was loaded. Everyone knew that.

"That's junior partner Christina to you," she purred. There was a slight pause and a rustling of sheets. "Have you told her yet? I want to make the announcement soon."

Patrick groaned, though this one had nothing to do with sex. It was the sound he made when someone wanted him to do something he didn't want to do. "Babe, you know I need a day or two. We have the presentation on the Tremon Industries trial coming up. I need her to do all that research shit for me. And you know no one writes an opening argument like Gemma."

Yep. That was what she'd been doing. She'd been up all night working while he was fucking Christina Big Tits, and apparently promising her Gemma's job. There was an odd thumping in her chest and she realized it was her freaking heart. She could actually feel it pounding. She knew she should move, but her feet felt stuck to the floor. This couldn't be happening. She'd worked her ass off. She was smarter than either one of the people in that bed.

A self-satisfied laugh came from Christina's throat. "Well, luckily my father has more money than god. As soon as I get that junior partnership, Giles and Knoxbury gets the representation contract for Daddy's film company. And you get me."

"Yeah. Maybe you should tell her," Patrick said nervously. "She's already like put down money for the wedding and stuff. I put her off as long as I could, but she put down ten grand to reserve some hotel for the wedding."

Nonrefundable. That deposit was nonrefundable, as was the designer wedding dress she'd nearly killed two women over at a bridal gown sale. She still had a scar on her forearm over that dress.

Her stomach took a nosedive. She'd been an idiot. She'd worked ninety-hour weeks, slaving over reports and evidence and filing briefs. And her promotion was going to a woman who spent more time on her nails than her work.

"I'm allowing you to head Daddy's legal team. You can get rid of the idiot blonde." Christina let out a long sigh. "And I want her fired. I don't want to have to look at your ex-fiancée every day."

Patrick's voice came out on a whine. She hated that whine. "Babe, I can't fire her. She's done nothing to get herself fired. She's smart as hell. Do you think she couldn't come up with a lawsuit? She was top of her class at Harvard. She's honestly kind of slumming here."

She wasn't slumming. She was where she wanted to be. She'd decided long ago that she would conquer Manhattan.

Except she wasn't conquering anything. She'd been chasing some fucking dream she'd had at the age of eight, and all she had to show for it was a going-nowhere job and a lying weasel of a fiancé.

She wasn't sure how it happened. One minute she was standing there, listening to them talk about how easily she'd been fooled, with Patrick arguing that they should use her a little longer, and the next she was being arrested by New York's finest and hauled out of one of Midtown's nicer apartment buildings, a good-sized chunk of Christina Big Tits' stylish brown hair still clutched in her palm.

"Sweetheart, you're going to have to get in the car now." The cop gave her a sympathetic nod toward the squad car.

Her vision still seemed hazy. Red. Everything had been red for a while. Reality rushed in on her. She was being arrested and her future was gone. And all she could think of was her damn bag. She wanted her bag.

"My purse?"

The cop's partner, a solid woman, held up the bag. "I have it, honey. I'll take care of it until you go through processing. Do you have someone you could call?"

They had been sympathetic after they'd managed to pull her off Christina and had the whole story. Cops, it seemed, sometimes got the shaft, too.

Who could she call? God. She couldn't call anyone at the law firm. Everyone hated her. She'd been kind of a bitch because it was the only way to get taken seriously. She had no friends. She had no fiancé. She only had one person in the entire world who might care that she was in trouble.

"My mom." Tears started to fall. How was she going to tell her mother she'd ruined everything?

* * * *

Tallahassee, Florida

Jesse McCann looked over the map. They had days of open road ahead of them. No one but him and Cade. Normally he would be looking forward to the trip. It wouldn't be the first time they'd jumped on the backs of their custom-built bikes and spent weeks exploring the country and picking up women.

They wouldn't be doing that this time.

This trip wasn't about fun times with the man he thought of as his brother. This trip was about revenge.

Cade strode in, stuffing a gun into his backpack. They had spent the last year learning what they needed to know. They'd learned how to track a man, and they'd damn straight learned how to kill one.

"You ready?" Cade glanced up, a dark look in his eyes. Guilt weighed heavily on his face. Jesse would never forget the dark hole Cade slipped into when they'd learned how their foster mother had died. Cade had been with their mother the longest. Jesse had only had five years with Nancy Gibbs. Cade had come to their foster mother when he'd been barely nine. Cade lived with her longer than his own mom.

Maybe if Jesse had spent more time with Nancy Gibbs, he wouldn't have a juvenile rap sheet a mile long.

He hoped he didn't get an actual adult arrest when they finally took down the man who had caused his foster mother's death. It didn't matter. One way or another, Christian Grady would pay for what he'd done.

"I'm ready." Jesse had been ready from the moment he realized that Christian Grady was responsible for Nancy Gibbs's misery and her eventual death. Grady had bilked an elderly lady out of her life savings and left her to die in a rat-infested nursing home. Guilt burned in his gut. He'd been partying with Cade while she was dying. He'd called every other day, but he should have visited. He should have made sure. He should have fucking stayed at home and taken care of her.

And his heartache was nothing compared to what Cade must be feeling. Cade didn't know it, but Jesse had figured out his foster brother's past long ago. He'd heard Cade's nightmares. He'd put together the puzzle. What had happened to Nancy Gibbs differed vastly from the way Cade's parents and sister had died, but the guilt would feel the same. Cade's face was bleak as he pulled his gloves on.

"Stop it." Cade stared at him, a frown on his face. "I know what you're thinking. We didn't kill her. Grady did, and Hope McLean is going to lead us straight to him."

Cade nodded but didn't reply. It wasn't anything they hadn't gone over a hundred times. He hoped Cade actually listened to logic this time. They needed to concentrate on the plan. Christian Grady wasn't dead, though he wanted the world to believe he was. They knew damn well he was alive, and he couldn't be allowed to get away with what he'd done. They would use the man's wife to lead them to him. Eventually Grady would figure out Hope McLean was living in Bliss, Colorado, so Bliss, Colorado, was going to be their home for a while.

They had jobs. They had a place to live. They had a plan.

He climbed on the back of his bike and slid a long look at his best friend. He couldn't imagine what he would have done if he hadn't met Cade Sinclair. Died, he suspected. Gone to jail. Something bad. Cade might be fucked-up beyond all recognition, but Jesse meant to stand beside him. Cade had taught him that there was something more important than himself. Family. Family was everything. Not blood.

Blood didn't make a family. Commitment did. Love did. Cade was his brother.

"What do we do after this?" Jesse asked.

Cade sighed, the sound deep and low in his chest. "I don't know, man. I guess we come back to Florida and try to start our lives."

Jesse nodded and gunned the engine. He wasn't sure where the hell his life was going, but he knew one thing. Wherever the road took him, it was going to go through Bliss.

Cade took off, his bike revving before he hit the road. Jesse did what he'd done for the last ten years. He followed his brother and hoped for the best.

Chapter One

Bliss, Colorado
Six months later

"So let me get this straight, Miss Wells. In the week you've been in Bliss, you've had and lost two jobs."

Yep, she was on a roll. "Stella hasn't actually fired me yet."

But she would. Oh, there was no doubt in Gemma's mind that the firing would come. Waitresses weren't allowed to use Tasers on the patrons of the café. It might not have been on her employment form, but it was one of those universal things. There was also the fact that she'd been forced to leave her shift after the sheriff arrested her. She was sitting in jail in a crapass small town. Her life might have finally hit rock bottom. She'd thought she'd made it there before, but it turned out the sinkhole she was in was deeper than she'd imagined.

"She will fire you." Nathan Wright looked every inch the lawman in a khaki uniform that clung to his well-formed torso. He leaned against the gate of her small prison cell, looking perfectly comfortable conducting the interview with bars between them.

"I suspect so." And then the guy she'd Tased would sue the hell out of her. He wouldn't get anything. She could sell her collection of shoes and handbags, but everything else was gone. And he would pry her coffeemaker out of her cold, dead hands. She looked out and the deputy was currently using his overly large paws to go through her Chanel bag.

"You find anything, Cam?" Wright didn't bother looking back. He kept his eyes steady on her.

"She's got a stun gun, pepper spray, what looks like a rape whistle, an EpiPen, more pepper spray." The deputy shook his head as he pulled out a small air horn. "Why?"

She sighed. She didn't particularly want to answer a ton of questions, but the deputy was almost too hot to resist. Deputy Cameron Briggs looked like he ought to be playing linebacker for a pro team. "I'm allergic to strawberries, hence the emergency dose of epinephrine I carry around in case of random strawberry attacks, and one of the pepper sprays is my backup. The air horn is for bears. And it's a Taser."

What could she say? As her old law school teacher used to say, prior planning prevented a piss-poor performance, and she was kind of scared of bears.

Briggs held up the small device that had already gotten her in trouble. "This is a stun gun. A Taser has darts."

She shook her head. "Nope. I call it a Taser. It sounds better. Hey, I stunned gunned a dude doesn't have the same ring as I tased his ass. You say potato and all."

The sheriff frowned. "That is not right at all."

She shrugged. She didn't care about some textbook definition. People knew what a Taser was. That's what she was going to call it. "And yet it is what it is. That's my Taser."

"But it's..." Deputy Briggs shook his head at his boss and obviously made the choice to move on. "She's got just about everything in here except a gun."

"Keep looking." They would find it eventually.

Briggs frowned, his hand digging further until he came up with her petite .38. "Yep. Here it is."

The sheriff's head shook. "All right, then. I guess I should be happy you didn't shoot Max."

"Was he the asshole with the salmonella phobia?" That cowboy had been hot, too, but slightly insane.

"Oh, yes. His name is Max Harper. He's the man you tried to kill."

"Don't be a drama queen, Sheriff. I wasn't trying to kill him. I was trying to prove a point. He was yelling at Stella. Stella is a nice lady. She shouldn't have to put up with some jerk harassing her. And that burger was done. There was barely a hint of pink." The Harper fellow had been loud and obnoxious and a bit of a bully. She'd stood there and listened to him harangue Stella, and she hadn't been able to stand another minute of it. She'd walked right over to her purse, grabbed her Taser, and knocked the obnoxious hottie out. And then the strangest thing had happened. "You know the whole diner cheered, right?"

The sheriff's lips curved up in a faint smile. "I can imagine. But that doesn't make it any less of an assault."

Fuck. She was in trouble. Again. For the last six months, she'd been utterly adrift. She'd had enough to stay in her crappy apartment while she'd looked for a job. She hadn't even gotten an interview. Giles and Knoxbury was blackballing her. Hell, they didn't need to blackball her. Her face had been all over the papers. She'd even made the national morning shows. One of the damn neighbors had taken video on their phone and she'd turned into a viral sensation. "Midtown Meltdown." That was going to be the sum of her career.

When her mom had insisted on moving back to her Colorado hometown, Gemma had followed. It had been time to leave New York.

What was she going to tell her mom? She was thirty freaking years old, and she was worried about her mom thinking she was a loser. She'd lost two jobs due to her taciturn personality, and now she had the added threat of actual jail time.

"What can I do to make this right?" She was tired of screwing up. If apologizing to the paranoid jerk would keep her out of jail, then she would do it. She didn't have to mean it. She was a lawyer. She was used to putting on a good show.

She used to be a lawyer. Damn it. Her money was running out. Right now, she could afford her own tiny cabin close to her mom's. If she couldn't keep a job, they would be living on top of each other. She didn't want to add to her mother's burden. Her mother had burdens enough. This was supposed to be a lovely time for her, but Gemma was doing nothing but making life hard. For the first time, she had to wonder if she was here for her mom or herself.

The glint in the sheriff's eyes put Gemma on high alert. "Well, there might be a way we could work this out. I happen to be good friends with the Harpers."

She bet he was. God, were they going to try to con the city slicker? She sat in stony silence, waiting for the shoe to drop.

"When you first came to town, you were given the choice of three jobs. Why did you turn me down?"

She had settled her mother into her cabin, made sure her own was livable, and then started looking for work. Three places had been hiring: The Trading Post, Stella's Diner, and the Sheriff's Department. It had been a hard decision between the first two. She'd utterly ignored the third. "I turned you down because the last two office managers you hired were both involved in bloody killings. And at least three people have died like right here. It doesn't bode well for assistant number three."

"She's got a point, boss. This job is hours of pure boredom broken up by surprisingly frequent multiple murders." Deputy Briggs winked her way. "And I've made sure to kill away from the station house so the office manager doesn't have to clean up."

The sheriff gave his deputy a thumbs-up. "See. We would be respectful. And the first manager was my wife. She killed a son of a bitch who was attempting to kill me. And then Hope's son of a bitch was her psycho ex-husband. You won't ever have to save me. All we have to worry about are psychotic exes. You got one of those?"

"Nope," she replied. "Just an asshole, but he wouldn't screw up his suit to kill someone, least of all me."

"Then you're in the clear." He let the keys to the jail cell dangle. "What about it? You take the job, and we'll call this time served."

"I used to be a lawyer, you know. This is complete bullshit. I went to Harvard Law."

The keys disappeared, and Wright winced. "Wow. No one told me that. Maybe I should rethink this. I didn't realize you were a lawyer."

"Come on, Nate." Briggs practically begged. "Ever since Hope quit, nothing's getting done. Make an exception. It's obvious she's insane, but she's also our only choice. And you have to admit, she can handle some of the rougher parts of the job."

"Yeah, but can she handle anything else? Fine. Damn it. I hate lawyers." He opened up the cell, a frown on his face. "You can keep the stun gun and pepper spray. You're going to have to prove to me that piece of crap gun works and you know how to use it. And lose the air horn. It only pisses the bears off. And they make my head hurt."

She stood up, a little wary. "Just like that? You hire me, and I don't get hauled in front of a judge?"

He shrugged. "Things work differently here, Counselor."

She looked at the big desk in the center of the room. There was a radio, a mess of electronic equipment, and a sad-looking laptop. "I want a new computer. That thing is ancient."

Nate frowned. "I didn't realize this was a negotiation."

She looked around the office. It could definitely use a makeover. "Life is a negotiation, Sheriff. I want a new laptop with a high-speed modem. I'm willing to work ridiculously long hours because I won't have a life outside this job. You'll discover that I'm excellent at deflecting unwanted attention from you, so you'll have more time to do whatever it is you do. And I make the best coffee in the whole world. I'll bring my own coffeemaker. I need my afternoon latte."

"Please hire her." The deputy's eyes had lit up at the mention of coffee.

Wright nodded. "But we're going to need a new speed trap. Laptops aren't cheap." He held out his hand. "Deal?"

She took it. At least she'd be off her feet, and this place actually looked like it might need something she could give. It was a dead end, but it would be good to be needed for a change. The job at Stella's had only required a warm body with a minimum of brains and a whole lot of patience. She wasn't patient. And apparently she scared children, which was why the very sweet Teeny Green had shown her the door with the Trading Post's customary layoff package—a pound of fudge and a T-shirt.

She took the sheriff's hand. "Deal."

The doors to the station house opened, and Stella blasted through followed by none other than Gemma's victim, Max Harper, a second Max Harper, and a woman carrying a wide-eyed baby.

"You let my waitress out of jail this instant, Nathan Wright!" Stella's purple boots with embroidered stars rang across the floor.

"Now, we should talk about this, Sheriff. She did nearly kill me." Max Harper held the spot on the back of his neck where she'd touched him with the Taser. The big bull hadn't gone down quietly. And he'd seemed awfully surprised.

"Maxwell!" The pretty woman with strawberry blonde hair gave Harper a look that could freeze the balls off a man.

Cool blue eyes rolled. "Damn it, Rach. Stella and I were just having some fun."

Stella turned on the cowboy. "You called me a senile old woman."

The blonde gasped. "Max!"

Harper practically hid behind his second self. "I didn't say it like that, baby. I told her she was losing her damn mind if she couldn't see the burger was bleeding."

The second Max Harper smiled Gemma's way. "Hi, there. I'm Rye Harper, the sane half of us. Could you memorize this face so you don't forget it the next time you get a hankering to shoot a whole bunch of electricity through a man?"

Max frowned. "Well, if I had known she was going to use a goddamn stun gun on me, I wouldn't have agreed to this in the first place. I thought my eyes weren't going to uncross there for a minute. That wasn't worth the babysitting night, Nate. That shit hurt."

Stella turned on the sheriff. "You set this up because you wanted to steal my waitress. You manipulative son of a bitch. Are you the one who set the Farley boys on her so she had to leave the Trading Post?"

Those boys had been past obnoxious, asking questions for four hours straight. They never let up. She'd finally broken down, cursing, and was shocked that two teenage boys could cry like that.

Nate Wright let loose a big, shit-eating grin. "I had to promise not to arrest them for their latest 'rocket into space' experiment. Though I think it might have worked. I feel bad for that frog. I think he might still be up there somewhere."

Gemma turned to the asshole who had been making her life hell. "You are a manipulative, sneaky son of a bitch."

"That's 'Boss son of a bitch' to you." Nate Wright looked pleased with himself as the phone rang. "Now, you need to take the spare Bronco over to Long-Haired Roger's because the brakes are squeaking. The keys are in your desk." The phone rang again. Wright pointed to it. "And that's for you, Gemma. Welcome to Bliss."

The Harpers were arguing over Max's willingness to risk his body for a night of babysitting. Stella yelled at Nate.

And Gemma sat down at her desk. It was stupid. It was a little mean. It was the most trouble anyone had gone to over her in a long damn time. Nate Wright had plotted and planned and brought half the town into his machinations. She totally respected that.

"Bliss County Sheriff's Department." She used her most professional voice. And then listened in complete shock. "What do you mean aliens are attacking?"

"I'll be fishing," Wright said, grabbing his pole.

"I have to go set up that new speed trap. I'm going to call it Gemma's Trap. And I'd love a tall one of those frothy coffee things with all the caramel. Thanks." Briggs practically ran out the door.

She was left with a huffing Stella, a bickering Harper clan, and a pending alien invasion.

If her friends could see her now…

* * * *

"Hey, Cade, something's up with one of the county vehicles. I think Cam is bringing it in this afternoon. Do you mind taking a look at it? If you can't fix it quick, he'll need a ride back to the station."

Cade looked up from the Chevy he was working on and gave his boss a nod. Long-Haired Roger was known for his courteous demeanor and his lack of hair. "Sure thing."

His boss was a gentle man who knew almost everything there was to know about the way engines worked. And he had a new friend. The town vet had recently brought Roger a rescue…dog. They said Princess Two was a dog, but to him it looked more like a rat that had maybe been thrown up by a poodle. Princess Two had weird bug eyes and a pink bow attached to her head.

And she shook. A lot.

Jesse walked in from the street, a bag in his hand. "Lunch is here. Apparently we missed all the fun. The new girl at Stella's pulled a stun gun on Max Harper, and Nate hauled her off to jail. Did you hear about the way she made the Farley boys cry? What kind of a woman makes two boys cry?"

A fairly mean one. Cade hadn't gotten a look at Gemma Wells, but he knew the type. He'd already heard her story. Big city lawyer. Some of the women had been talking about her shoes and the purses she carried. She probably looked down on everyone and everything. And sure Harper could be an ass, but what the hell kind of woman stunned a man like that?

"She's a tourist." Cade walked to the small sink and washed his hands. He was covered in motor oil, but the smell was soothing. Even all these years later, the smell reminded him of his father. He shook off the feeling and the crushing guilt that threatened to overwhelm him any time he thought about his dad. "She won't hang around here for long. Hey, do you mind looking at the seal on that radiator?"

Jesse nodded and headed to the sedan they were working on. The owner was supposed to pick it up in an hour or two, but damn it was giving him hell.

Long-Haired Roger shook his bald head. "Naw. Gemma's not a tourist. Her momma was born here. I remember Miss Lynn Griffin. What a pretty thing she was. I even went out with her for a while, but then a musician named Donald Wells came into town and she left with him. She always wrote her momma, though. Nice lady, Lynn. She's come back home. I heard Don died a long while back, but she's been traveling. A bit of a gypsy, that one."

"And she brought her problem child with her?" Cade grabbed his burger and hopped up on the counter after tossing his oil-stained shirt to the side. Despite the chill in the air, he felt more comfortable without it on.

"Lynn was real sick from what they say," Roger explained. "I think her daughter was helping to take care of her. Do you have a problem with shirts, son?"

He shrugged. "Don't like 'em."

Jesse came back up, a wrench in his hand, eyes rolling. "He would be happier up the mountain, if you know what I mean."

Roger gave him a blank stare for a moment and then gasped. "Oh. Like up the mountain and off with the clothes. Well, that's fine, son, but you have to keep your pants on in here. I can't have a naked mechanic. Those boy parts dangle. You remember that."

Roger walked off, the tiny poodle-looking thing yipping away.

Jesse snorted, putting the wrench down. "It's done. It needed a jimmy. Boy parts dangle. Damn, I love that man. And I heard Gemma Wells didn't have much choice about staying in New York. The word is she got fired and had some sort of trouble. I have to admit, I'm intrigued."

He stared at Jesse. His best friend had become a wretched gossip since they'd settled into Bliss. He should have known Jesse would get involved with their neighbors. Even when they'd lived in big cities, Jesse found a way to build a community around himself. Jesse genuinely liked taking care of the people around him, and he particularly liked having a woman to take care of. Cade liked to join them for sex. He sighed. It was starting to sound pathetic even to his own ears. "Who have you been talking to?"

Jesse shrugged, picking up his drink. "Everyone. You know how it is. New people come to town and everyone talks."

Cade took a long breath. "Damn it, Jess. You saw her, didn't you?"

He smiled, a smug grin. "It was a brief glance, but she made an impression. Blonde hair. Blue eyes. Great tits. She seemed a bit lost though. She seems arrogant at first, but I would bet anything it's a shield."

He'd seen her and decided she needed a man who could take care of her? Jesse was getting more and more desperate. "Why did she have to leave New York?"

"Laura and Holly were talking about some incident there where she tried to kill someone."

Cade groaned. "Damn it. We are finished with the dangerous portion of our lives. I'm not hopping back in, and I'm not going to allow you to turn into a cautionary tale. Here's what we know about this chick. We know she's mean, and she tries to kill people. Stay away. The ski bunnies will be here soon. Once we get some powder on the mountain, you'll have your choice of women."

Ty could help out on that front. They'd become good friends with one of the EMTs who worked at the resort. Ty had assured Cade that once the Elk Creek Lodge was in full swing for the winter, the party would begin. Cade liked tourists. Well, he liked the nice ones. They came. They had fun. They left town.

Jesse stared at him. He tended to let Cade lead for the most part except with a couple of the women they'd shared, but there were times when he was as stubborn as the day was long. His mouth twisted into that grimace that let Cade know he'd pissed Jesse off. Still, Jesse took a long drink of his soda and sighed. "I'm sure that will be fun, brother."

Cade put the burger aside, his appetite gone. Jesse was the only real family he had left. Everyone else was dead, and he didn't make friends the way Jesse did. "We'll find someone. It's just not going to be a ball-busting, big-city girl."

"You forgot to mention that I'm a soul-sucking lawyer," a throaty voice said from the front door.

He stopped, his attention focused on the woman at the front of the garage. Gemma Wells was petite with honey-blonde hair, and she wore a Stella's Diner T-shirt and jeans that clung to her every curve. *Fuck*. Jesse was right. Her tits were nice. They weren't incredibly large, but they would make a good handful, and he would bet her nipples were a decent size. He liked nipples. He liked to twist them and pinch them and suck them into his mouth. He could spend an hour merely playing with a woman's breasts.

"Oh, and coldhearted bitch, vampire bitch, cast-iron bitch, pretty much everything goes with bitch." She crossed her arms over her chest. "And I didn't bust Max Harper's balls. Those are still on his body. Now, Bare-Chested Ape Man, if you could be bothered to look past my boobs, maybe we could have a conversation."

"Bare-Chested Ape Man?" Cade crossed his arms over his chest, mimicking her squared-off stance. Every damn word out of her mouth made his blood pressure tick up. And it, unfortunately, had his dick jumping, too.

"Well, I don't know your name and you seem to have zero problem with calling me names, so yes, you will be forever known as Bare-Chested Ape Man." She turned to Jesse, her eyes narrowing.

"Gemma Wells." Jesse grinned like the cat who'd swallowed the canary. "You're Gemma Wells. Sorry if I looked at your chest. You should know that I like your face, too."

A hint of smile crossed those ridiculously hot lips. "Fine. You get a name."

Jesse stared at her.

Gemma looked back at Cade. "He has a name, right?"

"Why don't you ask me politely, and I'll give you the courtesy of an introduction." Jesse's words came out in that low rumble that meant he was damn serious.

Cade felt a deep sense of satisfaction. There was no way the city girl would let a mechanic talk to her like that. She would unleash some serious vitriol Jesse's way, and Jesse couldn't stand an impolite woman.

Except she didn't hurl sarcasm his way. "Hello, my name is Gemma. What's yours?"

"Jesse, ma'am. Jesse McCann."

"You'll have to forgive me. It sounds like you practically know my life story." Her eyes were warmer as she looked at Jesse. What color were those damn eyes? At first he'd thought they were blue, but now there was a hint of green in there.

Jesse walked forward, holding his hand out. It was a good thing since he was pretty sure Jesse would need it to wipe away the drool. "It's a small town, Miss Wells. You're new. Pretty much everyone knows everything."

"I wouldn't say that." Cade kept steady eyes on her. "We have a few secrets here in Bliss."

She shook Jesse's hand. "I'm sure you do. Now, can you tell me where I can find someone called Long-Haired Roger?"

Jesse flushed as he pulled away. He hadn't been thinking. He had motor oil on his palm and a little grease. Gemma looked down at her now filthy hand.

Well, at least Jesse would figure out she wasn't for him. She would show that bitchy mouth off and prove she was the type of woman who wouldn't fool around with a couple of blue-collar guys.

"I'm sorry. I wasn't thinking. I'm sure I have something you can clean off on."

Gemma looked at her hand and then slowly drew it across the thigh of her jeans. Somehow the action of that small hand wiping filth off was deeply erotic. "Don't worry about it. I used to be a lawyer. I don't mind getting my hands dirty." She held out a set of keys. "Now, I've recently been blackmailed into becoming the office manager for the sheriff. He's a son-of-a-bitch, manipulative, rat-fink bastard. And his brakes squeak. Can you handle that for me, Jesse?"

Jesse's smile was slow. "Yes, Gemma. I can handle that problem for you."

He watched the invisible tether catch Jesse. Damn it, but he didn't like being left out. "And what would you have called him if he hadn't been able to come up with your name? If I'm Bare-Chested Ape Man, what would he have been?"

There it was again, that devil in her smile. "The Sweet One. Miss Stella tells me there's always one. Call the station when the car's ready, boys."

She turned and started to walk out.

"Hey, do you need a ride?" Jesse looked like he might offer to carry her all the way back to Main Street.

She didn't turn, simply let those hips sway as she walked to the door. "Nope. Both my legs work and the longer I stay away the less I have to hear about something called Reticulan Greys and their plans to take over the world. Apparently I should have skipped the law degree and gone straight to psychology."

The door closed behind her.

There was a dippy grin on Jesse's face. "I was right about her."

"The jury's out on that." She hadn't exactly been sweet as pie, but he could handle that. "We do know she's a little crazy."

Jesse's smile went wide. "Damn straight. I love a psycho chick."

He did, too, though this one seemed dangerous. He watched through the bay windows as she started walking back toward the sheriff's department. She walked in a straight line. She didn't look around. She tackled the walk as though it was a task to get through before she took on the next one.

Jesse stared at her, too. "Do you think we should go after her? Maybe walk her back?"

Somehow he didn't think Gemma Wells would love having an Ape Man trailing after her. She might call the cops and have him arrested for stalking. "No. I don't think she would take too kindly to that. Be careful with that one. She's as likely to bite you as she is to give you a kiss."

Nope. Gemma Wells wasn't for him. Still, he kept his eye on her until she turned the corner and disappeared from sight.

Jesse was quiet for a moment. "I'm interested in her."

"I thought we'd gone over this."

"No, you gave me a whole bunch of reasons why she scares you off," Jesse returned. "I thought the whole reason we settled down here was we were done with wandering and this is the kind of place that will accept us and all our weird-ass needs. It's months and all you want to do is play around with women who have zero interest in anything but sex."

"I'm not sure why that's a problem."

"It's a problem for me." Jesse crossed his arms over his chest. "I'm ready for something more."

"And you've decided you want more with a woman you met five minutes ago?" He didn't get it. She was gorgeous, but she was also obviously trouble.

"At the very least I want to get to know her." Jesse had his hands on his hips like he was squaring off for an argument. "How can we get anywhere at all if we don't try? She's stunning and she's single, and tell me you're not intrigued by all that sass."

"I'm not intrigued." Except he was a bit. She'd been smart and quick witted. She wouldn't be boring. He would give her that.

"You're a liar," Jesse accused.

He was, but he wasn't admitting to this lie. It would only get him in more trouble.

There was a brief knock on the door and Barney Osman walked in pushing his cart in front of him. He was dressed in his postal uniform and gave them a wide smile. "Hello, Jesse, Cade. How are you doing today. Got a couple of packages for the shop if you don't mind signing for them."

Cade took the paperwork and signed it while Barney pulled out the deliveries. They'd been in town for months and not once had Barney delivered to their cabin. They didn't get mail. There weren't people out in the world who sent them letters and packages.

"Here you go." He passed the clipboard back to Barney.

Barney settled it back in his bag and pulled out a small box. "Y'all are my last stop of the day, but I still have one package. Have either one of you heard of a woman named Gemma Wells?"

She was haunting him already. Jesse's head came up and a light sparked in his eyes.

"She's the new lady in town," Jesse said. "She's staying in the valley. I can deliver that for you."

Well of course Jesse could.

At least he knew what he was doing tonight.

Chapter Two

Gemma opened the door to her small cabin with a sigh. This was home for now. She was back to her childhood, moving from place to place. In the last six months she'd lived in New York, Chicago, and now Bliss, Colorado. She'd come to Colorado with a suitcase full of completely impractical shoes and bags, her laptop, and her phone— neither of which were doing her a bit of good. Everything else she owned was in a storage container in Brooklyn, and she wouldn't see it again for another couple of days when the movers finally shipped it. She didn't have anything to work on, and no one had called about her resume. Big surprise there.

Now she had another job. The sheriff had worked to get her, but how long would he keep her?

And why couldn't she stop thinking about Bare-Chested Ape Man and the Sweet One? The last thing she needed was for her hormones to go on all-out, full-on, call-in-the-troops alert.

She tossed her purse inside and turned back, looking at the slightly larger cabin next door to hers that her mother had rented. The front porch was empty, which could mean only one thing. She closed the door and walked around to the back. Twilight was encroaching, but that meant something different in Colorado.

Blues and pinks and oranges painted the sky. In New York, evening had simply meant the world got darker, but it was a nightly show here.

How long had it been since she sat and watched the day fade? The last ten years of her life had been one long press against the borders of time. Time was the enemy. Time had to be used. Every second of it. Gemma Wells, hard-nosed lawyer, fought against the whole idea of sitting and watching the sunset.

But she wasn't a lawyer anymore. She was a daughter, and she'd almost lost her mom.

"Hey, baby girl." Her mom turned her head, a serene smile on her face. How she managed her constant peaceful mood, Gemma had no idea. Her mom had spent years battling cancer, but there was no bitterness in her body. Even when she'd lost both breasts, Lynn Wells had simply told Gemma she was grateful for the time she had with them. She'd held a damn party to say good-bye to her breasts and invited all her hippie friends to read eulogies to her mammaries. She didn't understand her mom, but, god, she loved her.

Patrick had told her that party was ridiculous. He'd been embarrassed when she'd mentioned it to her coworkers.

"Hey, Momma." Gemma took the Adirondack chair next to her mom and let her head rest back, closing her eyes.

She bet Jesse McCann wouldn't have laughed. He'd probably have escorted her to the party and said good-bye to her mom's breasts, too. She could size up people pretty well. She'd had to learn to in her job. Jesse was the sweet one. Jesse was the one who could be easily led by his penis and would smile and thank the woman who led him.

Not the Neanderthal, shirtless dude, though. No. He was trouble.

"How was work?"

"Assaulted a man. Got fired." She was done prevaricating. Her mom would know the truth soon enough.

"Now, Gemma, that is not the way I heard it."

Or she'd already heard the story. Gemma sighed and opened her eyes. Her mom's brilliant blue eyes were staring right at her.

"Oh, thank the lord, the entertainment is here!" Naomi Turner rounded the corner, a tray in her hand. It contained all the new nightly rituals that had been implemented since they'd gotten to Bliss. A bottle of rich red wine, a tray of cheese and crackers and prosciutto. There were three glasses, and Naomi passed Gemma one.

"Thanks." Gemma took a long sip. Naomi Turner was a godsend. She'd been her mother's nurse in Chicago during her surgery and the subsequent radiation treatments. She wasn't sure how or why, but Naomi had agreed to come with them when they retreated to Colorado. She rather thought Naomi was running from something, but she'd been far too grateful to ask.

Her mom took her glass and shook her blonde hair. "I heard that the nosy sheriff had a hand in everything."

Naomi winced, her dark eyes turning slightly toward the front of the house. "Keep your voice down, sweetie. We have company."

A pretty woman with brown hair and sparkling eyes rounded the corner, another tray in her hand. "Oh, it's all right. I know my husband is a manipulative bastard. He told me what he'd done earlier today. That's why I made my spinach dip."

An ethereal brunette in a long cotton skirt, tunic, and Birkenstocks followed Mrs. Wright. "And I brought cruelty-free pita bread to go with the spinach dip, although you might simply want to eat the bread. The dip has sour cream."

Spinach-dip lady smiled. "Hi, I'm your neighbor, Callie Hollister-Wright. This is Nell. She thinks sour cream is evil."

The woman named Nell shook her head. "No, I simply think it's ignorant of the harm it does. But Gemma here is very good. Did you know she's a lawyer?"

Thank god. Someone in the world didn't think she was the second coming of Satan. "Thanks."

Nell had a serene smile on her face. "You're welcome. I'm involved in all the environmental cases going on in the area. I heard you worked on the Calvin Township case. I can't tell you how much I appreciate it."

Gemma reached for a piece of bread. "Yeah, though I'm surprised you've heard of it. We tried hard to keep Tremon Industries out of the press. Guess my old firm is laying down on the job."

Nell gasped and grabbed the bread from her hand. "You weren't representing the town?"

"No." Yeah, her reputation was going to hell.

Nell sank to the ground in a single, graceful motion, crossing her legs, a stubborn expression on her face.

Callie Hollister-Wright grimaced. "Sorry. She's protesting you now."

"Oh, dear." Her mom stared at the now-protesting woman with a worried look on her face. "Should we do something?"

Callie shook her head. "Not unless she starts singing. Now, I would like to apologize for Nate's evil plan to get you to work for him. All I can say is, apparently he's been plotting ever since Lynn called Stella and said she was coming home and you were coming with her. He's shorthanded right now with Logan in Dallas. Hope, his last office manager, recently got married and she's working out at her new husbands' ranch. I'm way too busy with the twins to help out. Laura and Rafe are trying to set up a new business. Holly says she has PTSD every time she walks into the station house since she almost got killed by Russian mobsters there. And Jen doesn't need the money. Oh, and Zane, my other husband, told Nate he would cut his balls off if he poached Lucy, so you were really important to Nate."

"Your other husband?" Gemma needed that wine.

Callie smiled. "Oh, yes. They usually get along great, but it's hard to find good help in this town. It's why I wish Nate would have left well enough alone. Stella is going to give him hell, but he refuses to back down. He says he won you through sheer ruthless determination."

The sound of a car rolling up the gravel road distracted her for a moment. The valley was usually quiet, but it sounded like everyone was getting home from work at the same time today.

Her mom sat back. "Thank the lord. I thought something terrible had happened. It's just Bliss antics."

The woman in front of her seemed to be meditating, a low hum beginning in the back of her throat.

And her mother was missing the point. "Bliss antics? I was manipulated into assaulting a man, Mom."

Nell's eyes opened, a look of shock going across her face.

"It was Max," Callie explained.

Nell's eyes closed; her humming resumed.

Her mother shook her head. "Oh, this is delicious, Callie. Simply wonderful."

Naomi dug in to the spinach dip as well. "It's excellent."

"Lynn! Lynn, hon, are you back here?" A feminine voice floated over the yard.

Callie winced. "Stella. Darn it. I don't have the babies with me to distract her."

Stella marched into the backyard, a frown on her face. Her eyes narrowed when she saw Callie. "You."

"Married very poorly, obviously."

Wow, Callie just laid right down and let the truck roll over her. Well, Nate Wright seemed like a man who could handle himself.

Stella growled, a surprisingly feminine sound. "Don't you give me that. You love that man. So you should know that I intend to take him down." She looked at Gemma. "You don't have to work for him."

"I do if I don't want to go to jail." It had been a good play on the sheriff's part.

Stella huffed. "Oh, that man is all bark and no bite."

Naomi shook her head. "I don't know about that. He's already written me two tickets."

"That's his way of saying hello." Stella sat down on the porch next to Lynn. "I'm going to fix this, hon. I won't have your poor, sweet girl working for that horrible old Nate. And it's dangerous there."

Callie frowned. "Because nothing ever goes wrong at Stella's."

"We have the occasional baby birthing, but other than that we've been murder-free for twenty-one years. I'm putting that on a T-shirt and shoving it up Zane's overly muscled butt cheeks," Stella swore. "Callie, you know I love you and your family, but I am taking Nate down for this. He's corrupting poor, innocent city girls."

"I did Tase the guy." Gemma took a long sip of wine.

"She got him good." Cameron Briggs walked up. She'd thought she'd seen him coming out of a cabin a couple of houses down from hers. "Nate and I were there...eating a completely innocent lunch. We weren't waiting for Max to blow or anything. Nice. Spinach dip." He turned to shout back at someone walking up the yard. "Hey, come on, Laura. Stella won't hurt you. Just me and Nate, and Nate's smart enough to stay away. By the way, you are looking gorgeous today, Ms. Stella. I mean beautiful. Why the hell is Sebastian letting you work anyway? If I was your new husband, I would keep you in bed all day."

Stella stared at him for a long moment. "Flattery will get you everywhere." She sighed and patted her helmet of blonde hair. "As it happens, I like to work. The dining industry is in my blood. And if I left it in Hal's hands, he would turn the whole place into something called the Gastronomy Café. That's his dream. I don't think that sounds nice."

A gorgeous blonde walked up and took Briggs's hand. "Hey, everyone. Hey, Miss Lynn. How are you this evening? It looks like we're having a party."

Callie sat down next to Stella, who sighed and put her arm around her. "That sounds like fun. Why don't we grill up some steaks?"

Nell cleared her throat.

"And some cruelty-free tofu burgers and have a nice evening," Callie offered. "It's going to be too cold soon."

Her mom clapped her hands together. "That sounds lovely. We used to have get-togethers all the time when I was growing up. Stella, do you remember that year the circus came to town and Mel was certain the trapeze artist was an alien?"

They were off, laughing and reminiscing. Gemma looked around. The gorgeous blonde with Cam was calling Holly on her phone, inviting her over. She also called someone named Rafe and told him to bring beer. Naomi was telling some story to Cam. It was a party with her mother in the center, laughing and talking and belonging.

She was surrounded by people, and all she could think about was how alone she was.

Callie moved over, crossing to Gemma and sitting beside her. "Hey, I wanted to thank you for not killing my husband. He genuinely thinks this will be a better job for you. He studied you for a couple of days, and he thinks you're smart. He also wanted to see Max get taken down by another waitress. Rachel has become awfully nonviolent since Paige was born. I'm going to go and grab Zane. We'll pull our grill over. Zane will have Stella purring in no time at all. You want to join me?"

Gemma shook her head. She would have absolutely nothing to say to the sweet mom of twins. Callie Hollister-Wright was one of those serene women Gemma didn't understand. Rather like her mom. "Thanks, but no. I'm going to head back to my cabin. I'm not much of a joiner."

She wasn't a joiner or the type of person who had fun. Of any kind. At all. How long had it been since she'd gone out for an evening without some strict plan on how it would go? She used to go to happy hours and dinners with coworkers, but she'd always had an agenda.

"You managed to join with evil," Nell said.

"Yes." Gemma turned to Callie. "Is this party evil? Because I only join with evil."

Callie nodded, a grin on her face. "Lots of evil. You should stay. And we have booze."

Booze was good. But no. She was tired. She was out of place. "Thanks, but I think I'll get some rest. I had a long day. And a long walk. Apologize to Nate for me, but the shop called and they won't have his Bronco back until tomorrow."

She'd spent the afternoon answering the phone and listening to a couple of tourists complain about the sheriff's ticketing practices and reorganizing what had to be the world's oddest armory. It was more like a locked closet where the sheriff kept the rifles, handguns, and Kevlar vests. And his fishing poles, a truly random selection of game console controllers, and a complete selection of X-Men comics. And all the while she'd waited to see if Bare-Chested Ape Man and the Sweet One would call.

She'd been disappointed. The owner of the shop had been the one to update her. Had she expected them to go out of their way to talk to her? She had a lousy reputation. Ape Man had been warning his sweet friend off when she'd walked in. She'd taken one look at his gorgeously cut chest and his emerald-green eyes and then realized he was talking about what a bitch she was.

It was better they hadn't called. She wasn't good at relationships.

Hell, she wasn't good at sex.

"Oh, I hope you reconsider," Callie said.

She didn't fit in here. That was fine. She wasn't going to stay forever. She nodded and Callie stood up, walking off toward her cabin.

Naomi gave her mother a shoulder squeeze and winked Gemma's way before heading back into the house. "I'm going to throw together a salad."

Lynn smiled her way. The rest of her friends were beginning to set up what looked to be a fun, impromptu get-together. "Do you want to put together something for the party, sweetie?"

Gemma put the wine down. "This isn't a good idea. It's best I keep to myself. I don't think these people are going to like me."

Her mom sighed and closed her eyes. "It's difficult for people to like you when you don't like yourself, dear."

"I like myself." She was smart. She was ambitious. Sure, she'd trusted the wrong man, but even that would blow over eventually. Not everyone would remember that she'd had a complete breakdown after years of pressure. Everyone did, right? She would serve her time and find another firm. Where she could work seventy-hour weeks and ignore everything and everyone except her career, and put all her money and effort and soul into building that career that sucked more life out of her.

Yeah, she didn't like herself very much, either.

Her mother simply waited.

"Fine. I'll try harder. But don't expect much. The mechanics at the shop already think I'm a head case." Had she meant to sound so glum?

Those blue eyes opened now, calculation plain in the orbs. Her mother, the matchmaker, was in the house. "Mechanics? The single ones?"

"Mom, they hate me."

"I doubt that, dear. Did they seem like nice young men? I have to admit, unattached males are rare in this town. I think it has something to do with most of the women having two husbands."

"Yeah. What's up with that? Deputy Briggs was talking about his partner, and I got sad because that man is too hot to be gay, but then his girlfriend walks in and there's the partner Cam is talking about, and they both kissed her. And someone was talking about Hope, the last office manager, and how she recently got back from Vegas with her two husbands. Has Vegas changed? I think all this is completely illegal."

Illegal, but she could make a case, maybe. The argument started to run through her head. She could practically see the judge's face when she tried to argue that nature created a woman to accommodate multiple husbands. After all, a woman had a couple of places for a penis to go. Darwin. Yes, she would argue pure Darwinism.

"It's always been this way in Bliss. Back when I was a girl, it was only Fred and Brian and their wife. They ran the Circle G and raised James and Noah, who are now married to Hope. And I can see you already have a whole Supreme Court case planned in your head."

Her mom knew her well. "It would be a fun argument."

And honestly, did it hurt anyone?

What would it be like to be pressed between Jesse and Bare-Chested Ape Man? *Damn it.* She needed to find out his name.

"I always wondered why you went into corporate law. When you were younger, you always helped people."

Gemma sighed. Her mom wouldn't understand. Her mom loved the vagabond lifestyle. Her mom hadn't been an awkward kid forced to make new friends every time they moved and deal with being the girl in school with mismatched clothes and hand-me-down shoes. Her mom and dad hadn't had an ambitious bone between them. They'd chased ephemeral things like love and joy and the perfect song.

Gemma had been forced to live in the real world. The real world kind of sucked. Now she was in a whole town that lived the way her mom did. She was right back where she'd been as a kid. The girl who didn't fit. "Corporations can help people, too."

Not often. Next to never. But sometimes. The biggest case she'd managed to work on had been the Tremon Industries case, and the EPA had practically cleared them of all wrongdoing. Gemma felt bad for the people of Calvin who had suffered, but Tremon hadn't caused it.

She was reminded that she wasn't alone by the low hum of Nell's protest. Was she going to start the singing thing now?

43

She got to her feet. It didn't matter. She had nothing to do with the case at this point. Christina Big Tits had likely grown back her hair and taken over Gemma's place as secondary counsel. But hey, Gemma had a new job, too.

"I should go."

"I'm sorry." Her mom looked up. "I shouldn't have mentioned it, sweetheart. You had to follow your heart. I understand that. I'm grateful for this time we have now. I love you. This will all work out."

She nodded, but still didn't want to stay. "Okay. I'll see you in the morning?"

Her mom looked disappointed. It was an expression that was on her face all too often lately. "If that's what will make you happy, dear. Just know that everyone is here if you want to join us."

Gemma got up. Not everyone was here. Would she stay if those two men had been here? Probably not.

Callie came back, a baby in her arms. Nate was with her, holding his other son on his chest like a cute suit of armor.

"Now, Stella, I have a baby," Nate said.

Stella growled, but then cooed at the kicking baby anyway. Nate winked her way.

And Nell stood. She walked straight up to Gemma and reached for her hand. "I have decided to be your friend."

Callie leaned in. "You asked when you should worry. It's time. Worry. Like a lot."

She stared down at her hand in Nell's. Was she supposed to do something? Would it be totally rude to walk away now?

Nell released her with a beatific smile on her face. "There's nothing to worry about. I can teach you."

"Uh, thanks." It was definitely time to go.

Gemma turned and started to walk off. She would go to her cabin and hide all night long. She could sit and stare at the TV or read some dumbass magazine because the last thing she was going to do was anything productive. And she wasn't going to make friends. Even if she wanted to. She wasn't the type of person who sat around and talked and grilled food. "Why the fuck am I here? Crazy, dumbass town."

She plowed right past Zane Hollister and his portable grill, turning to start an apology, but she smacked straight into a wall of masculine flesh. Jesse McCann looked down at her, a grin on his ridiculously perfect face.

* * * *

Jesse had to stop himself from touching her. Nothing more than a light touch, a grasp of her hand. But he forced himself to not reach out to her. After a nice long discussion with Cade about getting involved with a potentially violent woman, he'd decided to give his brain a chance to catch up with his libido.

Her breasts brushed against his chest as she plowed her way through them, the hard nub of her nipples apparent because she wasn't wearing a damn bra. His dick immediately began composing a letter to his brain.

Dear Brain—Hurry the fuck up. I'm dying here. Sincerely, your Dick. P.S. The balls are pissed off, too.

"Sorry about that, Gemma." At least he didn't sound as completely idiotic as he had before. The pretty blonde in front of him made his brain take a nosedive. He didn't know a damn thing about her except that she had a craptastic attitude, but then so did Cade. It was Jesse's lot in life to be surrounded by difficult people.

"It's okay." The words came out in a breathless puff. She shook her head and backed up.

She was still wearing those jeans with the stain on them. It was nothing more than a small trail of grease, but it had transferred from his hand to hers and then to her clothes. A tiny piece of him marking her.

He could think of other ways to mark her.

"Is she giving you trouble?" Cade stood there, holding the package they'd brought, Jesse's whole reason for forcing them to come out here.

Jesse made sure a smile stayed on his face. Gemma wasn't the trouble right now. Cade's past, however, was giving Jesse fits. If Gemma were a normal, everyday, sweet-faced tourist with the same heart-shaped ass and boobs that would fit perfectly into his hands, Cade would have been all over her. Even if she'd been a bit cantankerous, Cade would have seen it as a challenge. They would have plotted and planned how fast they could take her from mean girl to purring kitten. But Gemma was different. Gemma had struck a chord in Cade, and now Cade was a big old pussy who didn't want to get his fingers burned.

"Not at all," he replied shortly. He hadn't wanted Cade to come with him on this particular mission, but his brother had insisted. "It looks like you're having a party."

Gemma shook her head. "No. Uhm, my mom is in the cabin next to me. This is all about her." She was charmingly graceless, her hands fluttering as she gestured back toward the larger of the two cabins. She sucked her bottom lip between her teeth, a sight that went straight to Jesse's cock. "They showed up to talk to my mom and Naomi. Not me."

He was about to ask who Naomi was when Cade stepped up. "Well, did you expect them to come for you when you call their town dumbass and crazy?"

And just like that she went from slightly off kilter to ice queen. Her whole body stiffened and a hard look came into her eyes. "I didn't expect anything. Well, I expected you to be half naked. Look, the Ape Man found a shirt. Nice."

"Well, I need protection from you, sweetheart."

Jesse sighed. "You both need flak jackets. I get it. You're both all wounded and shit. Fine. Cade, why don't you go and see if Zane needs help with that grill?"

Cade stared at Gemma like she was a bomb that was about to explode. "I think he's doing fine."

"Please." Jesse bit the word in a way that wasn't at all polite. This situation was more serious than he thought, but Jesse felt Gemma's pull, and he wasn't sure if he was willing to turn away. He needed some time alone with her.

Cade's mouth turned down. "You're sure?"

"I am."

An almost sad look came over Cade's face, and he passed him the package. "All right then."

"Cade?" Gemma asked as Cade stalked off. Her blue eyes trailed back toward him.

So she wasn't entirely uninterested. "Cade Sinclair, though Bare-Chested Ape Man suits him fine. He's often wearing much less than what you saw in the shop. Roger makes him keep his pants on."

Gemma's mouth dropped open. "He's a nude guy, nude person, nudist?"

God, he loved it when she got flustered. The veneer stripped away momentarily, and he got a glimpse of the woman under that perfect surface. "They like to call themselves naturists. He's always worn as little as possible, but a couple of years back we were seeing a woman who liked the lifestyle and Cade took to it."

Her cheeks were flushed the prettiest red. Her skin was fair. He would bet her ass would take a spanking beautifully. "I don't understand much about this place. Like you two. You were both seeing the same woman?"

There wasn't distaste in the question, merely a simple curiosity. Somehow, the minute Cade walked away, the tension in her had deflated like a balloon slowly releasing its air. Jesse smiled at her and nodded toward her front porch. "I'd love to explain it to you, sweetheart. Will you sit with me for a minute?"

She huffed. "If you stop calling me sweetheart, maybe I will."

He turned and let his face go cold. "That was rude and unbecoming of you. It's a term of endearment meant to be affectionate, nothing more. I'd like us to be friends. If you're utterly uninterested in being friends with me, tell me now and I'll walk away."

The roundness of her eyes told him she wasn't used to being talked to in such a frank manner. "I'm sorry. I would prefer it if you didn't call me sweetheart. My ex-fiancé called me that and he didn't mean it. It bothers me."

"Excellent. Then I won't call you sweetheart. You could have simply told me and I would have understood. Is it all terms of endearment you're against? Or just that one?" He started to lead her toward the porch, making sure she didn't stumble over the uneven ground. He sat down beside her, giving her plenty of space, setting the package beside him.

She seemed to think about it for a moment. "I don't see why you can't call me Gemma."

That was easy. "Because everyone calls you Gemma, and I want to be special. I want to call you something that only I call you because I think it could help to bond you to me. I'm interested in seeing you. I'm interested in taking you out and talking to you, and eventually I would very much like to get you in bed."

There it was again, that ridiculously sexy flush. "Wow. You put it right out there for all to see."

He shrugged. "I don't lie to myself. Why should I bother to lie to anyone else? I learned a long time ago that lying about what I want will get me in trouble."

A flash of challenge came into her eyes. "You don't lie?"

"I don't."

There was a laugh, but it held no humor. "Fine. Tell me something bad about yourself."

Honesty. He was actually glad she'd given him the opening. It was best to put his cards on the table. "I spent some time in jail. You should know that right off."

Her eyes flared with obvious surprise. "Jail? I thought you would tell me something dumb like you care too much. You know, like on a job interview where they ask you about your flaws and you turn it into a strength? Jail? Why?"

"I did eighteen months in a youth center for stealing a car. I was trying to fit in with a group of boys who had formed a tight-knit group."

"A gang?" She asked the question, but he didn't sense any judgment in the words.

"Yes. My mom had died and my father left without a word. I was living on the streets and I thought being in a gang sounded better than being on my own. I stole a car as part of my initiation. Turns out I am a horrible criminal, and I got caught not a mile from where I'd stolen it." He shook his head. "It was a minivan. It smelled like old milk, but it had been LoJacked so dumbass me went to juvie."

"Eighteen months? That's a long time. How old were you?"

"I was thirteen."

Outrage replaced the surprise on her face. "Thirteen? They sent you to juvie for a year and a half and you were only thirteen? That's ridiculous. Who the hell was your lawyer?"

Damn, but he wished Cade had seen this side of Gemma. It might make it harder for him to turn away. "I was a big kid. At thirteen I was a tad under six feet, and I always built muscle fast. I also already had this." He scraped his hands over the scruff of his beard. He shaved every day but by afternoon he always had some stubble back. "And I was a street kid, darlin'. I couldn't afford a lawyer past the one they appointed to me."

"You shouldn't have spent time at all for a nonviolent offense," she argued.

"I think they wanted to make a point, and I didn't have anyone who would fight for me at the time. I was damn lucky they found a foster parent for me when I got out or I would have spent the rest of my teen years in a halfway house."

"Is that where you met Cade? In juvie?"

He laughed at the thought. "No, honey. Cade was as straight as an arrow. I met him in the foster home. He lost his parents and his sister when he was nine, but he needs to tell you that story. We were raised by a woman named Nancy, and she saved me. She and Cade. They became the family I never had."

She stared out at the party starting to take shape across the yard. Why wouldn't she go over there? What kept her apart from everyone else? He wanted her to be honest with him, but he knew patience was going to be the key with Gemma Wells.

"Is that why you share? How does it work?" She shook her head, her eyes widening. "I meant that in a nonmechanical way. Emotionally. How does it work? I mean, is it casual?"

Oh, how he wanted to explain the mechanics to her. He was damn fine with mechanics. "Sometimes it's just sex. We've had a couple of relationships, too. Nothing that lasted more than a year or so. We lived with a woman once. She moved on because she said it didn't look good for her career to live with two men. She was a doctor."

"Ah. He's opposed to evil career women." She looked over to where Cade stood laughing with Zane and Cam.

"That's not really his problem, but again, it's his story to tell. His past was rough. I might have gone to prison, but at least I got out. Cade gave himself a life sentence a long time ago. Give him a little

49

time."

An almost serene look came over her face. "Nope. He doesn't like me. I should know. I get it all the time. Look, I appreciate this. But you two share and I recently came out of a relationship, so it wouldn't work."

"You recently came out of a relationship?"

She nodded. "Yes. Like six months ago."

"That's not recent. Six months is moving-on time, baby. As for Cade, well, we've also had relationships separately. And honestly, if he sat down and talked to you like this, I think he would see you for what you really are."

"And what's that?" The question sounded more like a challenge.

"He would see that under all that hardness, you're soft inside. You're trying to protect that part of you that you're afraid will get you in trouble. You're afraid of everything. You're scared of anyone getting close because you've been hurt. I don't know if it was one spectacular ache or a series of minor ones, but they affected you. And they affected him, too. If he sat his ass down for ten seconds, he might see how much alike you are." He frowned. Everything he said was true, he simply wasn't sure it would help Cade. It might make him run even faster.

She stood up. "Look, I don't know if you think you're some sort of amateur shrink, but think again. I am who I am. I'm not hiding away or anything. If you think you can come in and change me, you're wrong."

It was time to figure out if this could potentially work. No relationship with him could work without some softness. "Sit down, Gemma."

She stared at him for a moment and then made the decision. She sat back down, her mouth set in a mulish line. Rather like Cade. Why the hell was he here? He must like stubbornness.

"I'm willing to put up with a lot of shit. It's expected in a relationship, and quite frankly, I know I'll be the easy one to deal with. But I expect honesty, respect, and some politeness. I get that you won't always be polite. I won't either. I want passion, and that doesn't always leave room for courtesy, but I expect you to start being more polite to the people around you. This isn't New York. This is small-town Colorado, and you're going to put people off with the gruffness. You had to be that way in New York. You don't here. I've told you I'll be honest, so let me state this flat out. Any relationship with me is going to involve a little discipline. I tend to keep it to the bedroom, but if you're mine and I catch you being blatantly rude to the people around you, I'll likely spank you."

It wasn't only her face that flushed this time. Her whole body went bright pink. And her pupils dilated. Her breath hitched. "That would be assault."

No, she wasn't scared at all. "Only if I did it against your will. If you were mine, we would have all sorts of rules. They would be set up so we both know how to make each other happy. We would talk about it. You could stop me, but you wouldn't want to. I would make sure of it."

She went quiet, and Jesse decided she'd had enough honesty for the day. It was time to back off and let her think about it. And it was time to go and work on Cade. He stood up and handed her the small package. It was addressed simply to Gemma Wells in Bliss, Colorado. The elderly mail carrier had asked he and Cade if they knew who she was. Jesse had jumped on that chance. And now it was time to let the whole thing go and allow Gemma to make the next move. It would be frustrating, but he wasn't going to push her.

"Think about it. That's for you. I told the mail carrier where to send anything else you get. If you want to talk some more, you come and see me." He started to walk away. He could smell the delicious aroma of sizzling steaks.

"I like *baby* and *darlin'*. I wouldn't have said I like *darlin'*, but I like the way you say it. It's the accent, I think. And for some reason, *baby* sounds sweeter than babe. But not *honey*. My mom calls me *hon*. So does Stella. *Honey* makes me think of maternal women trying to feed me." She stood up, clutching her package.

He didn't even try to stop himself now. He hugged her, wrapping his arms around her and letting himself breathe in her scent.

"Are you smelling my hair?" Gemma asked.

"Yep." Honesty.

"You're kind of kinky, aren't you?" She said it with a laugh. "And I shouldn't have called you the Sweet One."

51

He pulled back. "You have no idea, baby. And I can be very sweet. You just have to get me in the right mood. Good night."

He turned and walked away, more hopeful than he'd been moments before.

Chapter Three

Cade watched from his place at the grill. Jesse had started his whole herding thing. It was the way he handled a woman he was seriously interested in.

Damn, was Jesse going to fall for Gemma Wells and finally leave him behind? He wasn't an idiot. Jesse had been ready for something serious for the last few years. Cade was the one holding them back.

Jesse would never understand why Cade wouldn't, couldn't do the whole relationship thing.

"Jesse seems interested in the new girl." Zane Hollister flipped over the steak he was grilling, his eyes trailing back to where Jesse was hugging Gemma. Really hugging her. Like rubbing himself all over the woman.

"Looks like it." Cade glanced around. Shouldn't there be some beer around here somewhere?

"Hmmm."

He didn't like the sound of that. "What does that mean?"

Zane shrugged. "I thought you two were, well, partners."

They were, but Jesse didn't blindly follow him. It would be easier if he did. Jesse tended to prefer to take a backseat, allowing Cade to make most of the day-to-day decisions because he didn't care, but when he put his foot down, the man didn't move.

What the hell was he going to do if Jesse put his foot down over Gemma Wells? Would he be forced to make the decision he'd dreaded for the last couple of years? Would he leave and not look back? Would he finally be alone—like he'd always known he should be?

"We're best friends. We've shared a woman before, but that doesn't mean we always will." He'd never expected to share a family. He'd kind of expected to be that sort of sad-sack best friend who hung around way too much and creeped out Jesse's wife. And then they'd come to Bliss and Jesse had started talking about a real family, a shared wife, and kids they both raised. *Fuck*. He loved Bliss, but it terrified him, too.

"You don't like Gemma?"

Cade stared back her way. She clutched the package in her hand as Jesse walked away. It was the softest he'd seen her, her blonde hair nearly glowing in the light from her porch. She was a little thin, and not in a healthy way, but she had curves in all the right places. If she did belong to him and Jesse, he would cook for her, make sure she filled out those sweet curves.

He couldn't think that way.

He was terrified of her. She was exactly his type—the type to rip his heart out when things went bad. "I don't know her. I don't throw myself in the way Jesse does."

Jesse was walking toward him with a grin on his face. Gemma turned and disappeared inside her house.

Zane tested the steak, cutting slightly in the middle. "You've been here for a couple of months, and you haven't even tried dating anyone."

"Oh, I've tried. I don't think you've noticed, but there's a distinctly low available female to male ratio in this town." He and Jesse had actually been interested in a couple of women. They'd hit town and it had seemed like they were kids in a candy store. The town was full of attractive, sweet women who looked like they could use a man or two to take care of them.

The trouble was every woman they got interested in was

unavailable for one reason or another. Lucy Carson reminded him of his sister who'd died in the same car accident as his parents. Hope McLean had flipped his switch, but she was married to James Glen and Noah Bennett. He'd been attracted to Holly Lang, one of the waitresses at Stella's, but he'd decided to keep his head on his body after a single, deeply confusing conversation with Alexei Markov where he wasn't sure if he was supposed to keep the balls of his eyes off the Russian's girl or his grill. Either way, the dude sounded serious, so he was giving both a wide berth. And he'd heard some horror stories about how thorough the doc could be during a physical when he was pissed off. Yeah. Holly was safe from his roving eye.

Then the new girl comes into town, with her honey blonde hair and swaying ass, and she turned out to be such a hot mess. *Fuck*. She moved him in a way the others didn't. He kind of liked a woman with the right amount of psycho chick.

Things with a woman like Gemma Wells would go one of two ways. Either she would view them as nothing but a hot fling or she would want way more than he was willing to give. The first would please him but hurt Jesse, and the second would hurt them all. Why her? He loved intelligent, ambitious, creative women, and they tended to see him as a Neanderthal.

Bare-Chested Ape Man. Yep, that was him.

The fact that he came with a built-in partner, ready for a permanent ménage, had totally aided in his quest to find a little sex. He could see the personal ad: Bare-Chested Ape Man seeks incredibly intelligent mate to share with his over-the-top Dom partner. Must like being topped in the bedroom and small spaces since neither makes a decent paycheck.

Yes, he would get a ton of hits on that one.

"You look morose again." Jesse stared at him, a frown on his face.

Great. Now he was Morose Bare-Chested Ape Man.

"He's waffling," Zane said. "I've seen it a hundred times. Done a bit of it myself."

Zane Hollister was one of the happiest men Cade had ever met. He was also one sarcastic bastard, but he seemed like a guy who had it all together. "You waffled about marrying Callie?"

The big guy's eyes went soft as he looked over to where Callie and Nate were playing with their twins as they talked to a couple of women Cade didn't know. "She's pretty much perfect, you know. The first time I met her, I was in a bad place. I was a stupid asshole and chose my career over her. I chose my friend over her. The second time, I was in an even worse place, and I was practically certain I was bad for her."

Cade felt himself smile. Not because he was happy that Zane and Callie had trouble in the past, but because it was easy to be shocked by it. They all seemed happy. The Harpers, Stef and Jen, all of them. But every family had its own problems. The strong ones came through it. His family never had the chance. He'd made sure of it. His family had died. All of them. "What made you realize you could be good for her?"

He was merely curious. He wasn't good for anyone, but he was interested in how Hollister had known.

A wide grin crossed Hollister's scarred face. "Who said I am? She's the best thing that ever happened to me. I might not be good enough for her, but I try every day to be the best husband I can be. Now I have the twins and I have to be the best dad, too. I didn't even have a dad, but I have to step up to the plate, you know. I have Nate to rely on. Nate did have a dad. We talk it over. We figure out what Nate's dad would have done and do the exact opposite."

Jesse laughed. "I think I learned that lesson young. My dad walked out. The most important thing about being a father is to be there for your kid."

Cade felt the pit of his stomach roll. His father hadn't walked out. His father had fought. His father had tried so hard before the water had taken him, before his eyes had gone a glossy blank.

He forced the image down. Jesse was thinking about kids? Cade thought about them, but in a vague, undefined way. Kids were something that might happen in the distant future.

But he was almost thirty. The distant future might be here now.

He didn't like to think about the future. Today was what he had. He'd learned that a long time ago. Parents, even when they loved a kid, didn't always show up for baseball games and school plays. Sometimes, parents walked out the door and they didn't come back.

Sometimes kids walked out the door only to discover the ones they loved and left behind were gone forever.

He wasn't ready. He didn't want to give Gemma a chance, no matter how pretty she was or how much she moved him. He had to acknowledge for the first time that he might never be ready. There might be something inside him that was simply broken. He'd used Jesse as a crutch. If Jesse wanted to move on, then good for him. It wouldn't have worked long term anyway.

He was surrounded by working ménages, but he didn't think it would work for him. He might have some issues. And damn Gemma Wells for making him see them.

He'd been fine. He'd been happy. He'd been settling in, but no, now Gemma was forcing him to think.

"What's wrong with him?" Zane asked.

Jesse had found where the beers were stashed. He took a short sip, keeping the shit-eating grin securely on his face. "That's his thinking face. Don't worry about it. It won't last too long. Cade prefers to shove his problems as far under the surface as possible. Every now and then he's forced to confront them, and that's the look he gets."

He shot his best friend the bird and decided he'd had enough of this damn party. He stalked off toward the car.

He heard Jesse groan and begin to follow. "I'm sorry."

"No, you're not." He wasn't sorry, and he wasn't wrong, either.

"I am sorry about putting it out there like that. It felt like we were among friends, and I was teasing you a little. Okay, a lot."

He rounded on Jesse. Cade might be avoiding his past, but Jesse was sorely overestimating their future. "You think I didn't see you with her? What are you doing? She's not a good-time girl. She's going to get serious, and she'll do it fast. What the hell is going to happen when she figures out what you make for a living?"

Jesse's eyes rolled. "Not every woman in the world thinks a man is nothing more than a dick and a paycheck. Besides, she's not exactly a catch herself. She doesn't have some great job."

And that wouldn't last forever. She wouldn't let that degree go to waste. Not for any real length of time. She'd spend the winter here in Bliss with her mother, but by the time spring rolled around, she would be in a big city somewhere with a high-powered career. She wouldn't go to her company's parties with two mechanics on her arm. "She will. She's going to leave."

"Maybe we can make her want to stay."

"God, that is naïve. It's not going to happen." He hated to bring it up. Hated that he had to be the asshole who tore down his friend's hopes. "She won't stay here because of us. What is that woman going to think when she finds out you spent a good portion of your teen years in prison?"

A hint of a smile showed up on Jesse's face. "She'll think I should have had a better lawyer. She was quite mad about it, but not because she looked down on me. She thought the sentence was overkill. I kind of think so, too."

"You told her?" He'd only met her hours before.

Jesse took a step forward. "I did. I like her. I would rather get all the crap out of the way. It's better to be honest up front. Go knock on her door and talk to her. Ask her flat out what she thinks about blue-collar guys. Tell her that you've been hurt before and would prefer to avoid it. Just talk to her. No bullshit. And when she tries to avoid questions, top her."

Holy shit. "You got into the discipline stuff with her? Damn it, you haven't even asked her out. Or did you? The way you're going the engagement should happen sometime next week."

Jesse's whole body stiffened. "I was honest with her. I didn't ask her to marry me. I have no idea if we're even compatible, but I would like to try. I'm tired, Cade. I'm tired of constantly being on the move. Since we turned eighteen, we've been like gypsies."

"We had a job to do." He wasn't going to be ashamed of it.

"No. I get that. I'm talking about before. Always moving on to find something new. The next town, the next party, the next woman. I want to settle down."

That was Jesse, brutally honest, even when it fucking hurt like hell. "And she's the one?"

Jesse's frustration rolled off him in waves. "How will we know if we never fucking try? I'm not saying anything except that I want to try."

And Cade didn't. He just didn't. She was beautiful and kind of crazy, and she scared the fuck out of him. "Then you should try. You should ask her out."

It had been years since they'd dated a woman separately, but maybe the time had come. Who the hell was he to hold his friend back? Jesse was his ride or die. He had been since that day they met fifteen years before. Jesse had followed him, even when Jesse's instinct at times had been to lead.

"I don't want to date her without you," Jesse said evenly, obviously holding on to his emotional state. "But I will. You have a week to think it over. I'm going to get to know her a little. Nothing formal. You can work with me or you can think about it. If you can't even try, then I'll ask her out myself."

The idea of watching Jesse settle in with a woman stirred an odd jealousy. He would be jealous of Jesse for finding something that might work. He would be jealous of Gemma for taking his friend.

God, he did need to think. His first impulse had been to tell Jesse to ask her out right away, but maybe he owed Jesse the courtesy of time. "All right. One week."

But he still turned and walked away from the party. If he was going to think, he'd better start now.

* * * *

Gemma watched them. She couldn't help it. She had been reduced to peeper status.

Jesse and Bare-Chested Ape...Cade...seemed to be having some sort of argument. Over her, almost certainly. Cade wasn't interested. That much was obvious. He couldn't stand her. She had that effect on some men, a lot of men. She wished she knew why he'd decided she was trouble. What sort of rumors were already going around?

The door to her cabin opened after a single brisk knock. Naomi walked in, peeking around the door. "You have been holding out on me. Who was the sexy cowboy you were hugging?"

She didn't look back. She'd gotten used to Naomi's nosiness. It was almost comforting. "He's not a cowboy. He's a kinky mechanic. And he's an ex-con. Sort of."

Naomi sidled up to her, their shoulders touching as she looked out at the place where Jesse and Cade stood talking. Jesse had a beer in his hand. They were so gorgeous. Cade looked like a male model, all perfection and cheekbones and classic good looks. Jesse was the embodiment of a bad boy. She would bet he had a few tattoos. Damn, but she would like to see them.

Zane Hollister stood between them, watching the two like he was observing a tennis match.

"How is someone a 'sort of' ex-con?" Naomi asked.

Cade was frowning, that lean body of his taut with obvious tension. Jesse's shoulders moved up and down. She wished she could see his face. "Juvie."

Naomi snorted. "Baby con. If he didn't go back, it doesn't count. Those are two beautiful men. What do you think they're saying?"

She could guess. "Well, Cade is saying, 'why do you want to date that crazy city girl?' And then Jesse says, 'because she's pretty and I'd like to spank her ass when she spits bile.' Then Cade's all 'let's find a nice girl to spank.' And Jesse says, 'all the nice girls are taken. We're stuck with the beyotch.' I don't know. He might not say beyotch."

Naomi laughed. "Spank you? Are you kidding me?"

"Nope. He said he would spank me when I was rude." And her whole body had gone on full-scale alert, praying he would start right then and there. Damn it. She'd read one too many erotic romances. It was her only guilty pleasure. She was crazy about over-the-top alpha males, but she knew they were fantasies. She'd been ready to try some role playing with Patrick in an attempt to amp up their sex life, but that had gone spectacularly wrong.

Naomi bumped Gemma's hip with her own. "Hmmm. That explains it. If he's into slapping ass for violating courtesy, you're going to be his dream woman. He might never have to stop smacking your ass."

Gemma growled a little Naomi's way. "Like you would know. Oh, shit. That's not good."

Cade strode away from Jesse, his face a mask of irritation. Yep, he wasn't happy. Not at all. He was damn pissed. What had put that look on his face? Jesse followed, clutching his beer. She would have to remember he liked beer. Maybe she should buy some so she would have it if he came over.

Damn it. She didn't need to remember anything because she wasn't falling for his line of crap. It was all an act. No one was that honest. And she wasn't going to even start thinking about pleasing another man. She'd done everything she could to make Patrick's life next to perfect, and he'd taken advantage of her. She wasn't going to do it again.

Naomi turned from the window. "I don't know what's going on with those two. It doesn't look good. Do they have names?"

Gemma forced herself to turn away. She didn't want to. She probably would have watched them until she couldn't see them anymore. But it was for the best. She didn't need to get involved with anyone. Even if she really wanted to.

He'd talked about spanking her. He hadn't said the words, but he basically meant he wanted to top her. She'd read about it. Thought about it. Dreamed a bit about it. She didn't honestly want it. It was only a fantasy, and fantasies weren't meant to be lived out. Disappointment lay down that road.

But he'd seemed sure of himself. It had been a truly shocking moment. When he'd said he would spank her if she got out of line, her whole damn body had responded, and not in a bad way. She'd wondered what the relationship would mean. Could she depend on him? Could she tell him all the problems she had and expect him to help figure out how to solve them? Her brain went a million miles a minute. Sometimes it was hard to concentrate on just one thing. She struggled, but she persevered. And it would be easier if someone was checking up on her. It was like the gym. She needed accountability. But no one cared enough to put up with her shit.

And they shouldn't. She knew she was hard to handle. Focus was the key. "The one who hugged me is Jesse McCann, and he's apparently a bit of a pervert. The one who's running away is the man formerly known as Bare-Chested Ape Man. His real name is Cade. Sinclair, I think. Apparently he likes to be naked. Like a lot. This place is weird."

Naomi grinned. "This place is awesome. So you're being pursued by a nudist and a Dom?"

"I don't know if he's a Dom. We didn't actually get into that."

"Oh, if it looks like a Dom and quacks like a Dom, it's a Dom, and that man would look good naked. Both of them, actually." Naomi sighed. "Are you still not over your ex?"

She laughed at the thought. She'd been over Patrick about two seconds after she'd caught him with Christina. What she hadn't gotten over was the loss of her career. "Not at all. I can't believe I even wanted to marry him."

"Why did you?" Naomi's gorgeous brown eyes went from laughing to calculating in a single instant, and Gemma was reminded of how intelligent the nurse was.

And she was spurred on by Jesse's honesty. Of all the things that had happened to her today, his flat honesty was the most affecting thing of all. "He was a safe bet."

Naomi sighed and crossed to her small table, looking down at the box there. "That doesn't sound romantic."

It wasn't. "Think of it more like a merger. Patrick and I wanted the same things. We understood the same world. We didn't hate each other." The sex had been bland, but she wasn't absolutely sure that wasn't her fault. Christina hadn't had the same problem. Another reason to stay away from Jesse and Cade and their ridiculously hot sexuality. "It was an easy relationship. Well, except for the part where he was a cheating, job stealing weasel. Other than that, I was almost completely in control."

Naomi shuddered. "That sounds horrible. Why would you do that?"

She'd asked herself the question about a million times and could only come up with one answer. "Because the love thing isn't real."

"Your momma would disagree."

She would. Her mother would tell her how much she'd loved her father, but now all Gemma could see was how much she'd grieved. "I was young when he died. I mostly remembered how horrible it was. We didn't know he had cancer until he went into the hospital. We thought it was a cold. Pneumonia, maybe. And then they told us it was stage-four lung cancer. I watched him die. I watched her watch him die. I don't see anything great about love."

Naomi's eyes filled with tears, and she walked to Gemma. "Then you weren't looking hard enough, hon. I'm glad you didn't marry that man. It would have been a mistake."

Damn straight. "Especially since he was fucking Christina Big Tits at the time." Gemma got out a letter opener. She should at least open the package. Jesse had brought it for her. What if it was actually from him? Her heart rate sped up. Another good reason to stay away. She was serious about the love thing. She didn't want it. But he was too tempting. And Bare-Chested Ape Man was, too. Damn him. "Patrick and I lived in the same world."

Naomi sat down. "Your world is narrow from what I can tell. And not particularly pleasant. Why aren't you joining the party?"

Because those people scared the crap out of her with their babies and happy lives and small-town world. Everyone knew everyone else. Everyone seemed to accept everyone else. It was a façade. She wasn't a dumbass. If she scratched the surface, she would probably find out that Callie hated Rachel Harper and had affairs with half the town, and sweet-faced Nell was really a horrible person. At least Max Harper was honest about his assholiness. "I don't have anything in common with them."

"Did they give you a class in self-delusion at Harvard?" It was a rhetorical question since she didn't wait for an answer. Naomi held up the package, studying it. "Who knows you're here?"

"I left a forwarding address, but that was to Mom's place in Chicago." The package looked to be tightly sealed. Gemma started to slice through the tape. "It's probably from someone at my old firm. They could find me pretty easily. I didn't exactly get a chance to clean out my desk. After Christina Big Tits pressed charges, they fired me and wouldn't let me back in the building."

A single eyebrow arched. Naomi wasn't past thirty-five, but she had the motherly attitude down. "I suspect that is not her real last name."

Someone had been damn serious about the package staying closed. The whole thing was wrapped in thick tape. "It might have been Fake Tits. Not sure."

Naomi leaned forward, her dark eyes sympathetic. "You know this wall you've built around yourself is going to have to come down someday."

"I don't see why." She freed one side and went to work on the other. She'd worked hard to build those walls. Taking them down would be a poor use of her time.

"Because you're never going to find happiness if you don't."

"Happiness is overrated. Ask my mom." Her mom was the reason she didn't believe in happily ever after. Her mom had done everything right when it came to picking her husband. And he'd died anyway. No forever for her mom. No joy. Just an aching sadness and a hole that couldn't be filled.

"Honey, you should ask your mom. I think you would find she wouldn't have changed a thing about her life. She's worried about you. I am, too."

She finally pried the box open only to be met with a layer of plastic. What had she left behind at the office? No pictures. She hadn't had any. They'd sent her expensively framed degrees to Chicago, and they now sat in a box on the kitchen counter. Would they send all the office supplies she'd kept? "Don't be worried about my love life. Worry about my career. I haven't gotten a single callback."

Naomi was like a dog with a bone. "Jesse seemed like a nice man. Why didn't you stay and talk to him?"

"Because I don't want to get my heart ripped out." She pulled back the plastic and gagged a little. *Fuck*. She hadn't left that in her desk. "Looks like someone else had their heart ripped out."

Tension prickled along her spine. There was no blood in the box, only an organ that had been surgically removed, if the neatness of the incisions was any indication. Someone had sent her a message. A heart. Dead and unmoving. A useless thing, a bit like her own.

Naomi put a hand over her nose and looked inside the box where the brownish-gray heart lay. Nothing else. Just a heart. "Okay, gross. I'll be right back."

"Don't get my mom." She followed Naomi to the door. "You don't need to get anyone. It's a prank."

Naomi shook her head. "It's a threat. Calm down. I'll be discreet."

Naomi strode off the porch and made a beeline for Nate Wright. He waved a hello to her as he cuddled his baby close. Gemma frowned as Naomi discreetly whispered something to the sheriff that caused him to hand off his son and start walking toward her cabin. As though he had sonar hearing, Cam Briggs perked up and started following, too. The rest of the party continued, but the two lawmen had laser focused in on her.

Nate had a fierce scowl on his face as he climbed her steps. "Seriously? You've been on the job for less than twenty-four hours and you've picked up a crazy?"

Gemma shrugged. She hated to admit it, but she actually would feel better if Nate knew about it. It was a heart. A freaking heart. She buried the fear deep. It wouldn't help to show it. "You know how to pick 'em, boss."

Cam smiled, the buttons of his shirt open and showing off tanned skin. "I'm excited. It's been boring around here since Hope killed her ex. What have we got? Creepy letter? Voice mail threats?"

Nate looked into the box. "Heart in a box."

Cam, the asshole, actually fist pumped. "Awesome. Who'd you piss off, Gemma?"

Honesty. It was the word of the day. "Pretty much everyone who's ever met me."

Nate turned to Naomi. "You're a nurse, right? I'll have Caleb take a look, but I would appreciate your input. Is that thing human?"

Naomi took another look at Gemma's present. "It's too small to be human. I think we're probably looking at a canine heart."

"Someone killed a dog?" That was horrible. A sweet puppy had been murdered so some asshole could scare the crap out of her?

"You were okay when it was human?" Cam asked.

"No. I'm not okay with any of it, but I like dogs more than most people." Dogs didn't sleep around on her and take credit for her work. Maybe she should get a dog. She'd never been able to have one in New York.

Naomi shook her head. "It's a cadaver heart most likely. It might be a swine heart. You can buy them pretty easily. Or sneak one out of most teaching hospitals. It's been preserved. Formaldehyde. Ick. This is why I didn't go into research. I hate the smell. Who would send you a heart in a box?"

"I don't know." She suddenly felt weary. She'd been forced to walk away from her job, but it looked like it had followed her to

Bliss. She turned away. She meant to keep up the tough-girl attitude, but she didn't have to stare at it. "I'll make a list of the cases I've worked on. There are a few where I was either lead or secondary counsel, but I almost always had face time with the clients or the opponents. Some of them were pissed off." She hated to beg, but she felt the need. "Could we please keep this quiet? I would prefer to just be the bitch, not the bitch who gets hearts in the mail."

"I have to talk to Caleb, but he won't mention it." Nate pulled a set of latex gloves out of his pocket. Gemma could only imagine how much he must love his job. "Who gave this to you?"

Fuck. She did not want to bring him into this.

"McCann. I saw him walk up with it." Cameron Briggs was way too observant.

"He said the mail carrier was asking Long-Haired Roger about it." Had she called the man Long-Haired Roger?

A long look passed between Nate and Cam.

"He didn't do this," she insisted. "Did you check and see where it was posted from?"

"It looks like it came out of St. Louis. But that doesn't mean a thing," Nate replied as he started to tape the box back up, carefully making sure he had every bit of packing material. "And I didn't say Jesse McCann had anything to do with it."

"But you thought it." She'd seen that look pass between them.

Cam took over. "Jesse's new in town. And he's had a run-in with the law."

Gemma felt her fists clench. "That was stricken from his record the moment he turned eighteen. It is absolutely unacceptable for you to use that charge against him."

"Whoa, counselor." Cam's hands came up in self-defense. "I didn't say I was charging him with anything. I merely stated that he has a record, and he brought the box to you. I have to look into it. And as far as the legal records are concerned, his charges are gone. I happen to be more thorough than simply checking what's easily available."

That surprised her. "You're a hacker?"

The big blond deputy gave her a thumbs-up. "Hacker, profiler, former FBI agent, now small-town deputy."

She wouldn't have pegged him as FBI. He was too laid back, too, well, happy. "I still don't think it was him."

Nate started toward the door. "I don't think so, either, but I'll look into it. And you seem damn ready to defend him. You two got something going on?"

Nope. Just a whole lot of hot thoughts that she had no intention of acting on. "No."

Nate's eyes narrowed in suspicion. "Because if you do have something going on, I think you should tell him about this before he finds out on his own. I'll keep it quiet for now, but these things have a way of coming out. Men around here don't like it when their women hide things."

Gemma rolled her eyes. "I am not his woman. Come on, Sheriff. What century do you think we're in? Even if we were dating, this would be my problem and I would want to keep it private."

"Have it your way. I'll ask him about it, but I won't let on." Nate turned, gesturing for Cam to come with him. "'Night, ma'am."

Cam slapped his boss on the back. "She's going to get spanked. I heard Jesse was the type."

Naomi shook her head. "Damn, the men here are fine. And you might get spanked, lucky girl. But seriously, think about this. You don't know that man. Jesse McCann might look nice, but looks aren't everything. The sweetest-faced man can turn on you in a heartbeat. Be careful, okay? I'm going to go back out there or your momma is going to start asking questions. Lock your doors. Better yet, come stay with us."

She wasn't going to be run out of her rented, temporary home. "I'll be fine. I don't have my gun back, but I have a whole purse full of other weapons. This isn't the first time someone's tried to scare me. It won't be the last. Now go on. My cell is charged, and the sheriff and the deputy live right down the road. I'm fine."

Naomi hugged her and left.

But she wasn't fine. She was scared, but she was also alone so she had to hold it together.

She fell asleep wondering if Jesse had a dark side. Or if Cade was the type of man to send a woman a message to stay away.

Chapter Four

Gemma stared at the red-haired doctor as he examined her gift from the previous day. She stood in the Bliss Clinic's version of a lab. It wasn't much more than a converted storage room, but the equipment Dr. Caleb Burke was working with looked pretty top of the line. He stared into a microscope at a piece of tissue he'd taken from the heart.

All in all, not the way she'd thought she would spend her first day on the job.

"We had a nurse look at it last night." Nate leaned against the countertop next to a container marked EBOLA CURE. "Naomi happened to be there. She thinks it's not human."

Should they be standing so close to anything called Ebola? "Uhm, I didn't know there was an actual cure for that."

Caleb's head came up and he glanced her way before shrugging and going back to his microscope. "It's SweeTarts. Cassidy Meyer likes them. When I tried to give her mints she wouldn't take them. Apparently the flavor winter green is an alien trap. Now when she gets the Ebola, as she puts it, it's SweeTarts for the win."

Gemma looked at Nate. "Someone in town has hemorrhagic fever?"

Shouldn't they be more worried? She got that this was a laid-back place, but damn.

Nate waved it off. "Cassidy's always got something. She's a character, as we like to say here in Bliss. Doc always checks her out and then gives her something to calm her down."

"So she's crazy."

Doc's head was back up, a glare in his eyes. "You want to define crazy for me? Because I've discovered we're all crazy in our own way. I can give Cassidy candy when she has an episode or she'll get a bunch of drugs that won't change the fact that she's simply different from the rest of us. She's happy and she's healthy, and who cares if she's also a hypochondriac."

Doc could go cold when he wanted to. She held her hands up, giving up that fight. "It's cool with me if she wants to pretend to have a bunch of diseases. I have told many a guy I had explosive diarrhea to get out of a bad date."

Nate snorted. "So what do you think, Doc? Was the nurse right?"

"It's definitely a cadaver heart. I would say swine. It's something you could pick up from a medical supplier if you had the right contacts, and those wouldn't be hard to find. All you need is some cash." He turned to her. "The good news is the pig was already dead. The bad news is someone is trying to send you a message, and not a good one. Usually when you get a body part of any kind sent to you anonymously it means you've pissed someone off," the doc said.

"Had a lot of experience with it, huh?" She had to ask the question even though her brain was running about a hundred miles a minute. It had been going all night.

"Absolutely," the doc agreed. "Though mostly it was bodily excretions."

"He's been sent a lot of shit through the mail," Nate explained. "But that was back when he was a complete asshole."

"Nah, someone left a big load on the doorstep of the clinic a couple of days ago. Pretty sure it was Max because his yearly physical was last week." Doc shrugged. "I will admit to being overly thorough with him. If anyone deserves an embarrassing rectal exam, it's Max. After all, he's ninety percent asshole."

Nate snorted at that. "Well, I don't think anyone would disagree with you, and we all know Quigley can drop a deuce. But none of that solves the problem of my brand-new office manager's stalker."

She sighed. "We don't know it's a stalker."

"You think someone who likes you sent you a heart?" Doc pointed to the Ebola cure box. "You need a SweeTart?"

She rolled her eyes. "Fine. It's someone who's unhappy with me. That could be a whole lot of people. I was a lawyer in New York City. Everyone hates me."

"I'm going to need you to be more specific," Nate insisted.

"Who would send you a heart?" Doc asked.

A crazy person. Only a crazy person would send a damn heart. Or someone who had a very specific point to make.

Nate seemed to catch on to what Doc was saying. "Did you work any cases involving medicine? You were a litigator. You sued people or defended companies who were being sued. Some of them had to involve pharmaceuticals, right?"

"Several." She'd made a list the night before. "I can probably give you the names of half a dozen people who wouldn't mind scaring the shit out of me, but there's only one who actively stated he would find a way to kill me."

A single brow rose over Nate's eyes, and she was certain he was perfecting that "dumbass said what" look he would use later on his boys. "You didn't think to mention this until now?"

She shrugged. "I didn't want to make a big deal out of it."

Doc pointed her way. "I get her. So tell me about this nurse because I could use a nurse. I don't know why I'm having trouble finding one."

Probably because they walked in and saw that he had developed a cure for Ebola that he kept in a plastic cereal container. Still, she wasn't sure Naomi would want to go back to Chicago. "You should ask her. Mom's getting better every day. She won't need her full time soon. But she's going to need benefits if she has to put up with your sarcasm."

"I would think she's used to it. You've been around her for months, right?" Doc challenged.

It was fair. "But she would also have to deal with that Mel guy, right?"

The negotiations had begun.

Nate stepped between them. "Hey, could we figure out who's trying to murder my admin before we deal with Caleb's staffing issues?"

"Says the guy who actually has an admin," Caleb pointed out. "Fine. But I'm going to talk to her."

He stepped out of the room, leaving her alone with her new boss.

"I'd like a list of names," Nate said.

She'd already made one. She'd sat up the night before and written down what she could remember about all the cases she'd worked on. Only one stood out. "I worked on a case when I was a first-year associate. This dude claimed he'd invented some new material that they were using in heart valves. A major medical company said it was their intellectual property and they didn't owe him anything."

"I take it you worked for the company."

"That's me. Always on the side of evil. You know evil needs a lawyer, too," she said. "Anyway, I might or might not have found a teeny tiny loophole in the contract that the firm might or might not have used to ensure the dude who probably developed the material in question didn't get a dime off of his hard work."

Nate stared at her. "Might have?"

"It was a job. I was good at it." She wasn't going to apologize. Even if she kind of felt bad about it now. "I don't remember his name, but he figured out I was the one who found the loophole and he sent some nasty notes."

"What do you mean by nasty?"

"The usual. I'm going to kill you. Blah. Blah, blah. You're going to burn in hell. Yadda, yadda. That kind of stuff," she admitted.

Nate sighed. "We're going to have to work on the fact that you're good at burying the lead. I'll need that list and everything you can remember about the case."

"Sure. I'll make a project of it." She looked at the sheriff. "Still happy you blackmailed me? You know karma's a bitch, right?"

A smile tugged the sheriff's lips up. "Somehow I think you'll be worth it."

That surprised her. "What makes you think that? I really did help a firm screw that guy out of his own work. I wasn't joking about that. It was my job to find the absolute best outcome for my client."

"And what happens when you start to view my office and this town as your client?" Nate mused. "You see, this town works on you. I should know since I wanted to leave it once. I thought for sure I didn't fit in here, but Bliss…well, this town finds a way to change a person."

"I don't change easily." She didn't want him to think she would be some softie after a few weeks of clean mountain air and sunshine. "I'm going to work for you while I find a way back to my life. My real life."

"I'll take that bet." Nate settled the Stetson on his head. "Let's head back to the office. I'm ready for a nap."

She bet he was. The place was weird, and she didn't understand these people.

Still, she grabbed some Ebola cure before she went because Cassidy was right. SweeTarts were delicious.

* * * *

Jesse glanced inside the window of the Sheriff's Department and caught sight of Gemma frowning at a filing cabinet. She was dressed in slacks and a blouse that had likely cost more than he made the previous week. She bit that sexy as hell bottom lip of hers and then shook her head as though giving up.

"You going in?" Cameron Briggs walked up the sidewalk, passing him on the stairs that led to the outer door. "Is Long Haired Roger having problems?" He looked inside, his hand on the door. "Ah, it's Gemma that brings you out today."

"How's she settling in?" He'd given her a day to think about whether or not she wanted to see him. He was planning on getting to know her this week, letting her see how he liked to treat the women he dated without scaring her off. He wasn't the kind of guy who wanted to fuck around on the weekends and not see his lover outside the bedroom. He wanted to know her, to be a part of her life.

But only if she wanted the same thing, too.

Cam grinned. "She's awesome. I mean Hope was great. She was, but she was also super nice and that doesn't always work in law enforcement. I always worried about leaving Hope alone when we had someone locked up because she could be taken advantage of. Not Gemma. She could be a cop."

"You leave her alone with criminals?" He didn't like the sound of that.

"They are locked up and with Gemma around, they're going to stay that way. Hope and Callie were suckers for a hard luck story, but Gemma ignores the crying like a pro." Cam sighed, a contented sound. "She actually got a guy to confess on her first day. I don't think he actually did the crime, but she had him ready to confess to anything. She's awesome."

Well, at least she seemed to have found her place at work. "I like her, too."

"Then why are you standing out here instead of going inside?" Cam asked.

Because he wasn't sure he should go inside. "She's been through a lot. I don't know that she's ready to date again. I know Cade's not ready, but I'm not sure he ever will be. Did you ever think about what you would have done if Rafe hadn't been ready to share Laura?"

Cam's hand came off the door and he stepped down to Jesse's level. "We fought in the beginning, you know. We didn't get together here in Bliss like some of the others so the idea of sharing her at all was foreign. It cost us years. It wasn't until we came here that we realized it was a real possibility."

"Cade's never minded sharing a woman," Jesse said, a bit wistful. He'd known what he'd wanted for years. "I always thought when it was time to settle down, we would find a woman and start a family. Turns out Cade never had that plan."

"Yeah, well, you know what they say about the best laid plans. They often go astray and there's usually a gorgeous woman involved. If Rafe hadn't been ready, I would have gone after Laura myself," Cam admitted. "At some point, you have to put her first. If you want to try with her, then make the decision that even if Cade's not interested, you're still going to go for it. It can't work any other way."

"I feel something for her I haven't felt...well, I've never felt it." Their chemistry was off the charts and he couldn't help but explore it.

With or without his best friend. "I would regret it for the rest of my life if I didn't try to figure out if we could work."

"Then you should start by walking in there." Cam hopped up and opened the outer door.

There was a knot in his gut that Cade wasn't with him, but he had to try. Up ahead, Gemma had a huge stack of folders on her desk and she was shaking her head.

He walked through the doors and she looked up, holding one out.

"This is the worst filing system...." Her hand came down and those big blue eyes widened. "Oh, hi. Sorry. I thought you were Nate coming back from lunch. Cam, this filing system is terrible. You know the alphabet has an order, right?"

Cam merely walked past him toward his desk. "I was unaware. I'm glad to know that. There's a reason Nate put the whole thing in your capable hands."

She put a hand on her hip and glared Cam's way. "He did that because he's lazy." She pivoted, facing Jesse. "Sorry about that. Office stuff. Can I help you?"

That bravado of hers was such a shield. He had no doubt she could handle herself with the best of them, but there was something in the way she softened around him that let him know she wanted a place where she didn't have to be tough.

He wanted to be that place. "I wanted to see if you would come to lunch with me. It's nothing fancy. Just Stella's."

She shrugged like it didn't matter. "I like Stella's. And I haven't eaten yet."

"I asked if you wanted to go with me," Cam pointed out. "You said you were waiting. What exactly were you waiting on?"

Cam was a bastard, but he'd let Jesse know she'd been waiting on him. He'd mentioned he might come by for lunch sometime this week. Had she waited yesterday, too?

Maybe she was more ready than he suspected.

She sent Cam a look that could have frozen fire. "I had a phone call I needed to take and I took it so now I can go to lunch. Thank you very much."

She grabbed her purse and joined him.

"I'm glad you were free." He didn't want to embarrass her. "I was worried I would miss you. I normally would take lunch around 11:30, but I was trying to finish the Bronco. It's outside. I'll walk back."

"Or I can take you." She started walking beside him. "Is Cade with you?"

He wanted to smack his best friend. "He had to work through lunch."

"Oh," she said, pressing through the door. She walked down the stairs and got to the sidewalk before stopping and turning to him. "You sure you want to go to lunch with me on your own?"

Coded language. Do you want to date me without Cade by your side? Such a wealth of worry in that question. He took her hand in his. "There is nothing I want more than to take you to lunch. I want to spend time with you. If it's okay with you, maybe we can start with lunches every day. Long Haired Roger doesn't mind when we take lunch as long as the work gets done."

She seemed to think about it for a moment as though deciding how to handle the situation. He was pleased beyond measure when she nodded.

"I would like that, too."

"And if Cade came with me occasionally?"

"I would be okay with that." She looked down to where his hand was on hers.

He pulled away, not wanting to push her. This week was about getting to know each other. "I'm glad. Let's get lunch and I'll tell you all about how I fixed the Bronco."

Her nose wrinkled. "That sounds terrible. Tell me about how you came to Bliss."

"It's a long story."

She started toward the café. "Then it'll be a long lunch."

He moved beside her, more hopeful than he'd been before.

Chapter Five

"Good morning, Gemma."

Gemma thought seriously about ducking under her desk. Nell Flanders was the single most tenacious person she'd ever met, and she'd gone three rounds with a superior court judge. Nell Flanders had walked in every morning for the last week and placed two things on her desk: A muffin of unknown origin and a picture of a person Gemma's former profession was—in Nell's words—seeking to murder for corporate profit.

Calvin Township was a small community with exactly one employer, a tanning mill owned by a large conglomerate. It boasted one school, one stoplight and twelve people with small cell carcinoma. Given that the town only had a population of one hundred and fifty—and three of the twelve were children—it was logical that the EPA had investigated.

But they hadn't found anything. And she was no longer even with the firm.

"This morning I have brought you a vegan cornmeal raspberry muffin. It was made with my own hands, so we can be sure it's cruelty-free." She placed a picture of an adorable girl with pigtails in front of Gemma. "And this is Mikayla. Her life is not cruelty-free because Tremon Industries poisoned her water supply with chemicals and now she has tumors on her kidneys."

God, Nell was killing her. "I feel for her. I'm sorry, but the EPA tested the site themselves. Everything was within regulations. Maybe the standards need to be tightened, but that's not my job. And neither is this. I don't work for Giles and Knoxbury anymore. I work here, and Nate has been careful about his recycling practices. He does as little paperwork as humanly possible. His laziness is saving trees."

"I resent that!" Nate yelled from behind his halfway opened door.

Cam looked up from his computer. "He also resembles it."

But Nell wouldn't be swayed. "Then the EPA is wrong. Or they're lying."

"I still don't know what you want me to do."

"You're a lawyer."

They'd gone over this a couple of times. "Yes, in New York. I'm not licensed to practice here, and the mayor came by my cabin and told me the town has a ban on practicing lawyers within the city limits. I don't think that's legal, but if I bring it up to a judge, I might be driven out of town. When you think about it, it's a good play."

Nell frowned. She was a sweet-looking thing, Nell Flanders, but Gemma wasn't fooled. There was a ruthless determination behind all her syrupiness. And besides, syrup stuck to everything, clinging and making even skin difficult to clean. "Enjoy the muffin. I have to make my rounds and then Henry and I have a protest scheduled for noon. The Stop 'n' Shop is trying to evict a long-term resident for absolutely no reason. I have to stop it. See you tomorrow."

Nell walked out, and Cam smiled Gemma's way. "It's going to be a fun afternoon. She's talking about a raccoon, you know. It's been living in the men's room. No one actually goes into the men's room at the Stop 'n' Shop because it's supposed to be haunted, but now the raccoon has reached mating age and they get downright nasty, if you know what I mean."

She didn't. She didn't understand a damn thing in this place. And she hated the way Mikayla's eyes seemed to be staring up at her. She put the picture in the top drawer of her desk along with Billy Sims, aged eight with leukemia, a fourteen-year-old named Sandy who needed a kidney transplant, and two twins with bad asthma. All from Calvin Township. All within two miles of the Tremon Industries plant.

"Why haven't you thrown those pictures out?" Cam asked, his blue eyes sympathetic.

She couldn't. Someone had taken those pictures. Someone loved those children. And she couldn't throw out their smiling faces even though it didn't mean anything to her own life. It didn't. She hadn't caused the problem. And she couldn't solve it. "I'm worried Nell will give me a quiz at the end of the week."

Cam snorted and reached for the muffin. She'd been tossing them to Cam every morning, but she slapped him away this time. Nell had made it for her. And she was hungry. Screw her diet. How many calories could it be? It was vegan. "Get your own muffin-making stalker."

Cam frowned but went back to his desk. He glanced out at the street and sighed. "I would argue, but that coffee you make is too damn good. The night shift is complaining, however. They have no idea how to use that monstrosity of a coffeemaker."

"It's a beautiful machine. I got it instead of a car." She couldn't help but smile. She already liked working with Nate and Cam. They were the dysfunctional brothers she'd never had. "I'll bring up the instruction manual and try to show them how before shift change tonight. And why don't we hire another deputy? Aren't those guys from Creede?"

Cam's eyes moved toward the empty desk. The one she wasn't allowed to clean out. The one time she'd tried to go through it, she'd gotten yelled at. They kept that desk like a shrine to the person who used to sit at it. "They're filling in on the nights when Nate and I both have off. Sometimes Rafe does it and Rye Harper takes a turn. Logan's coming back. He needs some time. He's on sabbatical."

She felt her eyebrows creep up. Finally, someone who wasn't perfectly adjusted. "Where I come from, a sabbatical means someone's gone a little crazy."

Cam's face went cold, and she knew she'd stepped into a whole pile of shit. "He's not crazy. And he's coming back." Cam turned, his shoulders locked, dismissal evident.

Yep. She'd screwed up. Now was the time to simply get back to her work. It wasn't her fault the deputy had his panties in a wad. She'd made a dumb joke. How was she supposed to know this mysterious Logan person had actually gone crazy and gotten sent away to some sort of rest facility? Cam joked all the time. He made fun of her.

And she could have told him his ears were too big and Cam would have played along. But Cam wouldn't let her joke about this mysterious Logan. Logan was his friend. Cam protected him even from dumb jokes.

Jesse McCann was a stupid bastard who was having way too much of an effect on her life. She could actually hear him telling her to reach out and apologize, to make things nice between her and Cam again.

Every day he'd shown up at the station house. Twice he'd taken her to Stella's and eaten lunch with her. Twice he'd shown up and sat in the break room and had a cup of coffee. Once he'd brought her a lunch Cade had cooked. Homemade lasagna that made Cam's stomach rumble and Nate sniff around asking if there was more. Did Cade know she'd eaten his food? He might not have liked it. He might have been creeped out by the fact that the whole time she'd eaten that delicious lasagna, she'd wondered if he'd cooked it in the buff. She'd had a vision of Cade in an apron with a spatula in his hand, and she'd gotten freaky excited.

Only once had Cade accompanied his partner. They had both shown up with ice cream cones. Chocolate, mint chocolate chip, and rocky road. No vanilla for those boys. They'd given her first pick. They'd sat on the front steps and ate while she and Jesse talked and she and Cade stared at each other.

And Jesse had kept up his eternal lectures on politeness and friendship and damn it, Cam was kind of her friend. She'd worked for years at Giles and Knoxbury and didn't consider a single person there her friend, but one week in a craptastic jailhouse and she was soft on everyone.

"I, uh, kind of assaulted a woman. That's why I got fired." The words were out of her mouth before she could call them back. Apology by way of confession.

79

Cam turned, a half smile on his face. "I know. I saw the YouTube video. You have a killer left hook, by the way."

Embarrassment flashed through her system. "Damn it. I was hoping that hadn't made it out here. Stupid Internet. Anyway, all I was trying to say is, I understand the need for a sabbatical. I wasn't making judgments. I come off that way, but I'm not. I've screwed up enough that I can't judge anyone. I got put on a seventy-two-hour psych hold. They were going to take me to jail, but I cried and talked about hanging myself with my Chanel bag and, sure enough, I got three days at Bellevue before they decided I was neurotic and not crazy."

There was a snort from the deputy. "Yeah, we sent Logan to Dallas to get his shit together. He was out of control. But he's going to come back, and you'll like him."

She probably would. She would, at the very least, understand him. And she envied him. When she'd lost control, she'd lost everything. When Logan had done it, he still had a job and friends waiting on him. And she'd kind of like to meet him. Was she considering sticking around here? No. But maybe for a while. Maybe she could view Bliss as her psych ward. Take six months and recover and then reclaim her real life. She liked the sound of that. And if she had some raucous sex in the meantime, good for her.

Cam gestured to the front door. "Your other stalker is here. And he's brought a friend."

Sure enough, she stood and could see Jesse walking toward the double doors. And Cade was right behind him. Her heart nearly skipped a beat. She had to stop this teenager crush thing she had going. It was silly. She actually wanted to run to the bathroom and make sure her hair was fixed.

Nate came to the door of his office, lazily leaning against the side. "Your friends here again?"

Dear god, he was kind of like a disapproving father. "I didn't invite them."

"Yes she did." Cam was obviously taking on the tattletale role.

She turned to Cam. "Did not."

"She did that giggling thing girls do when they're totally into a guy," Cam explained. "And she practically blew her ice cream cone yesterday. It was gross. She was licking and practically inhaling it."

She had the strongest urge to smack him. "That's not true. I hadn't had ice cream in a long time. I enjoyed it. And it wasn't gross."

"He wouldn't have thought it was gross if Laura did it," Nate pointed out.

Cam shrugged. "Laura's hot. Gemma's, well, she's Gemma."

And she'd tried to spare his feelings why? She flipped him the bird. "Screw you, Cam."

The doors opened at the perfect moment to have Jesse catch her cussing at Cam while she flipped him off. Jesse's whole face darkened, his mouth turning down. Cade shook his head like he'd always known she would be trouble.

Nate sighed. "Don't look at her that way, you two. Cam was being an ass. He deserved it."

Cam looked back and forth between them. "I can't help it. I can't find her hot. She's like my little sister."

Jesse's focus went right to Cam. "Keep it that way."

Nate leaned over and whispered. "Tell him about the package. He's going to find out." Nate had been on her for days to tell Jesse and Cade what was going on. He straightened up. "You two have her back in an hour."

Nate walked away. Cam winked her way and then walked off to the break room, leaving her alone with a still-frowning Jesse and Cade. Jesse stared at her, obviously expecting some sort of explanation. Cade simply waited as though he'd only been hanging around because she was going to screw up at some point in time.

She felt stupid. The morning had been comfortable, pleasant even. She was fine with the minor skirmishes with Cam. They felt good, like she was connecting and finding a weird place for herself, but now she felt dumb again. She'd been fooling herself. She couldn't live up to whatever Jesse seemed to expect from her. She sat back down at her desk and tried to give them a calm smile.

"Was there something I can help you with? I can't go out to lunch. I have a lot to do."

"Nate said you have an hour." Jesse loomed over her.

She could smell the aftershave he'd used. His face was clean right now, but by afternoon that sexy beard of his would make an appearance. The one time she'd hugged him, his beard had scraped against her skin, a delicious sensation.

But she was already too crazy about him, and when he figured out she wouldn't get with his game plan, he would move on to a more acceptable female. It was better to get out with her pride intact. "I think I'll skip lunch today. I have to go through all of Nate's mail and book his travel for the big conference."

"You can take an hour, Gemma." There was a hard edge to Jesse's tone.

"I don't want to."

"Why?" he asked.

He was so frustrating. Most guys would shrug and move on, but not Jesse McCann. He wanted to talk about it. The man loved to talk. He'd missed his calling. He should have been a shrink. He was always asking her why she felt the way she felt. "I…"

He held a hand out. "You think about what you're going to say. You give it some real consideration. If you're about to spit something nasty out, you should know that it won't go over well. We've had a nice week. We've been talking and getting to know each other. Let's not screw it up by you getting pissed off."

"I'm not the one who was pissed off," she shot back. "You walked in and got mad that Cam and I were teasing each other."

Jesse leaned over the table, his lean body an instrument of both intimidation and temptation. "You were flipping him off."

Cade stepped up. "Jeez, Jess, give her a break. Cam can be an asshole. She was fucking with him."

Jesse turned to Cade. "I want her to start fitting in here. She can't do that if she flips off everyone who makes her mad."

A smile curled Cade's lips. "I don't see why not. This town has plenty of cantankerous people."

Actually, now that she thought about it, it was true. Jesse had said he wanted her to fit in to Bliss and that he was trying to help her, but the truth was, he was trying to make her fit in with his vision of what a woman should be. She felt heavier than before. She hadn't realized how much she'd looked forward to seeing Jesse every day, and now she had to give him up.

"I don't want to go out. You two should find some other idiot to run these games on. I don't want to have anything to do with all this discipline shit."

Jesse stared at her for a minute and then turned and walked right out the door. Well, that was easy.

Blinking past an entirely annoying set of tears, she turned back to her laptop. At least it was over. She could go back to concentrating on what was important. Doing her job and finding a way to get back to her real life. This whole relationship stuff was way too rough.

"Discipline shit?" Cade stood in front of her.

She nearly groaned. Why hadn't he left with his friend? He hadn't been happy to be around her at all. He should be thrilled. "Go away."

"You would like that, wouldn't you?"

She turned her eyes up, looking into his way too perfect face. "Yes. I would like it if you would leave."

"Damn it." His fingers came out, catching a tear. "Don't do this to me, Wells. You're the tough bitch. Stay the tough bitch."

She slapped his hand away. She could do that for him. "Get out of here. Go follow your friend."

He turned to walk off. The door slammed behind him, and she was blissfully alone.

Which was where she should have been all along. With a deep breath, she turned back to her work, thankful that Cam and Nate weren't around to see what a fool she'd made of herself.

* * * *

Cade nearly stormed out the door, pausing in between the inner and outer doors to catch his breath. She was everything he'd thought she was. Bitchy. Career obsessed. Self-centered. A little vulgar.

The last part didn't bother him a bit. He kind of liked her smart mouth. He often thought some of the women Jesse picked up were a bit dull since they never talked back. He wanted a bit of brat in his woman.

And she wasn't truly self-centered. The couple of times he'd sat and listened to her, she'd had real conversations with Jesse. She'd talked about the world and her mom and what books she'd been reading. She'd listened to Jesse, allowing him to change her mind about a few things. She was stubborn, but she wasn't stupid about it. When Jesse had a good argument, she'd followed him. When he didn't, she'd told him what she thought, challenged him. Hell, she'd talked about some things that had gone over Cade's head, and he'd found himself looking the issue up on the Internet so he could understand the arguments she made.

Fuck all. He liked her. And that whole episode with Jesse didn't ring true, damn it. He'd watched her. She'd been horrified that he'd found her flipping Cam the bird. Cade had flipped Cam the bird on more than one occasion. The guy could be a dick, but he was just having fun. Cade thought it was actually a good thing that Cam was fucking around with Gemma. It meant she was starting to find her place. But Jesse overreacted and allowed his temper to flare.

Cade looked out and Jesse was standing at the street corner, his body a complete study in tension. Jesse didn't allow himself to lose his temper. He kept it under rigid control. But sometimes that temper was on a hair trigger, and Jesse had shown signs of it all week long. He'd been testy, on edge. The only time he'd been his calm, serene self was when he was around Gemma, as though she had some magical effect on him.

Then she'd spit bile his way. He was pretty sure Jesse had taken that all wrong. That single tear on her cheek gnawed at Cade's insides.

Gemma Wells put on a good front, but what if that front hid the softer woman on the inside?

He wasn't going to do it. This was his out. He would walk right out there and commiserate with Jesse on what a close call he'd had. He'd call his friend Ty and they could meet him at the Elk Creek Lodge for a few drinks, and before long they would have a nice safe woman between them and Jesse's cares would melt away. They would go on the way they always had. Sooner or later the shine would fade off this town, and they would hop on their bikes and drive away.

Yes. He would do that.

Except his goddamn traitor feet weren't listening to his brain. He turned and marched right back inside.

Only to catch her dabbing at her eyes.

"What the fuck is wrong with you?" Cade spat the question. "He's been nothing but nice to you and you treated him like crap."

"Do we have a problem here?" Nate Wright loomed in the doorway, his eyes narrowed.

Gemma flushed. "No. No. Not at all. I just didn't want to go to lunch."

"I don't like the tone of your voice, Sinclair." Nate ignored Gemma, using that lawman look on Cade. He wasn't that much older than Cade, but Nate Wright reeked of authority.

Gemma stood, her mouth a flat line. "He was leaving, Sheriff. Don't worry about it. I can handle him."

She walked around her desk and took him by the elbow, trying to lead him out.

Cade wasn't sure he wanted to be led out.

"Please. Please don't make a scene." Gemma looked up at him with those big blue eyes. They were shining with tears again. She was trying to hold it together. It was plain to see.

So Jesse was freaked out at the street corner and Gemma was hanging on by her nails. When had he become the goddamn go-between? He allowed Gemma to drag him along. When they got to the small space between the inner and outer doors, she turned on him.

"Please go away. I don't need to get fired again. I like this job. I don't want to have to go around begging for another one."

What the hell? "You think Nate was mad at you?"

She sniffled. "I think Nate likes to run a tight ship and my personal life is causing him trouble."

How fucked up had her life been before? "He was pissed at me because of the way I was talking to you. He was trying to protect you. He wasn't going to fire you, but he might have roughed me up."

She stopped and looked back through the windows. Sure enough, Nate was still watching them. "I don't know."

"I do. I know a protective brother when I see one. I say brother because he might beat the shit out of me if I used the word 'father figure.'" He couldn't help himself. He reached out and held her arms, rubbing up and down, forcing her attention back to him. "Tell me what's going on. I don't mean between you and Cam. That was the two of you playing. Tell me why you said what you did to Jesse."

"He doesn't want me."

Cade groaned. "That's the stupidest thing I've ever heard. Do you know what he planned for you today? A picnic. It's going to be too cold next week, so he has a nice spread laid out in the park."

She shook her head. "You don't understand. He doesn't want me. The real me."

He crowded her a bit. They were too close. There wasn't a lot of room. He could feel the heat of her body, smell the citrus shampoo she'd used. She was wearing a white button-up shirt, but it was thin and he could see her nipples, chafing against the cold—or responding to him? "Who's the real Gemma?"

She swallowed once, her eyes on his chest. "What you said before. I'm a bitch."

And he was a loser if he went by what some of his other girlfriends had said. He didn't want to understand Gemma, but he did. Maybe even better than Jesse. He put a hand out and forced her to look at him, tilting her chin up. "I think you hide behind that term a whole lot."

A bitter smile tugged at her lips. "You're wrong. I really am. I don't always say the right things. Hell, I almost never think the right things. I liked flipping Cam off. I can't be this perfect, polite lady Jesse wants, and it's going to hurt us both if I try. I have the sweetest mother you can imagine. Always courteous. Always nice. I have no idea where I came from. So please, leave me alone."

"Tell me you don't want him."

Those eyes slid away from him again. "I don't want him."

Top her when she lies. Jesse had been drilling it into him. He'd never had the taste for dominating a woman the way Jesse did, but it roared to life with Gemma. He forced her chin up, looking her straight in the eyes. "I don't like it when you lie."

A spark leapt in those blue orbs. "I don't like it when you talk."

"Are you going to like when I spank your ass?"

Her face heated up. "Nate is still watching."

Damn. Jesse had been right. She was interested. And his cock was hard as a rock, harder than it had been in months. All for her. Gemma Wells was like a weed, wrapping herself around him, strangling out the voices that told him why this was a terrible idea.

And he suddenly didn't give a fuck that the sheriff was watching. The sheriff needed to stay out of this. "Let him watch. He can handle Callie his way and I'll handle you in mine. Now tell me again. This time try not to lie."

"I want him, but I don't think it can work."

"Why?" He could give her a thousand reasons, but he was interested in what she thought.

Her hands played at his waist and then she seemed to force them to her sides. "Because I can't be the woman he wants. It's not fair of him to try to change me. And I don't want anything serious."

"Because you don't want to get serious with men like us?"

"Because I'm not good for anyone. Damn it, Cade, I don't have a job and I don't have any prospects for one. Brush off whatever fucking chip is sitting on your shoulder. I don't care what you do for a living. I want someone who wants me, but that's neither you nor Jesse. You don't want me at all, and he wants some perfectly polite princess."

"Don't want you? You think I don't want you?" He could put that rumor to rest. He pressed her to the wall, grinding his pelvis against hers. His cock swelled, the close heat of her body perfectly torturous.

She was forced to hold on to him now. Her hands clutched at his waist as she tried to stare down at the place where their bodies touched. "Why? You don't even like me."

It felt good to be close to her. "I don't have to like a woman to want her. And I don't hate you. I'm a little scared of you. You think you're not good for anyone? God, baby, you have no idea. Does this whole thing have to be so damn serious?"

She shook her head, licking at her bottom lip like she was staring at some dessert she wanted a bite of. "No. It doesn't. It can just be fun, right?"

Keep it light. Don't fall for her. He might be able to have her, if he followed the rules. He pressed in, enjoying the feel of her against him. She was so much smaller, but her breasts were plump and round. "We can have a lot of fun, you and me and Jesse. You have to talk to him. Tell him what you want."

A hard voice broke through the tension. Jesse stood in the doorway, looking in. "I think I can tell what she wants. A little fast sex, Gemma? I hope that's what you want because it's all Cade is going to offer. That's all he offers any woman. I'm the one who takes care of our women. He just fucks."

Cade rolled his eyes and reluctantly pulled away from Gemma. "Good to know you have a high opinion of me."

Jesse shook his head. "It's true and you know it."

Gemma was right back to her ice-princess self, all that hot and flustery anticipation gone in the wake of Jesse's judgmental eyes. "I'm going back to work. You'll both understand if I would prefer to not see you again."

She started for the door. Cade was about to reach out for her, but Jesse was faster. He pulled Gemma to him, his eyes hard as he looked down at her. Cade glanced back and now both Nate and Cam were watching.

"Careful, she has a couple of protectors," Cade pointed out.

"They better not come between us," Jesse said. "You need to make it plain to those men in there that we're involved. You haven't told them, have you, baby?"

"We're not involved. I think you made that plain," she replied.

Jesse softened a little. "I was being a jealous asshole. And I'm sorry. You were playing around with Cam. I took it the wrong way. Then I walked back in to apologize and you were close to Cade and you told him you only wanted sex. I could give you more, Gemma. Give me a chance. I am sorry about walking out. It was a dumb thing to do. I got mad and I had to step away. Forgive me."

He put his forehead against hers, and she calmed down.

"It won't work." But her hands came up to cup his face.

Cade felt a brutal jealousy take root in his gut. She'd rubbed against him, gotten all hot, but she showed Jesse real tenderness.

Probably because you've never been anything but an asshole to her. You're lucky she talks to you. You can get your shit together and figure this thing out or those two are going to leave you in the dust.

"Give it a chance." Jesse hugged her close. "I'll be at Trio tonight. If you want to make a date of it, I'll be waiting."

Cade couldn't stand it. He hated being on the outside. He fucking hated the fact that she wasn't looking at him. Damn it all, he'd fought it for a week, but he did want her. "I'll be there, too."

She finally looked his way, a half smile on her face. "Will you?"

Jesse nodded, never taking his eyes off her. "He will. He'll screw up again, but you'll see, he's going to come around. We can give you what you need. Think about it. I hope I'll see you tonight. If you want to make the first move, come to me. If you want me to handle it, stand by the jukebox and I'll know you're ready."

"I don't know if I should."

Cade watched them. They looked good together. Gemma softened around Jesse. Jesse lit up around her. What was he doing?

"Don't think. Just be there." Jesse turned to Cade. "I'm going to go clean up. I'll see you back at the shop."

Gemma looked miserable as she turned and walked back in.

He was left alone, with his best friend walking one way and Gemma walking the other.

He looked back in to see Cam and Nate beginning to surround her. They would be friends to her. Jesse was wrong about that. She was fitting in nicely. Maybe even better than Cade had since he'd held himself apart, allowing Jesse to make connections and befriend people. Cade had dragged Jesse all over the damn country and every time Jesse made a home for them and then Cade forced them to take off again.

He was the one who shouldn't show up tonight. He glanced back in as Gemma waved the men off and sat back down at her desk. Did she even have a lunch with her? He'd sent one with Jesse on the days he'd met her here. He'd fried chicken for today's lunch, exactly the way Nancy had taught him. He'd thought about Gemma the whole time he'd done it. Usually he only thought about Nancy and his mother when he cooked, both gone, both because he'd been irresponsible.

He didn't deserve Gemma. Hell, he didn't deserve Jesse.

But he still went to the park, helped Jesse pick up, and he quietly marched back to the sheriff's office. It took fifteen minutes, but when Laura Niles walked in, he handed her the cooler and asked her to make sure Gemma got her lunch.

Then he walked back to the shop and got to work.

Chapter Six

Jesse watched the town crazy walk into Trio. Well, one of the town crazies. Bliss seemed to be full of them, but this particular crazy was more sad than funny. And Jesse wasn't sure Michael Novack wasn't the tiniest bit dangerous. Novack was dressed in a flannel shirt and light jacket and jeans. It was what he always wore.

He took a long drink of his beer as the former US Marshal strode in and took a seat at the bar. Yep. He intended to keep an eye on Michael Novack because he knew what a dangerous man looked like. He'd stared at one in the mirror for months. Sometimes he wondered if chasing after Christian Grady for all those years hadn't changed something fundamental inside him. There was still an ache in the pit of his stomach because he hadn't been the one to take the fucker down. That had been Hope and Lucy.

How much worse was that ache for Cade? He'd lost two mothers. Cade had two whole families and they were both gone. Did he sit up at night wishing he'd been the one to end the life of the man who killed Nancy Gibbs? And how about the man who had killed Cade's parents and sister? Jesse knew it was all bullshit, but Cade blamed himself for their deaths. How long would it be before Cade forgave the child he'd been?

"Damn it. Lucy caught sight of him, and I swear to god that girl is drooling." Cade sat back with a long sigh. "That girl needs a keeper."

Jesse watched as Trio's cutest waitress fumbled with her tray. Lucy wasn't the most graceful woman in the best of circumstances. Add inexplicable sexual attraction to the mix and she was downright clumsy.

Jesse winced as the tray in her hand wobbled and the single glass began its long dive toward the floor.

Luckily, Zane was damn fast. He caught the glass and managed to only spill a bit of what Jesse suspected was the town doc's whiskey. Doctor Caleb Burke sat at a long table with his girlfriend, Holly, and his partner, Alexei. On the other side of the table sat Holly's best friend, Laura Niles, and her boyfriends, Rafe and Cam.

Zane turned, and Jesse could hear Michael grumble his order. It was the only way the man talked, in a low mumble that was something between a growl and a moan.

"I don't get it." Tyler Davis sighed as he slid into the booth beside Cade. "Look at her. It's like she could eat him up. What the fuck is wrong with me?"

Jesse shrugged. "Dude, according to most of the female tourists around here, there's nothing wrong with you. Aren't you like, rolling in the tips and shit?"

He genuinely enjoyed giving Ty a hard time.

Ty Davis was one of those sun-kissed blond gods who generally set Jesse on edge, but Ty was brainy with the slightest edge of nerd. It made up for his pretty-boy good looks. "I do not take tips, asshole. I'm a paramedic. I don't have a tip jar on my med kit. Do you know how pissy people get after they break a leg while skiing? Trust me. They're thinking lawsuits, not tips."

Cade smiled, that shit-eating grin that let Jesse know he was about to say something wretchedly sarcastic. "He wasn't talking about the medical stuff, Ty. How are tips after the sex stuff?"

Ty went a great shade of pink.

"Sex stuff?" Lucy asked, her breath huffy. She was wearing the Trio uniform, jeans and a tight white tank top with the bar's logo, two beer steins with a glass of red wine in the middle. It was a slightly salacious logo that always reminded Jesse that relationships in Bliss tended to consist of two foaming beer drinkers and a single curvy female. Lucy fit the bill. The tank top molded to her plump breasts, but unfortunately, Lucy had been firmly placed in the sister category. And she was kind of a bratty sister. "If we're talking about sex stuff, we must be talking about Ty."

Ty's blush deepened. "Damn it. Do we have to get personal? I'm not the only one around here who has sex."

Lucy cocked her hip and set her tray on the table. "Well, I'm not having any, so we're not talking about me. And these two have been working around the clock. I think you're the only one at this table having sex."

Cade's head hit the table and a low moan came out of his mouth. "God, I miss sex. I miss sex with hot blondes."

"You would not have to miss it if you would stop being stubborn." Jesse missed sex, too. But the fact that Cade was joking about it gave him hope. He hadn't missed the fact that Cade had left the park with the cooler in hand after the lunchtime debacle and then shown up without it at the shop. He'd gone back and made sure Gemma had food for lunch.

Cade was falling into the trap. Jesse knew what Cade was scared of. He simply didn't intend to let it stop him. Gemma would be good for both of them. A soft, sweet bunny of a woman wouldn't get Cade off his ass. Gemma would challenge him. Gemma would make him see the light.

If she showed up. He found himself watching that door. He was damn happy that every now and then Cade turned and glanced at it as well.

Ty's head came up as though he was greatly relieved they were no longer talking about his love life—which resembled a TV sitcom. It came in short bursts and had zero chance of containing a long-term plot. "Are you talking about Gemma? She's a hot blonde."

Jesse felt his eyes narrow and his spine straighten like a dog who'd gone on full "protect my fucking turf" alert. Ty was a womanizer. Ty liked to bed almost any woman who would let him. He better not be sniffing around Gemma.

"How the hell do you know Gemma?" Jesse asked.

Ty leaned back as though realizing he was walking through a minefield. "She and her mom rented two of the cabins Cole owns. They're right there in the valley. It's the two cabins he hasn't let go of yet. He had me take them spare keys."

Cole Roberts owned the Elk Creek Lodge, the ski resort that was located outside Bliss. He was Ty's boss and one of the wealthiest men in the county. He'd recently taken over for his uncle, who was now retired and spent all his time fishing.

Lucy's sweet face contorted a little. "He has you playing his super now? When is River going to let you go full time so you don't have to work at that lodge? It's a bad influence. You're going to catch something terrible from one of those women and you'll die exactly like I always said you would. Of a venereal disease." She winked Jesse's way. "River and I have a bet. I picked syphilis. She's got gonorrhea."

Ty had two jobs, and one of them was working with a company that provided guided adventure tours around the area. It was obvious which one Lucy preferred.

Ty shook his head and sighed. "I would think River would be more circumspect now that she's gotten married. And that's precisely why I'm not working there much anymore. Matt takes most of the tours I would have taken. Another reason to not like him."

Lucy's nose wrinkled in a way that let him know she wasn't fond of the guy either. "We grew up with River. I don't know if you met her yet, but she's awesome. We're worried about her brand-new husband, but there's not a lot we can do. I'm still not happy that Cole Roberts is turning you into a courier."

Ty's eyes rolled. "No one else was around. I get bored. I took her the extra key. I tried to talk to her a little, you know, get to know her. She took the key and slammed the door in my face."

Good. The last thing he needed was Ty trying to hit on Gemma. He doubted it would work. He was pretty sure Gemma was interested in what he and Cade had to offer, but he was a straightlaced man. He believed in tradition, and that meant no fourths.

Lucy looked back to the long table and sighed. "Do you need anything? I have to go and make sure the champagne is ready." Her eyes grew wistful. "I've been told something nice is going to happen tonight."

Jesse looked over at the small party in the back of the bar. Laura and Holly and their men were all smiling and having a great time. He could take a wild guess at what was about to happen and why they would need champagne. It seemed to be a theme going around Bliss. Hope McLean and her men had recently gotten back from eloping in Las Vegas. There had been a huge party out at the Circle G not two weeks before. It looked like either Laura or Holly would be next.

"I'll take another beer, sweetheart," he told Lucy, handing her his empty mug.

"Me, too." Cade finished his off.

"I'd like the usual," Ty said.

Jesse and Cade both snorted. Ty's usual was a piña colada.

Ty frowned. "I like sweet drinks."

Lucy simply winked his way. "I know you do, Ty. Be right back."

Lucy walked off, Ty's eyes following her every move. His eyes went hard when she stopped in front of Michael Novack and her whole body took on a flirtatious air. Novack simply continued frowning. Jesse looked at the man with his thick beard and longish hair and hoped he bathed regularly. If Novack hadn't hit rock bottom yet, he couldn't be far away.

"What the fuck does she see in him?" Ty complained.

"I heard Novack nearly shot two people who walked on his land. He said he thought they were bears, but I don't believe him. I think he's a damn powder keg waiting to go off."

Cade leaned back against his seat. "I heard they were nudists on a nature hike."

The gossip mill was one of the best things about Bliss. "I heard it was aliens. Mel tried to talk to him, but Mike apparently doesn't believe in them. Mel's been leaving him pamphlets."

*You've Been Probed. What to do Next...*was his favorite of the recent rash of pamphlets the town's citizens had been putting out. Earlier today, Nell had come by Long-Haired Roger's auto shop and left a flurry of *Eat Vegan or Die Horribly* flyers. Jesse thought Nell was getting desperate.

"I don't care who they were. That man is on the edge. Why the hell is he still here?" Ty complained.

As far as Jesse had heard, the former US Marshal was here because he didn't have anywhere else to go. He'd lost his fiancée when she'd turned criminal and sold out the man they'd been charged with protecting. Michael's fiancée had been willing to let Alexei Markov die, and she hadn't cared if the town doc and Holly Lang had gone down with him. According to the gossip, Michael had quit his job the next day and rented a cabin and he hadn't been seen for a month. When he'd emerged, he'd grown a beard and a paranoid attitude. And Lucy had promptly gotten a crush because, it seemed, she liked a bit of crazy.

Yeah, Jesse understood that.

His own bit of crazy walked in. The door to Trio swung open, and Gemma Wells entered with her swaying hips and crazy, bee-stung lips and that surly attitude, and fuck all, his cock did a dance in his pants.

She was here.

"Have you actually asked Lucy out, Ty?" Cade asked. His back was to the door, but he watched Jesse. Jesse nodded toward the wretchedly hot blonde as she moved through the crowd.

Ty sighed. "It's like she said. We grew up together. Not here in Bliss though. We grew up in Creede. It's a town north of here. As long as I can remember it was me and Luce and River. I guess I thought of them as friends for the longest time. Or maybe I thought Luce would always be there so I could do what I wanted and when I was ready, I would settle down with her. I waited too long. Now she laughs when I talk about us dating. And to be honest, I don't actually ask women out. It just kind of happens," Ty said, defending himself.

Jesse spoke, though he was actually busy drooling over Gemma. She took off her coat and revealed a tight V-neck sweater and skirt. "So you fall into their vaginas? Do you trip or is it a controlled fall?"

"Dude," Cade said with a laugh, holding up his hand. "Nice one."

Jesse high-fived his partner and nodded again, trying to force Cade's attention to where it should be focused. Gemma had entered the bar on her own. And she walked right past the jukebox. What the hell was that supposed to mean? "She's alone, but I think she's going to give us a little hell."

Cade turned, his eyes widening as he caught sight of Gemma. "Damn, look at that. But she's not alone."

"I don't fall in. I am careful about what vaginas I enter. Wait. That sounded bad." Ty shook his head.

"No, it sounded like Ty." Lucy put a beer in front of Jesse. "And who's the gorgeous girl with Gemma?"

Ty turned, looking toward the bar where Gemma and her friend were settling in. "Oh, that's Naomi Turner. She's a nurse."

"She's been coming into Stella's with Lynn almost every day. She seems nice." Lucy glanced around the bar.

Naomi was her shield. No doubt about that. Even as Jesse stared at her, Gemma's eyes slid his way and then she turned as quickly as she could when she realized he was watching. Nervous. She was a pretty deer who wanted to be fed by hand but wasn't sure she was safe.

Cade sighed. "You're the one who is always telling me to be patient."

He didn't want to be patient. He wanted to walk right up to her, grab her, and take her right back out the door. He'd been patient all week, giving her time and space, and now he wasn't sure he could stand another minute of it.

But she was sidling up to the bar and not the jukebox. She'd brought a friend with her in case she needed an out.

All he could do was wait and watch and hope she was brave enough to take that step.

Ty shook his head as he sipped his frou-frou drink. "I've heard that girl is trouble with a capital T."

Yep, Gemma was trouble, and Jesse figured they were the solution. He and Cade. It would be different if they were the kind of guys to fall into a girl's vagina and then fall right back out like Ty, but Jesse had changed. Jesse wanted to get in a vagina he really cared about and spend a long time there. They could be good for her.

He had to convince her of that. And then he had to convince Cade. Yeah. He might need another beer.

* * * *

"Is he looking this way?" Gemma tried to not look back. It was hard. Her eyeballs seemed to have magnets and those two hot mechanics were pulling her sight their way. The minute she'd entered the bar, she'd caught a glimpse of them and her heart rate had tripled. She'd debated whether to come at all, but in the end, she couldn't stay away.

They were ridiculously gorgeous. She still couldn't forget seeing Bare-Chested Ape Man shirtless, showing off one of those chests that should only exist in the movies because it wasn't fair to females across the globe. With his dark hair and piercing green eyes, Cade was stunning.

And then there was Jesse—the sweet one. He had light brown hair that brushed the tops of sculpted shoulders and a scruffy beard that made her wonder what it would feel like on her skin.

She shouldn't have come out. She wasn't going to that jukebox. No way.

Naomi turned slightly, as though she was looking for something behind her. When she turned back, there was a grin on her face. "Oh, yeah. He's looking your way. So is his friend. Where are my two hot men?"

Naomi might envy her, but she wasn't thinking about all the complexities. It was far too complicated. Jesse wanted a relationship. Cade wanted a little sex, but he didn't honestly like her. She liked them both, but she wasn't going to hang around.

Maybe she could spend some time with them. Just not forever. Forever was an idiot's dream. But she still had needs. Lots of dirty, filthy needs.

And some not-so-dirty needs. She needed time away from thinking about how she'd screwed up her life and how her mom had a second chance. Would she get a second chance? She'd almost lost her mom. It had been easy to forget all about her own personal horror story when she'd been concentrating on her mom and the rounds of chemotherapy she'd been through.

"Are you okay? You went pale." Naomi put a hand on her arm, feeling for her pulse. Naomi took her job seriously.

Damn her Swedish ancestors. "Sorry, I pale easily."

Naomi grinned, even white teeth gleaming from her lovely face. "Yeah, you white girls do that."

She returned her smile with a wink. "Bitch."

"Back at ya." Naomi looked down at her cell phone. "She hasn't called. Maybe I should call."

Gemma put her hand down on the phone. "Don't. She wanted you to have a couple of hours out. She's fine. She has your number. She has Doctor Burke's number. Actually, he's sitting right over there."

He got up and so did a gorgeous dark-haired man. Alexei Markov, former mobster and a key state witness in some high-profile trials. Everyone in Gemma's office had followed those trials, watching them like a gory soap opera. He'd been a spectacular witness. Charming and intelligent, he'd won over the juries. It was odd to see him here in small-town Colorado.

Holly, her fellow waitress from Gemma's two-day stint at Stella's, looked up as the men surrounded her. A hush fell over the whole bar. The music that had been rocking the walls was suddenly at a lull.

Gemma's stomach took a long, slow dive.

"Hey, guys." Holly got a faint grin on her face. "What's going on?"

The big Russian got to one knee. "My *dushka*, Caleb and I have questionings for you. We wish to make offer you can't to be refusing."

Caleb grinned. "Sorry, baby, I let him watch *The Godfather*. But you're not going to refuse us, are you?"

"I don't know the question yet, so I don't have an answer," Holly shot back, but there were tears in her eyes.

Both men pulled out velvet boxes and diamond rings flashed.

"Yes." Holly didn't wait for the actual question. She simply started kissing them. One and then the other.

Patrick hadn't proposed. Hadn't bought her a ring. She'd brought it up over lunch one day. She'd laid out the business plan of their marriage and presented it to him. He'd agreed. No romance. No protestations of love.

Cam stood up. "Excellent, now we'll show you how two men

who don't mind talking do this thing."

That was why Cam had been smiling all afternoon. Cam was getting engaged, too. She wanted to be happy for him. She liked Cam. All she could think about was the date. Tomorrow's date, really. It was burned into her memory since she'd sent out two hundred and fifty "save the date" cards with tomorrow's date on them.

Cam's partner, Rafe, got up beside him, both men looking down on Laura Niles, who put her hand to her mouth, tears pooling in her eyes. "Laura, it's been a long road, but every turn led us right here."

"Every stop sign and detour didn't matter because we had one destination in life. You." Cam reached out and touched her hair.

"We're here now, and we won't ever leave again. Laura, will you marry us? Will you build a life with us, a home, whatever family we're blessed enough to have? Will you grow old with us and stare back at the life we were granted, happy it was a shared one?" Rafe asked.

"Oh, yes." Laura accepted her rings.

Caleb looked at Holly. "What they said."

Holly shook her head and hugged him. "I love you exactly the way you are, Caleb. You, too, Alexei."

The whole bar erupted in a long cheer.

Tomorrow was supposed to be her wedding day. She'd planned that wedding out with the same type A-fueled adrenaline she'd used on her career. She'd found the perfect venue, the perfect dress, the right band. She'd concentrated on a wedding, but those people in the bar would have real marriages.

A warm hand covered hers. "Are you okay?"

She shook her head. It wouldn't help to think about it. Six months ago she'd been ready to get married, on the cusp of becoming a junior partner, had her whole life ahead of her.

And it hadn't meant a thing.

She'd worked her ass off, done everything right, and it hadn't paid off. Her mother had followed her heart and it had all gone wrong. And she still told Gemma to do the same.

Follow her heart? She hadn't listened to it since she was a girl.

"It's okay to be upset, Gem," Naomi said. "I know what was supposed to happen tomorrow. Your mom had that wedding invitation on her refrigerator. When I first met her, she told me she had to live long enough to see her baby get married."

There they were. Those tears that she always seemed on the edge of. Every time she was about to fall into self-pity, she thought about her mom. She took a deep breath. It was past time to pull up her big-girl panties. She wasn't getting married tomorrow. She wasn't a lawyer anymore. But she was still her mother's daughter. "Well, it's better this way. We get to spend more time together."

Naomi sighed as though slightly disappointed. "Yes, you do, hon."

"What can I get for you, ladies?"

Gemma felt her eyes widen. God, they grew them hot in this town. She'd seen him around the valley and at the barbecue in her mom's yard, but she hadn't actually met him. The man in front of her was at least six and a half feet tall, with emerald green eyes and pitch-black hair. His face was scarred, but it was oddly lovely on him, as though pain had molded him from picture perfect into something infinitely more interesting. She had to find her voice.

"Vodka tonic."

The Bartender God winked her way. "Sure thing. You're Gemma, right? The new office manager at the station?"

"Through nefarious means, yes."

A brilliant smile crossed his face. "Excellent. You give Nate hell, hon. And you should know that all your drinks are on the house. I know how hard it is to deal with that man."

She couldn't help it. She smiled back. "You're Zane Hollister." Callie's other husband. Callie had been into the station several times, but Zane hadn't stopped by. They lived not a quarter of a mile from each other. He'd cooked dinner in her mom's yard while he'd talked to Cade. She worked for the man's partner, but she hadn't taken the time to meet him.

He gave her a salute. "I am indeed. I'm the one who's going to make sure you don't kill your boss. Lunches are on the house, too. You're part of the family now." He turned to Naomi. "How about you?"

"White wine spritzer. And heavy on the spritzer. Just one. Thanks." That was Naomi. Always in control. It was probably a good thing in a nurse.

"Will do." The wretchedly hot bartender turned and started mixing drinks.

And Gemma sat there for a minute. She didn't buy the family business. It wasn't true. He'd only said it because they needed someone to man the phones. "Part of the family" was one of those things someone said to get a person to do what they wanted. That was all. Bliss wasn't any different than the real world. It just liked to say it was.

And where were all the non-hot guys? It was stupid. She was in a rural small town. It should be filled with men she would never sleep with, but no, not Bliss, Colorado. Bliss, Colorado, had to be the world's epicenter for sexy men.

She took a sip of her vodka tonic when Zane passed it to her, her eyes wandering. So many beautiful men.

And she couldn't even handle Patrick. No. She shouldn't be sitting here thinking about Jesse and Cade and whether or not she should go to the jukebox.

Like they truly wanted her anyway. There weren't a whole lot of available women. The men left had to double team. But they hadn't latched on to Naomi, and Naomi was gorgeous and sweet.

"Miss Turner." The doctor set his empty glass on the bar along with a delicate martini glass. "It's nice to see you out and about."

Naomi turned his way, a big smile on her face. "Lynn insisted. She said she wanted some alone time."

Her mother had been stubborn about it. They'd been in Bliss for almost three weeks and her mom had finally pushed them out so she could be alone. Or so she would know they were out having a good time and being social.

Doctor Burke leaned against the bar. "She knows what she wants. She's been through enough. She should have her way now. As long as she makes her checkups, she's going to be fine." The doctor gave Naomi what Gemma thought was supposed to be a smile, but it kind of looked like a shark sizing up his dinner. "Which is why you should seriously reconsider my offer."

The first stop they'd made in Bliss was at the Bliss County Clinic run by Dr. Caleb Burke, who happened to be Dr. Caleb Sommerville, ridiculously wealthy and well-trained doctor. She'd studied up on many of these people before she'd let her mother come here. The doctor had been a plus for the town.

Its reputation as the murder capital of the US had not recommended it.

But her mom wouldn't be deterred. She'd wanted to come home, and she'd fought cancer for years, so Gemma had come with her.

Years when Gemma had been chasing money and position. It was during that time her mother had fought for her life. The cancer had invaded her breasts. They'd started with lumpectomies and then mastectomies.

And all the while Gemma had been in New York trying to conquer Manhattan and making an idiot of herself.

"I have all her records," the doctor continued. "I'll help in any way I can." His lips suddenly curled up. "And if you're around for a while, maybe you can come to the wedding."

Naomi's face lit up. "Oh, are you getting married? I hadn't noticed."

He flushed a deep red, but it was charming on him. "I wanted to do a private thing, but Laura and Holly are best friends, and they should have a double wedding, you know. Well, I think I'm getting married. I mean, I am, but maybe not legally. No. Wait. Alexei's got mob people after him and his real fake name is still Howard. I think it has to be me, right? And I have the money. And speak English. Well, mostly. Yeah. I'm signing the papers, but it's Bliss, so we're all getting married."

"I am confused." Gemma tried to follow him, but it wasn't happening. And she hadn't had a damn drink yet.

The doctor tossed his hands up. "Absolutely. It's weird, right? Except now I've had sex so many times with Alexei like right there that it feels weird when Holly and I do it alone. I mean, we do. Alexei works some late hours and I need to get my freak on, you know. But it's weird. I can safely say that I never thought I would get married to a waitress and an ex-Russian mobster. Though I'm not married to Alexei. Right? There's no actual sex and stuff so we're not married. Fuck. I might be marrying Alexei. He gets his English wrong a lot. We could screw up and end up married to each other."

Gemma sighed, all the while thinking of the two men behind her. Were they still behind her? Had they given up? Did they think this was her way of flipping them off? Because it wasn't. It was her way of being terrified.

Naomi laughed a little. "Well, if you do end up married to Alexei, I for one will pay for tickets to that show."

The doctor flushed, and the ridiculously hot bartender slid him another round.

"Ladies, don't tease the doctor. He has a rifle loaded with tranquilizer shots, and he's not afraid to use it."

Gemma was interested in that because if the doc could get away with it, she wasn't sure why everyone had been horrified about the Taser. "You tranquilize the citizens of the town? Is that like on a random basis or just the people who annoy you?"

The doctor waved a hand. "God, no. Max Harper would never be awake. No, I only use it on Mel when he gets out of hand. And you're one to talk. I had to have a whole checkup session with the Harpers to assure them Max suffered no ill effects from his close encounter with high voltage. Nice work, Wells. Maybe you can hold the tranquilizer gun during the wedding. Holly wants to release doves. It could go wrong if Mel decides they're aliens. And Naomi, think about my offer. I could use a nurse. It's only a matter of time until our next trauma."

The hot doctor nodded, took his drinks, and walked off. The gorgeous bartender winked their way and turned to take the next woman's order. So much hotness in a small area.

She didn't have a future. The truth beat at her at the most inopportune times.

"This place is weird." Gemma took a long drink of her vodka tonic. She still wasn't sure she understood this town, and she didn't like the feeling.

Naomi sighed and looked around. "I don't know. I like it. It's different from Chicago. It's softer here somehow."

Chicago. Her mom had spent more time in Chicago than anywhere else, but it wasn't home. Gemma didn't have that one place where she could always go. Her whole life had been a blur of small towns and big cities, and those years on the Renaissance Faire circuit.

Lynn Wells had only been in Chicago to visit a friend, but she'd been forced to stay for two rounds of chemo before she'd gone into remission. And then she'd told Gemma she wanted to come home. To Bliss. This was where her mother felt safe. Gemma wasn't sure she would ever have a place like this.

Silly name, Bliss. A misnomer since there was no such thing. She'd figured that out long ago.

But she was wondering if there wasn't such a thing as an orgasm. Cade had asked her if it all had to be so serious. Why did it have to be? Because Jesse said so?

She glanced behind her. Cade was gorgeous. She wanted to see him in his full glory. She wanted to see him walking around without a stitch of clothes on.

And Jesse. Jesse smiled and the whole damn world lit up. She'd tripped over her heels the other day going to lunch, and Jesse had thrown his body down so she would fall on him and not the concrete.

Patrick hadn't noticed when she'd had her gallbladder out. She'd taken a cab from the hospital. Somehow she didn't think Jesse or Cade would have allowed their woman to do that. Of course, they also seemed like men who would use the phrase "my woman." Neanderthals. Ridiculously wretched-hot Neanderthals.

The jukebox wasn't that far away.

"Damn, that's a serious face." Naomi leaned in, a smile on those beautiful lips. Maybe if she looked more like Naomi she would already be over at the jukebox. Maybe if she hadn't let herself go, she would feel comfortable enough to walk over and take control, but she'd indulged for six months. She'd gained ten pounds and lost most of her designer wardrobe. She'd left it behind in New York because she didn't need it. Her hair was back to its normal color and it brushed her shoulders, though she usually shoved it in a ponytail.

Gemma shrugged. "Not really. It was a passing thought."

Naomi leaned forward. "Why passing? Look, Gemma, if you want them, I think you should go for it. You need to have some fun."

She wasn't sure she knew what fun was. Zane picked up a bottle of gin in front of her, his hands working to pour the proper amount. Family, huh? If they were "family" then he could answer a couple of questions. "Zane, what do you know about those two guys at the table behind me?"

He looked straight at her. "There are five tables behind you. I know all the guys."

Asshole. She rolled her eyes, biting back a grin. "The one right behind me."

He sighed, staring out over the bar. "There are three men at that table."

She hadn't even noticed there was another man in the booth. "Black hair. Doesn't like to wear a shirt. The other one's scruffy, but in a sexy way."

Zane slapped at the bar, his enthusiasm apparent. "That's Cade and Jess. Excellent choice. The other one's a man-whore. Jesse's good people. I don't know as much about Cade, but I know they're close. And Nate said they've been sniffing around you."

She didn't care about how "good" a man he was. Well, she did, but she didn't. And she probably shouldn't get anywhere near him. "Nate needs to stop gossiping."

"Ain't happening, Gemma. Get used to it." Zane went back to work.

Naomi leaned over. "Those two men are practically eating you up. What are you going to do about that?"

Nothing. She wouldn't do a damn thing. Except she wanted to. Every nerve in her body longed for touches and caresses. She was only human. And she'd completely ignored the need to be skin to skin for so long it was becoming a real problem. She craved it. She worried that if she ignored it long enough, it might go away, and she would spend her life without arms around her.

Four arms around her. Two mouths kissing her. Legs entangling.

She forced herself to stop thinking about it. She couldn't. She needed to worry about the asshole who'd sent her a heart in a box and the letters she'd received since. They'd come a couple of times this week, filled with nastiness and vague threats. She'd narrowed it down to three cases. Nate and Cam were checking into it. It was weird to give up control like that.

"So how is your job going? Is it as bad as you thought?" Naomi asked.

"It's okay." She was shocked to find out that she meant that.

Running that office was kind of fun. In the week she'd spent on the job, she'd talked a woman down from a tree, overseen the installation of a new vending machine, calmed Nate down when the aforementioned vending machine stole his money, learned how to tie a fly-fishing lure, and enjoyed a batch of cookies from the woman she'd previously talked down from a tree. Cassidy Meyer was a little crazy and she'd taken to the tree when she'd learned her half-alien children were marrying a woman who didn't like beets. After a long talk on a cell phone with a man named Leo, she'd coaxed Cassidy down. The wedding was months away. Her future daughter-in-law had plenty of time to prove her humanness.

Another wedding. She hated weddings. Even alien ones.

Naomi continued on. "Can you see yourself there long term? I mean, shouldn't you try to find a job with a law firm? Have you thought about what you want to do?"

Had she thought about it? Lots. She'd also thought about the fact that anyone who looked her up on the Internet would likely find the words "Midtown Meltdown" and read about how she'd been discovered by the NYPD wrestling with Christina Big Tits. Yeah, law firms across the country would go crazy over her. They might like her as a client, but not as a member of the firm. "I want to spend time with Mom for now."

There was a long sigh from her friend. "I know your mom is thrilled to spend time with you, but she wants you to be happy, too."

Happiness was a chimera. It didn't exist. Happiness was a fairy tale. "I'm fine, Naomi. I need a little time."

Yes. She needed time, not another set of problems. She wasn't going to indulge herself with them. It would only bring more heartache. She didn't have anything to offer them. She wasn't terrifically good at sex. She had a bad reputation around town. Jesse wanted someone polite. Cade called to her, but she knew better than to answer.

She didn't have anything to give to a lover, much less two.

Her phone rang. Unknown number. It could be the cabin. Her mom had a cell phone, but there was also a landline in the cabin, and Gemma hadn't put the number in her phone yet. She picked it up. "Hello."

"Gemma? Gemma, babe, god it's good to hear your voice. It's been too damn long."

She closed her eyes. Patrick? Her whole body clenched as though she'd taken a blow to her gut. He called her the night before their almost wedding? *Motherfucker*. "What do you want, Pat?"

Naomi started beside her. "Patrick?"

His voice came over the phone line. "Sweetie, I want to talk to you. I need to talk to you."

Did they need to talk? Maybe he was moved by the fact that this should have been the night before their wedding. Did he need closure? She didn't. Not over him. She hadn't loved him. She hadn't even liked him most of the time. "Don't worry about it. It's fine, Pat. I'm fine."

He stopped. "It's not fine."

She felt the beginnings of a headache. "What's going on? You don't call me for six months and then you decide to get in touch the night before our wedding was supposed to happen?"

"Was that tomorrow?" He laughed a little. "Shit."

The asshole had forgotten the wedding she'd paid for? "Good-bye. Don't call again."

"Don't hang up. I can get you your job back, babe."

She stopped. *Damn it.* It was the one reason he might be able to give her that was a bit compelling. The partners seemed to be blackballing her.

Her job. It had been her obsession for so long that she couldn't flick her finger over the *hang up* button the way she should.

His voice came over the line, cajoling, tempting. "I can make it happen. All you have to do is give me some of your time. We can talk this out."

"Fine, talk." She wouldn't stay. She would stay long enough to restore her reputation and then she would find another job. And she wouldn't have anything to do with Pat. The very idea made her nauseous. Especially now that she'd seen Jesse and Bare-Chested Ape Man. Cade. Cade was a man. Pat was a nice suit with overdone hair.

"Not on the phone. I want to meet with you." He was using his flirtatious voice, a perfect example of a nasally whine.

It was deeply easy to ignore. "Not happening. I can't come to

107

New York."

"It's okay, babe. You don't have to come to New York. I'm coming to Colorado. I'm at LaGuardia right now. I can be there by morning. Is there a Hyatt out there? Could you make me some reservations? And I need you to pick me up in Denver. How far away is this Bliss place?"

"I'm not picking you up." She wasn't going to drive for hours. "And it's a long way. You should rent a car or better yet, forget it. I don't want to see you."

There was a long sigh. "You know that's not true. Babe, I am coming. I have a few things to talk about and they're serious. But I have some personal stuff to talk about, too. I didn't love Christina. Look, I made a terrible mistake with her, but I'm only a man. Our sex life wasn't satisfying. She was excellent in bed. I think we need to sit down and talk. Sex isn't everything, right? We can get a class for you or something."

Humiliation washed over her. "Fuck yourself, Patrick."

She hung up the phone. He wanted something, but it wasn't to help her out. He was playing an angle.

"Wow. That sounded rough." Naomi shook her head. "Why would he call?"

Because he needed something, and she wasn't going to give it to him.

A throaty chuckle filled the air, and she couldn't help but turn and look their way. Jesse and Cade were laughing, talking to each other and that messenger her landlord had sent the other day. She thought he'd said his name was Ty something. They were relaxed and happy and perfect.

She was a mess. But maybe she could have a night. Patrick needed something from her, but she needed something he'd never been able to give her. If she hadn't made him feel like a man, then maybe she'd never truly felt like a woman. She needed to feel wanted.

One night. Was it too much to ask? She glanced back at the jukebox, its lights blinking their invitation. All she had to do was walk over to that jukebox and wait. Then she could show those two men that she could please them. She could take some pleasure for herself.

Naomi looked back at the booth and then to Gemma. "Are you sure?"

Was she sure? Nope. Not at all. But she wanted to try.

Naomi gave her a hug. "Go for it, sweetie. You need to stop worrying and live in the moment for a while. I'll see you tomorrow."

Naomi gave her a wink and left. She was on her own. And she had two men to take down.

Chapter Seven

Jesse felt like pouncing. Maybe if he just jumped her he would feel better, but he simply took another sip of beer and watched as Gemma stepped up to the jukebox. Her booted foot tapped against the hardwood floor and that heart-shaped ass swung back and forth.

She was there. She knew what it meant and she was standing there.

"You're drooling."

He shrugged. He didn't care if Cade caught him drooling. She was drool worthy. She was also a puzzle. He liked puzzles—interlocking pieces that individually meant nothing at all but as a whole created something lovely. He stared at Gemma the same way he would an engine that wasn't functioning properly. A woman was like a car. She could look beautiful on the outside, but if she hadn't been taken care of, she wouldn't run properly. Someone hadn't taken care of Gemma Wells. "She's alone now."

Cade's eyes slid off Gemma and back to his beer, his fingers tightening around it. "Yes, she is."

Fuck. He could feel Cade pulling away. Gemma was standing there. He didn't have time to discuss Cade's problems. If he didn't get a move on, Gemma might think he'd set this up as some sort of joke. "We need to go in."

She was alone. Her friend had left, and Gemma was all by her lonesome, listening to some music, waiting for him.

Cade stared at her. "I don't know. I don't have much to offer her. You were right about that."

Jesse kept his cool. "I was merely talking about the way you've been up to this point. And here's the deal, you were right, too. This doesn't have to mean we end up married to her. Let's take this one day at a time. She's standing right over there. She's saying yes."

"She's saying yes to you. She always kind of frowns my way. Maybe she's putting up with me to get to you."

Jesse nearly groaned. There weren't many women in the world who were so crazy about one man that they would take on his crabby best friend, too. Gemma was interested in them. She was interested in ménage. Jesse figured if he ended the night with his cock up Gemma's pussy, then it meant she was okay with his lifestyle choice. And if she wasn't, then he would have to show her. With his tongue and his fingers and his filthy mouth. He simply needed to get Cade on board. "You kind of called her a bitch."

Cade nodded toward Gemma. "She still calls me Ape Man from time to time."

Ty tipped back his beer. "Half the women I sleep with call me something different. I just say yes."

Jesse was pretty sure he shouldn't take relationship advice from Ty. "What can it hurt? We ask her to dance."

Cade's eyes widened. "What can it hurt? Ask Max Harper."

Jesse slid out from his seat. "I'm going in. I'm not afraid of her. I'm faster than Max Harper. I intend to evade her stun gun and any other weapons she might have on her person. And if we leave her there for too much longer, she'll likely walk away. I won't let that happen."

Those weapons might be plentiful. She was deeply prickly, but he'd seen some softness underneath her sarcasm. He'd seen the hurt in her eyes when Cade had talked about her. She'd put on a good front, but she couldn't hide it all.

He had to treat her with real care and patience. And he had to make her comfortable enough to bring Cade in. If he had to, he would take care of her on his own and then try to work Cade in. She wouldn't wait. If he backed off now, he could lose her, and he didn't want to lose her. Over the last week he'd grown addicted to her sass and sarcasm. When he'd walked in and seen her grinning at Cameron Briggs, he'd wanted to plant his goddamn fist through the man's face. He wasn't possessive. Or at least he hadn't been before. He'd had no problem with women coming and going, their effect on his life as transitory as his existence seemed to be.

But Gemma needed roots. And he intended to provide them.

He walked up to the jukebox, keeping a decent distance between them when all he wanted to do was cuddle against her backside and sway to the music.

"Hey, Gemma."

She smiled, her lips curving up in a satisfied grin that told him she hadn't been unaware of him. "Hi, Jesse."

She'd sent her friend away. She was standing at the jukebox. He should put an arm around her and lead her out of the bar. They could go back to her place, and he could be inside her before midnight. And still he had a hard time walking out and leaving Cade behind.

"Can I buy you a drink?" Jesse asked. What he wanted was to buy some time.

"No." Gemma turned to him. "But I can buy you one."

There it was. He smiled, catching on to what she was doing. She wanted to control the situation. He could go along with that for the time being. "I would like that."

She turned and walked back to the bar, simply expecting him to follow. Again, he could do that for the time being. He hopped up on the seat beside her.

"Zane, could you get my friend a drink? I'll take another one, too." Her voice was completely steady. She looked like quite the seductress. Sexy smile on those gorgeous lips. Honey blonde hair flipped back.

And her hands were shaking.

Yes, someone had damn straight not taken care of Gemma Wells.

He put his hand over hers, curling their fingers together. She looked up, a little startled at the contact, but she relaxed, her hand still in his. "How's your momma doing, Gemma?"

He could see plainly that she hadn't expected that, either. She seemed to fumble for a moment. Had she expected him to come on to her with tired old pickup lines and easy come-ons now that they were getting down to the nitty gritty?

"She's good." The husky seduction was gone the minute she talked about her mother. "She's happy to be back here. I guess I never thought about it, but she considered this home all these years. I wonder why she stayed away for so long."

Zane slid their drinks in front of them, breaking the oddly intimate moment. Her hand slid out of his and reached for that vodka like it was a lifeline.

"But I'm sure you don't want to talk about that. Let's talk about you." She chuckled.

He would adore that throaty sound if he thought it was honestly directed at him. But he could see it for what it was. An act meant to bring about a reaction in him. "I'm not that interesting, darlin'. I would rather you told me how the rest of your day went."

She bit her bottom lip. "Is it just the two of us then? I guess I scared the Ape Man away."

"My name is Cade, Gemma. And I try not to leave Jesse alone. He tends to get into trouble." Cade slid into the seat beside Gemma.

Thank god. He'd worried Cade would stay away, but he'd pulled his sneaky moves and crowded her from the other side.

And Gemma was right back to looking like a deer in the headlights.

"How about an iced tea for me?" Cade told Zane.

Gemma took a long breath and seemed to gather her wits about her. "I would have thought you were a beer guy, Cade."

He turned to her, smiling slightly. "I like a beer from time to time, but I think I need all my faculties to deal with you, baby."

She knocked back a third of her drink, giving Cade a jaunty smile. "Well, I think I can handle you with one hand tied behind my back."

Cade whistled. "I would watch it. You start talking about rope and Jesse over there is likely to give you a demonstration. It won't be just one hand, though. I assure you, he'll have you trussed up and unable to move so fast it will make your head spin."

Jesse couldn't miss the way Zane Hollister started watching those two like they were the nightly entertainment. The bar owner's hand went out, grabbing the phone and dialing a number—most likely his wife's. Callie Hollister-Wright was a sweetheart of a woman and she was also the filter through which all of Bliss's gossip flowed.

"I think I'll pass on the hard-core bondage. I'm not exactly submissive," Gemma shot back.

And she was wrong about that. "Submissive doesn't have to be a lifestyle choice. It can be something you indulge in, like that ice cream the other day. It can be a way to relax, to unwind, to enjoy yourself."

She gave him a bright smile. "I think I'll decide that for myself. Unless there's something you need to tell me. Are you playing a part? Are you playing the reasonable guy until we get involved and then you'll turn into an asshole?"

Cade piped up. "I'm easy. I'm exactly what I show myself to be. I'm a mechanic. I like beer and burgers and the occasional action film."

She snorted a little. "Well, then, we're not going to do well, are we? I like good vodka and romances. And I like to read. Guess we're not compatible."

Jesse sort of wanted to punch them both. "Only if you're both completely unwavering. Gemma, do you require a man who drinks vodka?"

She sputtered a little. "Well, no."

One down. "Cade, if the woman you're interested in wants to see a romance film, what do you do?"

Pure stubbornness came over Cade, his whole body setting in hard lines. But at least his damn mouth didn't lie. "I go see the film."

Gemma stared straight ahead. "And he probably complains the whole time. He would ruin it for me."

Poor baby. Was that how she'd been treated? "He wouldn't."

Cade softened immediately. "Hell, no, I wouldn't. If I liked her, and she liked some dumb romance movie, then I would like it, too, because it brought her pleasure. And if she didn't want me to tie her up, then I wouldn't. I can be vanilla if I have to be."

She shrugged, her eyes not meeting his. "And I might be more open than I let on."

The tension in the air seemed to deflate a bit. Jesse leaned in. She was still on the edge, but Cade's words had an effect. She'd been hurt. That was obvious. Maybe she needed a dual approach. Not good cop, bad cop exactly, but more like soft lover, take charge lover. Damn, but she needed both.

Jesse let his hand slide over hers again. "I like beer, too, but I would always get you what you want. This doesn't have to be an all or nothing thing. You see that, right? We can have a nice time. We can take care of you and still get what we need."

She took a long breath, shaking her head and pulling back her hand. "I don't know. I just want to have some fun. Cade said it didn't have to be serious."

But that wasn't what she needed. She needed more. "We don't have to start picking out rings, but it's also not merely a good time. I want to see you on a regular basis. I want to give this a shot."

"I want to try, too, but I can't promise anything." It was more than he'd gotten out of her in a whole week of careful courting.

He looked at Cade, whose eyes had grown heavy. The minute Jesse started mentioning anything permanent, Cade's eyes darkened and his mouth turned down. Had he expected that they would never settle down? *Damn it.*

Cade nodded her way. "I'm going to head home. I don't think I should be involved. The two of you have something going, and that's fine. I don't think I'm a relationship kind of guy. You two have a good time."

He slid from his barstool and walked back toward Ty.

Fucking, fuck, fuck, goddamn fuck. Jesse took a long breath. What the hell had Cade thought would happen? He'd made himself plain. He wanted Gemma, and he didn't want a one-night stand. Had Cade thought they would spend the rest of their lives on the road, screwing women and partying because he didn't want to face the past? He set his drink down. Cade had been his friend for too long. "I need to talk to him. He's got a lot on his mind. Will you be okay here?"

She turned to him, her face a mask of indifference. "I'll be fine.

Go talk to Cade. I need to head home any way. I'll talk to you later."

She wouldn't call. She wouldn't talk to him again. He started walking away, utterly sure that she would dismiss him entirely. And she wouldn't try again. She'd taken a chance and goddamn Cade had let her lead the way. Her fears were leading them all down a path because Cade couldn't let it be.

Did he have to make a choice? Or should he take a chance that might lead them to something good?

Cade had walked away. That didn't mean Jesse had to follow it. Gemma was special. He felt it deep in his bones. He'd connected to her the moment she'd walked in their goddamn door. For the first time in years, he had to make a decision.

If Cade was out, then he was out. Damn it, Cade was his friend, but he couldn't give up his whole future for him.

He turned around. He marched back to Gemma. "Dance with me. I'm a spectacularly shitty dancer, but I want to dance with you."

Her face was suspiciously red as she turned to him. "That's probably not a good idea."

"It's a great idea." He held his hand out. "It's the best idea I've had in years. Maybe you've had better, but as for me, this is it. I know one thing, Gemma Wells. I want to dance with you."

"I'm not a good dancer." She sniffled, just a little.

He gave her his surest smile. "Then we're well matched, baby, because I've got two left feet." She put her hand in his but didn't move off her barstool. "Gemma, baby, he's as scared as you are." She started to turn right back to her vodka tonic, but Jesse reached out and put a hand to her chin, pulling her eyes back to his. "You be braver than that. You look at me. You tell me what you're feeling."

Big fat tears pooled in those eyes, nearly breaking Jesse's heart. "I don't understand you two."

He gave her what he hoped was an encouraging smile. "You don't have to right now. It takes time to understand, especially two men. But neither one of us truly wants easy sex. If that's all you're looking for, then I need to walk away, too."

"I don't know what I want. Do I have to know what I want tonight?" She wiped away the tears on her cheeks. "Damn it. I was supposed to get married tomorrow. I didn't love him, but I planned a whole life around him. It fell apart and I lost my job and my fiancé and my life in one day. I thought I could not think about it tonight, but in typical Gemma fashion, I fucked up and picked the man who doesn't want easy sex, and the one who might have wanted it walked away. So you should go. I'll drink my way out of it."

He wanted to groan. He fucking attracted difficult people. He was a magnet. And he couldn't stand the sight of her crying. "Can we compromise?"

She turned back awfully quick. "How?"

He moved in, letting her feel the heat of his body, his lips close to hers. She was curious. He would place a big-ass bet that her fiancé hadn't satisfied her on any level. "I don't want a one-night stand."

"And I don't want a commitment."

A standoff, yes, but one he could deal with. He let his hand cover hers again. "Open-ended affair. I want you. I wanted you the minute I saw you. I've been hard as a rock since you walked into the shop. It's more than your curvy, gorgeous, fuck-me body. I like how smart you are. A woman like you can make a man better. I want that, Gemma. Cade wants it, too."

She didn't pull her hand away. "You don't know me at all. And I don't think Cade feels the same way. He walked away."

He tangled their fingers together, enjoying the feel of her soft skin against his. "So did you. The only reason we're having this conversation is that I'm the reasonable one."

Her lips tilted up. "The sweet one."

He could handle that title. "Yes. The sweet one. And you're the fuckable one. And Cade's the one who handles all the bad shit. It can work, Gemma. It can work for the long term and it can definitely work for a night. But I want you to go into this whole thing with an open mind."

She sighed, her hand squeezing his. "I'm a bitch."

So she'd been told, probably by many people, but Jesse was going to set her straight. "No. You're smart and sexy and don't compromise when it's not necessary. I'm asking you to compromise now. You're a smart woman. Make a quick list. Put me and Cade on one side and your pride on the other, because that's what we're up against—your pride. You add those numbers up real fast. You tell me if I should stay or I should go. Factor in the fact that I don't want to go."

He stared at her, sending her his will. He wasn't sure he would be able to leave if she told him to.

He was betting a lot on her, but then, he was a betting man.

* * * *

Jesse McCann was going to make her crazy. It was supposed to be a simple plan. She was supposed to smile his way, and then he would do anything to get into her pants. Easy, breezy plan that almost any man would follow.

But no, Gemma Wells had to pick the guys who wanted more.

Or the guys who wanted to play games.

She was scared out of her mind. They weren't acting like she thought they should. Cade couldn't lie and take some sex and dump her in the morning?

And Jesse should have been happy with one night's fuck. He was supposed to be her rebound man. He was supposed to be that guy she took all her frustration out on and then sent on his way.

And she would have woken up and felt emptier than she did right now.

He was right. She was smart. She could think her way through this. What did she know?

They hadn't played games. They'd told her what they wanted. She didn't know what she wanted except she wanted someone to want her. They wanted her. They weren't willing to take her under her terms.

Did she even like her terms? What the fuck were her terms? She'd gone into the whole thing with the thought that she would be in control. She would make all the decisions. That had never worked for her before. And why would she have goddamn terms? This wasn't war. She wasn't sure what it was, but she knew she didn't want to fight with them.

Cade's green eyes haunted her. She couldn't use the term "them." He was gone. Would something with Jesse work when Cade didn't want her?

"What do you want, Gemma?"

Jesse's voice flowed over her. He was soothing where Cade set her on edge. Jesse calmed her, his very voice a silky smooth seduction most of the time. Then there were times when he would growl her way. Would he be able to top her? Would he let her be in control when she needed to be?

She liked both. She needed both. She didn't even want to be in control, she simply didn't know another way to be. Neither of her previous two lovers had wanted to be in control. Patrick had been practically lackadaisical.

Jesse had been honest. *Fuck*. Honesty stripped away her armor. What would be left? Be brave. Jesse had asked her to be brave. She'd been in hiding for six months. Could she be brave?

She was Gemma Wells. She'd put herself through Harvard. She'd given up huge chunks of her soul for a job that had taken everything and given nothing back. Years of her life had been wasted on people who would never have been as honest as these two men had been in the last ten minutes.

And she'd sent one of them away.

She really was a masochist.

What did she want?

She wanted a couple of minutes of pure joy, and they were offering it, but it came with risk. Nothing good came without risk. She might wake up tomorrow and look like an idiot. They might be lying. Was she willing to take the risk? What was the balance? Her pride versus the potential of some happiness.

"Don't go." The words sounded almost foreign in her mouth. She'd said them, but she wasn't sure she recognized the woman who had spoken. She'd changed in an instant. No. She'd started changing a long time ago, six months in fact. She hadn't acknowledged it until this moment. "I don't want you to go."

Jesse smiled that brilliant, light-up-the-whole-goddamn-world smile. She had no idea how a man his size, with those muscles and his badass looks, could have such a sweet smile. "I'm glad. Can I talk to you about Cade?"

His friend. He wanted to plead his friend's case to get into whatever the hell they were starting. Two men. Two amazing men.

119

She got off her chair and looked around the bar. Cade was waving good-bye to the blond guy she'd slammed the door on a couple of days back. She needed to think about being nicer to people. Cade said something to the waitress and then turned. He caught her eye, but his slid away, his whole body turning for the exit. Was she going to let him walk out that door? He'd wanted her earlier in the day. She'd felt his cock press against her, rubbing her right in every way. He'd wanted her, but there was a haunted look in his eyes at times. She'd seen it in her own. Could she let him go because she didn't want to face him?

Fuck no.

She had no idea what she was doing, but she ran across the bar and found herself standing in front of him. Jesse followed her, his body bulwarking hers. And she stared, not a damn word coming out of her mouth.

Cade stared down at her. "Gemma? What do you need?"

Nope. Nothing. She looked at him, feeling the weight of the whole bar staring at her like she was the lead actress in their favorite soap opera. She glanced around. They were totally the center of attention. She was being an idiot. He'd walked away. Why was she chasing after him?

Jesse put a hand on her shoulder. "Don't think about them. They're nosy. Go on, darlin'."

Go on. Yep. Go on. Did she want to go on? Yes. She did. She wanted him, even if it was only for a night. She was a Harvard Law grad. She knew lots of words. Why did they fail her now? "Do you want to dance?"

Dumb. That was dumb. There wasn't any music. The jukebox had gone silent five minutes before and no one had approached it since. She was so stupid.

Cade turned from her, his hand going into his pocket. He walked away, her whole soul flattening. She didn't even get an answer.

He walked straight to the jukebox, putting some money in and in a few seconds, a slow, sultry beat started to pound out. Cade turned back to her, holding out a single, callused, deeply masculine hand. God, she was fascinated by that hand. "Are you sure? I don't know what I can offer you."

She wasn't sure of anything except the fact that if she walked out now she would hate herself forever. She might be able to forgive herself if she got played, but not if she didn't try. She'd always tried. She'd wanted to be a lawyer so she'd applied to Harvard. She hadn't let the fact that she didn't have the money faze her. She'd gone for it. When she'd decided she wanted to marry Patrick, she'd told him they should get married.

She'd spent her whole life chasing what she wanted. Why couldn't she ask for this?

"I'm not sure of anything." She didn't bother to hide her emotions. He'd been honest. She could be, too. "I'm scared out of my mind, but I want to dance. And I want a night with you both. Is that too much to ask? I won't require anything from you but tonight, Cade Sinclair."

She felt Jesse's arms wrap around her waist. Pure pleasure. She was drawn back into his heat, his body. And Cade crowded her front. He put his forehead to hers, nuzzling her sweetly.

"I'll dance with you. I should warn you, I'm not good. But I'll dance as long as you like." Cade pressed his body to hers, his hips swaying lightly. Jesse moved behind her.

The sweetness of the moment assailed her. She let one arm wrap around Jesse and the other drift around Cade as the music flowed over her. Her feet moved in time over Trio's hardwood floors. She barely noticed when other couples joined them. Couples? Trios. Laura Niles danced with her men, her body moving easily. Alexei Markov held Holly Lang as he swayed to the music. And Caleb Burke kind of, sort of, moved behind her.

And she was surrounded by Jesse and Cade. She knew she should feel self-conscious, but it was hard when all she wanted to do was melt into them. Jesse's hands molded her curves, skimming along her hips. Cade, who said he couldn't dance, moved with such grace, his lean body picking up the beat and giving her something to follow. His chest pressed against hers, making her nipples peak. It wasn't a dance so much as a seduction. Jesse and Cade surrounded her, not leaving an inch between them.

While the music played, she didn't have to think. She didn't have a past. She didn't care about the future. All that mattered was the moment, and the moment included two men.

She let her arms tighten around them.

"That's right." Jesse's breath heated her ear. "Touch me."

Every inch of her body heated up. She felt drunk, but she hadn't had that much to drink. She wasn't drunk on alcohol. She was drunk on them, on what they represented.

A new beginning.

Tomorrow was supposed to be her wedding day. She should have been preparing to walk down the aisle, but tonight she felt. Felt.

Every choice she'd made had been logical—from where she'd decided to work, to her groom, to the dress she'd bought.

She let her head drift back, leaning against Jesse while she pulled Cade in. There was nothing logical about this. She wasn't planning on staying in Bliss. She had nothing in common with the men.

Except she wanted them, and they seemed to want her.

She didn't have to put a time limit on it. She could get her heart ripped out. She could completely fuck up. The world could end. Anything could happen.

And that was okay.

She suddenly didn't need to know what would happen the next day or the next. She could live in the moment. She could embrace this weird life. No commitments. No promises. Just life.

Was that what her mother had been trying to teach her?

It didn't matter. She took a deep breath and gave in. She wrapped her arms around Cade's big body. He was so tall he made her feel petite. And Jesse was broad and built like a linebacker.

"Are you ready to get out of here?" Cade asked.

She nodded. "Can we go back to my place?"

"We can go anywhere you want." Jesse's lips played along her ear.

It was crazy. It was wild. It was everything she needed tonight. "Yes."

Yes to them. Yes to the night. They led her outside. She followed with no thought to anything but the moment she was in.

Chapter Eight

Cade bundled her into her coat, deeply aware of how hard his cock was. This was a bad idea. He was thinking with his dick and not his head, but all the blood in his body was in his cock, so he was fucked. She'd given him permission. Jesse was giving him permission. He could enjoy her body tonight and Jesse would take care of her in the morning. It was exactly what he wanted.

Why was he still nervous?

"Where's your car, baby?" If Jesse had a single worry, he wasn't showing it. Jesse kept a hand on her, moving from her back to her elbow as he started to show her out the door.

"McCann! Sinclair!"

Cade turned at Zane's sharp bark.

The big bar owner stared at both of them. "You take care of her. She's Nate's secretary."

Gemma frowned, her pretty face scrunching up. "I'm the office manager."

Zane smiled. "Fine. She's Nate's office manager. You two understand what I mean. Nate or Cam should be giving you this lecture, but Nate's at home with the kids and Cam is doing god knows what to his fiancée in my broom closet. I'm putting a lock on that in the morning. So it's up to me. She isn't without some men to watch out for her. You take care of her or we'll have a long talk. Go on, then."

Cade understood exactly what he meant. He'd been warned to treat Gemma right or Zane and Nate and possibly Cameron Briggs would come after him and Jesse. Gemma worked for the sheriff and that was a small, tight family. Just because she was a new employee didn't mean she wasn't protected.

"Does he think I'll be late for work?" Gemma asked as they walked into the cool night. She turned, staring back at the bar. "I won't be late. Or do you think they have morality clauses? I didn't actually sign anything yet, so I didn't read the employment terms. That's ridiculous. They can't expect me to not have a life outside of work."

Jesse stopped her. Gemma fairly vibrated with nervous energy. Jesse gave her a reassuring smile. "He wasn't disapproving. He was warning me and Cade that he would kick our asses if we hurt you."

She frowned. "Why would he care?"

She'd lived alone for way too long. "Because you work for his partner. That makes you like family. We're a small town here. We're isolated. We have to watch out for each other."

"Especially with all the murders and stuff." Jesse said it like he was talking about a bit of bad weather.

"Yeah, I read about those. It doesn't bode well for my future employment." She glanced back at the bar. "I don't understand this place. And I don't have a car. We only have the one car and Naomi took it."

She'd been walking to work all week? He didn't like the sound of that. It was a long walk from the valley community of cabins into town. Even further to the shop and the small apartment he and Jesse shared. She needed a reliable form of transportation. He could look around and see if there was something he could get for cheap and then fix up for her.

He stopped himself. He wasn't her boyfriend. He couldn't make decisions like that.

"Come on, baby. We brought the car tonight. Cade can drive.

Neither one of us finished a single beer." Jesse took her hand.

Cade stopped them. "How many did you have, Gemma?"

He wasn't about to take advantage of a woman who'd had too much. He would see her home and make sure she was safe.

Even in the low light, Cade could see Jesse roll his eyes and mouth the word "coward."

"A vodka tonic. And two sips of the second one. I'm fine." She seemed awfully sober. And she didn't exactly look like a woman looking to party. She looked nervous. Unsure.

About what?

"Have you had dinner?" Cade asked.

Jesse jumped on it. He wouldn't let her go hungry. Jesse was already taking on his role of indulgent caregiver. He loved having a woman to take care of. "We can go to Stella's. Or we can stop by the store and we'll make you something."

She leaned over and kissed Jesse, her lips meeting his in a little bump. It wasn't the world's sexiest kiss. It was awkward, but Jesse let her explore, his hands coming out to cup her waist. She kissed him for a minute, getting more aggressive as the seconds passed. "I don't want food. Take me home."

"Yes," Jesse said, his voice going deep.

She turned back to Cade. Her face had lost its vulnerable look and a hardness had taken its place. She put her hands on Cade's chest. "Good, then let's go and get this party started."

She went on her tiptoes and pressed her lips against his, the deep lack of passion overwhelming him. She was kissing him, but it seemed to be a practiced move. He stood there and allowed her to kiss him, his mind working. What was her game?

She stepped back and nodded as though she'd done her part and it was time to move on to the next phase of the evening.

Definitely not a woman who had easy affairs. It was obvious she was trying to look like a seductress, but he didn't buy it. Her movements were stiff, her smile forced.

Jesse sent him a look, his brow furrowing. At least they were on the same page.

Cade reached out and took her hand. Earlier in the day, he'd crossed the street from the shop and headed to Polly's Cut and Curl. If

125

a man needed to find out about a woman, the local beauty parlor was the place to go. Polly had gotten the scoop from Teeny, who'd talked to Callie, who had heard it from Stella that Gemma had not only been engaged, but that the whole thing had ended in a disaster that cost her everything. Was she trying to rebound with the small-town yokels?

He followed Jesse and Gemma to the classic car he'd spent years restoring. It was his dream car. He'd scrimped and saved and lovingly put together every piece of that car. It had been his father's at one point, the only thing he had left of him. After his parents had died, Nancy had put his father's prize possession into a garage and kept it there for him. He could remember the moment when she'd come for him. It had been at his parents' funeral, in that odd time after they and his sister had been placed in the ground, when he'd gone to his home where everyone was gathered, but he'd felt alone. He'd hidden in that Camaro. After the accident, it had been hard for him to feel comfortable in a car, but the Camaro hadn't worked in years.

And then Nancy had been there, sneaking into the car with him. She'd been his mom's best friend. The rest of his family didn't have a place for him, but Nancy stepped up. She'd sat in that car with him until long after everyone left.

She'd promised to take care of him and the piece of crap car his father had loved. Even after she'd lost her money, she'd found a way to pay for the garage. Now this car was all he had left of her, too.

How would Nancy Gibbs have handled Gemma Wells?

Jesse opened the door, but Cade was faster. Jesse had pushed them into this. He could do the driving, too. He helped Gemma into the backseat and followed after her.

Jesse frowned as Cade slapped the keys into his hands. "Asshole."

He wasn't about to feel guilty. "It's not far away."

Gemma sat in the backseat, looking forward as though she'd figured out she was in a car with two men she didn't truly know. He had the most insane urge to push her boundaries just a little.

"Hey, do you do this often?" he asked, sliding in beside her. He knew the truth. He would bet his life she'd never done anything like this before, but he wanted to see if she would lie.

"Often enough." There was that brassy tone, the one she seemed to use on everyone until she forgot to and showed her softer self.

Little liar. He put a hand on her knee. She stiffened slightly before taking a deep breath.

"So you sleep with a lot of men?" It was time to put it more baldly. Gemma seemed to appreciate a direct approach.

"Cade!" Jesse admonished as he turned the engine over.

"Hey, you're the honesty guy," he pointed out. "It's a fair question. We're practically strangers and we're heading back to her place to have sex. I would like to know what I'm getting into. For all I know she's one of those female serial killers. She could be luring us back to her lair with the promise of sex and all the while she intends to kill us and use us for fertilizer."

She turned to him, her mouth hanging open. "That is the stupidest thing I've ever heard. I'm not a serial killer."

He shrugged. "It's Bliss. I have to ask. So how many men have you slept with?"

"Cade!" Jesse hissed his name, a warning.

He wasn't listening. "It's a fair question."

Even in the low light, he could see her flush. "How many women have you slept with?"

"Fifteen. Wait. Are we talking actual penetration or like oral and stuff?" She huffed. How did she expect to get naked with them in the next fifteen minutes if she couldn't even talk about sex?

She was quiet for a moment.

"Gemma?" Maybe he'd pushed her too far.

"Two. Okay. Fine. It's two," she spat out. "Are you happy now? I slept with my boyfriend in college and then he turned out to be gay, and then I slept with my fiancé and he turned out to be an asshole. Maybe you should think about this because I don't have a great track record in the happy customer department."

There she was. Bitchy. Honest. Funny. He hated the hard shell, but he was intrigued by the woman he was beginning to glimpse underneath. He was fascinated, and that was dangerous. He should walk away. He couldn't, and if he did, he probably wouldn't be welcomed back. If he wanted any kind of a place in the relationship she and Jesse were starting, he had to be there in the beginning.

Because she was like a turtle. She'd poked her head out and

looked around and decided to give them a try. If they turned her down, she would go back into her shell.

"Why only two?" He kept asking questions he didn't want answers to.

She turned toward the window, watching the night go by. "I only had the two boyfriends."

Jesse drove down the long paved road toward her cabin. "I think what Cade is asking is why did you choose only two? You're a beautiful woman, Gemma. You're what? Twenty-six?"

"Thirty." The word was flat, but Cade heard the satisfaction behind it. Jesse knew how to make her comfortable. "I don't know. I didn't have time for it. I knew from a young age that I wanted to do something special. I studied hard. And my parents moved around a lot, so I was constantly adjusting to new schools or sometimes to homeschool if we were on a commune. My parents wanted me to get a life education, but I wanted to score high on my SATs."

Now she was talking. He scooted closer to her. She didn't move away. "That must have been hard. No high school boyfriends then?"

"No. My dad died when I was twelve. Mom settled down for a few years and I spent all my time studying. The first time we had high-speed Internet was the greatest day of my life." She relaxed against him, her body sinking into his. "Look, I love my mom, but she was all about finding herself, and that meant I was in some weird situations. I know that communes are supposed to be these perfect places, but I was a teenaged girl without a dad."

Vulnerable. She would have been incredibly vulnerable. Cade knew how that felt. In the warm darkness of the car, it was easy to pull her into his arms, to let his body comfort hers. It didn't have to mean anything. He could walk away in the morning. He wouldn't even have to feel guilty because Jesse would take care of her. He could cuddle her tonight and go about his business in the morning.

Her face turned up. "Why did you get in the back with me? Did you want to play twenty questions?"

He had an honest answer for that. "If I'd let Jesse hop in the back with you, he would already have you flat on your back with your legs spread. I wanted to wait. I wanted to be able to watch when he gets you naked."

"Maybe I would get him naked first," she said, a hint of challenge in her voice. She brought herself up, staring him in the face. "I don't want to talk. I don't want to open up my damn soul and tell you my story. I want to have a good time. Can you help me with that?"

He knew he was being deeply perverse, but he didn't like the sound of being Gemma's good time. It wasn't fair so he let it go. He gave her his easiest, most laid-back smile. "I'm right here, darlin'. You come and take what you want."

She put her hands on either side of his face, drawing him down. He was game. He let her lead for now. She pressed her mouth to his, her tongue drawing along his bottom lip. His cock jumped. He had zero intentions of going first. That was for Jesse. Jesse was the one who would stay with her. Jesse was the one who would be her man. But he liked being close to her. The scent and warmth of her called to him. She moved him, and more than merely his cock.

He kept his hands off her, afraid that if he touched her, he might do what he'd tried to avoid with Jesse—put her on her back and get balls deep inside. This was a warm-up for his friend. That was all.

Her hand trailed down his torso, making his flesh quiver everywhere she touched. He didn't like clothes in the best of circumstances. He down right hated them now. He wanted to feel her hands on his chest as they kissed. He wanted to make out with her until they couldn't see straight, and then Jesse would turn her into his arms and Cade would watch them kiss. They would get her so hot she would beg them. They would take her to the edge over and over before giving her that one push that sent her to heaven. Yes, they could play all night long. That was what he wanted. A full night of pleasuring Gemma, passing her back and forth like a sweet sex toy he shared with his best friend.

He loved the buildup. He fucking loved foreplay. Fucking was an art form and it took time to get it right.

Gemma didn't seem to have the same philosophy.

Her hand went straight to the fly of his jeans. She was awkward, pulling at it. She left his mouth, her face turning down as she tried to get his jeans open.

"Hey, slow down." He wasn't ready. She couldn't possibly be.

"No need. We can do it here," she insisted.

"I think I should have a say in that," Jesse said on a low growl from the front seat.

Fuck. He wasn't going to step on Jesse's toes. He pulled back. "Let's get to the cabin."

She was so aggressive. She finally got his fly open, and her hand covered his hard-as-a-rock cock. "You don't want to wait."

But he did. She was moving way too fast for him. She started to pull at his jeans. For the first damn time in his life, he wished he wore underwear. It would have provided him with a temporary buffer from her forceful hands.

"Gemma, we're almost home." He could see the valley up ahead. One turn and then he could pull her out of the car and they could set everything on the right footing. He could slow things down. Jesse would take charge. They would get her where she needed to be, wet and wild and wanton.

"Do you have a condom." Her voice was all husky command. She wasn't asking. She was telling him he should have a condom.

Jesse stopped the car in front of her house. "Gemma, get out of the car."

She wiggled, her hands moving under the flouncy cotton skirt she wore. He watched in equal amounts of arousal and horror as she came up with her black lacy panties in hand. She winked and tossed them his way. "Come on, Cade. Where's the condom? We're going wild tonight. No holds barred, crazy sex. Let's go."

Those panties told the tale. They were lovely, all lace and seduction. They were meant to get a man's blood hot, but he wasn't concerned about his blood. He could fuck her right now and all night long. But Gemma's blood was in question because those lovely panties were perfectly dry. He put them right to his nose and all he could fucking smell was the fabric softener she'd used on them.

She wasn't anywhere close to being ready for sex. Why the hell was she pushing for it?

Jesse opened the door and frowned down at both of them. Cade simply looked up at him and handed him the panties. Jesse seemed to know immediately that something was wrong. Cade wasn't surprised. Jesse knew damn straight what a pair of close-to-the-edge woman's undies should feel like. They'd brought many a woman to the breaking point before they'd eased the panties off and slid inside.

His unruly cock was wailing at him, but he needed to figure out what was going on with Gemma. This was supposed to be fun, not a race to see who made it to the finish line first. Jesse held her panties, sending him a "what the fuck" look.

Cade shrugged. He had no idea what was going on. He tucked his cock back in, carefully zipping back up.

"Are you going to kiss me or what?" Gemma asked, aggressively moving toward him.

Kissing was still a good idea. She needed a whole hell of a lot of kissing. She needed kissing and petting and possibly a tongue teasing into her pussy before she was ready for sex. She slammed her mouth on his, and her hands went right back to his jeans.

He pushed her away. "Damn it, Gemma. Slow down."

She stopped, her body going completely still. She took a moment and then smoothed her hair back. "I'd like to get out now."

Good. They needed to get inside so they could lay her out and show her what foreplay was. He'd love to meet her previous lovers because they obviously hadn't taught her pleasure. Cade slid out of the car, forcing his big body out of the backseat and onto her driveway. He could breathe again. The night air cooled his skin. He reached his hand back in to help Gemma out, but she didn't take it. Awkwardly, she struggled out of the car. She nearly fell over, but Cade caught her. She pushed away from him as quickly as she could, steadying herself on her impractical heels.

"Thank you for the ride home." Her face was a polite blank.

"What?" He looked at Jesse, completely at a loss.

She didn't reply, simply turned and walked toward her door, digging in her purse for her keys.

He'd been dismissed. That much was clear. She was shutting them out. Gemma climbed the two steps to her porch.

"You didn't do anything," Jesse said, his eyes never leaving her. "If I'd gotten in the backseat, she would have done the same thing to me and I would have reacted the same way."

Cade had the sudden, desperate need to go after her. It didn't matter that he was scared. It didn't mean shit that he knew he wasn't good for her. He couldn't walk away. "Gemma?"

She didn't turn around, merely stood at her door in the gloom of the night, trying to force her key in.

"You can go if you want to, but I'm going to handle this." Jesse had a frown on his face. "She's about to find out she's not in charge of this."

Jesse started toward her, and Cade followed, hoping he hadn't fucked everything up.

* * * *

Jesse checked his temper. He was righteously pissed off, but he needed to handle Gemma with care. "Let me do that."

She was struggling with the key. She obviously couldn't see the lock since the light on her front porch was out. She shouldn't walk up alone when she couldn't see. Anyone could charge her from the dark, and she wouldn't know what hit her.

"I've got it." She cursed as the keys fell out of her hand.

Jesse got to them before she could. "Baby, let's go inside and talk about this."

"He doesn't want me," she replied. "You two are a packaged deal. I get that. So why don't you both run along?"

Something was going on with her. She'd been on edge all night, but he wasn't going to let her ruin this. "We're going to go inside and sit down and talk about this like rational adults. You weren't even aroused."

She frowned. "How the hell would you be able to tell?"

He held her panties up. "These are bone dry, darlin'. They should be wet."

She gasped and reached out for her underwear. "Give me those."

"No." He shoved them in the pocket of his jeans. "Now, you don't want to go inside? We can do this out here, but you might want to keep your voice down."

Her jaw firmed to a stubborn line. "I am not doing anything out here."

"You were ready to assault Cade a few seconds ago in full view of your mother's cabin."

"Assault is a strong word," Cade said, standing well outside her range of fire. Chickenshit.

"Assault?" The words dripped with sarcasm. "He was as hard as a rock."

She needed to understand. "But he wouldn't have touched you because you weren't ready, baby. Now, let's go inside and we can do this right."

Her body was brittle, her words even harder. "I tried to do it right. I'm not exactly a virgin. It didn't work out. No problem. Not everyone is sexually compatible. It's no big deal. There are more men in this town."

Cade groaned. "Gemma, don't do this."

"What the hell is this about?" He was starting to lose patience. "You watch what you say now. If you push me too far, you'll likely find yourself over my knee."

Her eyes narrowed. "I would love to see you try, McCann. Don't you forget what I did to Max Harper."

"Don't try it. It won't go well for you."

She was pushing him. Her foot tapped against the wooden porch, making a rhythm for his blood to pound to. "We'll see about that. Now why don't we both go our separate ways? Cade doesn't want me, and I know you can't get it up unless your friend is around."

A vision of stripping her and forcing her over his knee assaulted his brain. He would smack that luscious ass of hers until it was red and nothing but sweet words came out of her mouth. She would fight him at first, but he would keep going until she submitted. He would have her at his goddamn feet by the end of the night. She wanted to challenge him? She wanted to top him? Oh, she would find out just how dominant he could be.

And he would be right back in jail. No. He turned. His temper was frayed. He needed a break. He needed to think.

"That's right. Walk away. Guess your plan didn't work out."

He closed his eyes, the truth sliding into place. Gemma's walls were so high and so thick that sometimes he forgot they were there. She used that sarcasm and bitter wit like armor against the whole damn world. She wanted to be in control because she didn't trust anyone else to be.

He understood that. It had taken him years before he could open himself up to anyone. Cade still closed his own heart off. They were a fucking trio. Three people who were so damaged it seemed impossible they could work.

But he'd decided long ago he wouldn't let the damage of his past wreck his future. He could still remember Nancy Gibbs holding him. It was roughly a year after he'd come to live with them. He hadn't talked much, just waited to do something dumb and get kicked back to the street. Night after night he woke up, those months in the detention center playing in his nightmares. Nancy had held him while he shook and cried. He'd been sixteen, but in that moment, he'd finally gotten to be a little boy holding on to his mother.

Nancy hadn't backed away because he'd been bitter.

He was falling for Gemma Wells. It would be easier to walk away and find someone less difficult, but he had the bad feeling that her face would haunt him for the rest of his life, that no other woman would move him the way she did. She was smart and funny and strong. The bitter brattiness went with it like a car whose engine purred perfectly but had been marred with a horrific paint job. He wouldn't give it up. He would bring that car back to life.

Tenderness. Care. Gemma needed those. She needed his protection. Even from herself.

He turned back around and walked straight up to her. She backed away, her heels slipping. He caught her, hauling her close. "It's all right, baby. It's okay."

"Stop it." But she didn't pull away.

"Tell me what's wrong. Tell me why you're acting this way." He kissed her temple. She was small in his arms.

"He doesn't want me," Gemma insisted.

Cade was suddenly crowding her back, and Jesse felt something inside him ease. He'd half expected Cade to run, but he was here, giving her what she needed. "That's bullshit, baby. I want you badly, but I want you to want me, too."

Her eyes tightened, a look of consternation crossing her face. "I was all over you."

Cade slipped an arm around her. She was totally caught, and that was exactly how he wanted her. "But you didn't want me. Baby, I can tell when a woman wants me."

Jesse cuddled close. She seemed to be responding to the contact in a way she hadn't when she'd taken the reins. "Tell me about your sex life."

She tried to pull away, but they held her fast. "This is stupid."

"How about this? I'll tell you what I like and Cade will tell you what he likes, and then you can talk about your fantasies."

She sighed. "Why can't we just do it?"

He chuckled. "You would like that, wouldn't you? That would leave you in control because you wouldn't have to put anything on the line. Well, I don't think I want to play that way. Hush and listen. Cade, you go first. Touch her while you talk."

"I like to go slow." Cade's voice proved his words true. He spoke in long syllables, drawing out each word as his hands cupped her breasts. "I don't want to roll on and roll off. I want to play with you for a long time. You'll be our plaything, a perfect doll we pass between us. I want to see every inch of you. I want to play with these nipples."

Jesse had to move back slightly to make room for Cade's hands. A soft moan puffed from her mouth as Cade's fingers tightened over her shirt.

"I'm going to suck on them," Cade promised. "I'm going to gently bite them. You'll squirm because it hurts but it also feels good. You're going to go crazy. Your breasts will be so sensitive after I'm done."

Jesse took over. "And the whole time he's playing with your breasts, I'll touch your pussy." He let his hand slip under the waistband of her skirt, gliding over her taut belly and finding the valley of her sex. He could feel the heat coming from her pussy. She wasn't dry now. Slick moisture coated her clit, making it easy for him to slide his fingers over her. She wasn't where he wanted her yet, but she was getting there. And she seemed to like dirty talk. "I'm going to touch this jewel with my fingers and my mouth. I like to eat pussy. It's my favorite meal. I can eat this pussy for hours. Don't you see what you're denying us if you go too fast?"

"Yes." Her voice was a breathless whisper, her hips moving against his hand. She was getting wetter by the moment.

"Good sex should start slow," he explained. "We'll get to the

Lexi Blake

point where you trust us enough to toss your skirts up and fuck you senseless, but not yet. We're going to fuck you so long and so hard that all you'll have to do is look at one of us and this pussy will get wet because you'll know what we can do to you."

Cade kissed her ear. "With our fingers and our mouths and our cocks. We can fill you up."

Jesse sighed. She was finally responding. "Tell me what you want."

She leaned into him, her voice almost too low to hear. "I want to submit."

His cock jumped. "Darlin', I can help you with that."

Chapter Nine

Why the hell had she done that? She'd just said it, like she was commenting on the weather and not asking for kinky sex stuff.

She'd done it because they tricked her and they were still tricking her. Damn. Her whole body went limp again, their hands lulling her into a sensual haze. She'd tried to get it over with, but no, they had to talk. She'd been ready to push through and get to the part she wanted to get to—that moment when they would cuddle her. Patrick had hated it, but she thought these two might like holding her.

Neither one was behaving the way he should. But then again, her body was misbehaving, too.

"You want to submit?" Jesse's voice rumbled along her skin, causing her to shiver. His damn voice wasn't the only thing making her quiver. His fingers skimmed her clitoris, parting the petals of her labia.

She should clear that up. It was a dumb fantasy brought about by romance novels and the desperate need to not be in control for five damn minutes. "It was a joke."

She nearly squealed. They moved in perfect time. Cade's fingers tightened on her nipples while Jesse pinched her clit.

"Don't lie to us." Jesse twisted his fingers slightly. There was a sharp pain that shifted into heat and a restless energy. "Tell me."

"I want to try it."

Their fingers eased up. Cade dipped into her bra, warm hands cupping her breasts. "Why did you try to go so fast?"

"Men like fast." Men wanted to get in and out. They liked a woman who could keep up with them.

"I don't," Jesse said. "I like slow. I like all night long."

"Patrick liked to get to sleep." Damn it, she hadn't meant to say that.

They both stopped.

"Who the hell is Patrick?" Cade sounded oddly outraged.

"Is he the man you were supposed to marry tomorrow?" Jesse asked.

He was the man she'd been ready to marry and who'd called her, not even bothering to remember it was supposed to be the night before their wedding. He was the man who had taught her about sex. Two-minute Patrick.

She nodded. "Yes. We were supposed to get married, but I found him with another woman."

Jesse leaned over, pressing his lips to hers in the sweetest kiss. "Hold that thought. Cade, distract her while I open this damn door. We're giving the whole valley a show. I think I caught the glint of binoculars a minute ago."

Embarrassment flashed through her system. Everyone was watching her?

And then Cade whirled her around and dragged her close, those strong hands pulling at her hips. His mouth came down on hers. She knew she should protest. She started to push away, but her hands met the most perfectly sculpted chest.

Cade was made of pure muscle, but his mouth was gentle on hers. "Give me your tongue, baby."

She opened her mouth to respond, and he took immediate advantage. His tongue slid against hers. She'd been kissed before, but not like this. Cade took over, forcing her head back. She'd been worried when she'd kissed him before. It had been nice, but nothing special. This was what had been missing. Cade held her, his arms a cage that locked her in and wouldn't let her go. She wasn't in control. She wasn't dominant. She softened, her whole body shivering at the thought of giving in to these men.

And she was damn glad Jesse still had her panties because if they'd been on, they would be wet. Her pussy was practically melting. Cade ate at her mouth, devouring her like she was a sweet treat.

She nearly protested when he moved back, the loss of his mouth on hers so terribly rough. But he leaned over and picked her up, his arms going under her knees. He hauled her against his chest like he was picking up something small that weighed next to nothing. Cade, who didn't want anything serious, held her like she was infinitely fragile.

She wasn't, of course. She wasn't some flower. She was more like the rock that anchored things down than some pretty, petite flower, but for a moment she envisioned herself as soft and deeply feminine. She gave in, letting her head rest against his chest, pretending this was her right as his lover, to lean on him, depend on him, to know he would take care of her.

Dangerous thoughts. The world didn't work like that, but for tonight, she was going to pretend.

Jesse turned the light on, illuminating her tiny cabin. No one had updated the décor for years. The living space seemed trapped in the seventies, but somehow Jesse looked right here. He looked like he belonged in the rustic setting. Cade carried her to the couch.

"My bedroom is back there," she said as he sat her down.

Jesse shook his head. "I suppose Patrick always did it in a bed."

She wrinkled her nose. Yeah, she should probably stop talking about Patrick. New lovers didn't like to hear about the old ones. She needed to write down a whole set of rules. "I don't want to talk about Patrick."

She wanted to kiss again. She'd never liked kissing. It was awkward and messy and she never knew how to hold her head, but when Cade kissed her, he moved her where he wanted her. She wanted Jesse to kiss her. She wanted to feel the scruff of his beard against her face.

What would it feel like on her pussy?

Jesse whistled. "Damn, darlin'. I would give a lot to know what you just thought. Your whole body flushed, but we do have to talk about Patrick. Now take off your shirt."

"What?" Were they going into therapy? "I don't think I want to be the only one naked."

Jesse shook his head. "Cade's been naked since he set you on the couch." He looked at Cade, a wry smile on his face. "How the hell do you manage that?"

She looked up and felt her mouth drop. Cade was naked. He was super naked. So damn beautifully and gloriously naked. Why did he ever wear clothes?

Cade shrugged. "It's my superpower. I don't like clothes. Gemma, here's the deal. I like to be naked when I'm at home. I actually would rather be naked wherever, but Nate passes out tickets, and let me tell you, they are liberal with the fines here."

Well, of course he liked to be naked. He was perfect. Six feet two inches of perfectly muscled male god stood in front of her. Every inch of him was defined, from his broad shoulders to his washboard abs and lean hips to powerful legs. Her mouth actually watered. She'd kind of thought cocks that big were a myth, like Big Foot and vampires. She'd been pretty sure they were photoshopped into porn videos, but no, Cade's was vividly real and pointed straight her way.

They wanted her to talk? She could barely breathe.

"See, now I'm getting jealous," Jesse said, frowning.

Fuck. She was screwing up. She'd screwed up all night long. This was what she did. This was why she concentrated on her job and not the stupid emotional stuff—because she was hideously bad at the emotional stuff.

"Hey, hey." Jesse got to his knees in front of her. He forced her to look into his seriously blue eyes. "I was joking, baby. Why did you get tense? Baby, I was only teasing. You can't help but look at it. People can see it from space."

She laughed, tears forming in her eyes because she was in way deeper than she thought she was. Why did they have to be so sweet? "I don't want to screw up."

His eyes closed, just briefly, and when he opened them again there was a soft ferocity there. "You aren't a screw-up, Gemma, and I'll beat the living shit out of anyone who tells you otherwise. This is why we need to talk about Patrick and everyone else who put you in this place where you're terrified of making a wrong move."

Cade sat down beside her on the couch, his utter ease with his unclothed state on display. He sat next to her, putting a hand on hers like they were just two friends talking and his incredibly large dick wasn't forming a lightning rod drawing her eyes in. "It isn't wrong to screw up, G. It's normal. I screw up all the time, and Jesse laughs it off. No one's going to throw you out if you prove yourself to be human."

But that wasn't her experience. So much of her life had been about perfection, and she'd placed herself in the position. She would have lost her scholarship if she hadn't made straight As. Her internship for a circuit court judge had been fraught with peril, his nastiness coming out if she'd put three sugars in his coffee instead of two. And the firm. God, she'd walked a tight rope every day, always having to be the best.

"I don't know how to be any other way," she admitted. "I think it's me. My mom and dad were great. They just didn't understand me."

"Take off your shirt. That's where I want to start," Jesse said.

She managed to get her eyes off Cade's cock long enough to stare at the floor. Now that she'd seen Cade, she wasn't sure she wanted to get naked. "Can't we turn off the light?"

"No," Cade said. "Give me the shirt, Gemma."

For a good-time guy, he seemed awfully bossy. "Jesse's still dressed."

"We're going to have to have a long talk about the meaning of the word submission, darlin'. We can have it one of two ways. We can have it with your shirt off, or we can have it with your ass in the air," Jesse explained.

She shook her head. "Why would my ass be… Oh, you'll spank me if I don't take my shirt off."

"There's that Harvard-trained brain." Jesse sat back, a hard glint in his eyes. "I'm going to explain myself just this once. I want you naked because I want this to be intimate. I think you'll be more honest with your clothes off. I intend to strip away every bit of your armor."

Cade smiled her way. "I want you naked because I would like to see your tits."

"You might not like them." That was her real fear.

Jesse groaned. "Damn it, Gemma. Cade promises he will like your tits."

"I will be very good friends with them," Cade said, his face looking lighter than it had in days.

It was the grin on Cade's face that did it. He was enjoying the play. He wanted to be here, where just moments before she'd wondered if he wanted her. He did. He was comfortable, and she didn't want to ruin it.

She pulled at the bottom of her shirt.

Jesse held his hand out, taking the shirt and putting it to the side. "And the bra. Tell me about sex with Patrick while you take off your bra."

He was an impossible man and he was also an immovable object. She reached around, trying to unhook her plain-Jane white bra that didn't match her underwear. She wished she'd bought a nicer one, but it didn't seem practical since no one could see her bra. She'd needed to spend money on the outward trappings of success, and no one at the firm gave a damn if undies were lacy and silky, not even Patrick, who often had simply screwed her without taking her bra off.

"Focus, Gemma." Jesse's sharp command brought her back to reality.

Oh, yes. She was supposed to talk. She took a deep breath, forcing herself to calm. Her hands were shaking. She would never get the damn thing off this way. Patrick. They wanted to know about Patrick. "I thought we were okay. I didn't love him. I know that's probably wrong, but I didn't even want to love him. I liked him. He was charming, and we were going to the same place."

"Tell me about sex." He said the word "sex" like it was a decadent dessert he wanted to lick up and savor.

"Tell me about sex." Cade echoed Jesse's words, but punctuated them by putting his steady hands over her shaking ones. In a single twist, he had the bra undone.

"It was quick. That seemed right at the time. My whole life was that way. I'm not the type of person who stops and smells the roses, Jesse. I tend to tromp all over the roses as I rush to make the subway."

Cade slid the bra over her arms. She was half naked with two men. Maybe she wasn't quite the woman she'd been before.

"I like to smell the roses," Cade said. "And I damn well like playing with them."

She leaned back because Cade crowded her, his head going down to her chest. He seemed to be taking the whole "making friends with her breasts" thing seriously. And he appeared to want to be good friends, intimate friends. She gasped as he sucked a nipple into his mouth.

This was what arousal felt like. Holy hell. Her pussy actually quivered. "I think I'm ready now."

Jesse stood, slipping his own shirt over his head. "Not yet. Did you submit to him?"

She nearly laughed, but Cade's mouth was doing amazing things to her nipples. She had to fight to speak. "Uhm, no. I was in charge of that relationship. Well, I thought I was. I had empirical evidence to support the claim. Patrick started at the firm a year before me, but I worked with him. Honestly, he needed a lot of help. He let me do all the work. We had a big case and he got promoted. And then I worked under him."

"Cade, get that skirt off her," Jesse commanded.

Oh, he shouldn't have made fun of Cade's super-sized man part. Jesse had one of his own. His cock bobbed as he stepped out of his boxers. She didn't protest the loss of her skirt because she was too busy studying Jesse. His cock was thick, with a plum-shaped head. For the first time in her life, she actually wondered what a cock would taste like.

Okay, so now she was actually totally naked and there were two other people in the room with her and they were naked, too, and she wasn't a toddler waiting for a bath. Crap and balls, she was going to have sex. With two men. Really soon.

"Go on, Gemma." Jesse stood, looking down. His hand covered his cock, stroking himself. He got even bigger, the thick stalk of his dick elongating.

"Jesse, I'm ready." She was ready. There was no question about it. Her heart was pounding. Her mouth was dry because she was pretty sure every available ounce of moisture in her body was now pooled in her pussy. Could a person get dehydrated from sexual stimulation?

His lips curled up. "Not yet. Tell me the rest."

Cade tossed her skirt aside and thrust his face between her breasts, nuzzling her as he spread her legs wide.

"How am I supposed to talk when he's doing this to me?" Her legs were around his torso. He was cradled between her thighs, and he started kissing his way down her body.

Jesse didn't move, simply continued staring down at her as his hand stroked up and down his cock. "Consider it a challenge. If you stop talking, he's going to stop playing."

Fuck. First she gets Two-Minute Patrick, with the skinny balls, and now she got the Big-Dicked Brotherhood, and they seemed to have perfected their torture methods. "Fine. Patrick got his promotion because he passed off my work as his own."

Jesse's eyebrows climbed his face. "How did that happen?"

She'd been stupid. She could see that now. "At the time, we'd recently gotten engaged, and it seemed like a sacrifice I was making for us as a couple. He'd been there longer. He was up for the promotion. I wouldn't have gotten it because I hadn't been around long enough. Oh, my god. What is that!"

Stupid question. It was his tongue. Right there on her hoo-haw.

Jesse grinned. "Cunnilingus. Otherwise known as oral sex. Eating pussy. Tasting girl pie. Need I go on? He's going to stop in a minute."

She didn't want him to stop. Her voice came out in a strangled singsong. "So I gave up the work to him. I backed him. And we went on. We did everything a power couple should."

"Sex, Gemma. What was it like beyond rushed?"

"Well, it sure as hell didn't involve this." She nearly screamed as Cade speared her with his tongue. He dove right in, sending his tongue straight up her pussy. "Why is he doing this? I don't think this can taste good."

Cade's head came up. His perfectly sensual mouth was glistening with juice. "You taste fucking incredible. Did that asshole tell you you didn't taste good, baby?"

She shivered, wishing he would go back to the oral sex thing because she was pretty sure she was addicted to it now. "He didn't like it. He said it wasn't sanitary."

"Sex isn't sanitary." Cade crawled back up her body. "It's nasty and filthy and glorious. This is what you taste like."

Before she could protest, he covered her mouth with his. He forced her lips open, his tongue delving deep. He'd lapped at her pussy, fucked her with his tongue, and now he was kissing her like there was no tomorrow, sharing the cream of her own arousal with her.

And she tasted tangy with a hint of sweet, the flavor mingling with Cade's own masculine spice. Dirty. Nasty. Intimate. Perfect.

Cade winked at her as he broke off the kiss. "He was a liar. You taste like sunshine, Gemma."

Sunshine. No one had ever accused her of that. As Cade made his way back down her body, she licked her lips and eagerly opened her legs.

"She's beginning to learn." Jesse smiled down at her like she'd just gotten something the rest of the class had grasped long ago. "Finish the story."

She didn't recognize the whine that came out of her. It was a sex noise. She never made sexy kitten noises. "Jesse, please. I don't have to tell you the rest of the story. According to Cam, it's all on YouTube."

Cade sat back with a long-suffering sigh. "You are going to have to learn some discipline."

The look in Jesse's eyes should have scared the shit out of her, but it didn't. She suddenly knew that no matter what happened, he wouldn't physically hurt her. He might spank her ass, but he wouldn't hurt her. She'd wanted to try this, and now she'd found a man—or two—who might be able to handle her. If it wasn't for this whole "bare her soul" thing, she would be perfectly happy.

But he seemed serious. "Fine. I'll tell you the whole crappy tale."

"Yes, you will. With your ass in the air." Jesse twirled his hand. "Turn around, darlin'. Present that ass to me."

She stopped, her body on full alert. Holy crap balls. He was serious. She looked at Cade, hoping he would save her, but he was on his feet, standing next to Jesse, waiting for her to turn around and "present her ass."

The whole cabin was still, nothing but her own heartbeat sounding through the place. She had a decision to make, and she was good at making decisions. She needed a white board. She was good with white boards. Decision matrix. She should think about this logically. "Pros and Cons of Allowing Her Ass to Get Whipped." She could see the whole thing in her head.

"Gemma, darlin', are you going to rejoin us?" Jesse asked.

"Stop." Cade shot Jesse a look. "I'm interested in whatever the hell it is she's thinking."

She grimaced. "I was making a decision matrix in my head about whether or not I should let you spank me."

They would run. Most men did. They caught a whiff of her special brand of crazy and they hightailed it to the next bland, cosmetically altered bimbo they could find. This was why she wasn't honest. This was why she kept her damn mouth shut.

Cade and Jesse looked at each other. Jesse shook his head. "Yeah, I gotta hear this. Go on. Pros?"

Why hadn't she done it? She'd felt sexy and hot and super close to that orgasm thing other women talked about but seemed to elude her. Now she felt silly. But they were smiling at her, and it didn't seem like they were making fun. It seemed like she amused them. It was a change. "Well, I thought the pros were that I'm curious and you seem like you would like it."

Jesse's grin got bigger. "I will, baby. Go on."

"And I think if I let you spank me, you might be in a better mood and you might let Cade go back to the whole lips and tongue thing."

"Eating your sweet pussy." Cade offered his version of the right words. "And yes, as long as you give him what he wants, he will allow it. And what's more, I suspect he'll give you a little cock."

She wasn't sure that part would work. It never had before, but the tongue thing was definitely worth it.

"And the cons?" Jesse asked.

She bit her bottom lip. "I think I might scream, and that would be unladylike."

Jesse laughed long and hard, but his eyes were so soft as he looked at her that she didn't think he was being mean. He got to his knees. How was she already comfortable with their nudity? He leaned over and kissed her swiftly. "Put that sweet ass in the air. Just a few swats while you tell me the rest of the story."

He wasn't going to let up. And she didn't want to back down. "All right. How can I turn around if you don't move?"

He kissed her again, growling a little. "You are the cutest damn thing I've ever seen. I am crazy about that smart mouth of yours because you are always going to give me a reason to spank that ass. Now say something sweet and then do as I told you to."

She wasn't used to saying anything sweet. What would he think was sweet? "I want this to work."

He kissed her nose this time. "It will, baby. Now go on."

He confused her, and so did Cade. They both watched as she slid off the couch and got to her knees. She was on all fours, with them at her back. Trust. They wanted trust, and this was way more than she'd trusted anyone. They were looking at her bottom. It wasn't her best feature. Maybe they would look at her butt and decide it didn't need any erotic torture.

"Will you look at that?"

She recognized Jesse's low growl only to be followed with Cade's smooth tones.

"How can I look at anything else? But she's not talking."

There was a loud crack, and then she was gasping. He'd done it. He'd spanked her. He'd laid his hand on her ass. Pain blossomed, spreading its wings and turning into heat. Her ass felt like it was on fire, but she didn't mind. And she needed to talk. She had to concentrate. "We were engaged for a long time."

Another smack. There was no other word for it. Jesse smacked her ass and then held his hand there as though allowing the skin to soak up the heat. "Keep going."

"But we didn't live together. He said it wouldn't look good around the firm." God, now that she was saying the words, she felt dumb. They would have lived together after they got married. No one would have questioned it. Two of the partners were married to women who worked at the firm. He hadn't wanted to live with her.

Another smack and a low groan came out of her mouth, but she continued with her story. "We started working on a case about a year ago. Tremon Industries. They were accused of polluting a town's water supply, but the EPA reports didn't back the claims. It was a high-profile case. Patrick had me do most of the work."

"I don't like this Patrick fellow," Cade said as Jesse landed another smack.

"He sounds like an asshole." Jesse gave her three more in rapid succession.

Her eyes watered. Her skin came alive. It was like nothing she'd ever felt before. She was playing with the edge of pain, but it made her feel so awake when she'd been asleep for months and months. She didn't want it to stop. She wanted the spanking part to flow into the sex part and then to the cuddling part. She wouldn't think past that. That would flirt with disaster. She'd had enough of disaster. She groaned out the words as Jesse struck the fleshy part of her ass. "I worked hard. We were making a motion to get the whole case thrown out based on lack of evidence. I worked for six months on those motions and the presentation. I finished up and went to Patrick's place. I was sure I would get the promotion to junior partner because they listened to Patrick."

He slapped her ass again but held his hand there. Then she felt the comfort of another hand on her back, smoothing the skin between her shoulders. Cade. Jesse's hands caressed her backside. Four hands soothing her. Jesse had been right. This was more intimate than merely telling them. She would have given them the story in flat details with no emotion, but she could hear feeling in her voice as she spoke now. "Patrick and Christina talked about me when I found them in bed together. They made fun of me and how easy it was to fool me. And then I did something stupid."

She felt someone, Jesse most likely, lay a kiss at the base of her spine. "What did you do, darlin'?"

"I kind of had a complete mental breakdown, you know, one of those times when everything goes red, and I didn't even think about what I was doing and I ended up being arrested by the NYPD after attempting to take off Patrick's balls with my bare hands. He was a complete chickenshit and locked himself in the bathroom, so I had to fight Christina Big Tits."

Jesse laughed, a rich sound. "You're going to have to make an effort to learn names."

"I don't care about her name," she replied. "I did care about the seventy-two-hour mental health hold they put me in."

"You didn't do anything wrong. They messed with you. You messed back," Cade said.

She'd lost her job, her apartment, her future. Maybe it was simple in Cade's world, but it hadn't been the right play in hers. "That's my sex life. Two lovers, one of whom is now perfectly happy with a man named Harry and their three Welsh corgis, and Patrick, who used me and said I wasn't good at sex. I think a lot of people thought I wasn't good at anything emotional. They called me the Ice Princess."

She'd had to be. Any emotion would have been used ruthlessly against her. Had been. The meltdown had been her first emotional outburst and she'd been fired.

She gasped as a hand slid through her labial lips, splitting them and stroking.

"They were wrong. There's nothing cold about you. You're pure fire. Now show Cade what you can do with your tongue while I get a taste of this pussy and prove to you you're not an Ice Princess." Jesse slid between her legs. "Sit on my face, baby."

It sounded like a terrible thing to do, but Jesse pulled at her hips, forcing her back until her pussy was right over his mouth. Then she knew she couldn't be an Ice Princess even if she wanted to. She was melting. His tongue slid along her pussy before he sucked at her labia. So good. So damn good.

Cade stood in front of her, his huge cock in his hand. "Come on, G. I'm dying here."

Her previous insecurity roared back to life. "I'm not good at this."

He smiled down, his face softer than she could ever remember it being around her. "Yeah, you are, or you will be. You're Gemma Wells. You're the best at everything. At least that's the way I hear it. It's just sucking a cock. Surely a woman who managed to put herself through Harvard Law can handle one little cock in her mouth."

Bastard. He'd made it a challenge, and she couldn't back down from that. And it wasn't exactly little. Far from it. Still, she leaned forward and bumped it with her nose. Awkward.

Yet Cade didn't pull away, only shifted back to give her space.

149

"Lick me. You like what Jesse's doing to you? I want you to taste me, too."

A simple request. She put her tongue out and licked. His cock flesh was warm and soft over the hardness of his erection. It wasn't her first blow job, but it was the first time she'd been sober when she gave one. And the first straight guy she'd given one, too, although she would admit her closeted undergraduate lover had been a connoisseur. He'd actually taught her a few things, but Patrick had thrown her off track by telling her he didn't like the way she did it.

Cade didn't seem to mind. He groaned and tangled his fingers in her hair. "That's right, baby. Eat me up."

It was exactly what Jesse was doing to her pussy. Eating her right up. She tried to focus on the task in front of her. Jesse sucked at her clit, but before she would fall over the precipice, he would back off. One more bit of delicious torture. But she had someone to torture, too. She licked at the head of Cade's cock, drawing it into her mouth and then letting it go only to draw it back in and sink deeper. She did it over and over again, satisfied with the way he moaned and pushed further in each time. She relaxed her jaw, allowing herself to take more and more of that hard cock into her mouth.

She was close. Jesse's tongue worried her clit while he pushed a finger deep inside her. She felt electric. She wanted to pass it on to Cade. She sucked him deep and didn't let go. She hollowed out her cheeks, making pass after pass around the dick in her mouth.

"She's killing me, Jesse. Her mouth's so good, so fucking hot. I'm not going to last."

That was what she wanted. She wanted to taste Cade the way he'd tasted her. She wanted to do the same thing to Jesse. She wanted to get both of her men in front of her and suck them in turn. Jesse curved his finger up and hit some amazing place and she finally understood what it meant to come. It meant every muscle in her body lighting up like a firecracker and pleasure shooting through her veins.

But she didn't let a little thing like her first orgasm stop her. She had a job to do. She felt Cade's cock swell in her mouth, and he unleashed a fierce groan. Warm fluid filled her mouth. She drank it down, loving the taste. It was Cade. He'd told her this wasn't serious, but it felt like a revelation to her. She glanced up and saw a look of deep peace on his face as he petted her hair. She'd put that look on his face. Often in her life she was the one who caused men to seek relaxation, not be the source of it.

She wasn't given a moment to think as Jesse pulled at her hips. "My turn. Ride me, Gemma."

* * * *

He fucking loved that almost panicked look in her sky-blue eyes. It told him she was aware of what was going on around her. He'd made a study of Gemma Wells over the last week and had decided that more than anything she needed to be drawn into the present. Her brain, it seemed, was always working. If she didn't have a problem to fret over, she made one up. She needed to be constantly working through something, focused on something.

He wanted to be the object of all that flustery, fussy, obnoxiously hot feminine energy.

He pulled at her hips, forcing her to move down his body. She scooted down, her pussy coming in contact with the skin of his chest, leaving a trail that crossed his torso. She hadn't been wet in the car, but she didn't have that problem now. She was soaked. She'd come all over his mouth. At the end, her pussy had been so fucking greedy. She'd squirmed, forcing his tongue higher and higher into her.

Cade had been right. Sex with Gemma was messy and nasty and glorious. A relationship with her would likely be the same. Fraught with peril, stress and this amazing heat that sizzled between them.

She was difficult. She was righteously impatient. She had the brattiest mouth he'd ever met. She was so sweet deep down that he ached for her. She was the fucking one.

"Ride me." He wanted her in control this first time. It was obvious her previous sexual history was a bit of a horror story. He wanted her to get what she needed, to feel comfortable enough to explore sex with them. Cade had played his part. He told her how amazing her mouth was, how hot she'd gotten him.

A look of rabid determination crossed her face. Maybe having her on top was a mistake because her impatience was showing. She gripped his dick and started to guide it to her pussy.

"Stop," Cade said, his voice hard. "Condom. He needs a condom."

She nodded and reached out. Damn it. She was going to do it. She took the condom Cade gave her and ripped open the package.

Yep, he'd made a horrible mistake and one he couldn't take back. She started to roll the condom over his dick in a precise, methodical manner that had him gritting his teeth. Slowly, too damn slowly, she began. She pinched the top, leaving space. He would bet she'd mastered that move in an attempt to get an A in sex education class. She'd probably practiced on a banana, but the banana likely hadn't wanted to die because she was taking so long.

Still, the look of triumph on her face when she finished was worth his pain. "I did it."

"Yes." He cupped her hips, adoring the feel of her curves under his hands. If she minded the fact that his hands were callused from daily work, she didn't show it. She was purring like the sexy kitten she was. She was purring for him.

"Go on, G. I want to watch you fuck him." Cade's monster was already hard again. The minute Jesse was done, he'd be right back at her. And he thought he could stay uninvolved? He was looking at Gemma like she was the damn sun in the sky. Ever since that moment when it had become brutally obvious that Gemma had a soft, awkward interior, Cade had been with them. Oh, Jesse had no doubt that later he would run like the scared boy he was on the inside, but tonight would bond them all. Cade could run, but Jesse doubted he would be able to hide for long.

Because she was like a drug, and he was already addicted to the way she shifted between lazy sarcasm and the slightly manic energy that was the real woman inside. Or maybe they were both real. He didn't care. He simply wanted her.

And she wanted him. Or at least she wanted to prove she could fuck him. She'd finished with the condom and now she straddled him, her hand holding him, positioning herself to take him. In typical Gemma fashion, she was moving way too fast. She impaled herself on him, taking him balls deep in one push.

Her eyes widened, her mouth dropping open slightly. "Oh, my god. That kind of hurts."

Damn straight it probably hurt. She hadn't had sex in forever, and he would bet her limp-dicked ex-fiancé had never fucked her hard. She was tight as a drum around him. "Hush, darlin'. Give it a minute."

She was biting that deliciously plump bottom lip. "Are you sure men don't like it fast? We could do this really fast."

Cade got to his knees behind her, between Jesse's spread legs. His arms came around Gemma's chest, his fingers playing with her nipples again. "No, Gemma. Real men like it slow. Real men like to watch you come, and you can't do that when you always go so fast. Slow down, baby. Enjoy it. How does he feel inside you?"

She frowned but made no move to shift off him. "You guys are too talky."

He was going to have to spank her again. After. "Gemma."

She moved her hips. "He's too big."

"I'm exactly the right size, baby." Jesse reached out and toyed with her clit. She'd responded so beautifully before. She was still incredibly wet. All she needed was the tiniest bit of time.

Her head fell back, caught against Cade's shoulder. "That feels nice."

Her hips moved again, more strongly now.

The muscles of her pussy gripped his dick. God, she was the one torturing him. He was going to go slowly mad with her long grinding movements. She said she didn't have a lot of experience, but she felt like a natural. Cade continued to twist and play with her nipples. Her hips moved in a sensuous dance.

He let his hands move to her waist, guiding her up and down on his cock.

She gasped. "It feels good."

He watched her through slitted eyes, all of his concentration on not blowing before she'd come again. "Does my sweet Gemma like to be impaled on a big hard cock?"

Gemma didn't say anything back, but those hips pumped. Up and down. Harder and harder.

"She does like it." Cade's voice was a low growl. "She likes fucking. Her little pussy likes to be filled up with cock. One day her ass is going to be filled with cock. She'll have a dick up her ass and one fucking her pussy. How are you going to like that, G?"

She seemed to like the idea. She picked up the pace. She rode him, thrusting down and pulling up, moving like she couldn't stand that whole two seconds when he wasn't fully deep inside her. She ground down, and her whole body stiffened.

He fucking loved watching her come. She was so beautiful in that moment when she simply let herself go. He got the feeling she would fight him most of the time. She was too smart, thought too much, but he could give her this. He could give her this glorious moment when nothing mattered except the fact that he was making love to her.

She had her moment and then Jesse took his. The muscles of her pussy milked him, drawing him out in blissful jets. His body was electric in that moment, fused to hers and connected to Cade. This was what he'd wanted all along.

His woman. Their woman.

Gemma fell forward, a heap of sweet femininity in his arms. He was still tucked inside her body. He never wanted to leave.

Her eyes opened, sleepy and languid pools of warm blue. "I like to cuddle, Jesse."

Oh, sweet trust. Gemma would never have made that statement three hours before. It was a request and one he would never deny.

"I think I can help you there." He wrapped his arms around her as Cade stroked her back.

He was going to cuddle her for a long time. He was going to cuddle her until she believed this could work.

Chapter Ten

Cade could feel the water. Cold. It was like ice slithering over his skin. Consciousness seemed to come in bursts. Pain here and then blissful darkness. Another flash and the shivering cold. Finally, unwillingly, his eyes came open.

Pain. It filled his world and made all thought difficult. Where was he? Why was he wet?

"I'm stuck, Cade."

His sister. He heard his sister's voice, but it was different. She was always bitching at him. He never did anything right. He was always in her business. He was the little brother. It was his job. But Annie didn't sound mad. She sounded almost sad.

And what was the rushing sound?

"Cade, you have to get out of here." Pleading. He almost never heard that from his close-to-perfect sister. She was everything Cade wasn't. Perfect grades. The apple of their parents' eyes. She never got in trouble. She was going to some fancy college.

Except maybe she wasn't because they were stuck in a car and water was rushing in.

"Cade!"

155

He finally turned and looked at her. She reached out for him. "What happened?"

His sister's hands found him and he turned to her, though it hurt to move. There was a ghostly light coming from the dashboard and he could see her. She had everything ahead of her. A brilliant future. A wonderful life.

The light in her eyes faded, and he was alone.

Cade came awake, sitting straight up in bed. Despite the fact that in the dream he'd been cold, sweat coated his skin. He hated that fucking dream. Deep breaths began to calm him down. It wasn't the first time he'd been in that place. It wouldn't be the last. He could still taste the river water that had coated his throat that night. The water had come from every angle, encompassing him like the vines of a carnivorous plant. They tried to drag him down to the depths.

Where his parents and his sister waited for him. Where Nancy now resided in his dreams. Though she had died in a nursing home, he saw her in the river now. Forever lost with his family.

Gemma stirred beside him. She turned as though realizing her comfy pillow had other things to do, but all she had to do was turn to find another. Jesse sighed in his sleep, and his arm went around Gemma's shoulders.

Cade glanced at the clock on the bedside table. It was after nine. It was the latest he'd slept in forever. He tended to get up at the butt crack of dawn, but then he also tended to wake up numerous times at night in a cold sweat because of the dreams. He almost never slept more than two or three hours at a time before he woke up, but he'd finally fallen asleep at two in the morning the night before. Apparently fucking Gemma numerous times had calmed his brain enough that he'd managed a whole seven hours of uninterrupted sleep.

He stretched and looked down at the sleeping couple. He could get back in bed. He could climb in and roll Gemma over. He could be inside her before she was awake. She would greet the day with his cock thrusting deep, rocking them both to pleasure.

Yeah, he wasn't going to do that because not a damn thing had changed. He didn't want to settle down. He didn't want to get into that bed. It wouldn't be fair to Gemma. He'd told her what he wanted. A little fun. A night of sex. He'd gotten it. He still wasn't good for her.

But maybe she's good for you, you stupid fuck.

He wasn't listening to his potty-mouthed inner voice, either. He simply wasn't built to do the family thing. Shit like that didn't work out. Sure, it might for other people, but he'd made his bed long ago, and he knew he would sleep in it alone.

And he *would* be alone. Jesse wasn't going to hop on his bike this time and follow Cade.

As quietly as he could, he snuck out of the bedroom and nearly screamed at the sight of a small woman standing at the stove. Lynn Wells glanced back, her eyes widening slightly, but then she shook her head as though he were a naughty boy and not a six foot plus naked man. "Cade Sinclair, you put on pants when you walk into the living room."

"Don't bother," another voice piped up. Naomi sat on the couch, her ebony hair shining in the early morning light. "I like the view."

"You hush now," Lynn said. "That weirdly large man part does not belong to you. I'm rather surprised my daughter didn't run when she saw that thing."

This was another dream. Yep. It was another horrifying dream. Damn it. He needed to wake up.

Lynn turned, a spatula in her hands. "Cade, I am serious. That nude thing is fine on the mountain, but I do not need to see it. Pants. Now."

Naomi winked at him as she tossed him the jeans he'd slung over the couch the night before in his haste to get naked so Gemma would wrap her lips around his dick. And now her momma was standing at the stove. He shoved his legs into his jeans and zipped them up. He crossed the space between them, picking up his shirt along the way.

"I am sorry, Mrs. Wells." He felt like a sixteen-year-old caught by his girlfriend's mom. "Obviously I didn't expect anyone to be out here. I'll be on my way. I've got to get to work."

He felt the heavy weight of judgment in those blue eyes. They were so similar to Gemma's eyes that Cade felt himself flush with shame. Would Gemma look at him the same way the next time she saw him? The night before those blue eyes had been warm. Would they go back to arctic because he was the man who'd fucked her and left?

"It's Saturday, Cade."

He shrugged. "Cars still need fixing on Saturdays."

Naomi whistled. "Damn."

He'd stepped into something. Lynn picked up an egg and cracked that sucker in two. "I talked to Roger last night. He said the shop is closed on weekends."

He thought seriously about making a run for the door. He was fast. He could run and keep on running. He could run straight to the shop, hop on his bike, and flee Bliss altogether. He would leave the car to Jesse and Gemma.

His father's car. Damn it. The minute he'd brought that car out here, he'd screwed up. He should have kept it simple. Just him and his bike and whatever transitory experiences he could have. He should have taken shit jobs for long enough to save some money and move on to the next town, but no, Jesse had talked him into fixing up the car and now he had more than two keys and had to deal with judgmental mothers and their horrible cooking techniques. He shook his head. "Give me those eggs. You've already got shell in there."

Lynn passed him the bowl and ceded her place with what he would have sworn was a look of triumph. "I was trying to make French toast. It's Gemma's favorite."

"Does Gemma have cinnamon?" He took stock. There was a loaf of sour dough bread but nothing else.

Lynn laughed. "Cinnamon? No. Gemma doesn't cook. I brought over the bread and eggs and milk and some vanilla."

Naomi shook her head. "Gemma believes cooking is setting her microwave timer. And she screws that up most of the time. I'll get the cinnamon."

Naomi glided gracefully out the door in search of cinnamon.

Cade got rid of the shelly eggs and started over, neatly cracking them with one hand. "Do you have a whisk?"

Lynn opened a drawer and handed it to him. "Who taught you to cook?"

"My foster mother. She was a great cook." She'd been surprised when he'd shown an interest. He'd never told her, but he hadn't cared about cooking at first. He'd wanted to be around her. He'd hated being alone. Alone meant thinking about everything he'd lost. Over time, he'd grown to find cooking soothing.

"Tell me something, Cade. Is your friend still in bed with my daughter?"

Oh, how he wished he hadn't slept in. If he'd followed his pattern, he would be safely at home and Jesse would be the one dealing with the suspicious mom. "Yes."

"Will he wake up and run, too?"

"I wasn't running. I just have things to do." He whisked the eggs. Like figuring out what the hell he was going to do when Jesse moved in with Gemma. It was going to happen. Jesse had been in heaven last night. He'd finally found exactly what he'd always wanted—a woman he could top during play and who challenged him outside of the bedroom. There was zero question that Jesse was falling for Gemma, and Cade wasn't sure where that left him.

"Does Jesse have other things to do?" Lynn asked.

"No, ma'am. Jesse will take care of your daughter." He poured the proper amount of milk into the egg mixture. He noticed the small bottle of vanilla Lynn had brought and picked it up.

"Gemma tends to think she can take care of herself."

He tried to concentrate on his mix but found himself thinking about Gemma. It was pretty much all he did these days. "She's wrong. She needs someone to look out for her. She's smart. Maybe too smart. She doesn't consider the bad things that can happen. She seems to think that if she does everything right, she'll get what she wants. Sometimes that doesn't work out."

"Are you talking about that business with her fiancé?"

"Ex-fiancé. That bastard used her and tossed her aside."

Lynn's eyebrows arched.

"Damn it, I'm not doing that. Gemma and I have a deal. I haven't lied to her. And I can't even sneak out now. You manipulated me into cooking, so don't compare me to him."

Lynn shrugged, a little light in her eyes. "I might have heard you're a good cook. Most good cooks can't stand to watch a bad one screw up food. You can't blame me. She's my only child. And I think you're right about her. She's too smart for her own good sometimes. I never liked that Patrick. He was too slick, but Gemma thought she could handle him because she was smarter."

That was where she'd gone wrong. "Book smarts doesn't always equal street smarts. He ran a con on her. He got her to do all the work, took the promotions and accolades, and planned on dumping her when he couldn't use her anymore."

"I've always wondered about that," Lynn mused.

"Wondered about what?"

"If he actually intended to dump her. I guess I'll never know."

Cade put the bowl down and checked the burner. Lynn had it way too hot. Did Gemma have sugar? He could make a caramel sauce. Gemma liked sweets. He'd noticed it. Her eyes lit up around decadent desserts. And she seemed to be addicted to Trading Post fudge. "It doesn't matter. He was cheating on her. He used her. She needs someone who can watch out for her, keep away the people who would use her. If she'd been with me and Jesse, Nate would never have been able to pull that manipulative crap on her."

Lynn waved that off. "I think working for the sheriff is going to be good for her. I feel better knowing she's at the station house. Nate and his deputy are already watching out for her. They checked her locks the other day and made sure she got home when they realized she was walking. Either Cameron or Nate drops her off and picks her up. Such nice men."

Nice men who should have pointed out the problem to him or Jesse. This was Bliss. The men of Bliss had taught him long ago that they had to stick together or the women of Bliss tended to run all over them. He and Jesse had received the lecture of a lifetime from the entire male population after the Christian Grady incident. And Jamie Glen had damn near broken his nose for not bothering to mention he knew Grady was in town. It didn't matter that giving her a ride was a friendly gesture. If their woman needed something, they should have been told. Jesse's woman. Damn it. "Jesse or I will take her from now on, until we can find a car for her. I thought she had one."

Lynn smiled brightly. "We have one between the three of us, but Gemma insists on leaving it behind, and Naomi has been looking for a job, so she needs it right now. I think she's going to take the doc up on his offer. The clinic is close to the sheriff's office. They can carpool. I'm grateful to the sheriff. He's been incredibly kind to us since the nasty threats started."

Cade stopped. "Threats?"

Lynn nodded. "Oh, yes. Gemma's had some nasty letters in the last few days, but nothing that compares to the heart in the box. She thinks it has something to do with a case she worked on when she first started at her firm."

Cade felt a vein over his right eye start to throb. "Heart in a box? Tell me you're talking about a heart-shaped box of candy that some asshole sent her. Was it expired?"

"Oh, it was expired all right. Doc Burke assured me it was probably from a cadaver."

So Nate and Cam and now Caleb all knew something about Gemma that no one had bothered to tell him. That spot over his right brow ticked away. He couldn't have heard the word cadaver. "Someone sent Gemma an actual heart and no one bothered to tell me or Jesse?"

Lynn sighed and waved it all off. "Well, Gemma didn't want to bother you with it. Nate wanted to haul Jesse in since he was the one who brought the box to her, but Gemma asked him to question you about it in a way that didn't alarm the two of you since what you had was casual. I guess she was right since you were going to leave. Do you have something wrong with your eye?"

Nothing spanking the ass of one naughty blonde wouldn't solve. Jesse. He needed to wake up Jesse so Jesse could start punishing her in a manner that would assure the next heart in a box she received would be immediately brought to her men's attention. Man's attention. Fuck it. He could figure it out later. Right now all that mattered was he'd fucked her the night before and not once had she bothered to mention to him that someone was sending her creepy serial killer love letters. Somewhere in between all the moans and groans and "yes, please, yesses," she could have worked that fact in.

And he and the sheriff were going to have a long talk.

"I think you should get that eye checked out. When Naomi comes back, she'll take a look." Lynn smiled like they were talking about the weather and not the fact that her daughter had received a death threat. There was no other way to interpret it. He was ready to go and wake Jesse up when Naomi walked back in, carrying the small bottle of cinnamon. Almost as soon as the door closed, it slammed opened again and Nate stood in the doorway. He was red in the face, as though he'd sprinted the hundred yards between their cabins.

He held a hand out. "You slept with Gemma?"

Lynn folded her arms across her chest. "I don't think there was much sleeping involved."

"Heart in a box," Nate blurted out. "Gemma got a heart in a box and three threatening letters, and I didn't break the code because you weren't sleeping with her."

"What?" Jesse stood outside the bedroom. At least he'd had the good sense to wrap a sheet around his waist.

"Get dressed, man," Cade said. "This is not a conversation you need to have looking like that."

"What's wrong with your eye?" Jesse asked.

Cade turned back to his cooking. Soothing. He needed soothing. "Nothing. And I'm going to need more eggs."

* * * *

Jesse stared across the table at the sheriff. "And you didn't bother to tell me, why?"

The last ten minutes had been an exercise in patience. He'd woken up, realized Cade was gone, and gotten out of bed to try to call him. He'd wanted to talk Cade into coming back before Gemma woke up, but when he'd walked out into the living room, he'd realized Cade wasn't his problem.

Nate took a long sip of the coffee Naomi had made and sat back. "You weren't sleeping with her at the time."

He wasn't going to buy that excuse. "I had made my intentions plain."

"And Gemma was skittish," Nate replied. "She asked me not to tell you. I honored her wishes because she hadn't made any sort of commitment to the two of you. When your car was spotted last night and was still here this morning, I got here as fast as I could because now you meet the criteria for being her man. Dating does not equal commitment."

Jesse wasn't completely convinced. "By your rules, Ty is responsible for about twenty women."

Nate rolled his eyes. "Ty isn't responsible for himself. Damn it, Jesse, you have to understand my position. She's my employee. She asked me not to talk to you about it."

"But you did talk to me about it." Now that he looked back on the last few days, Jesse could see he'd been carefully interrogated. Nate had asked him about how he'd come to handle the package, giving him some lame-ass story about potential mail fraud. He should have known something was up.

"I did. And I honored Gemma's wishes right up to the point where you became responsible for her."

"He's also been taking her to and from work," Cade called out from the kitchen.

Nate shrugged. "She needed a ride. She's working the day shift all next week. I expect her to be there at nine."

"She'll be there." She would have a sore ass, but she would be there. "Now, what have you figured out about the threat?"

Naomi and Lynn were sitting at the table, praising Cade for his culinary skills. He'd apparently made some fancy French toast and now he was in good with Gemma's mom. *Bastard.* From what he'd heard, Cade had been halfway out the door before Lynn had stopped him. He'd thought the night before had been a turning point, but Cade had still tried to run.

At least he didn't have to tell Gemma. It was a damn good thing because she had a whole lot of explaining to do.

"She thinks it has to do with a case she worked a couple of years back," Nate explained. "It was an intellectual property case. She was an intern, but she came up with the argument that won the case. A man claimed that he invented a new material used in heart valves. The big medical tech firm that marketed it claimed they invented it. Gemma won the case for the medical firm."

"And now this guy is angry." At least he understood the heart imagery. "What are you doing about it?"

Nate nodded. "Rafe called some friends with the New York FBI field office. They're looking into it. This guy's name is Paul Johnson. According to records, he lives in an apartment in Buffalo, but the package was sent from St. Louis. That's easy enough to do."

"And the letters?" He couldn't help but notice that Cade was leaning over, listening in even as he flipped pieces of toast.

Nate sighed. "They came from all over the country. One from Virginia. One from Pennsylvania, and the last from Oklahoma. No rhyme or reason. They all say the same thing. I hate you. I want you dead. Blah blah blah."

"It's good to see you're taking it seriously." Jesse went through a mental checklist of the private investigators he and Cade had hired to track down Christian Grady. They'd gone through three utterly useless PIs before they'd found the Dawson brothers of Dallas, Texas. The twins had not only managed to find evidence to support that Christian was alive, but they'd tracked Hope McLean to Bliss. Ben and Chase were still on his speed dial.

Cade put down his spatula, sending Jesse a look that told him he was thinking the same thing.

Nate shook his head. "We are taking it seriously. Come down to the station later, and I'll walk you through everything I've done. I wasn't being blasé about the threats, but there's something off on the whole thing. Why don't we give Cam a call? He can explain it better."

Lynn sighed as she looked out the door. "No need. He's running this way. Cade, we're going to need to set a few more places."

Nate shrugged. "That's the valley. Get used to it. We're all up in each other's business. I'm surprised it took him so long to figure it out."

Sure enough, Cam was at the door in two seconds. He wore a pair of pajama bottoms, his sneakers, and nothing else. He took a deep breath as he walked in the door. "Gemma got a heart in a box."

Well, at least now Jesse knew the parameters of the bro code around these parts. "Yeah, I got that."

Cam's eyes went to Nate. "Damn it. I shouldn't have slept in. I saw the Camaro last night and I figured it was time to tell them, but I thought I should wait until morning."

"I appreciate that." He would have been way more pissed had all of this come to light before he'd gotten inside Gemma. "Now, you two better give me one good reason why Cade and I don't pick Gemma up and haul her off someplace safe."

"Because I want to keep my balls on my body," Cade muttered.

Naomi laughed. "He has a point. She's not leaving her mother."

Jesse could fix that problem real fast. "Lynn, pack your bags. We're going to leave this afternoon."

Lynn finally looked at him with something other than vague amusement. Her eyes widened and she stood. "You can't order us to leave."

Oh, but he could. "Watch me, ma'am. I care about your daughter. I can and will do whatever I need to do to protect her and her family, and if that means pissing the both of you off, then so be it. We can do this one of two ways. You can pack or we can pick you both up, shove you in the car, and neither one of you will have your things."

Cade had a half smile on his face, as though he wanted to see how that particular plan would work out. "You're forgetting Naomi."

"No, I'm not. Naomi is the reasonable one. I give her logic and she'll go pack." He'd figured that out after five minutes' worth of conversation at the diner one day.

Naomi smiled slowly. "I do believe in running when it's time. I'm not sure it's time yet, Jesse. Why don't you talk to Laura and Rafe? They've been working on this, too."

The whole damn town had known, but no one mentioned it to him. He rather liked his plan.

Lynn stared at him. She was an older, more peaceful version of Gemma. "You would really do it."

Cade stepped in. "He would and I would help him. No matter what I said before, I wouldn't let anyone hurt Gemma. If she needs to disappear, then we can make that happen."

A serene smile came over Lynn's face, and she sat back down, picking up her fork. "Let me know what you decide."

"Just like that?" Cade asked.

"Just like that," she replied. "I like a protective man. And I certainly want one for my daughter. But she will not be as reasonable as Naomi and I. She'll think she can meet this head on."

Nate sat back, seemingly unaffected by the swirl of emotion around him. "Why don't you take a look at the case and then decide.

I'm sorry we didn't bring you in earlier. If it makes a difference, Cam thought we should, but I didn't want to break Gemma's trust before I had to. She's a skittish one. She needs to feel safe."

"And she doesn't feel safe with us?" He wasn't sure he wanted to know.

Naomi answered that one. "She didn't want to scare you away. Look, you don't understand the world she's been in. I do. She was ambitious and working in a cutthroat place. She learned to hide any weaknesses. It doesn't say anything about you. It says something about the people she knew."

He softened a little. How hard had it been on Gemma, always having to be perfect, never allowing herself a moment's weakness? Not even with the man she'd intended to marry.

"Don't," Cade said, pointing the spatula his way. "Don't you go soft on her. She lied to us."

"She didn't lie." Her mother attempted to defend Gemma.

There was no defense. "I asked her every day how her day was and every day I got the same line of bullshit. 'It's great, Jesse. Couldn't be better.'"

Lynn sighed. "So she lied a little."

He looked at Cade. "I'm not going soft. She's going to feel it, but I'm also going to listen to her." He looked at Nate. "We'll be at the station at noon. I want to talk to everyone who has a toe in this thing. For now, I'm going to wake our sleeping princess and let her know how much trouble she's in. Cade?"

He hesitated for the briefest moment before pulling the skillet off the burner. Cam looked down but was blocked by Cade's spatula. "Don't you think about it, Briggs. That's for Gemma."

Cam shook his head. "Why does everyone feed Gemma? She's tiny. Do you know how many calories it takes to keep this body going? No one ever thinks to feed Cam. I'm headed to Holly's. I smelled banana bread."

Nate perked up when banana bread was mentioned. "I'll go with you. Thanks for the coffee. I'll see you both at noon. We'll all be there. Hey, don't you run. I want some of that bread, too!"

Nate and Cam started a foot race to get to Holly's cabin.

Jesse was beginning to understand that this was the way things worked in the valley. The small valley nestled on all four sides by mountains contained a village of cabins, and the neighbors had formed a tight community. If he lived here, he could expect any one of them to pop by during the day.

They were bastards, but damn if he didn't want to be a part of this.

Gemma and Cade needed it, too. They simply didn't see it yet.

Cade followed him back to the bedroom, where he would make his intentions plain.

Chapter Eleven

Gemma came awake to the feel of hands on her body. It was nice because that was pretty much the same way she'd fallen asleep. There was no need to open her eyes. It was way more fun to play a game. Who was touching her breasts? Jesse. His touch was firm, commanding. Cade was the one skimming down her legs, teasing her there and making her shiver.

Heat rushed through her system. She wasn't bad at sex. Patrick had been bad at sex. Johnny had just been gay. He was probably really good when it came to sex with another man. She couldn't blame him for that. But Jesse and Cade were good. Excellent. Amazing. And they'd taught her that she was good, too.

She finally let her eyes drift open. There was Jesse. At one point in time, she would have described her perfect man as clean cut and well-dressed. She would never have said her dream man wore low-slung jeans and had the sexiest scruff.

Of course, she also never would have said that her dream man was two men.

Cade crowded her from behind. She could feel his erection pressed against her back. He hadn't left. She was surprised at how relieved she was. He was still here. Even as she'd fallen asleep the night before, she'd worried that Cade would leave.

She felt her lips curl up, allowed her body to move, her torso toward Jesse and her legs tangling with Cade's. "Good morning."

Jesse kissed the tip of her nose. She loved when he did that. "Good morning, sunshine. Did you sleep well?"

She'd been warm and safe between them. She'd been able to forget everything. She'd forgotten about her job and Patrick and her wedding and the letters. She'd simply been. No thoughts, just a perfect wave of feelings. "I slept like a baby."

He cuddled her, his chest brushing against her nipples while Cade nipped at her ear. A girl could get used to this.

"I think you slept like a baby because you don't have anything to worry about now, do you?" Cade's words rumbled against her skin.

She had a whole lot to worry about, but she didn't want to bring them into her crap. "That's right."

Jesse kissed her, his tongue tangling briefly. "I'm glad to hear that. We have a lot to talk about this morning. Baby, you know you're my woman now, right?"

Jesse's girl. She smiled. Yeah, she could sing that song. She tried not to think about the fact that Cade had stilled behind her. At least he wasn't running. The night before she'd wanted to keep things casual, but that was before they'd had sex. Made love. *Damn.* She'd made love for the first time. Sex for Gemma had been something she thought she should do. It had been a thing on her checklist. She'd decided she should lose her virginity and she'd found Johnny. She'd decided to get married and that included sex.

But making love was a completely different thing. It didn't matter that she'd thought the idea of being some man's woman was Paleolithic. It felt right.

"Yes." She wasn't asking for a ring, but she did want to explore this thing. It was so far from her past experiences that she had to see where it would take her. Besides, she didn't have anything better to do. It might be years before she could go back to New York and practice law. That was her goal, of course. It would be stupid to give up her education, but in the here and now, she could spend time getting to know Jesse and Cade.

And she would definitely spend the time making love with them. She kissed him again.

Jesse pulled back. "Hey, don't you want to talk?"

She shook her head. They talked way too much. "No."

His expression had turned distinctly serious. "I like to have things laid out. I like to have certain rules. I need to know that my woman would come to me if she had a problem."

If she had a problem he could fix, she would definitely go to him. But her problems were best left in Nate's hands. Jesse couldn't do anything. It would only worry him. Or worse, it could make him think twice about being involved with her. And it would give Cade exactly what he needed to run. "I will. Now, please make love to me."

Jesse groaned.

"Come on, man," Cade implored.

"Now who's soft on her?" Jesse asked, looking over her shoulder.

She could practically hear Cade's grin. "I'm not soft, man. We can take it out on her ass later. I'm hard. So fucking hard. I walked back in this room and my cock took over."

"Damn it," Jesse said with a resigned sigh.

She wasn't sure what that particular argument was about, but it didn't matter. Jesse kissed her, this time with purpose. He rolled her on her back and dominated her mouth. She softened underneath him. She needed this. She didn't have to think when Jesse took over. The voice in her head that constantly questioned whether she was good enough, went silent when he tugged on her hair and forced her to focus on him. His tongue invaded, sliding against hers while he covered her skin to skin.

"My turn." Cade's fingers tangled in her hair, and he forced her his way. He brought his lips to hers, immediately sucking her bottom lip between his. "This mouth makes me crazy. I think about your mouth constantly. I think about all the shit you spew out of this mouth and then how damn sweet it can get at times."

His tongue came out, drawing along her bottom lip and then teasing her tongue. It didn't matter that this kiss was messy, that their tongues were playing and Jesse watched. She didn't feel stupid or awkward like she had before. She felt sexy and powerful.

Jesse left the bed, the loss of his weight shifting her closer to

Cade. Cade surrounded her, inhaled her. And he was dressed. She wasn't used to a dressed Cade. She pulled at his shirt. He got up to his knees and tugged it over his head, tossing it aside before falling on her again.

She breathed him in. "You smell good."

A smile creased that perfect face of his. "I was cooking. French toast with a caramel sauce. I would have done it as a caramel brûlée, but you don't have a torch."

She also didn't have food. He must have gone out and bought the ingredients. Not only had he not run, he'd calculatedly come back to her. She pulled him close, wrapping her legs around him. She pushed at the waist of his jeans. Yesterday she'd taken forever to heat up, but this morning she knew what awaited her, and her pussy was ready. She could feel herself getting wet. She needed to feel him thrusting into her, becoming a part of her. She wanted it quick and hard and oh so hot, and then they could sit down and eat Cade's breakfast and, for a moment, she could pretend they were a family like the ones she saw all around her.

Dangerous thoughts. She wouldn't ever speak them. She wouldn't let them know that she was already falling hard, but she could play out the scenarios in her head. And she could have them this morning.

Cade got to his knees, shoving his pants down and freeing that magnificent cock of his. "Jesse?"

His partner was right there. He handed Cade a condom. He had a tube of lubricant in his hand. He must have brought that himself because she sure didn't have any. He looked down at her, his eyes warm. "Do you have any idea how fucking gorgeous you are? You look beautiful lying there, your legs spread and waiting for some cock. Tell me what you want."

"I want you and Cade."

Cade stroked himself, his gorgeous body displayed for her. There was something savage about the fact that his jeans were around his hips. "That's not what he wants, baby. Tell me you want some cock. Tell me you want this big, hard cock in your pussy."

It was a challenge, and she always rose to the challenge. If they wanted her to talk dirty, then she could talk dirty. "I want that big, hard cock in my pussy and in my mouth. I loved the way you tasted. You think you can cook? Well, let me tell you something, Cade Sinclair, I've never tasted anything as good as your cock in my mouth."

His cock actually jumped. His skin flushed. His pupils dilated.

"Suit up before you jump her," Jesse said, shaking his head. He winked down at her. "Overachiever."

Cade sheathed his dick and pounced. He covered her body with his, his mouth nearly slamming on hers. She spread her legs further, giving him access. He wasn't gentle or smooth. His cock surged in, pushing deep inside in one long thrust.

"Fuck, yeah. I needed that." Cade swiveled his hips, forging in until he was as far as he could go. "Damn, Gemma, you can take every inch, baby. Do you know how good that feels?"

She felt drugged. Yeah, she knew how good it felt. It felt like pure intimacy.

"Cade, turn her over. I want to play, too."

Her eyes widened at Jesse's command. Before she could protest, Cade had neatly shifted her over so she was riding him. He kept himself buried deep.

She felt Jesse's hand on her back, pressing her forward. Cade's hips moved, fucking her in little strokes. She rubbed her clit against his pelvis, the sensation beginning to build.

"Hold still for a moment, baby," Cade said, gripping her hips. "Jesse wants to play with your ass."

Ass. Lube. She did the math. "Uhm, I don't think that's a good idea. I don't think my particular ass works that way. But this is nice." She rubbed against him again. "Jesse can wait for his turn."

A loud crack sounded through the air a split second before her ass cheeks caught fire. Jesse didn't sound amused. "You lean over and put that ass in the air or we will begin the inevitable discussion right here and now, Gemma. You want me in a good mood when we start talking. I promise you that. You're fucking two men. How did you think that would work?"

She gritted her teeth against the sensation. Jesse smacked her ass again, a jarring erotic pleasure/pain.

"Do that again, man. She clamped down so hard." Cade pulsed

inside her.

Jesse spanked her one more time, and then she felt the cool lube hit her skin. Jesse parted her ass cheeks and touched her. There. Right there. Where no man had gone before. Where she'd pretty much thought no man would ever want to go.

"Shh, hush now." Cade wrapped his arms around her. "Let him play. If you don't like it then we don't have to. But I am curious as to what you thought would happen."

He had the sweetest grin on his face. She shuddered as she felt Jesse massage the ring of muscles that comprised her asshole. "I thought you would take turns."

"I don't want that." Jesse's voice went deep and low. "I want to share. I like to share. I grew up alone. I know it makes me perverse, but I like sharing. I like knowing I'm not alone in taking care of you. I like knowing Cade is right there, in case I can't provide you with something. This is who I am, Gemma."

She had to bite her lip. He was asking her to accept him for who he was. In a normal person that would include putting up with his control issues or the fact that he liked to sleep with the fan on, but no, Jesse McCann had to add a rider to this particular contract. Anal sex. Accept me, accept my cock up your ass. Yeah, she could see that particular contract.

He pressed in and she groaned. Intimacy, pure and simple. She'd worried it would feel like a rectal exam, but she'd been wrong. Maybe it was the fact that she had a huge pulsing cock in her pussy or the fact that Jesse was talking like no doctor had ever spoken to her.

"You're fucking tight, baby. Cade's cock is stretching you. Think about what it will be like when this is a dick in your ass. You'll be so full. You won't be able to breathe, but we'll do it for you. We'll do anything to make sure you let us fuck you like this. We'll get addicted to it. I'll just look at you and I'll be able to feel how tight this hot asshole can get."

He rimmed her, stretching her as Cade moaned and fucked into her.

She already felt full. So full. So close to the edge of pain, but firmly in a state of pleasure. When she'd read up on erotic games, this wasn't what she'd imagined. This was more.

"That's right. Fuck my fingers, baby." Jesse's fingers scissored inside her. "Fuck, Cade. She's a goddamn natural. She's actually fucking my fingers. She took two fingers beautifully. She's going to be an anal goddess."

Gemma couldn't help it. She laughed. Of all the titles she'd ever aimed for in her life, she might end up being proudest of Anal Goddess. And she was more determined than ever to please these men who had given her so much. She moved her hips, pressing down to take Cade all the way. She pushed back, fucking against Jesse's fingers.

She found a lovely rhythm. Over and over she moved, letting herself go, allowing herself a freedom she'd never had before. She let go, trusting them more than she'd trusted anyone in her life. She rode the sensation and her whole body went up in a grand wave of pleasure. She felt Cade's shout of completion as she fell forward, her body against his.

But they weren't done. Jesse groaned behind her. "Damn it, Gemma. Get back on your knees. I'm dying here."

She was breathless as Cade kissed her and rolled out from under her.

She was happy. She let them manipulate her whatever way they wanted. She was a sweet Barbie, ready for their pleasure. She heard the sound of a condom unwrapping.

"Do you have any idea how hard that is to do with one damn hand? But I'm not about to take the time to go wash up. We can do that later. I have to have you now." His cock thrust in.

She moaned as he filled her up. Jesse slammed into her, fucking her hard. She would have said she couldn't come again, but the feeling built. And she was missing something. Damn it. One time and she already craved it. "Put your fingers back in."

Jesse never let up. "What?"

"I need your fingers. Please play with my ass. I want you to."

He groaned again, his fingers sliding deep. "Damn it, Gemma. You're going to kill me."

But he didn't stop. He fucked her hard, his cock sliding in and out in time with his fingers. She gasped as she felt a hand on her clit. Cade. He stood at the side of the bed, pinching and working her clit as

Jesse fucked her pussy and her ass. Overwhelmed. She couldn't handle another minute and screamed as she came for a second time that morning. Cade held her up so Jesse could finish, groaning as he pressed in as far as he could go.

Jesse gently pulled his fingers out and rested against her back.

A sense of complete peace swelled. This was right where she wanted to be. In that one moment, she didn't need anything beyond this place and these men. And she wanted her promised breakfast.

"What do I have to do to get breakfast in bed?"

Jesse pushed himself off the bed. "Well, first off you can explain to me why I had to hear from Nate that someone's threatening you."

The sweetness of afterglow fled. "What?"

Jesse stared down at her. "I want you to think long and hard about what you're going to say to me. I'm in a damn good mood right now. I'm close to forgiving Nate and Cam. I'm close to deciding that you simply don't understand what it means to be in a relationship and that I should cut you some slack. I'm going to go clean up." He reached for his pants, covering that cock that already seemed like it was waving at her again. "How much slack I give you depends on what you say to me when I walk back out."

She watched him disappear into the bathroom, unsure of whether to be scared of him or righteously angry that he seemed to think she owed him an explanation. He'd known damn well what was going on the minute he walked into the room, and he'd screwed her senseless anyway.

Cade lay down beside her, facedown, his finely muscled backside on full display. "Don't do it, G."

She reached for the sheet because she felt her nudity now. She heard the shower come on. "Don't do what?"

He turned to look at her. "Whatever it is you're going to do. You'll piss him off more. And he won't go away. He'll come after you."

She climbed out of bed, walking to her closet. She'd thought to eat breakfast without the encumbrance of clothes. She'd briefly had a vision of sitting naked on Jesse's lap while Cade fed her, but they'd been trying to trap her. Rat fink bastard men. It wasn't their concern.

She grabbed some underwear, fighting back tears. Damn it. They thought they wanted to know, but they didn't really. As soon as the novelty of the sex wore off, they would realize how much trouble she was. Jesse would want someone "sweet," and Cade would want to be free. By bringing them into this crap, she was probably cutting their relationship time in half. She knew it wouldn't work out, but she'd thought she could keep them for a little while longer.

She shoved her legs into her jeans.

"What are you doing?" Cade rolled over, his head propped on one hand, looking like the most delicious centerfold ever.

"I'm getting dressed."

He sent her a knee-weakening smile. "That's your first mistake. You should walk into the bathroom and hop into the shower with him. Tell him everything. Or you can wait and I'll heat up breakfast and you can tell us both what's going on."

"I thought this was casual." She pulled on a bra. She used to be able to go without one, but since she'd lost her job she'd given up on things like exercise and eating properly, and it seemed to all go to her boobs. Damn it. Even when she did get her old clothes out of storage, she wouldn't fit into them. She grabbed a flannel shirt. She used to wear designer everything. She used to be somebody. Now she just pissed men off.

"It isn't casual for Jesse." He frowned. "And I don't know what it is for me. I need some time to figure it out. I'll be real honest. I never planned on settling down. I still don't know if I like the idea."

Harsh words but honest. She wondered if this was brought on by the revelation that she was in trouble. Maybe he didn't like the idea that she was the kind of person other people hated, sometimes on sight. "Well, I was surprised you were still here this morning. I kind of thought you would leave."

He sighed. "I tried to."

Honesty sucked. It was kind of a kick in the gut. "Well, no one's stopping you. The door is that way."

His face screwed up in the sweetest grimace. "Yeah, your mom and Naomi are out there. The first time I tried to leave, they caught me in all my glory."

She felt every inch of her skin go up in flames. "My mother is out there?"

"Yeah. She wasn't real happy with me, but then I made her breakfast and Jesse threatened to kidnap both of you after he found out about the whole heart thing, so now I think she thinks I'm the reasonable one."

Her fists clenched at her sides. "You came back in here and fucked me while my mom sat in the other room listening in?"

Cade seemed to finally realize he was in trouble. "Baby, your mom knew we fucked. And I don't think she's listening in, although she probably heard because you make a ton of noise. And damn, you're cute when you blush." He sat up. "Gemma, don't look like that. I love the noises you make. They're hot."

Tears threatened. They hadn't even bothered to tell her. No, they'd come in with a plan. She could see that now. What she'd thought had been passion had been a careful dialogue meant to trick her into saying she was Jesse's woman so when she lied about nothing being wrong they could trap her. She was done. She needed to breathe. She thought briefly about climbing out the window, but it was awfully small. She needed to take a long walk and cool off and figure out how to deal with this crap. It felt like every man in her life had betrayed her this morning.

"Don't you walk out of this house." Cade moved fast. He was reaching for his pants as she opened the door.

Sure enough, her mother and Naomi were sitting at the small kitchen table. Her mom looked up and smiled. Naomi gave her a big thumbs-up, but Gemma didn't want to talk or hear about how hot her two rat-fink bastards were. She wanted to get away.

There was a brisk knock on the door. That was what she needed, more company, more people to see what an idiot she'd been.

"Honey, what's wrong?" her mom asked.

Naomi stood up. "Don't be embarrassed. We didn't hear that much, and what we did hear sounded pretty damn good. I know I'm jealous."

Well then they obviously hadn't heard the fact that this morning's lovemaking—fucking—session had been one long power play. She threw open the door, ready to blow right past whoever stood on the other side.

She stopped. Patrick stood there dressed in what he would likely call casual chic. Perfectly pressed slacks. Flawless dress shirt. Thousand dollar shoes. A pair of designer aviator sunglasses covered his eyes, but he slid them off as he looked at her.

"Gemma? Holy crap. What happened to you?" Patrick asked, his voice a shocked gasp.

The bedroom door opened and Cade sort of fell through it. He was trying to get into his jeans, but he tripped as he hit the doorway. "Gemma Wells! You do not walk outside this cabin. I swear to god I will spank your ass, and I don't have Jesse's practice with it so it will probably hurt like hell."

The shower shut off. Any minute Jesse would walk out and she would be surrounded by men she should never have slept with. She took the easiest way out. She grabbed Patrick's hand and hurried down the steps. She immediately saw the rental car in her driveway. A Lexus. Naturally.

"Let's go."

Patrick beeped the car. "Where are we going?"

"Anywhere but here. Now get a move on or you're going to have to deal with two angry men."

Patrick slid into the driver's seat. Gemma buckled her belt. She couldn't miss the smooth smile of satisfaction that crossed Patrick's face. He winked her way. "Looks like you're in trouble again, babe. Lucky for you, I'm here."

She watched in the rearview mirror as Jesse and Cade charged out of the cabin. Jesse only had a towel wrapped around his waist. She was worried, for a moment, that he would start running after them, but both men stared at the car, scowls on their faces.

Gemma took a deep breath as Patrick turned back toward town and wondered if she hadn't made a terrible mistake.

Chapter Twelve

"So, do you want to explain to me what you're doing in this crap hole?" Patrick asked, pushing the plastic menu away.

The better question was why she was sitting with her ex-fiancé when there were two half-naked men at home. Angry men, she mentally corrected. Really angry. Probably done with her men. That was what was waiting for her. She took a long breath, banishing the tears that threatened to fall. She wasn't going to cry around Patrick.

"My mom grew up here." She looked down at the menu and wondered what the special was. Sushi. Thank god. The way Hal prepped, she might actually die from eating it.

Patrick sat back, giving her a high-voltage smile. "I forgot about that. It's easy, you know. You're so intelligent that it's hard to believe you came from such humble roots. God, I drove into town, if you can call it that, and wondered how bad it'd gotten that you'd end up here."

She put the menu down. Like being from the city meant a person had brains. She'd met more incredibly intelligent people here in Bliss than she'd ever known in New York. "It's a nice town. I came here to be with my mom, who is recovering from cancer."

"And the guy climbing out of the bedroom?" Patrick's eyebrow arched.

"Not that it's any of your business, but his name is Cade."

"You're seeing someone?"

Gemma leaned forward, ready to dispense with the bullshit. "Why are you here, Patrick?"

God, it was supposed to be her wedding day. She should be getting ready to walk down the aisle to meet her picture-perfect groom and start her well-planned life.

Her picture-perfect groom leaned toward her. "I made a mistake, Gemma. I knew it the minute you walked out."

Pat might look good in photos, but she could see through him now. "Well, it's six months later, so you couldn't have been too sure."

"Babe, you have to understand. That scene you made was all over the papers. The partners were horrified. I couldn't simply go back to you. I had to think about how it would look. I had to play a long game."

He couldn't go back to her? As if she would have had him. She looked up at the clock. Straight up noon. She'd forced Patrick to drive around for what felt like forever before she settled on hiding out at Stella's. Maybe she should have driven into Creede, but she was half hoping they would come after her. What was she doing?

She should call Jesse. No. She wasn't going to call Jesse. Damn it. This was what happened when she acted on emotion. She should have sat down and made a decision matrix and decided what to do from there. But no, she'd run on pure fear and now she'd probably wrecked everything.

"Earth to Gemma?"

She'd nearly forgotten he was here. And why was he really here? She didn't buy the whole long-game crap. "What?"

"See, there's the Ice Princess. I worried she was gone for a minute. You walked out of that cabin looking all soft and flustered and, god, feminine. I nearly didn't recognize you."

Yeah, she could guess why. "Packed on a couple of pounds, huh?"

His head shook vigorously. "They look good on you. When the hell did you get boobs? I mean it. You look damn fine, Gemma, but I need the real you. I need the killer lawyer."

"Why?"

"Because I can get your job back," he said with a smug grin. "I didn't come here empty handed. Look, that whole meltdown thing is history. The partners realize what they lost. I'm here to talk to you about coming back."

"Are you kidding me?" Her job? She'd never thought they would even consider it.

"Not at all. Look, they had to hire two people to do your work, and they still weren't as efficient as you." He reached across the table, his hand covering hers. "And they aren't the only ones who miss you."

So soft. His hand was actually soft. It shouldn't have shocked her. She'd gone on weekly manicures with the man. She couldn't imagine Jesse or Cade sitting around and letting someone clip their nails. Their hands were rough, callused from hard work. She shivered when she thought about how those hands made her feel. Safe. Wanted.

She pulled away from Patrick. It felt wrong to have him touch her. "What happened to Christina?"

She winced when she realized she'd left off the "Big Tits" part of Christina's moniker because it really was rude.

He had the good sense to look ashamed. "She went back to the West Coast. The partners sent her there. She was far more trouble than she was worth. And I was an idiot. I got cold feet. I should have talked to you about it, but you can be intimidating."

"Yes, talking to me would have been better than sleeping with someone else."

Stella walked up to the table, a notepad in her hand and a smile on her face. "Hey, there, hon." She looked to Patrick, her smile fading. "I was sure you would be with Jesse today. Or Cade. Who's your new friend?"

No judgment there. Damn. She felt like a kid who'd gotten caught with her fingers in the cookie jar. A blush crept up her throat. She didn't owe Stella any explanations. None.

Patrick smiled that photo-ready smile of his. "I'm Patrick Welch, her fiancé. I've come to rescue the princess and take her back home where she belongs."

Gemma groaned, wanting to barf a little. She used to think he was charming. "Ex-fiancé. And Jesse and I have a casual relationship."

Stella's blonde football helmet of a hairstyle shook. "That's not what I heard, hon. And I hear that man is hopping mad. He's been calling all over the county looking for you. Now I understand why. So is it true? Are you heading back to the city?"

Patrick leaned forward. "I thought you were involved with the one named Cade. Who the hell is Jesse?"

She ignored him, speaking to Stella instead. "I don't know. Patrick here claims he can get my job back. I worked hard for that job. It's something to think about."

Stella's eyes turned soft and sympathetic. "You do need to think about it. It can be hard to choose between your personal life and your career. Hell, sometimes it's hard to choose between your personal life and your pride. Remember this. There's no corner so small you can't find your way out of. And don't you let this slick talker sway you. You do what's right for Gemma. Now, what can I get for you?"

Patrick frowned up at Stella. "I suppose I'll try a salad. Can't mess up a salad. Get me the Cobb salad, strawberry vinaigrette on the side."

God, if she was even thinking about going back to New York, she needed to get down to her fighting weight. They might like curves in Colorado, but she would be judged for them in New York. "I'll have the same but nix the strawberry and give me oil and vinegar on the side."

Stella's foot tapped. "She's allergic to strawberries, you know."

Patrick shrugged. "I'm not. I would suggest you don't get the orders mixed up."

Stella turned back to her. "Yes, you need to do a whole lot of thinking, hon. I'll be back."

"The service here is horrible." Patrick waved her off. "Now, let's talk about how soon we can get out of here."

It was too freaking much. And she hadn't eaten a thing all day. She needed to sit down and cry. She only did it once a year, and she'd already done it back when she'd gotten dragged from Patrick's apartment. It was six months before she was scheduled for another crying jag.

"I'm going to the bathroom." She scooted out of the booth and started walking toward the ladies' room.

She was a woman who scheduled her emotions and who had no idea how to deal with them when they didn't get with the plan. What the hell was she doing? Why hadn't she jumped on Patrick's offer? Not to be with him, of course. She was utterly over Patrick Welch. She wasn't even tempted. He had nothing on Jesse and Cade.

She noticed the man they'd been sitting next to at Trio the night before. Blond and hunky, he looked up from his burger and then back at Patrick. He frowned and sighed as though he'd always known she'd be trouble.

Tears blurred her vision as she pushed past the door and into the small bathroom. Just two stalls, but she already felt better. That man was probably calling Jesse right now telling him she was hooking up with a tourist.

Stella was right. She was in a corner, and she didn't know how to get out. She wasn't even sure what she wanted anymore. She should want to go back. She should want her damn career back, but all she could think about was Bliss. And when she honestly thought about doing that job again, all she could see were pictures of those kids. No matter what the EPA said, something was wrong in that town and those children were suffering. Damn Nell. She was happier when those freaking kids had been names and ages on a page. She hadn't thought about their pain. She hadn't thought about what their parents must be going through.

She was the Ice Princess. When the hell had she started to melt?

"Oh, Beth, honey, you were totally right." A pretty brunette walked through the door, followed by another brunette, though this one was visibly pregnant.

"I know a woman on the edge when I see her." The pregnant one smiled shyly. "Hi, I'm Beth. This is Hope. You must be Gemma."

Hope? Ah, the woman who'd had her job before. "How did you know?"

"We might not get off the G much," Hope said, "but we listen to gossip on a daily basis. Are you okay?"

Gossip. Yeah, she understood that. And she also understood that women loved to kick each other when they were down. She dried her eyes. The crying jag would have to wait until the scheduled time. "I'm fine. I just have something in my eyes."

"Do you need to talk about it?" The concern in Hope's brown eyes was almost enough to get Gemma crying again.

But she'd been played too many times before. "There's nothing to talk about. I must be allergic to something."

"Is that the man from the YouTube video?" Beth asked.

Hope nudged her friend, her voice going low. "You can't ask that."

Beth looked at her with guileless eyes. "If I don't ask, then how will I know?"

"It's none of your business." She hadn't meant the words to come out harshly, but they did and Hope flinched.

Beth didn't. Her eyes narrowed slightly, and she leaned against the counter. "It's okay."

"Pardon?"

"You're safe here," Beth said softly. "We gossip and pry, but we do it to help each other. I wasn't born here. I come from a tiny town in Texas, and I grew up surrounded by some of the meanest women you can imagine."

Gemma shook her head. "Oh, I can imagine a lot."

Beth's hand drifted to her belly as though she gained comfort from the contact. "They called me Mouse. When I was little they ignored me. When I got bigger they liked to make fun of me. And they always loved to kick me when I was down. I often had something in my eyes. It's hard. Even now it's hard to think about it."

There they were again. Stupid tears. She didn't have a group of girlfriends she could talk to. She'd never had a group. When she'd been younger, her parents had moved so often, she'd never formed strong friendships. Later, she'd concentrated on school because it was easier.

At the time she thought she was taking the hard road, eschewing the normal rituals, but now she wondered. Homework didn't require emotional finesse. Homework never broke her heart.

"She's right, you know." Hope put a hand on her arm. "You are safe here. We haven't met, but I talk to Cam all the time, and he thinks you're great. Cam and Nate are crazy about you. I did my job, but I admit I wasn't like some gung-ho girl. I felt bad when Cam started bragging about all the things you're doing at the station."

Beth gave her friend a half hug. "You were worried about your crazy ex."

Hope shook her head. "It wasn't that. Well, not altogether. I never took on big projects like she has. And she's good with Mel. I'll admit, he scared me at first."

Gemma snorted at the thought. Mel was so not scary. "He was freaked out that the Trading Post couldn't get fresh beets in. Apparently the ones at Jack's in Del Norte are actually an alien ploy. I found a co-op through Nell and I called in an alien expert to pronounce the beets both organic and alien free. Don't look at me like it was some big thing. The alien expert is from Durango. I got him to come out by promising to buy one of his books. The Bliss County Library is now the proud owner of Alvin Marple's *Aliens and Us: The Truth About Roswell, Area 51 and The Today Show.* Apparently he's sure NBC is run by Reticulan Greys."

Beth grinned. "See, you fit right in. Now you don't have to tell us anything, but we're here if you want to talk."

"Full disclosure," Hope said, holding her hands up. "I happen to know you're sort of getting involved with Jesse and Cade, and you should know that I adore them. They saved my husbands' lives a while back, but that doesn't mean I won't listen to you bitch about them. Even heroes can be jerks."

"They saved someone?" Jesse had mentioned why they'd come to Bliss, but he'd left out that part.

Hope's eyes got misty. "Oh, yes. My ex sent some men to kill Jamie and Noah, but Jesse and Cade intervened. They risked themselves. They're good men. You couldn't do better. Now, how did they totally screw up? Because that look on your face isn't about some job or the town. That's a 'man done me wrong' face."

Beth nodded her friend's way. "Hope would know. Several men have done her wrong. At least one is dead. She can advise you."

Gemma deeply envied their obvious closeness. What if she could find some of that for herself? Was it worth taking the risk? "We've been sort of dating. Nothing serious until last night. I still don't think it's serious with Cade. He told me he only wants sex."

Hope laughed. "Yeah, that's what Caleb told Holly. He's engaged now. Men lie, Gemma. Well, maybe they don't lie, but they aren't very smart. Go on."

Could they actually help her understand what had gone wrong? "I didn't think they needed to know that I've gotten a couple of letters."

"Why would they need to know about your mail?" Beth asked.

Hope sent her a look. "I doubt she's talking about junk mail."

"I consider it junk," she replied. "In my former line of work, we get people who don't like us, and threatening letters are part of the gig."

Beth whistled. "I got the spanking of a lifetime for doing the same thing. I know it seems reasonable to keep them out of it, but it isn't worth the fight. You have to tell them."

Had she made the wrong move? "Nate told them. And then they tricked me into admitting I should have told them without telling me what I should be telling them, and they made me scream with my mom in the next room. Not an angry scream, if you know what I mean."

Hope's lips quirked up. "Yes, I would kill Noah and James if they did that."

Beth shrugged. "Trev would have done me the courtesy of offering me a gag. He has several. But let me ask you something. Have you been casual about them all this time? Really think to yourself. Were you seeing them because you had nothing better to do or were you interested?"

She'd been interested. If she was honest with herself, she'd been interested from the moment she saw them. Her heart had fluttered when she'd walked into the shop. Cade had been male perfection, and Jesse was so bad-boy biker hot she'd hardly been able to stand it. She remembered her first thought had been to wonder if they were taken and how nice it would be to fall into a typical Bliss relationship. "I was serious. I am serious. But it's complicated."

She had a chance to go back to New York and rebuild her career. She couldn't give that up. Could she?

Hope leaned over and gave her a hug. It was…nice. No fakey hugs from Hope Glen-Bennett. Hope pulled her close and squeezed her. "You need to decide what you want. But you were wrong. You should have told them. If they care about you, even a little, then imagine how they feel right now knowing that you didn't tell them. Knowing that Nate and Cam have been doing the job that should be theirs."

She didn't completely understand this. It was some code that was foreign to her. Maybe it would be best to pack up and leave with Patrick right away, but she knew she couldn't. She would have to see them. Talk to them.

Figure out what she wanted.

"Thanks," she whispered, her arms embracing Hope.

Beth smiled when Hope let Gemma go, her arms coming up. "Me, too! Hope and I were talking about the fact that we need another girlfriend. Friendships are like romantic relationships. They come in threesomes. It's Rachel, Callie, and Jen. Then there's Laura, Holly, and Nell. It's just me and Hope because Lucy works so much she can never go out with us. And she hates game night. You can be on our team."

"Don't let it scare you," Hope assured her with a laugh. "It's mostly a way for the women to get together and drink. Although Beth won't be doing that for a while. And neither will Jen Talbot. She's only been pregnant for a few months, but she's already cranky about missing cocktails."

Beth winked as she pulled back. "I'm glad I have someone to go through it with." She reached into her purse and pulled out a card, pressing it to Gemma's hand. "You call me if you need anything. Or if you want to talk. I hope you stay."

"You're okay?" Hope asked.

She was as okay as she could be. "Yes." She was going to have to swallow her pride and talk to Jesse and Cade before she made any real decisions. And she had to deal with Patrick. "I'm good. And thank you for the talk."

She followed them out, kind of wishing she could sit down with them instead of dealing with her ex. She looked at him. His salad was in front of him, but he was attempting to talk on his cell.

"It's going to be fine. Yes. We'll be back in a couple of days. Don't worry about it. You told me to get this done and I'll do it. I just need time. Yes, I know what's at stake." He looked up and his eyes flared. "I'll have to call you later." His expression was right back to that smooth smile he plastered on his face at every client meeting. "Big case."

There was always a big case. She sat down and looked at her salad. She didn't want it. She wanted a burger and fries and maybe a vanilla shake. Hal made perfect vanilla shakes. She picked up the fork in front of her and forced herself to eat a bite of ham and lettuce.

"Gemma," Patrick's voice went soft, his eyes huge in his face. "Gemma, babe, don't panic."

Why would she panic? "What?"

And then she felt it. Her tongue got thick, swelling in her mouth.

"That was my fork."

She took a long breath of air, knowing damn well it might be her last.

Chapter Thirteen

"You're sure?" Jesse asked, his hand on the door to the station house. Despite the fact that Gemma had run, Cade still felt his partner's will. Jesse had spent every minute of the last few hours looking for her. And he'd spent the last few hours with his heart in his throat. "Because I could come with you. I'm sure Nate can reschedule this meeting."

"It's his day off, man. He's doing us a favor. Someone has to figure out how deep the shit she's in goes. And one of us needs to find Gemma." They had called all over the county. They'd checked anywhere they thought she could hide. And come up with nothing.

Jesse pulled the door open and then closed it again. "Why did she run like that? And with him?"

He felt his whole body sag. He probably understood in a way Jesse couldn't. Everything had become real this morning. And it scared the shit out of Gemma. Jesse didn't get it. He was ready for the whole relationship thing, but she wasn't. Not entirely. She might be ready to have sex and date, but they had both pushed her this morning. "She's a private person, I think. She was horrified everyone knew what she'd been doing. Especially her mom."

Jesse sighed, a long, deep sound. "I didn't think about it. I was too mad. And honestly, I don't understand why it's a problem. Her mom obviously knows we're making love. I wanted to stake a claim in a way she couldn't dispute."

Despite the severity of the subject, he felt his lips tug up. "I think Gemma can dispute anything you throw at her. She's not exactly a shrinking violet. You underestimated her. Now, I need to find her so we...so you can talk to her." He'd almost said we. He didn't need that. He was close to the edge. He didn't need to start thinking that way.

Jesse's eyes narrowed. "You were right the first time, Cade. *We* need to talk to her. Go find her."

"And if she's thinking about getting back together with her ex?" That was Cade's greatest fear. Smooth Asshole Lawyer Dude would waltz back in, and Gemma would make a decision matrix based on what they could offer her. Lawyer Dude could offer her fancy cars, jewelry, and apartments in the city. Cade could offer her non-commitment and orgasms. The good news was, Asshole Lawyer didn't give her orgasms. The bad news? Cade had a tiny fucking apartment that smelled like motor oil. He had to hope she really wanted the orgasms.

"She's not getting back with him." Jesse, it seemed, didn't have the same fears. "She wouldn't get back together with that asshole if he offered her the moon. She's got way too much pride. We have to hope we didn't wound that pride too much this morning. When you find her, tell her I intend to hug the fool out of her before I spank her ass. And tell her I missed her. She was only gone for a few hours, but I missed her."

The door closed behind Jesse, and he was left with a hole in the pit of his stomach. Jesse was in love with her. He hadn't said the words, but there was no doubt in Cade's mind. If Gemma returned his love, where did that leave a coward who was terrified of commitment? Where did that leave a man who cared about them both but knew damn well he didn't deserve either of them in his life?

His cell chirped, announcing he had a text.

Gemma's here. Stella's. Who's the jerk?

Ty. Well, at least someone had found her. He typed back, his thumbs forming the words.

Ex. Keep an eye on her. Don't let her leave. On my way.

Cade strode toward the diner, his mind a damn mess. Did he want to confront her?

Gemma Wells was going to drive him completely and utterly mad. What the hell did she not get about the word "casual"? Casual meant things were to be kept on a superficial level, and he got to enjoy the sex without being too serious about any one woman. It meant he kept floating through life. No problems. No connections. No woman who forced her way into his thoughts.

So why couldn't he think of anything but her? Why did he know deep down that no other woman would ever be as beautiful as Gemma Wells was when he slid inside her? He could still see her face as Jesse played with her ass. She'd viewed it as a challenge and she meant to win. She made his cock jump every time she crossed his mind. He was fucking hard all the time. There was that wonderful peace that happened for two minutes after he came inside her, and then the need built again. She was maddening, obnoxious, tart and sweet at the same time.

And she was going to get her ass whipped.

He couldn't sit there in the station house and listen to Nate and Cam talk about all the ways someone wanted to kill her. He would go slowly insane because he knew she was somewhere out there with a man who'd broken her heart once before. Jesse would have to give him the rundown later. What he wanted to do was find Gemma, pull her over his lap, and smack her ass until she never thought about running out on him again.

He'd never spanked a woman in his life. That was Jesse's thing. Cade's thing was fucking them and then quietly sneaking out and leaving the tender care part to his partner.

His rage at her as she'd left this morning was only tempered by the deep sadness he'd felt at the same time. Gemma made him feel. He'd managed to waltz through life caring for only a few people, but that had started to change the minute they came to Bliss. What should have been a short mission of vengeance turned into something far more dangerous. He'd started to put down roots.

Everyone he loved with the exception of Jesse was dead, and it was his fault. He didn't deserve roots.

"Cade!" a deep voice called out.

Cade waved as he crossed the street. James Glen had turned out to be one of those damn roots he couldn't afford. James stood with his partners in the Circle G, Bo O'Malley and Trev McNamara.

He always thought it was surreal to see the former pro football star hanging out around Bliss. He'd seen Trev on TV and in magazines. Now he wore a cowboy hat and dealt with cattle.

"Hey. We heard rumors you were looking for someone." Bo O'Malley was a big cowboy with a sunny smile and a happy disposition. "We can help you out with that. Our girls found your girl."

Trev tipped his Stetson toward the diner. "Beth and Hope are redecorating the ranch house, and they claim they can't plan without Stella's pie."

James frowned. "There's nothing wrong with the ranch house."

Bo's baby blues rolled. "Dude, that place hasn't been updated since 1968. I don't even know how that fridge is still working."

"I like it," James replied.

Trev ignored them. "Beth said they backed you and Jesse up, but you better think twice before you make a girl look bad in front of her momma again. They're already protective of her. Beth said she's in. That means something here. Don't piss those women off, Cade. They stick together."

James went a little white. "I swear I think they write this shit down so no one ever forgets. I think that game night they've been having is actually a plotting session on how to take us all down."

"Oh, you do not want Gemma joining in on that." He couldn't imagine the shit Gemma would come up with. "She's evil. I mean that in the sweetest way."

Bo gave him a slap on the back. "So you better walk the straight and narrow, man, or we're all in trouble."

"I don't see how we made her look bad in front of her momma." He was still confused. Lynn hadn't had a problem with it. "Her momma now knows how well we take care of her."

All three other men groaned.

"Dude, she knows how well you doubly penetrate her daughter.

192

It's not the same. Women are weird about stuff like this. They don't talk the way we do," James explained.

Yeah, he didn't understand that part. "I don't understand that. We're involved. Jesse and I have been dancing around her since she showed up in this town. We're dating. I've cooked for her. I made her lunch two times this week. Everyone knows where we were going with that. It's not a big deal. But we haven't. You know, the both of us. Not yet. She's never done that. It takes time."

What the hell was he doing standing around here gossiping about his damn sex life? It was right on the tip of his stupid tongue to tell them how happy he was that he and Jesse would be her first. And that she was an anal goddess. Most women shrunk away from it. Not his Gemma. She rose to the challenge. She'd fucked the fingers in her ass, begging for more. God, he wanted to fuck her ass. She really was a damn goddess.

"Preparation phase," Trev said with a hazy grin. "I miss that."

Bo laughed. "He's gotten misty eyed over everything since our wife got pregnant." The two men slid each other a long, meaningful look. They shared a family. It was more than mere friendship. It wasn't two buds sharing a six-pack and meaningless women as they partied their way across the US. They were building a life.

That was what Jesse wanted. He wanted a family. He wanted a home with Cade and Gemma. Gemma would be the center of the whole fucking world. She was a woman he could trust with the title. But Cade wasn't a man to be trusted. The thought of a kid depending on him made his stomach turn. And his heart flop a little. A baby who reminded him of his mom or dad. A baby with his name.

His family was gone. His sister dead. His foster mom dead.

But what if he could start over again? What if he could be better this time?

"I swear, you're as hormonal as Beth," James said, laughing.

Trev laughed with him. Cade had never met a man as comfortable in his own skin as Trev McNamara. The way Cade heard it, the man had gotten there the hard way, but the happiness Trev had now made Cade think it had probably been worth it.

"You just wait," Trev said. "Wait until Hope gets pregnant and our kids run around like wild men all over the G. You'll get sentimental, too."

"Yeah," James said, his voice going emotional. "I likely will. I remember how good it was for me and my brother. It was our little kingdom. I've never known freedom the way I did when Noah and I were young. It would have been even better if we'd had more brothers and sisters."

A home. A real home. A home where Gemma yelled at them when they did dumb shit and welcomed them into her arms at the end of the day. A home she would make the nicest in Bliss because Gemma didn't do things halfway. If she loved a man she would be fierce, and she would never fall out of it. She would love that man or men until the day she died if she let herself. And if she had children, she would protect them with everything she had.

Like his mom. And his sister. And his foster mom.

How many amazing women would he be blessed with only to watch them die? How many chances did the universe give?

"Cade?"

Bo's voice startled him out of his thoughts, and he shook his head. "Sorry."

Bo smiled that sunny smile of his. "No problem. I was asking if you could take a look at Beth's car. It's acting up again. Not that she drives it much."

Beth liked to cycle. She'd been known to ride her bike from the G into town, her torso encased in a brilliant yellow reflective shirt. He and Jesse knew cars better than anyone in Bliss. It was their natural place. "Sure."

James flashed a grin. "Come out on Sunday and bring Gemma with you. We'll have a nice dinner. The girls seem to like the hell out of Gemma. We can try to convince the women we're good boys."

Yep, Gemma was getting him in trouble. "I'll let Jesse know. And thanks for the tip. Ty's watching her. I better go and collect her."

The other men nodded and waved him on his way.

He took a deep breath. The idea of sitting around a dinner table with friends and their wives, as he and Jesse showed off their girl, didn't scare him the way it should. And that did scare him. He didn't want to need her the way he did. She was starting to get her claws in, and they went deep.

What the hell was he going to do? Stay or go? Fight or flight?

If it came to a fight, he would like to take out Lawyer Asshole. That might make him feel better.

The door to Stella's opened and Hope Glen-Bennett nearly knocked him over.

He braced himself, his hands out to steady her. "Whoa, there."

Her eyes were wide with panic. "I have to find Caleb. He's not answering his cell phone, but he forgets it from time to time."

Caleb? Caleb was the town doctor. If Hope needed Caleb, someone was in trouble. *Fuck*. Beth was pregnant. Trev and Bo had just talked about their child, their eyes misting at the thought of a future, and now she was in trouble. This was why a man should think twice before getting involved. It could all go wrong in the blink of an eye.

Hope pushed at him, turning toward the clinic. "I have to go. You need to get in there. It's Gemma."

Hope pushed past him and started sprinting.

Nausea swept across him as he looked at the door. Gemma? She hadn't said Gemma. He'd heard her wrong. But what if he hadn't? What if Gemma was in trouble and he was standing out here like a dumb asshole?

Adrenaline took over. He didn't even feel himself move. One minute he was standing outside the diner, and then next he was surrounded by chaos.

There was a crowd in the middle of Stella's, like the world had shifted and there was a gravity well that was situated right in front of the bar seats. At least ten people crowded around in a circle. It was like an arena, and he feared Gemma was the gladiator in the center.

"What's she allergic to?" Ty's voice rose above the crowd. Strong and loud, he was ordering people around in a way he wouldn't do in anything but his professional life. Ty always sounded so strange when he was working. He lost the immature, devil-may-care lilt to his voice and a cool competence took over.

Cade pushed through the crowd, elbowing the audience aside. Gawkers. He pressed forward, needing to see the truth. It wasn't Gemma.

Ty was on his knees on the floor, his head down. Asshole Lawyer stood above him, his shirt still perfectly pressed, as though he would walk into court any moment. He wore a frown, but other than that, he couldn't tell the fucker was affected at all.

His eyes caught on the body on the floor under Ty's hands. A mess of bloated flesh lay there right in the middle of Stella's. Red, swollen skin. Wearing the clothes Gemma had tossed on right before she'd run from him. Cade felt like his feet were planted in concrete.

This isn't happening. Dream. This is a dream. You'll be in the river soon. You always end up there.

He needed to wake up in Gemma's bed and realize this was all a nightmare.

Asshole Lawyer's nasally voice cut through Cade's brain. "Strawberries. She's allergic to strawberries. Even a little could kill her. She used my fork. I didn't see it until she'd already done it. Who uses someone else's fork? Oh my god. Tell me you can save her. She looks horrible."

The fucker winced as he looked down at her, like she was a plague he didn't want to catch. Cade's whole soul wanted to be with her. Bad or good. He would go with her. He wanted to hold her, but he was afraid. She looked incredibly fragile.

Ty's hands were working, lifting her up. "Where's her purse? If her allergy is this bad, she should have an EpiPen. I need it."

"She left her purse behind," Asshole said, averting his eyes. "She was kind of in a hurry."

She'd left her purse behind because she was eager to get away from him.

Ty's hands tightened around her. "Gemma? Gemma, stay with me. Someone get my kit. I might have to trach her."

Tracheotomy. Ty might have to put a hole in her throat and shove a tube in it so she could breathe.

Ty looked up, his eyes lighting with hope when he saw Cade. "Cade? Cade, get down here and help me."

He felt like time sped up again. He'd been locked into place, but this was happening and he couldn't hesitate. Ty seemed to think it was okay, so he could touch her, let her know he was there. She needed him. He dropped to his knees and put his hands on her. No matter what she looked like, she was his Gemma. She was beautiful.

Gemma's eyes, her beautiful blue eyes, had narrowed slits. Her whole face was swollen. She turned toward his, her hand coming out. Red blotches covered her perfect skin. Gemma gripped his hand.

It killed him to see her this way. She always seemed larger than life, like nothing could truly touch her, like she was deep down stronger than the world around her. But he was reminded that she was human. She was a woman who needed someone to coddle and protect her.

"Baby, baby, stay with me." He'd sent her off with this fucker who hadn't taken care of her. He'd done this. He was going to lose her, too. He would hold her hand and she would slip away. She would join the others. Tears blurred his eyes. *Stay with me. Stay with me.*

"What the hell?" Stella's voice rang out. Her boots sounded across the floor as she ran. "Oh, god. Is that Gemma? Hal!"

"Someone needs to get my fucking kit." Ty held his keys out. "This is serious. If I can't get her breathing in two minutes, she's going to die. She needs some fucking epinephrine."

Asshole Lawyer simply stood there, looking around like he was waiting for a servant to show. Beth McNamara plucked the keys out of his hand and took off running.

Stella yelled back to the kitchen, but everything was an incomprehensible mess to his ears. Blood pounded through his system. His vision shifted down to just one thing. Gemma's eyes. They were small when they were always so big to him. Those eyes that watched him with mocking affection seemed to shrink, her flesh crowding them out. As he watched, they closed, the poison in her system shutting everything down.

He would go down with her. He would walk out and be done. The Rio Grande was minutes away. The river had always wanted him. It was where he belonged. When Gemma was gone, he would find her again there. It would be easy. The easiest thing he'd ever done.

Hal ran out, a small object in his hand. His knees hit the floor. "I have an EpiPen! We got it when Gemma started working here. We wanted to make sure she was safe."

Ty took the small syringe and had it in her leg before Cade could take another breath.

The door to the diner opened, and Caleb Burke ran in, Hope

following behind him. "What the hell's going on? Where's my patient?"

Gemma breathed, her chest moving in a shallow but sweet symphony of life.

Ty put his head down, his breath sawing in and out like he'd run a marathon. He moved away, his back against a booth. "She's in anaphylactic shock. Apparently, she's allergic to strawberries. Hyperallergic by the looks of it. She's had a dose of epinephrine. Her pulse was thready but steady now. She's all yours, Doc."

Caleb Burke started looking at his patient. Gemma's head fell back. Cade caught her, pulling her onto his lap as the doc looked her over. Cade took a long breath, forcing himself not to cry. Never once, even when death had seemed imminent, had she let go of his hand. Cade held on to hers gently, though he wanted to squeeze tight. Anything to try to keep her here with him.

"Wow. She still looks horrible. When will that go away?" Asshole stared down at her.

And Cade lost it.

Chapter Fourteen

Jesse looked down at the letters Cam laid out in front of him. They were protected by plastic evidence bags, but it was easy to read the typewritten letters—and way too easy to see the intent behind them.

"Has she gotten letters like this before?" He had to check himself. What he wanted to do was beat the shit out of someone, anyone. It would make him feel better. Maybe not anyone. Maybe Patrick Welch, who had run off with his woman. Yeah, that would make him feel better. Patrick came from that world. From the world that had brought this crazy man into her life.

Nate sat down at the table in the interrogation room. He stared down at the letters, his blue eyes shrewd. Despite the fact that he was now the sheriff to a tiny county, Jesse heard he'd spent years undercover with the DEA. When Nate Wright's eyes got that steely gaze in them, Jesse could damn well believe that was true.

"Apparently it's a job hazard in her former occupation." Nate nodded toward the door as Cam walked in with Rafe Kincaid and Laura Niles.

Rafe looked down at Jesse, a rueful smile on his face. "I wanted to tell you. I think the whole getting-in-her-pants thing is overrated.

We should have told you days ago. If you care about a woman, you care about her whether or not you're sleeping with her."

Laura's lips turned up in a smile as she sat down beside Jesse. "I heard Rafe was outvoted. The rumor is the men all got together a couple of months back and banged out an agreement on how to act. I would love to get my hands on a copy of that agreement."

Cam huffed out a laugh. "Rumors. Do you honestly believe if the men of Bliss got together for a guys' weekend, we would do anything other than drink beer and fish? Well, except for Trev. He drank a lot of coffee and sat around with that perpetual look of amusement he has on his face. I swear that man's blood count must be half caffeine."

Rafe's shoulders moved up and down in a negligent shrug. "Besides, if we did have some sort of agreement, we would never be so foolish as to write it down. We would memorize it."

Nate reached for his coffee mug and grimaced. "Cam made the coffee this morning. I was kind of hoping Gemma would come in with you. She's the only one who can work that thing. Is she with Cade? Tell me you weren't too hard on her."

He didn't think he'd been hard at all. He'd cajoled her into admitting she belonged to him and then he'd given her a crazy strong orgasm and explained how she could get out of her punishment. He'd been a total softie. He should have immediately put her over his knee, but he'd wanted things to go easy with her. "She left. Her ex showed up and she took off."

"She'll come back. She's not a girl to up and run without a good reason. I would also be surprised if she got involved with her ex again. I heard what he did to her. She would be far more interested in her old career than in reclaiming him," Laura said.

That career shit scared the crap out of him. He agreed with Laura. Gemma had seen an opportunity to make a point and she'd taken it. But why was that asshole here in the first place? Jesse had to hope Patrick was trying to win her back. That wouldn't happen. If he'd come to talk to her about going back to work? That was another story entirely.

Nate groaned and scrubbed a hand through his hair. "Yeah, well, Bliss rules or not, I shouldn't talk to you about this at all without Gemma here. I'm going to because I think Gemma overestimates her ability to take care of herself. Now, Rafe and Laura and Cam have been working up some ideas about this guy."

Jesse didn't care about ideas. He wanted facts. "Do you have a name?"

"Paul Johnson was the man who threatened Gemma after he lost his lawsuit over the heart valve material. Before you hop on your Harley for some of that vigilante justice you and Cade seem to like so much, you should know we've already tried to locate him. The last report we could find had him living in Kansas City two years back," Nate explained.

Rafe opened the folder he'd walked in with. "According to his ex-wife, he took off sometime after the case was over. She said he'd decided to leave the rat race behind and get in touch with nature."

Jesse stared at the hate-filled letters again. "Looks like he's ditched that plan."

Laura put a sympathetic hand on his arm. "I don't know about that. Do you know what Rafe, Cam, and I used to do?"

Most everyone in town had a story. Laura, Rafe, and Cam's was a violent one. "You profiled for the FBI."

They had worked for the BAU. They knew their stuff, and Jesse was willing to listen.

"I've profiled criminals for years, and often with far less than I have here." She gestured toward the letters. "What I find interesting about these letters is the complete lack of passion behind them."

He couldn't agree. "I don't know about that. Putting a fucking heart in a box seems extreme."

Rafe picked up one of the letters. "I know it seems that way, but I've studied these letters. They're precise. He says the same things over and over. 'You'll pay the price for what you did. Lawyers are bad. Gemma is the worst of them all.' But the wording is almost polite."

"Men who are truly angry don't mince words." Cam pressed a couple of buttons on the laptop in front of him and turned it around so Jesse could see. "These are some of the transcripts from the depositions prior to the trial. They're expletive filled. He was truly angry. He had to be restrained at one point."

Jesse looked them over and had to agree. But talking and writing were two different things.

Rafe picked up where Cam left off. "We also have copies of the letters he wrote to Giles and Knoxbury, the law firm Gemma worked for. Again, he's very vitriolic. There's no politeness in these letters. They're full of bile and rage and centered squarely on what he lost. Most of his rage is directed at the firm, not Gemma herself, though he calls her out."

"If you'll note," Cam began, "he doesn't actually threaten her in a physical sense. He calls her morality into question."

Jesse skimmed through the notes. Sure enough, they were filled with a woe-is-me attitude that didn't completely jibe with the latest batch of letters.

"And there are some phrasing inconsistencies that bother me." Laura placed the second of the letters in front of him. "See here where he says this is "all your fault" but over here in the next one, the phrasing is "this is your entire fault." I know it sounds odd, but the second one is the way Word corrects a document. If he's that angry, why is he letting his processing program fix his grammar? And then in the third we're right back to "all your.""

He wasn't sure what changing the wording had to do with anything, but they were the experts. And he did trust them. They were friends. They wouldn't steer him wrong. "So what does all this add up to?"

Rafe and Laura exchanged looks, a whole conversation occurring in silence.

Rafe finally nodded as though agreeing with her. "I think it's a game. And I don't think Paul Johnson is at the heart of it. If you asked me, I would say if he's involved, he's nothing more than a pawn."

He didn't understand. "Why would someone do this?"

Laura shrugged, an elegant movement of her shoulders. "To scare her for some reason? To set up a potential lawsuit? I've been going through her cases. She had her fingers in some big legal actions when she left the firm. Tremon Industries, a lawsuit against a biochemical plant, two intellectual property cases. She wasn't lead on any of them, but she was crucial."

"I talked to some FBI friends in New York," Cam said. "There's a rumor that Giles and Knoxbury is being investigated. I've gone over this with Gemma, but she can't think of anything she knows that could hurt the partners. And according to those same friends, this kind of harassment is typical for a lawyer who works the kind of cases Gemma does. So we could be totally wrong and this guy is just expressing his anger."

He calmed a bit. "The heart shit still scares me."

Rafe's fingers drummed along the table. "It smacks of showmanship. It wasn't human. We suspect he bought it from a supply store."

He widened his eyes because that didn't sound right.

"Cadaver hearts are used for research purposes and for training in surgical residents, though many hospitals are moving to more technological methods," Rafe explained. "If there had been blood on the heart, I would be worried. I actually think it was a fairly sterile warning."

It still seemed awful to him, and he didn't want them to brush this off. "I would be happier if I knew where this guy was."

"Cam's looking into it," Nate said.

"If he pokes his head up, I'll find him. I already have access to all of the e-mail accounts he's used in the past, and I found one his ex-wife didn't know about." Cam smiled. "Hey, I wasn't always a straight and narrow fed. I've done some hacking in my time."

"I want to be kept in the loop," Jesse said. "Even if Gemma won't talk to me."

It was a real possibility. She'd been surprisingly angry this morning. He wasn't sure exactly how to handle her. He only knew he had to figure it out. There was no other option. He couldn't let her go.

She was it. He'd suspected it that first time she'd turned her tart mouth on him, known it last night when his heart had nearly broken at her deep vulnerability. He'd cared for women before, but he'd never longed for one. Gemma was inside him now, and he didn't want to get rid of her.

The door to the room opened, and Holly rushed in. Holly was manning the phones on Gemma's day off. The beautiful redhead was flustered. "Nate, we have a big problem at Stella's."

Her eyes trailed to Jesse, her mouth firming, and he knew.

"Gemma?" He stood, his heart threatening to thud out of his

chest. "What's happened?"

Nate and Cam were already on their feet, heading out the door.

"Just tell us all," Nate said as they moved toward the front of the station house. Nate picked up his Stetson and settled it on his head.

"Gemma went into anaphylactic shock," Holly explained. "Caleb is prepping her to go to the hospital, but a fight broke out. Caleb is pissed. If you don't get down there right now, I worry he's going to do something stupid."

Laura sat down at the desk. "Go, Holly. Go help Caleb."

Jesse didn't wait to hear another word. He'd heard Gemma and shock and hospital, and someone was stopping her from getting the help she needed. They shouldn't worry about Caleb doing something stupid. They should worry about him.

He ran. He heard Nate curse behind him and then both Nate and Cam were catching up to him.

"You try to remember that Gemma needs you," Nate said, his voice even though he was sprinting. "You help Caleb get her out of there, and you leave everything else to me and Cam."

All that mattered was getting to Gemma. What the hell was anaphylactic shock? What had happened? She'd been fine this morning. More than fine. She'd been perfect. What else was she hiding from him?

Nate made it to the door first, shoving his way through. Jesse's heart nearly stopped at the scene in front of him.

It was complete chaos. A man was thrown bodily right across the diner, and then there was a loud roar as another man launched himself.

"Stop him!" Fuck. Gemma's ex-fiancé. His nasally scream seemed to echo in Jesse's head.

He looked at the other man and nearly joined in the fight. Cade. Cade jumped on Patrick Welch, his face red with fury. Cade's fist flew back and he started pummeling the smaller man.

Caleb Burke hadn't gotten his trusty tranquilizers out yet. He was leaning over a prone body, protecting it with his own. His face came up. A truly wrathful expression played across his features. "Get that shit shut down now, Nate. I swear to god, if she comes to harm because of that, I will kill them both."

Jesse didn't give a shit about the fight. His eyes were on Gemma. Small. Vulnerable. Hurt. What the hell was Cade thinking?

"Holly, hold the door open." Caleb bent over to lift Gemma up, but Jesse moved into place.

"Doc, please." He couldn't let anyone else take her. She was his.

Caleb nodded and allowed Jesse to bend over and lift her up. "I think she's breathing well enough that we can move her now."

Nate and Cam were breaking up the fight, throwing their bodies in between the combatants and forcing them apart.

"Jesse?" Gemma's voice sounded harsh, forced out of her throat.

She looked like hell and yet he'd never seen anything so damn beautiful as those eyes opening up. "Baby, you're going to be okay."

He had to believe it. She couldn't not be okay.

"Gemma, you've had an allergic reaction," Caleb said. "We're taking you to the hospital. Ty has his truck ready. It's got sirens on it. We'll be there in no time at all." He looked at Jesse. "When we get her to the truck, you can ride along, but I have to be in the back with her. I don't know if she's had enough epinephrine. Do you understand? I need to monitor her and make sure she doesn't have any cardiac problems."

As it seemed the doc had had enough people getting in his way today, Jesse nodded. "All that matters is her safety."

"Cade?" She tried to look around. Her face was still swollen, red blotches all across her skin.

Jesse looked over at Cade, who had blood running from his lip. He seemed to be coming down from his volcanic rage.

"I need a doctor!" Patrick was saying. "Take that man to jail. He's insane. He attacked me for no reason."

"Cade?" Gemma was insistent.

"He's fine, baby. He's fine." Jesse looked back at his best friend. Cade wasn't fine, but there was not a thing he could do about it now. Cade was supposed to find Gemma, keep her safe. Not place her in more danger. He should have been carrying her out to Ty's truck, not starting a fight.

Nate looked over at Caleb. "You want to take a look at these two, Doc?"

Caleb flipped Nate the finger as he charged out the door.

Nate sighed. "Jesse, you tell Ty to come to the station house when he gets a chance. I think they're fine, but someone should look them both over."

Cade's eyes met Jesse's before he walked out the door. Pure and utter misery was plain on his bloody face. He didn't fight as Cam cuffed his hands behind his back and started reading him his rights.

Jesse turned because he couldn't help Cade now. He had to think of Gemma.

His choice had been made the night before. She was his woman. He would share her with his friend, but he would never put her second.

He handed her over to Caleb and hopped in the truck as Cam hauled Cade out and started walking toward the sheriff's office.

"Jesse?"

"I'm here, baby. I wouldn't be anywhere else."

As Ty took off, lights flashing, Jesse worried for the first time that this wouldn't work out. And he had no idea how to fix it.

* * * *

Cade let the cell door shut behind him, utter misery washing over him. What the hell had happened? One minute he'd been terrified about losing Gemma and the next Cam Briggs had been pulling him off Asshole Lawyer and shoving him into handcuffs.

Laura Niles sighed and walked up to the cell with a wet cloth in her hands. "Come here. Let me take a look at that. Rafe, will you get me some ice? Please tell me Cam didn't do this to you."

He let her wipe the blood off, though he wasn't sure he deserved anyone's tender care. "No. Asshole got in a lucky punch. Are they going to book me?"

The station doors opened again and Nate hauled in Patrick Welch. The lawyer looked terrible, his formerly pristine clothes a bloody mess. His hands were cuffed behind his back, and he was talking as fast as he could.

"Do you have any idea who I am? You fucking small-town idiots. Do you know what I'm going to do to this town? When I'm done there won't be a goddamn town. I will bury this place. I am going to slap you with a lawsuit the likes of which you've never seen. Have you ever even heard the term false arrest?"

Nate opened the cell door, giving the lawyer a wide-eyed look. "Now, they might have covered something about that in small-town idiot school. But I never did too well in school, son. That's how I ended up a sheriff. Ain't much learning needed here."

Nate had gone to an Ivy league school. He came from old money. Oh, it might have dried up, but his upbringing had been privileged. Nate was fucking with the lawyer. Why? Cade had started the fight.

"Sheriff, you should let him go." This was his fault. Patrick had been a jerk, worrying about how Gemma looked instead of whether or not she was alive. But Cade had been the one to throw the first punch.

"Shut your mouth, Cade," Nate warned.

"You should listen to him. He's the only one making sense." Patrick sat down on the small cot and wiped at his mouth, a sullen expression on his face. "It won't help him." He turned his gaze Cade's way. "I intend to sue you for everything you're worth, you piece of shit."

Cade stared out at the office. Cam was already writing up a report. And he had no idea how Gemma was doing because he'd been an asshole who couldn't control his temper. And as for Patrick taking everything he was worth, well, he wasn't worth much. He was worth way less than he'd been about an hour ago.

"Do you know how she is?" Cade asked quietly.

Laura stepped up. "I talked to Ty on the radio. Gemma's stats are good. Her heart rate is steady and she's breathing fine. Jesse's with her. Caleb is taking her to the hospital, but he told Ty that all she needs is some rest and steroids. He's going to keep a close watch on her. Ty's coming back here to take a look at you."

He didn't want any damn medical attention. He wanted to sit and rot in the cell and think about what the hell he was doing. He should never have gotten involved. He knew better. He knew what happened when he loved someone. He fucked up and they got hurt.

Gemma almost died. She would never have been in Stella's without her purse if it hadn't been for him.

The station doors opened, and Stef Talbot strode in along with his wife, Jennifer. The rumor was Jennifer Talbot was pregnant, but Cade couldn't tell. The artist looked slender and lovely, following her husband, who seemed deeply agitated. The man people around town called the King of Bliss, wore jeans and a Western shirt, but that didn't make him an ordinary cowpoke. Stef had power, and he didn't mind wielding it.

"Does someone want to tell me why my stepmother is crying and trying to tally up the damage to her place of business?"

Cade opened his mouth to talk, and Nate sent him a nasty look.

"I told you not to talk." Those words were an obvious warning from the sheriff's mouth.

Stef stalked his way. "Did you do this, Sinclair?"

Patrick piped up. "He sure as hell did, and I'm going to sue him."

Jen took a long look at the man in the other cell. "Babe, why don't we get the whole story before you try to take Cade apart? He's a damn fine mechanic. We need those around here. The snowmobile is busted."

"I don't give a damn about the snowmobile," Stef said, never taking those angry eyes off Cade.

He was kind of happy for the bars between them.

Jen came up and whispered something in her husband's ear that had him flushing.

Stef turned back to her. "Are you serious?"

She shrugged and gave him a half smile. "Rach says it works really well. I thought we could get some happy fun time in before I get too big."

Stef's hand strayed briefly to her belly before he turned back to Cade. "Fine. Talk. You have two minutes before I throw you out of my town."

"Do it. I was going to leave anyway." The look in Jesse's eyes had made that decision for him. Disappointment. Anger. Regret. All directed his way. At least one of them was there for Gemma.

Holly walked up, brushing the hair out of her face and passing Cade an ice pack. "Put that on your lip. It's swelling. Stef, according to Hal, who I just talked to, Cade was upset Gemma nearly died from anaphylaxis because this guy over here was eating strawberries in front of her. She's got a terrible allergy to strawberries. I called her mom, and she's on her way to the hospital."

Stef turned to Patrick. "Did you know she's allergic?"

Patrick didn't bother to look ashamed. "I'm not taking the blame for this. I like strawberries. They're a super food. I'm not going to eschew them because Gemma has a problem. It was her fault. She should have been more careful. Come to think of it, it was that dumb bimbo café owner's fault because she only brought one fork. I'll have to see about suing her, too."

Stef Talbot nearly grew fangs and claws. His eyes narrowed. "Nathan."

"Already on it. I have witnesses coming in to give their reports," Nate explained.

"Thank god, you're getting one thing right," Patrick complained. "I'll want copies of everything."

Nate stood in front of the cell, his hands on his hips. "I'll make sure you have them. According to all the witnesses I talked to, you started the fight, Mr. Welch. Now, why would you do that? Is it because you found out your ex-fiancée is involved with Mr. Sinclair?"

Jen grinned, her arm going around Stef's waist. "See, babe, told you Nate would handle it. You're not the only manipulative son of a bitch in the world."

Stef sighed, a satisfied sound. "Excellent. Nathan, let me know if you need anything. Talbot resources are completely available to you. And you. Think twice before you go after that bimbo café owner. She's Stella Talbot, wife of Sebastian Talbot and my mother in every sense of the word. You might think you're the big-time fucking lawyer out here in the sticks, but I promise you that stick will hurt when I shove it up your ass, and no amount of New York City lawyers will be able to get it out."

Jen gave Cade a wink. "Come out to the estate when you get a chance and take a look at the snowmobile. Bye, Cade. Tell Gemma we're all thinking of her and to expect the casseroles to start showing up at her place tomorrow. I promise no strawberries. Unfortunately, I can't promise the same of tofu."

They walked out the door, leaving Cade more confused than ever.

Patrick went a nice shade of green. "As in Talbot Industries?"

Nate leaned against Gemma's desk. "One and the same. And in case you want to go after the doc for not seeing to that tiny bruise

Sinclair gave you, you should know his birth name is Caleb Sommerville. Yes, those Sommervilles."

"The senator from Illinois?" Patrick practically gulped the question.

"Is his brother," Nate explained. "Now, do you still want to sue this town for everything it's worth?"

It seemed Bliss was worth way more than Patrick Welch thought it was and he backed off. "I think we can all agree this was a terrible misunderstanding."

Nate nodded. "I thought you might see it that way. Cam, you can stop. I think we're all going to agree to walk away from this."

Cam stopped typing. "Thank god. I hate paperwork. I'm going to call and see how Gemma is and when we can see her."

Ten minutes later he was free, but no one could let him out of the prison he'd put himself in.

Cade walked to the Trading Post, bought what he needed, and got his bike and a few things from the apartment he shared with Jesse. He went to Gemma's. The cabin was silent where hours before it had been full of life.

He worked until long past twilight. His cell phone was depressingly silent. He sat down on Gemma's couch and waited.

Chapter Fifteen

"You okay back there?" her mom asked, her neck craning around.

"I'm fine." Gemma looked out the back window of her mom's sedan. Utter blackness stared back at her. She'd never seen darkness the way it was here in Bliss. Velvet night dotted with diamonds. The night was soft here.

The road thudded beneath her, and she wondered where Cade was.

Jesse's arm settled around her, pulling her close. His scruffy cheek rubbed against the top of her head. She felt him kiss her hair.

When she'd woken up, Jesse had been right there. He hadn't left her side the whole time. He'd completely and blatantly lied to everyone, telling the staff that he was her husband so he couldn't be cut out of the loop. Caleb and Ty had gone along with it.

She was surprised at how much comfort he'd given her. She'd been alone for so long that she'd forgotten what it meant to lean on someone. After her father had died, she'd pulled away from her mom. She'd told herself she did it because her mom didn't need a kid clinging to her while she worked through her grief, but now she could see she'd done it because it felt safer to be alone.

Nearly dying had made her overly contemplative. And pointed out some harsh truths in her life.

She tried not to think about what she'd figured out. There was time enough to deal with that later. Though she would have to tell Jesse what she suspected because, like it or not, Neanderthal thinking aside, he was her man. He'd proven it today.

"She's all right now," Naomi said, her hands steady on the wheel. "The hospital wouldn't have released her if she wasn't okay. She'll be tired for a couple of days though. And she'll stay away from strawberries from now on."

Freaking strawberries. "It's not like I said I wanted a taste."

Her mother's head shook. "And you without your medication. She's had that medication on her person every day since she was six years old."

Jesse's arms tightened. "That wasn't smart."

She managed to shrug. "I haven't been smart for a while." The car got quiet for a moment. "Where do you think he is?"

Jesse's voice was low, meant for her ears only. "I don't know, baby."

He'd been frustratingly silent on the subject of Cade. She remembered that he'd been there. Cade had held her hand while she'd lain on the diner floor. He'd looked so scared, and not of her the way that massive ass Patrick had been. He'd been scared he would lose her. She'd felt his will, his panic, his fear. Then he'd been gone and Jesse had taken his place and she didn't know where Cade was.

"Did you call him?"

"No." The word came out gruff and unwavering.

Well, that told her something. She sat up, shrugging off his arm. "What happened?"

"You should tell her." Naomi made the turn that would take them to the valley. "You would be pissed if she didn't tell you."

One thing was for certain. "Someone better tell me something now."

Jesse tugged her back into his arms. "Doc told you to rest."

Stubborn man. "I can rest while you tell me where Cade is."

Panic was starting to flare. Would he leave? Had she been wrong about how he'd felt when he'd held her hand? Could he have been so horrified by the whole body bloating thing that he actually fled the county? She remembered how Patrick had reacted. *Fucker*. But Cade had gotten to his knees and held her like he wouldn't let go.

Jesse sighed. "Gemma, the last I saw of him, he was being hauled off to jail."

She leaned forward, her hand on her mom's seat. "Naomi, you have to get me to the station house. Damn it. How could you leave him there? What's his bail? How late is it? I think the boys from Creede take the night shift. I don't like them. They forget things. What if they forget his dinner?"

He could be sitting there in jail, rotting because he'd defended her.

"He lost his temper when he should have been taking care of you," Jesse argued.

At least she knew what he was angry about. "Ty was taking care of me. And Cade was with me the whole time until Ty gave me the EpiPen. He held my hand. It might be hazy, but I remember that part. It was Patrick, right? He punched Patrick."

It was the only explanation that made a lick of sense. And given the conclusion she'd come to, she kind of wanted to kiss Cade.

Jesse's chuckle held not an ounce of humor. "Honey, he didn't merely punch Patrick. As far as I could tell, he damn near killed him."

"Good for Cade." A sense of satisfaction filled her.

"That's what I said." Naomi sounded fierce.

"Me, too. Good for Cade. I hope he messed that no-good up." Her mother typically preached love and understanding, but she slapped at the dashboard.

"Does anyone here understand that what he did was wrong?" Jesse asked, obviously incredulous. "He should have been taking care of Gemma. He made things difficult for the doctor. He could have hurt you."

The time for honesty was upon her, and it was easier because it would get Cade out of trouble. "Jesse, I had my own fork."

Jesse stared at her. "What does that have to do with anything?"

Naomi stopped the car and both she and her mom turned.

"What are you saying, baby girl?" her mom asked.

She'd been over this a thousand times while she'd lain there in that bed. From the moment she'd been able to hold a comprehensible thought, she'd gone over and over the moment when she'd picked up that freaking fork and taken a bite.

"Stella brought me silverware. I unrolled it and put the fork and spoon and knife aside. I got up to go to the bathroom. I talked to Hope and Beth. I came back and my fork was right where I'd left it. Except it wasn't mine. Mom, seriously? Do I go around picking up other people's forks?"

Naomi answered that one. "You try to clean the ones they bring you in restaurants. I'll admit, it can be embarrassing at times."

For once her clean-freak status was a plus. Oh, it had failed her, but only because that weasel, tiny dicked, no balls ex of hers had played her properly. "I know how Stella cleans her dishes. I tested the temperature of the dishwater. Ten percent above health code. I feel comfortable eating at Stella's."

"I don't understand what you're saying, baby." Jesse's tone had changed to what she'd begun to think of as his About to Kick Some Ass voice. It was a slightly less sexy version of his About to Spank Your Ass voice, though she still found it awfully arousing.

"I'm saying Patrick got rid of the fork Stella gave me and put his where I would think it was mine."

She could practically feel him vibrating with rage. If she'd thought for a single moment that this was all some sort of a fun game for Jesse McCann, those ideas were gone. He really did give a shit about her. He'd been pissed at his best friend when Cade hadn't behaved the way he thought he should. He'd stayed with her, apparently choosing a rousing night at the hospital over getting his best friend out of jail.

She'd come between them, but in the best way. Not the best way. The best way would be sexually, but they both cared about her. They just didn't see eye to eye on how they should go about it.

She needed rules. God, she fucking loved rules. Well, the ones she made, anyway. "Rule number one—always make bail."

"What?" Jesse asked.

"We have rules for this relationship. You taught me that. You want me to be your woman? Well, I like rules and lists and matrices. If we live together, you better get used to a whole lot of whiteboards."

"She's not kidding," her mother said with a laugh. "She made me get her one when she was eight years old and trying to figure out what pet to get. Her father and I watched in utter horror as she made pros and cons columns and then decided after ten days of deliberation that she wanted a houseplant."

She'd been a mystery to her freewheeling hippie parents. She was cautious, unsure. She wanted the world to give her a money-back guarantee on life, but she was rapidly discovering that nothing worked that way—and it was okay. It was fucking okay to make mistakes and need a damn do over. It was okay to not be one hundred percent sure that she was on the right path.

Gemma sat back, a single moment of her life crystalizing in an instant.

She was twelve and her father was dying. She remembered how cold the hospital was, but she couldn't leave because this was her home now. Two weeks she'd spent as he choked and gasped his life away. Her mother had never faltered. She'd tried to send Gemma off, but she couldn't go. What if he died and she wasn't there?

She'd stood on a step stool and looked down at him, and he'd said three words to her.

Live. Live. Live.

She'd thought he was too far gone and didn't know what he'd been saying. She'd thought he was telling her what he wanted. That he wanted to live.

He'd been begging her. He'd been pleading with his too-intellectual daughter.

Live. Live. Live.

For so long she'd clung to that vision of her father, a dying man, holding on to something far gone. It had influenced her life, driving her to goals that had nothing to do with emotion. Her life had been a checklist, devoid of true passion. Absent of feeling. As she'd lain there clutching Cade's hand and praying for Jesse to come, she'd understood what her father had meant.

Live. Live. Live.

She'd pursued wealth and cultivated ambition. But she knew

what she wanted now. And she knew something else. She was Gemma Wells. And she would get it. Come hell or high water. She wanted Jesse McCann and Cade Sinclair, and she wanted to practice law in Bliss, Colorado, where they had an actual injunction against lawyers.

And that wouldn't stop her.

"Baby, are you sure?"

Gemma knew he was asking about whether or not her small-penised, couldn't-please-a-woman-if-someone-gave-him-a-road map-to-her-clitoris ex had actually intended to kill her, but she meant something else. "Yes. I'm sure."

There would be no more New York. No big city to conquer. Just Bliss. But she would find her place. She would build her home with a single-minded passion that had been lacking for years.

"Take me to Cade."

* * * *

Cade started when the door opened. He'd been sitting there for so fucking long, he'd kind of expected no one would ever show up. But the door opened and Gemma walked through, her blonde hair swaying around her shoulders.

"There you are." It wasn't the greeting he'd expected. She sighed and her eyes narrowed, but there wasn't any anger in her gaze. There was a soft satisfaction there. "I thought you were still in jail, but the Creede boys said you had been gone for a while. I was going to wake up Nate when I saw your bike outside."

He stood, looking around the cabin. He'd cleaned. Though she kept the place precision perfect neat, she sometimes forgot to dust. He'd stocked the fridge. He couldn't stand the thought of her having nothing to eat. He'd busied himself when he should have had the courage to go to the hospital and tell her good-bye. "They let me go. Your ex pissed off Stef Talbot and everyone decided to leave well enough alone."

Jesse's eyes became hard. "Where did that little fucker get to?"

He wished he knew. "I'm not sure. Nate warned me to leave him alone."

"Nate can bite my ass," Jesse said on a growl.

Gemma sent Jesse a nasty look. "You promised."

The grin that lit Jesse's face was perfectly feral. "Only for tonight. Tomorrow, he's mine."

Cade wasn't sure what that was about. Now that Gemma was all right, it seemed like Jesse wanted a piece of Patrick. And it was Jesse's right. Gemma belonged to him.

Gemma. He couldn't take his eyes off her. The last time he'd seen her, she'd looked like she was close to death. Now she merely looked tired. He would never be able to forget that she was fragile. No matter how much of a force of nature Gemma appeared to be, she was only a woman at heart, and she was as fragile as the other women in his life had been.

He should have left, gotten on his bike and fled the fucking scene of the crime. He'd stayed because he couldn't leave without making sure she was all right. He'd spent hours cooking for her, making sure that at least she would be well fed. The truth was he'd stayed because he needed to face her. He wanted to see that she'd finally realized what a bastard he was and then he would be able to go knowing she wouldn't feel bad about losing him. Then he could get on his bike and leave forever. He wouldn't look back. He would know that Jesse would take care of her, and he could drink and party himself to the death he deserved.

Except she walked right up to him and wrapped her damn arms around him, snuggling her head against his chest. "When they told me you'd been arrested, I was so worried about you."

Worried about him? She was the one who'd almost died. And he didn't understand a Gemma who didn't spit and claw like a riled-up cat. Shouldn't she be mad? "Are you okay? What did the doctors say?"

Jesse moved behind Gemma, his eyes finding Cade's. He frowned, but Cade couldn't tell what was going through his head.

"I'm fine. Mom and Naomi drove me home, but we went to the station first," she explained. "They told us that you were cleared and Pat was gone. That part is over. But we need to figure out why my sad-sack, scared of his own shadow ex would try to kill me. I don't want to do that tonight, though.

He stopped. "Kill you? I thought it was an accident."

Her chin came up. "Do you honestly believe I would steal his fork?"

Gemma had some OCD tendencies. When he'd cooked what seemed like a week's worth of food earlier, he'd made damn sure every single dish was sparkling clean. She might not dust the bookshelves, but her kitchenware was immaculate. Even when she never used it. She wouldn't drink after another person. She damn straight wouldn't steal a fork.

She sighed. "There it is. Did you know you get this tic over your right eye when you get mad?" Her fingers brushed the place, as though trying to soothe him.

"I never had it before I met you." She'd given him a damn tic. And it wasn't only when he was mad, though he was pretty freaking mad right now. Before he went off to drink himself to death, he would find that fucker, force a goddamn fork into some soft part of him, and then the asshole would know how wrong it had been to mess with Cade Sinclair's girl.

Because even though he was leaving, she would always be his girl.

"Stop. I know what you're thinking, but this is going to require more thought than beating the crap out of him." She pulled away. "I don't want to think about Pat anymore tonight. I want you to come outside with me." She pulled on his hand, and he wondered if she hadn't been damaged by the whole poisoning by strawberry incident.

She grasped his hand, tugging him out.

"Gemma, baby, I need to talk to you before I go." He had a few things to say to her and then he would leave her to Jesse.

She utterly ignored him, walking toward her front door.

Cade looked at Jesse. "What's going on?"

"No idea, but I'm going with it." Jesse followed them out the door. "Gemma and I have completely different ideas on how you should behave when someone tries to kill her."

Cade tried to stop. "I still don't completely understand that."

"She'll explain it later." Jesse followed them. "She's not big on vigilantism. I already tried. Tonight, we need to let it be. Tomorrow we can talk, brother."

The fact that Jesse was still calling him brother gave him a deep sense of peace. It didn't change what he needed to do, but he felt better about it. Jesse had done the right thing. Cade had lost it, proving once again that he didn't deserve joy and happiness.

Jesse continued, "Tonight, just follow her. She's made some crazy breakthrough. I would spank her ass, but I can't fucking Dom her tonight. I want to hold her tonight. I want to think we can work."

She kept pulling at him, drawing him out. He should pull away, but he couldn't let her hand go. He knew he should, but he held her tighter as she walked on to her porch and then to the grass. She turned the porch light off, sending the entire yard into complete gloom. Darkness pervaded and still he followed her.

"Look up." Her voice led his way through the dark.

He pulled back, trying to get her to stop. They needed to talk. He needed to explain to her why he should leave. It was the only thing to do. He would get on his bike and head out, leaving her to Jesse, who could love her with a whole heart and no crazy fucking violent rage between them.

She let go of his hand, the loss of her warmth a deep sadness in his soul. She walked away from him, turned and laid her body down on the grass, her face up to the sky. A look of wonder crossed her face. "Look up. I never look up. I wouldn't think to. Up didn't matter, but look at it. Tell me that doesn't matter. Tell me that is meaningless."

She might have gone over the edge. Gemma almost always rode that fine line between perfectly normal and neurotic nut job, and nearly dying seemed to have pushed her over.

His eyes had adjusted and he looked down at her. "Gemma, baby, I only hung around so I could make sure you were okay. I need to go. I'm not good for you."

But she was staring up. Jesse got to the ground and lay down beside her in the grass. A chill ran across his skin. It was damn cold, and she'd been sick and she was lying in the grass in the middle of the night.

"You can leave tomorrow," she said, a smile on her face. "Please stay with me tonight. Come on, Cade. I want one night. I want you to lie down and look up with me."

Frustration welled. Stay with her? Didn't she know how hard it was to leave her? Couldn't she see that the last few hours had been a living hell? He wanted to get it over with, to move on with his life. But he couldn't deny her. He couldn't look at those big, bright eyes and get on his bike and drive off. He sighed and gave in, getting to his knees and sinking down on his back beside her.

And he saw what she was talking about. A million stars blanketed the sky, brighter than anything he'd seen. They twinkled and winked like diamonds. He found himself staring up, wondering how he'd never seen it before.

The night was soft, a blanket cradling the earth.

"Isn't it beautiful?" Gemma's voice was a contented sigh. She reached out, linking her hand to his, pulling it over her heart. He felt another hand there. Jesse's. She held both hands over her heart.

"Of course it's beautiful. It's Colorado. Do either of you look around?" Jesse grumbled but Cade could feel him clutching Gemma's hand. "Am I the only one who smells the freaking roses? Gemma, you've got to spend the next couple of days resting, and I'm going to make sure you really look around and see the place we've been blessed with."

Jesse was right. Cade didn't look around. He didn't stop and stare at the beauty around him. During the day he worked, and at night he partied. He hadn't spent a ton of time looking around at the mountains and the stars above. In many ways, he'd been as single minded as Gemma, focusing on how to have fun and keep the ghosts at bay.

He looked back up at those night lights. Millions of miles away. Some were dead already, their light a mere beacon, proof that once the star had lived. Some still thriving suns. Those stars were always there, always above him, but the harsh light of the sun masked their existence. In the city, they were tiny, insignificant things, covered up by human lights, but here he could see the infinite.

He stared up. It should make him feel small, but somehow, with Gemma's hand in his, those stars above gave him comfort.

"Isn't it beautiful?" she asked again.

Cade turned his head. He could see Gemma's face, the curve of her cheek, the stubborn tilt of her chin. He rolled toward her. The stars were beautiful, but she was gorgeous. He laid his head close to her shoulder and let himself be still for a moment.

"It's stunning," he replied.

One more night. He could handle one more night. And then he would go. He was still bad for her.

But for tonight, he would rest and watch the stars.

Chapter Sixteen

Three days later, Cade had no damn idea what he was doing.

Oh, he was replacing Mel's ancient artifact of an alternator. It had blown due to its extensive old age and not, as Mel had claimed, because of alien vibrations from its recent abduction. This time, he claimed, they had taken his whole 1972 Ford pickup truck. He'd left it at Beaver Creek when he'd gone on a fishing trip. The next morning, he'd told the sheriff aliens had taken his truck. They'd done an exhaustive search and the truck had turned up later that day in the woods near Mel's cave.

Mel was certain that the aliens were now abducting precious vehicles, but Cade kind of thought Mel needed to lay off the "special" tonic he took when he was fishing. It was rotgut whiskey. Cade had tried it once, and he hadn't remembered where he'd left his car either.

No, he totally knew what he was doing with the truck. Gemma was another story altogether.

"I'm going on a run into Alamosa," Jesse said, picking up his helmet.

"You call if you find anything."

Jesse nodded, palming his keys. "Let Roger know where I've

gone. I'll pick up the new parts to the snowmobile on my way back. And I promise, I'm only looking. If I find the fucker, I'll let you know."

Patrick. He'd disappeared the night of Gemma's accident, and they couldn't find him. Nate claimed he didn't have enough evidence to put out an APB. They were stuck in limbo until they tracked him down.

Limbo. That was exactly where he was. He should be halfway to California, but Gemma had changed tactics and he had no idea how to handle her.

"I'm taking Princess Two to the dog park," Roger said, walking out with his baby thing in his arms. He'd dressed the dog today. In deference to the coming winter, Princess Two had on a pink and white sweater. "And then we're going to have a nice lunch at Stella's. Yes, we are. Yes, we are. Is Jesse picking up the snowmobile parts?"

"Yep. We'll have them this afternoon."

"Good." Roger was almost out the door when it opened. "Well, hello Miss Gemma. You are looking mighty healthy. Princess and I were real upset to hear about your trouble. Weren't you, girl?"

Princess answered with a weird howling sound.

Gemma stood in the doorway wearing jeans and a light V-neck sweater that showed off the beginnings of the slopes of her breasts. The jeans hugged her hips, nipped in at her waist. The sunlight came through illuminating her hourglass figure. Cade had been stuffing her every chance he got, feeding her to make up for years and years of harsh diets, and those curves were finally filling out. She looked soft, healthy, and so fuckable his dick threatened to burst free and make a run for her.

Two days of cuddling that sweet body and not sinking in were taking their toll.

Of course, if he'd had his way, he would be on the road and not forced to look at what he couldn't have again.

She talked to Roger for a moment and then he left, the door closing behind him. Cade was all alone with Gemma.

"Hi." That voice went straight to his gut.

Maybe now was the time to talk to her. After he got one thing out of the way. "You're supposed to be with Naomi."

"She's getting the full smackdown at Polly's Cut and Curl. I think it sounds horrible, but Polly's got a whole wrestling theme going right now. A smackdown is a full mani-pedi with a deep hair conditioning, a cut, and a styling. She could be there for hours."

Hours. Hours alone with Gemma when he needed to keep his dick in his pants. He had to find a way to ease out of the relationship without hurting Gemma.

Gemma walked across the floor, her hips swaying. "Whatcha working on?"

She walked into the bay and leaned over, looking into the engine. It put her heart-shaped ass on full display. His hands itched to cup those curvy cheeks.

"I'm replacing an alternator." The words came out on a high squeak that would have done a virginal schoolboy proud. He cleared his throat. "Jesse's gone into Alamosa."

"I know. I talked to him on my way in." Her head turned back, a smile playing on those lips that looked perfect wrapped around his dick. "Looking for Patrick?"

And she was too smart for their own good. They'd tried to keep her out of the loop. "Nah, he's picking up some parts."

She stood back up, crossing her arms under her breasts and shooting him a deeply cynical look. He only caught a tiny piece of the cynicism because her arms pushed her boobs up so they formed a glorious rack. "I'm not dumb. I know you're looking for him. I would be depressed if you weren't."

He felt his eyes narrow. Shouldn't she be yelling at him? "I thought you would be mad."

"I figured out that you and Jesse are different from the other men I've dated."

Since she'd dated insane douchebags, he was pretty satisfied with that. "How?"

She leaned against the truck. "In every way, but in this case, you like to take matters in your own hands, so to speak. Most of the other men I've dated would be happy to have the police looking. You and Jesse want to deal with it on your own."

"Well, there's not a lot Nate can do. Me and Jesse don't have to work within the confines of the law." Despite the fact that it was chilly outside, his skin was heating up.

She leaned over, closing the distance between them. "Because you care about me."

Because he was crazy about her, thought about her every second of the goddamn day, and dreamed about her at night. Her hand touched his chest, and he had to back away because, damn, he wanted to lay her out on the hood of one of the cars and pound away at her. And he couldn't because she was fragile and he was leaving.

"Gemma, baby, we need to talk."

She hadn't let him have his talk with her. Every time he tried, she changed the subject or sighed and put her head on his chest and looked generally wounded to the point that he gave in and held her. Two nights of cuddling her in front of the TV had yielded nothing.

Even Jesse wasn't listening to him anymore. He'd tried to talk to Jesse, but Jesse seemed as stubborn as Gemma.

She stalked after him, backing him up to where he had no place to go. His back hit the wall. "I saw Caleb today. He cleared me for…everything. I think Jesse intends to make another stop before he comes home tonight. Something about toys."

Damn. Damn. Damn. *Everything*. Everything meant sex and stuff. She'd been all horny and kissy and lovely, but Jesse wouldn't let her play until Caleb gave her the okay. Toys. Sex toys. Dirty, fun things to use on his girl.

Not his.

"G, you know I can't stay." He had to go.

She nodded, her eyes on his mouth. "I know. You're bad for me."

"That's right." At least she got it. His dick would have to chill out because she was starting to understand. "I'm not good for you."

She didn't back off. "No, you're a bad, bad man."

"Gemma, please." Her hand was on his chest, trailing down to his jeans, and he couldn't move.

"Yes, Gemma needs to be pleased. Gemma's had several very bad days." She pulled at the fabric of his T-shirt.

He tried to keep his hands up. "Bad idea. I'm leaving, remember?"

Those baby blues came up. "Do you have to leave now? You could wait a few days. Don't you have to give Roger some notice?"

This was what she did. Every time he tried to bring this incredibly important subject up, she started talking about all the problems with him leaving Bliss.

And yeah, he should give Roger notice. But not today. It was Tuesday. Friday was more of a day to tell someone about an inevitable departure. Two weeks. Yes. Two weeks from Friday. That would satisfy his conscience.

Gemma pulled the shirt free. "Don't you prefer to be naked?"

He did. He knew it was weird, but he liked the way it felt, and it would be dangerous around Gemma. Who he wasn't going to fuck. Nope. "That's a rumor."

"I don't know. I think I might like it, too." She pulled her sweater up, teasing him with inch after inch of perfect flesh. She pulled it over her head and tossed it his way with a sexy wink. She wore a lacy black bra underneath that barely managed to hold her breasts. They threatened to spill out over the top. One flick to the back of that bra and her breasts would be free. He could touch them, take them into his mouth. He could lick and suck those sweet pink nipples.

He reached over and handed her back the sweater. "Gemma, this isn't right."

She pouted a little. "But I told Jesse I was here to seduce you and he asked me to do it in front of the security monitors because he wants to watch it later. And I bought new lingerie."

Damn Jesse. He'd known Cade would have a hard time turning away Gemma. But he had to do it. His dick protested mightily, but if he ever wanted to be friends with her, he couldn't keep fucking her at every given opportunity. He needed to leave, and maybe in a few years he could look them up again. They would be married and maybe have a couple of kids, and Cade would be nothing more than part of their wild courtship, a thing to look on fondly. He could still be friends with them.

He needed to keep them the only way he could.

"Get dressed. I'll take you to lunch." He would talk to her over lunch, lay out all the reasons this couldn't work. He would tell her about his family, and she would understand.

She stood there for a moment, that previously flushed skin turning white. He caught a brief hint of tears as she turned and pulled the sweater over her head. She took a moment, and when she turned back around, she was perfectly composed. "I think I'll go join Naomi. I should get my nails done or something. I'll see you later. Tell Jesse I'll be at home."

Fuck. He'd hurt her, and he was trying hard not to. This was what he did. He fucked up time and time again. "Gemma."

She didn't turn, simply grabbed her purse and smoothed her sweater down. "It's okay. You said you were leaving. I thought I could make you want to stay. It was a stupid idea. I'm not some sexpot. I just…just forget this happened. I'm deeply embarrassed."

He caught her before she made it to the door. "Baby, it has nothing to do with how much I want you."

She turned her eyes up to him, tears falling. "Oh, I beg to differ. Please let me go. I won't fight you anymore. I got it into my head that you were leaving because you had some dumbass idea that you were cursed or something. But that's stupid. It's because of me. I'm difficult."

She was and he fucking loved her that way. "You're perfect, Gemma."

She snorted. Yeah, he loved that, too. "Hardly."

He was dangerously close, staring down at her with a hard cock and a soft heart. He couldn't help himself. He used his thumb to sweep away a tear on her cheek. "I am bad for you."

"I don't care."

He sighed. "You will one day. Or maybe not. But I do care. I cost some people close to me their lives. Every time I open up, someone gets hurt. I'm tired. I don't want to try again. Can you understand that?"

She nodded, her hands coming up to find his cheeks. "You're wrong. One day, you're going to meet the woman you love, and you will open yourself up and, god, I hope she makes you happy, Cade Sinclair, because if she doesn't she'll answer to me."

"Gemma."

"No, it's okay. You can't love me. It's okay. I still don't even know what I want. I don't trust that Jesse will stay. I'm holding on for dear life as long as I can because I'm pretty sure this is the most happiness I'll get. If a few weeks with the two of you is all I get, then

I want to take it." She pulled away. "But you don't have to leave town because of me. This is your home. I'm not going to make things difficult for you."

She didn't understand anything. "Seeing you will be difficult."

"I could leave. You were here first and all."

"It's not some contest, baby."

"Please don't call me that. And let me go, Cade. I made my play and it kind of sucked. I should have taken sex-kitten lessons or something. I'll try that on the next guy."

Oh, there was the bitch. Yep. The bitch got his cock hard while those tears kicked him in the gut. It was a perfect mix. One without the other and he could let her go. As it was, his hands tightened. "You are the only woman I want, and the idea of you stripping down for anyone but me or Jesse makes me fucking insane."

Her eyes narrowed, calculating the power shifting between them. His Gemma knew when she'd gotten the upper hand. "You don't have any right to say that to me."

He was so fucking weak. "I don't want to hurt you. I'm trying like hell not to hurt you. I want you bad, but I don't know if I can stay."

Her body moved into his. She might think she wasn't a sexpot, but she was a goddamn siren. Everything about her called to him. "I'm not asking for a ring."

"You deserve one." She deserved two.

"Can't I have a few weeks? Can't I have a few weeks where we simply let things flow?"

A horrible idea. He was already in love with her. If he let himself be with her for a few weeks, he might never be able to leave. A terrible idea and yet his head dipped down, his lips brushing against hers. He should have known this wouldn't work. He should have known he couldn't resist her. "I'm not a good man."

"Then be my bad boy." Her hands skimmed his chest. "Just for a while."

He would break her heart, and she would never know that she held his in the palm of her hand. Just for a while, he might pretend he was good for her. And he couldn't leave until that fucker Patrick was dealt with. Did he honestly think he could be around her and not kiss her and love her and fuck her? Memories. He could build memories of her, of the family he could have had if he was a better man.

"Gemma," he started.

She put a finger to his lips. "Don't. I only want to be with you. No promises. No regrets. No promise but the here and now."

She needed to feel wanted. He'd damn near crushed her by turning her away. She'd spent years discounting her value for anything but her brain and her ambition. Cade pulled her close, growling a little. She needed to feel sexy, and he could do that. She was the sexiest woman he'd ever met.

"Give me that sweater."

She hesitated. Cade decided to take a page from Jesse's book. She liked a dominant male. She liked to fight and scratch and struggle, but in the end she wanted to be taken down by a man who cared about her. He could be that man.

"I said give me that sweater, Gemma. I want to see your breasts."

"Are you sure?" she asked.

"I'm sure that if that sweater isn't on the floor in two seconds, I'll pull your pants around your ankles and we'll start with a spanking."

Her skin flushed a darling pink, her eyes dilating with desire. She pulled the sweater over her head and let it fall to the floor.

"That's what I want." He stared down at her breasts, letting his hand trace a line from her throat to the valley of her chest. Smooth curves beckoned him. "Take off the bra."

She fumbled a little, but got the bra undone. "What about you?"

He couldn't help but smile. "I'm supposed to be in charge."

She wrinkled her nose. "I might have issues with authority."

Cade pulled his shirt off, giving her what she wanted. "Can we agree to a little give and take? You give me that tight pussy and I promise you all the cock you can take."

She sighed, the tension leaving her body. "I might be demanding."

"I might be incredibly horny." He reached for her hips, pulling her close again. He loved seeing her in the sunlight. He shut the door but left the windows open. He didn't give a shit if someone saw them. He wanted her bathed in sunshine. He tugged the bra free, releasing her breasts.

He lifted her up. She was small, no weight at all in his arms. It was easy to get her right where he wanted her. He brought her nipples to mouth level and rubbed his face in her chest.

"Horny?" Gemma asked, running her hands through his hair. "Aren't you always horny?"

He loved the fact that her voice was light and teasing again. This was what he could give her. He could bring some lightness to her always ambitious life. "You have no idea how horny I get the minute you walk in the door, baby. My cock stands up and it doesn't go down until it gets what it wants. The last two days have been hell on me. I've masturbated more in the last couple of days than I did when I was fucking fifteen."

"You masturbated thinking about me?"

He glanced up, surprised she sounded amazed. "I've yanked my own cock since the day I met you. I pretend my fist is your pussy, but nothing compares to actually getting to have you. I'm going to have you today, aren't I?"

"Oh, yes."

He would have her. He was a bad man. He would take her over and over. He sucked a nipple into his mouth, reveling in the low moan that he wrung from her throat. He adored that moment when her brain shut off and she became soft and wanton. He whirled his tongue around and around the tight bud in his mouth. Gemma's legs wrapped around his waist, her back bowing.

He needed more. Without letting her nipple go, he carried her across the floor to where his precious Chevy sat. He tinkered with the engine whenever he had a chance. He laid her out on the hood of the car.

"Fuck, you're gorgeous."

He started to work the button of her jeans, dragging them down her shapely legs. She was left in nothing but a pair of black panties, and she didn't have the same trouble she'd had before. He leaned over and shoved his nose right into the *V* of her legs. Arousal surrounded him. He inhaled the spicy scent of her wet pussy.

"I don't know how you can do that." Her voice had gone husky. She looked down her body, her eyes wide as he brushed her wet pussy with his nose.

"I told you, I love the way you smell. I love how wet you get. I love the taste of you on my tongue."

And he loved the fact that she was inexperienced. Oh, he hated the fuckers who hadn't taught her pleasure, but he loved that he could teach her. "Ever done it on the hood of a car?"

"Uhm, no. Strangely, that didn't happen for me. Patrick would never do something so filthy."

Now he growled in earnest. "Don't you say his name when I'm fucking you. What name do you say?"

He half expected her to call him Bare-Chested Ape Man, but she merely smiled that mysterious smile of hers. "Cade. I say Cade, but I have two lovers so if I mess up and call you Jesse, will I get spanked?"

He stood, pushing off his own jeans and freeing his cock. "You better remember which man is which or you'll get the spanking of a lifetime. You'll get spanked and fucked over and over until you use the right name."

"Not exactly a reason to be good."

"I didn't say I wouldn't enjoy it." He hopped on to the hood of the car. He had a fantasy to play out. "Get on top, Gemma. Not that way. Sit on my face and take my cock in your mouth. You suck me. You suck me hard or I'll stop eating your pussy."

He could see the light hit her eyes. He'd made it a challenge because that was what she responded to. A little awkwardly, she shifted on the car, positioning herself right over his face. Her scent surrounded him. He reached up, putting his hands on her ass and dragging her down. This was where he wanted to be. He wanted to be tongue deep in her pussy four times a day.

He slapped her ass lightly when she hesitated. "Suck me, Gemma."

He sighed as he felt her tongue on the head of his dick. His balls drew up as her hot mouth closed over him.

He pulled her down, bringing her pussy onto his mouth. He dove in, licking and sucking. He speared up into her, seeking her unique sweetness. He drew out her cream, kissing and suckling every bit of her pussy. He sucked her labia in, laving it before moving to the other.

Gemma gave as good as she got. She sucked the head of his cock, forcing him to concentrate on the task at hand. Over and over she drew his cock in, running her tongue all over him before sucking hard.

He was surrounded by her. She occupied his every sense, leaving no place for the noxious doubt and guilt that usually stuffed him to the brim. He was filled with her. There was only Gemma.

He worked her clit, sucking at her and biting gently. His whole heart swelled when she pulled her mouth off his cock, groaning as she came.

He flipped her over, not giving her a chance to take him down. He wanted to get inside her, to make her come again, this time on his cock.

Her eyes were wide, and she gasped as he moved, making a place for himself between her legs. He spread her wide and remembered what he'd forgotten. "Baby, I don't have a condom on me."

Her lips curled up. "You don't fuck a lot of girls in the shop?"

"Never." His dick was an iron poker that threatened to slice into him if he didn't give it what it wanted. "God. I could go look in Roger's desk, but I don't think the man's had sex in years."

"Good thing I brought my own. Look in the pocket of my jeans." She cupped his ass, a languid smile on her face. "I was trying to be a sex goddess. I thought I should be prepared."

She was his sex goddess. He kissed her again and then scooted off the car and ran for her jeans. Just in time to see Max Harper start to walk up. Fuck no. That was not happening. Completely comfortable with his nudity, he ran for the door, locking it and turning the sign from "Open" to "Closed" as Harper tried to open it.

"Cade. Come on, man. I need spark plugs," he shouted.

Cade shrugged. He needed to get laid by the most gorgeous sex goddess in Bliss.

"Is someone there?" Gemma asked.

Harper rolled his eyes and then turned his back, a silent assent that sex was far more important than his spark plugs. But he wasn't leaving.

"Nope. We're good." His cock was still at full mast. Fuck, he loved this place. He didn't want to leave. He didn't want to leave her.

He didn't want to leave Jesse. He didn't want to leave Bliss. Home had seemed a place he'd abandoned all those years ago. He'd been drifting until he'd come here. What the hell was he going to do?

She sat up, the siren call of her soft body his undoing. She held a hand out, and it didn't matter anymore. No past. Just here and now with Gemma. He rolled the condom on and laid her out on the car his father had adored, the one he'd painstakingly reconditioned. His car. His girl. All was right with the world.

He spread her, her body welcoming him inside. He lined his cock up and pressed home.

"I love that. I didn't get it before." Her eyes shined up at him.

"It wasn't right before." He stroked into her, every thrust a pure pleasure. "I came with other women, but they didn't matter. Only you. Only you matter."

She was everything. Now he knew why his father had often locked the door to his parents' bedroom in the middle of the afternoon. Why his mother got that look in her eyes when his dad walked in the door. Love. A sweet, pulse-pounding love-lust that spelled out the meaning of his life. Loving Gemma changed everything.

She pulled in for a kiss. "Only you and Jesse. You're the only ones for me."

His girl. His best friend. His town. He could have it if only he was brave enough to take the chance. He thrust in and out, the decision meaningless at the moment. He could be a coward later, but for now, he would give her what she needed. He ground his pelvis against her clit, and she called out his name when she came. One more perfect thrust and he went over the edge with her. He pressed in, again and again, giving her everything he had. It was hers. It was all fucking hers.

He collapsed on her, loving the way she held him. He breathed in the scent of their mingled sex. All day long, he would look at this car and remember her.

There was a loud banging on the door. "If you two are done fucking, I need spark plugs for the lawn mower. I haven't mowed in three weeks and Rach gets mad when I lose Paige in the back field!"

Gemma squeaked and tried to hide, but Cade laughed. That was life in Bliss. He kissed her and climbed off.

"Get dressed, baby. I got a business to run."

He was deeply pleased with the gorgeous pink her skin turned.

* * * *

Jesse turned back down Main Street, his prey eluding him once again.

He'd heard Patrick had been seen in Alamosa, but when he'd gone to the better motels in town, the little fucker was already gone. He'd put the word out, but the lawyer was proving to be fairly good at covering his tracks.

Jesse stopped at the red light before turning up the road that led to the shop. Cade was still there despite the coward's best attempts at fleeing. Gemma had changed tactics on his ass, and Cade had no idea what to do. Jesse smiled a little. She was cutting Cade off at every pass.

Every day when Cade came to say good-bye to her, she hugged him and asked for one more night.

He wondered if Cade even realized they had practically moved in with her. The first night, they had lain there in the grass for a long time, staring up at the stars, and then they'd gone to her bed and cuddled her, passing her back and forth, hugging and kissing her until she'd finally fallen asleep.

And the next morning she'd gotten up and unpacked Cade's clothes and placed them in her dresser. He'd packed up again, and she'd convinced him to stay, and the next morning Cade's clothes had been right back in the drawer next to Jesse's. Cade hadn't bothered to pack again this morning. And if she'd played her cards right, Cade had probably spent a good part of the afternoon buried deep inside her, bonding with her.

Their girl was smart. And Jesse intended to protect her at all costs.

Long-Haired Roger walked out of the shop carrying Princess Two in his burly arms. A county Bronco was parked outside. Jesse cut his engine and kicked the bike into park. He removed his helmet as Roger walked up, Princess Two's bug eyes directly on Jesse.

"Hey, been trying to get ahold of you. Nate's in the shop talking to Cade. Seems like he's got some information on who's trying to hurt poor, sweet, Gemma." Roger's head shook, a long look on his face.

Roger was sweet on Gemma since she'd come into the shop the day before. She was supposed to be there so Jesse could keep an eye on her. She'd come armed with some books, but she'd then spent the whole time organizing Roger's office and filing his receipts, since apparently Roger didn't believe in a filing system. Now Roger was sure Gemma walked on water, and Princess Two had given her assent by not barking Gemma's way. In Roger's mind, it meant Gemma was good people.

Jesse stalked into the shop, wanting more than anything to get this whole thing over and done with. He wanted this settled because until she was out of danger, he couldn't concentrate on what he wanted to—convincing Gemma to stay.

Nate stood with Cade, his arms crossed over his chest. A short man with round glasses stood by his side. He had a smallish build. Jesse pegged him in his mid-forties, early fifties, with an intellectual bent.

Nate nodded as Jesse walked in. "Jesse, meet Paul Johnson."

Jesse stopped in his tracks, remembering why that particular name made him want to punch someone. Paul Johnson was the asshole Cam had been looking for. The one who had made the threats against Gemma years ago. "Paul Johnson?"

Cade put a hand out. "Stay calm and listen to what the man has to say."

When Cade was the voice of reason, Jesse figured they were all in trouble. He stared at Paul Johnson, who turned to him. The man was dressed in khaki shorts and a T-shirt proclaiming "Scientists Do It Methodically." He started to put a hand out, but seemed to think twice about it.

"Sorry, I guess you've read those things I said to Miss Wells."

"Damn straight," Jesse shot back. "And you should know she belongs to me. I don't take kindly to your threats."

The smaller man shook his head. "I wouldn't, either, though I think your language is very possessive. She's a free spirit, man. We can't own another soul any more than we can own the land and sky."

Jesse turned to Nate, who had an amused grin on his face. "What the fuck is he trying to say?"

Nate shrugged. "I thought about calling in Nell to translate. It seems Paul here has had a change of heart. He's given up his worldly possessions to walk the earth and do good things."

There was an oddly peaceful look on the scientist's face. "Karma is an amazing thing. It led me to take a look at my own soul. To take stock, so to speak. I would love to talk to Miss Wells, to make amends."

"And you think you can do that by sending her threatening letters and boxes of freaking hearts?" He wasn't letting the man in the same room with her.

Cade sighed. "Catch up. Does he look like a dude who would send her a cadaver heart? This has all been one big setup."

Setup? But why? "You think someone is trying to make it look like this dude wants to kill Gemma?"

"That would be my assessment," Nate said. "Cam found him yesterday and managed to get in contact. He came right in. Seems he's been on the road for over a year following the big music festivals from town to town. The heart in a box was sent from St. Louis."

"But I was at Peacenick in San Francisco that week," Paul explained. "It's a music and healing festival."

"Are we sure about that?" Jesse wasn't going to be convinced because the guy looked like he wouldn't hurt a fly. Appearances could lie.

"Oh yeah, there are several time-stamped pictures of him at the festival. He's easy to pick out of a crowd. He's at least twenty years older than anyone there," Nate explained.

"And I haven't used a computer in months, man," Paul said. "I'm all natural. This is a great town you have here. The vibes are incredible. Peace, man. This place radiates peace."

"It's got the worst murder rate per capita in the country." The last thing he needed was someone else from Gemma's past hanging around. He needed her to think about the future.

"Really?" Paul looked around like he was expecting someone to try to murder him any minute.

Cade seemed to pick up on Jesse's thought process. "Oh, yeah.

It's totally dangerous. We've even had a serial killer. Mobsters run amuck here. I heard there was a violent biker gang."

"Don't forget all the alien abductions," Long-Haired Roger chimed in.

"And our women would make your toes curl." Nate got a shit-eating grin on his face. "They like to keep a running tally of their kills. They have a club."

It was more like a support group. Jesse had mistakenly walked in on it one time. It seemed to consist of drinking coffee, eating cake, and talking through their feelings about being forced to kill in self-defense. Though he'd overheard Marie and Rachel giving tips on the best places to shoot a son of a bitch, as they called it. He'd tiptoed back out of that room right quick and prayed they didn't notice him.

Paul's eyes grew round. "Wow. I would not have guessed that. It seems beautiful. Serial killers. Yeah, maybe I should go. I don't need bad vibes. I heard there's an alt-rock healing festival in Santa Fe. I'm thinking about spending some time there so I can study to become a yogi. I think I can heal hearts from the inside, you know?"

"So you're not mad at Gemma anymore?" Jesse asked.

Paul's face fell momentarily. "I signed a bad contract. I thought I was smart enough to get out of it. I wasn't. She was smarter. She found a tiny clause in my contract, and by playing off some of the vague language, she cost me millions, possibly billions of dollars. When I think about it, I get upset. Yeah, I get mad. But there's not a thing I can do about it. I heard about what happened to her."

Apparently everyone had heard. He needed to figure out a way to get that damn video down. Gemma had to hate the fact that everyone could see her lose control like that. "I'm sure that made you feel better."

"No, it made me sad, but it could end up being a good thing. She's a great lawyer. Why do only the big corporations get someone like her? Why can't the little guys have someone like Gemma Wells? So she pissed off her firm. Maybe she should start her own. I always thought she would make a great warrior. Maybe that sounds dumb, but there are a lot of people out there who need a warrior." Paul shook his head. "Or a masseuse. You both seem pretty tightly wound. I can help with that. There's healing in these hands."

Nate put a hand on Paul's shoulder. "Let's get all the paperwork out of the way before you start healing people. Come on, Johnson. Cam should have some sort of report to make."

They left, the door closing behind them and a silence falling.

Roger sighed. "Well, he seemed like a decent fella. Don't much cotton to massage, though. I'm going to get some paperwork done. You boys let me know if you need anything."

When the door closed behind Roger, Cade turned, his eyes stark. "We're right back to square one."

"No, we know who we're looking for." Patrick Welch had attempted to build himself a fall guy. He'd probably known damn well that Johnson was in the wind. But why try to set up an accident? Why not simply kill her? It was an awfully complex setup for an accident.

"Do we? I've thought about this. Can't think of much else. Why does Patrick want her dead?" Cade scrubbed a hand through his hair.

"Maybe he wants her and he's trying to scare her enough that she goes back to him."

"He could have gone after her before now," Cade pointed out. "And he couldn't know she was getting involved with us. We weren't actually involved with her when she got the first package."

"Dear god, don't point that out to her." She was still arguing about the duties and expectations of being in a relationship. He was going to have to put a ring on her finger before she would acknowledge his right to protect her.

Fuck. He was going to marry Gemma Wells. He had to figure out how to keep her here because he truly believed this was the best place for her. Paul Johnson might be a weirdo, but he was correct. Gemma couldn't sit behind a desk at the station house for the rest of her life, but the crazy, high-pressure life she'd led before wasn't right for her, either.

Cade took a long breath, his head shaking. "You have to talk to her. I can't seem to do it."

"I saw her at lunchtime. She was coming in to see you. You should have talked to her then." Jesse studied Cade. His best friend seemed even more stressed than before. Had the afternoon not gone well with Gemma?

Cade paced, walking back and forth from the Camaro to the work bench. "There wasn't a whole lot of talking going on. She came in and showed me her breasts and I pretty much gave in."

Then the plan had come together. He needed to check those security tapes. He would love to watch Gemma work her magic. "Then you had a good afternoon. I'm afraid I don't see what the problem is. She told me Caleb cleared her. She's fine. If she wants a little sex, isn't it our job to give it to her?"

Cade stopped pacing and turned to him, his jaw set in a stubborn line. "You know I can't do this long term."

He didn't want to have this conversation. He was actually sick of the whole thing. "You talk to her."

"I've tried. Man, you know how hard I've tried. She turns those soft eyes up and asks me to stay."

"And what the hell is wrong with that?" He did not see the problem.

Cade groaned, a sound of frustration. "You know what's wrong with that. Damn it, Jesse. I'm not good for her."

Jesse was frustrated, too. "I'm sick of that argument, man. It's complete bullshit."

"No, it's not. I don't want this. I don't want a family. I had a family, and I fucked it up."

"You were nine years old, Cade. You were a kid."

"I knew what I was doing. I did it because I was a pathetic piece of shit who wanted attention, and they died because of it." Cade's face flushed, anger rising. "And I damn straight knew what I was doing when it came to Nancy. It doesn't bother you? We were out partying while she was dying."

Cade had the most fucked-up sense of guilt. It dragged him down every day. Jesse felt it necessary to point out a few of life's brutal truths. "I loved Nan. She was the mother I wished I'd had, but she was stubborn and too proud for her own good."

"What the fuck are you talking about?"

He acted like she was a saint and he was the devil who'd led her to her death. Cade liked to rewrite history. "We called her every other day. You think I don't remember? Even when we were on the road, you would make us pull over to call her. We had to buy minutes every week because you would gab for hours. You kept in touch. I kept in touch. And she spent all her time talking about the neighborhood and what television shows she was watching, and not once did she mention she'd lost every dime she had in a scam and was in a rat-infested nursing home."

"I would have known if I'd stayed with her."

How could he make Cade understand? "We were adults. Were we supposed to live with our foster mother forever?"

"We were supposed to take care of her," Cade replied.

"She didn't let us, man. You aren't responsible for Nan any more than you were the reason your parents and your sister died."

Cade turned, his face shutting down. "You can't understand."

He was also sick of that fucking argument. He could feel his blood pressure take a leap. "You think you had it bad? My old man died in prison. I never met him. Probably a good thing since he was up for killing a man in a bar brawl. My mother was a trailer park prostitute whose life took a nosedive—yeah, there's a place downhill from trailer park prostitute—when she got hooked on meth. I lived on the fucking street for years after she tried to sell my ten-year-old body to a john one night so she could get high. I ran. I kept running until I fucking found something good, so don't tell me I don't know how bad the world can get."

There was a startled intake of breath from the vicinity of the door, and Jesse's heart plunged to his feet. Gemma stood there with her friend, Naomi. She'd heard every word he'd said. He was honest, but he'd never intended to be that honest with her. His childhood had been a brutal walk on the razor's edge. By the time he'd entered kindergarten, he knew more about survival than most people had to learn in a lifetime, and he didn't want Gemma to see that part of him.

She stood there, stark white, and he wondered if she would turn and run.

Cade's mouth hung open. "Gemma, just because his parents had trouble doesn't mean he does. He's the straightest arrow I know."

"Shut up," she said in that commanding tone he was sure she'd used in many a court of law. She walked straight up to Jesse. "Am I the good thing? Am I the thing that stopped you from running?"

She got to him. If she was fucking with him, fooling around with his dumbass mechanic heart, he might lie down and die. But he was brave enough to tell her the truth. He wouldn't hide from it. He knew how shitty the world was, had seen it with his own eyes. And nothing changed unless a man willed it. He was going to will Gemma Wells into loving him. "Yes. I got nothing to run from, darlin'. I love you."

He waited for her to bite that bottom lip and explain all the reasons why they couldn't work out long term. She was way past smart, into the brilliant territory, and he rebuilt engines. She had a whole heart and he shared one with his best friend. She was whole, and he never would be if she told him no.

She walked straight into his arms, hugging him tighter than he'd ever been held. "Be sure, Jesse McCann. You be sure."

He buried his head in her hair, holding her close. "I've never been more sure of anything in my life."

She held him, her face buried in his neck. A long moment passed before she turned and reached out. "Cade?"

But he was gone. The door shut behind him. Jesse heard the purr of an engine starting and held Gemma tighter.

He might not have a whole heart, but what he had was hers. He had to pray it would be enough.

Chapter Seventeen

Gemma sighed with pleasure as Jesse thrust inside. She wrapped her legs around him, glorying in the feel of his cock sliding over and over that magnificent spot deep inside her body. She clutched him, needing to know he was close. She couldn't get enough of this. Years and years she'd viewed sex as something to get through. It was expected when she was someone's girlfriend.

This wasn't a task to be completed. This was something she needed like her next breath.

"That's right, baby. Give it up. I want to feel you come all over my cock." Jesse lifted up, holding himself on his arms as his hips moved in a rough rhythm. She stared up at him, loving the way he looked. He was gorgeous and masculine, with his hair all askew and that beard coming in across his face. His shoulders bunched into tight muscles. And all that masculine beauty was focused on her.

Everything inside her coiled and waited, spiraling up and up. She wanted to make the moment last. She didn't want to come down. She wanted to stay right here on the precipice with him.

But he was too good for that. He found her hot spot and his cock worked it, hitting it again and again while his hips swiveled, grinding on her clit. She'd only held out this long because he'd made her come twice before, licking her pussy until she'd screamed out his name.

She let go, her whole body shuddering as pleasure washed over her.

"That's what I need." Jesse lost his rhythm and started fucking her like a desperate man.

She loved watching him. His face contorted, and she was sure he was hers in that one moment, only hers.

He stiffened and jerked, riding out his orgasm before he let himself rest down on her body.

She held him, her hands soothing the muscles of his back. She'd thought Cade was hers, too. But he was gone.

Jesse's head came up, his eyes dark in the twilight. He'd left the curtains open, allowing the late afternoon light in, but it was rapidly moving to night. "Baby, he's going to come back."

She wasn't sure. She'd hated the fact that they were fighting over her. "What happened to his parents?"

Jesse hesitated and then with a reluctant kiss to the tip of her nose, rolled off her. He didn't go far, merely moved to the side and put a possessive hand on her belly. "You know they died, right?"

She knew most of their background, but it was in a clinical way, a series of dates and numbers without the emotion behind it. "Why does he feel responsible?"

"He doesn't talk about it, darlin'. It's the one thing he hasn't shared with me. I know what I know because I've read the articles about the accident and I've heard him when he dreams about it. His dad lost control of the family car in the middle of one of the worst storms in his hometown's history. Violent rains. A couple of tornados touched down. Pure grade A Florida Panhandle weather. The river they lived near flooded and the car went in. Only Cade came out. Search and rescue found him clinging to a floating tree trunk three miles down the river from his parents' car. He spent the night in that river. When he has dreams about it, he sometimes struggles to breathe."

Tears filled her eyes. How horrifying it must have been, a kid fighting to survive when he knew his parents were dead.

"His mom and dad died on impact, blunt force trauma. But his sister went into the river alive. Her seatbelt jammed. I've always wondered if Cade knew she was alive and couldn't help her. He carries this guilt around like a backpack. He seems to collect more along the way. He blames himself for you nearly dying."

Gemma turned over, looking him straight in the eyes. "That was your fault."

He gave her that look, the one that told her she would be in serious trouble if she didn't backtrack. She kind of loved that look.

"Fine. It was stupid." That day seemed like forever ago even though only a few days had passed. She felt different. Stronger. And way more willing to cop to her mistakes. "I was pissed, and I walked out. It's not Cade's fault. I'm stupidly organized. I make lists of the lists I need to make. I have a handbag that contains enough crap to run a third-world country. I knew not to walk out without it. I knew what could happen."

She just hadn't thought about it then.

His hand came out, cupping her cheek. "Then why did you do it?"

She wanted to give him a crap answer that wouldn't reveal too much of herself, but then he would likely growl and send her another of those patented looks. It was easier to tell him the truth. "There was a part of me that was thrilled when Pat showed up because I was mad at you and I wanted to show you both that you couldn't control me."

"That's my girl." He sighed and rubbed their chests together. "I'll spank you for that later."

He would, and she would enjoy it. "You really don't care that I'm a righteous bitch?"

"You aren't a bitch. You have certain aggressive tendencies toward making your point clear."

"Everyone calls me difficult." Even her parents had been at a loss with how to handle her, but Jesse seemed to have the magic touch. "My mom and dad took me to a shaman when I was five. He said my aura was hard to read." Even to the hippie kooks who tolerated everything from ancient aliens to obnoxious tourists, she was difficult.

He smiled that serene smile of his that tended to calm her down even during the worst situations. "You are difficult. You're headstrong and proud and so smart I can't keep up with your brain half the time, but that's not a bad thing. The best things in life are hard. Most of the worst stuff that ever happened to me happened because someone took the easy way out. I don't want easy. I want beauty, and beauty is something you work for. Baby, you're beautiful. You just don't know it yet. You don't know what you could be."

All she wanted to be was in between them. She was down a man. "Where do you think he went?"

"Probably to Hell on Wheels. It's a bar. I'll go looking for him in an hour or two. I'll drag him back home."

She liked the way he said home. She loved the fact that their clothes were neatly folded in drawers next to hers. She hated that Cade's duffel bag was sitting on the floor waiting to be packed up and carried away. "You can drag him back, but I don't think I can make him stay."

She'd had one lovely moment when everything seemed to fall into place. Just for a second, Cade had seemed perfectly satisfied. Even the knowledge that Max Harper knew she'd been laid out on the hood of a Camaro hadn't killed her afterglow. After they'd dressed, Cade had kissed her and walked her over to the Cut and Curl, and she'd had her toes painted a bright, deeply unprofessional turquoise and relaxed, thinking she'd found the way to Cade's heart. She would make love to the man until he saw things her way.

Then, not two hours later, she'd heard him talking to Jesse and they were right back where they'd been before. "I'm not secure enough to think this isn't about me."

"This is about Cade," Jesse insisted. "He cares about you. The problem is he doesn't care about himself enough. The fact that he's still here says something. Give it a little time. Don't give up on him."

She didn't want to give up on him. If Cade left, she wouldn't be whole, but Jesse was enough for the moment. "Is all that stuff you said about your mom true?"

He turned over. She wouldn't let him get too far. She put her head on his chest, her arm around him. She was happy when he relaxed and cuddled up to her.

"Yeah. It's true. But don't think everything was bad. Before she hit the meth, she wasn't a horrible person."

"She didn't have any skills, did she? Did she get into prostitution to feed you?"

His head came up, staring down at her like that was the last thing he'd expected to hear.

"I did a stint working for a court-appointed attorney in the city. I met a lot of prostitutes. Heard a lot of stories. They don't get into it because they love sex. They do it because they're hooked on drugs or they don't know how to feed themselves. You don't have to worry about me looking down on you, Jesse. You think because I worked in a fancy firm that I don't know how the world works, but I've seen it from all sides. People are just people. Good and bad. Poor and rich. They're all looking for that one thing that makes them happy."

He took a long breath, hugging her close. "See, that's what you could be, baby. Difficult and amazing. And yes, she took her first john because my dad was in the pen, and he'd left her with more debt than she could handle. We lived in a motel after dad was gone. I got shoved into the bathroom when she had clients. Her one thing turned out to be meth. She loved it more than me. More than herself. More than anything."

She sat up, staring down at him in absolute wonder. She had seen more of the world than she'd wanted to, but she'd never seen anything so lovely as Jesse McCann. He'd grown up in the worst of circumstances. He should have fallen into all the cracks that would have tempted him along the way. Drugs. Violence. Hate. Self-loathing. But he had avoided them all and come out with a kind heart, a heart that could love openly. His friend. His neighbors. Her.

She was a smart woman. She'd graduated at the top of her class. She'd gotten everything she could have wanted. But she knew when something better came along. One thing. She'd thought it was fortune and position. It turned out she was a woman like the rest of them. Love. She wanted love.

"I love you."

"What?" Jesse sat up beside her. "I tell you that my parents are a convicted killer and a drug-addled prostitute and that's when you tell me you love me."

She could do him one better. "I want to marry you."

His whole face softened, and he gave her words back to her. "Baby, you be sure."

She was sure. But she was sure of something else, too. "I love Cade, too."

He pulled her close, bringing her back down to the bed. "I want us all to be together. I love Cade like a brother."

She grinned. "Most brothers don't share women."

"They do in Bliss." He got serious. "I want to stay here. But if you need to go to New York, I figure my home is with you now. You have to know that even if Cade doesn't come back, I'll go where you go."

"I got a letter from the firm today." It had come by the hand of a deeply confused FedEx guy who had knocked on every door in the valley before getting to her. Apparently, overnight services didn't make it to Bliss County often. It had been a formal invitation to come back, with a letter from the head partner himself.

Jesse seemed to hold his breath. She knew she should tell him she'd already decided that the firm could fuck itself, but hey, she was difficult. "What'd they say?"

"They want me back. They're willing to reinstate me at a fifteen percent raise to go along with my promotion to junior partner." It was an amazing offer. Everything she could have dreamed of. She didn't have to apologize. She could walk back into Manhattan and reclaim an even better life than she'd left behind.

Jesse's face went blank. "All right. I think we should talk about this. I don't know if that firm is the best place for you. When do you have to give them an answer?"

"When Hell freezes over, but I'm not going to tell them that yet."

"Gemma?"

It was past time to put her brain to work. "It's too easy. They have zero reason to bring me back. Well, not any I've figured out yet. I've been going over and over this ever since I got that damn letter this morning."

"Well, they're bringing you back because you're good."

She didn't buy that. "You obviously haven't met many lawyers. At my level, we're all good. Quite frankly, there's always another up-and-coming genius, and most are way less difficult to deal with than me. It can't be that they're worried I'll sue. There's extensive evidence out there that I had a breakdown. I could fight the firing, but it would be a long, expensive suit, and I would probably lose. So that's not the reason."

"Then why?"

"I don't know. I checked my computer. I don't have anything suspicious on there." She sighed. "I thought for a minute that maybe I walked out with important data or something. But they confiscated my work laptop, and my personal one is fairly boring. Unless they want me for my mega scores on solitaire."

It was a conundrum.

"Didn't Patrick say they sent him?"

Yep. And that was another piece that didn't fit. "I called the firm and asked for him. I thought maybe he'd gone back and he'd just been dodging Nate. I used Mom's cell. It has a Chicago area code. I guess I was trying to trick him. I was told he's on a case right now in Buffalo. They either don't know he came here or they're lying about where he is."

None of it made a lick of sense. And she'd had another note in the mail, too. One that pointed out an entirely new problem. "And you might rethink the whole marrying me thing. My health insurance doesn't kick in until next month and the hospital bill for my stubborn fit is in the five figures."

"Hey, don't you worry about that. We'll make a payment plan. I might not make a ton of money, but I have some saved up. We'll take care of the hospital."

A sweet thought. He acted like they were a team. Like her parents had behaved. It was a scary thought. She'd given up on the whole "happily ever after" thing when her dad had died, but now she understood what her mom had been trying to tell her all along. What her dad had tried to tell her at the end. It would be better to have that ache than to be whole and empty. That ache her mother felt meant she'd been loved.

She sat back, her whole soul going soft. She would fight for Cade because this was a meaningful fight. And she should look into Calvin Township. They had craptastic lawyers who couldn't find their way out of a paper bag if it was open and there was a big arrow painted on the side. She couldn't take the case, but she could ask around and see if there was any way to help the town.

Her mind started working in an odd loop, making connections. The heart. The letters. The pictures. So little time in Bliss and so much debt already accrued. The offer. The easy way was often the worst way. The pictures. She needed to figure out a way to get those pictures Nell had shown her out of her head. Now that she was settling down, she couldn't help but think about those kids. There was only so much time anyone had. The idea of those kids having less time than they should have was unsettling. Sure the EPA had cleared the company, but the EPA wasn't infallible.

Jesse kissed her neck, working his way down to her breasts.

She was drugged by sex. That was why she wouldn't even think about her old job at Giles and Knoxbury. She'd turned into a raging sex maniac. If they had wanted her back six months ago, she would have run back to New York, but no, they waited until she'd gotten to Bliss and found a going-nowhere job where a crazy lady brought her muffins and guilt pictures and hot mechanics fixed all her girl parts up so she hummed just right. The firm had terrible timing. Not even Patrick's lame-ass attempt to kill her would get her out of Bliss now.

Timing. Location. Pictures. *Fuck.*

She sat up. "They didn't give a shit about me until I came to Bliss."

Jesse's eyes were glazed with heat. "What are you talking about?"

Her mind was a whirling dervish. She hoped she was making a lick of sense. "Think about it. Patrick didn't call me until I was here. The firm didn't care if I lived or died until I came to Bliss. Bliss, a town an hour away from the site of their biggest case right now."

"How do they know where you are?"

She'd been dumb. "I had one friend at the firm. And I wouldn't even call her a friend, per se. More like a work buddy I had lunch with every now and then. I was surprised when she called a couple of months back and asked how I was doing. I contacted her right before I came to Bliss to see if I could get her to sign the paperwork to close my storage shed. She asked where I was going, and I told her Colorado. She had to have been keeping tabs on me."

"What do you know that you shouldn't?" His eyes were sharp now, and he reached for his jeans.

"I don't know. I have to figure out what I know that they don't want me to know. It was a coincidence that I'm here at all. Mom wanted to come home." She sighed. "How well known is Nell Flanders as an activist?"

Jesse chuckled. "Uhm, I think she's very vocal and has a website called Activists Unite that connects that whole world. And she gives away recipes."

"So I come to Bliss and suddenly I'm connected with an activist who wants to publicize the Calvin Township case." She got out of bed. The stuff with Cade would have to wait. "I need to talk to Nell."

Jesse frowned. "Damn it. I'm going to have to eat tofu. I hate tofu."

* * * *

Cade took a long pull off his beer, wondering what the hell he was doing here. He'd ordered the beer an hour before and hadn't even gotten through half a bottle. He couldn't even drink properly anymore.

He shrank back in his booth as the door opened and someone he actually knew walked through. Michael Novack strode in, his dark eyes looking around the bar. He was dressed in jeans that had seen better days, a black T-shirt, and a beat-up leather jacket. He looked dangerous and mean.

Crap, he hoped Novack wasn't looking for Lucy. She took a shift here sometimes when the tourists were light at Trio. What Lucy saw in the man, he had no idea. But her eyes got soft when he walked in the room. Lucy seemed to be a little masochistic.

And so was fucking Cade Sinclair. He was an idiot and a masochist. He'd had every chance to get his shit and run. He'd walked straight out of the shop and gone to Gemma's with one thought. He would get his duffel and be gone before she could turn those blue eyes on him again.

And the first thing he'd seen was the enormous bill from the hospital.

And he'd come here because the dude who ran Hell on Wheels had always wanted to buy his Camaro.

He had the money to pay Gemma's bill. He did not have his freaking duffel bag.

What was he going to do? Walk in and hope that Gemma thought he was a fucking hero for selling his car? It had been an easy decision to make. He loved his dad, but his dad was gone. Gemma was here.

He loved Gemma.

He was stuck. He knew he didn't deserve her, and he still couldn't walk away.

A huge figure loomed above him, shutting out most of the light from the bar. Sawyer stood roughly six foot six, with the shoulders of a linebacker and a perpetual frown that would send most men running for their lives. His long black hair hit just below the shoulders, and despite the fact he worked the bar, he didn't pull it back or put it in a hair net. He let those locks flow and didn't bother with a shirt. His massive arms were on display along with a sleeve of some scary ass tats that ran from his right hand all the way up to the base of his neck. He wore only a leather vest and jeans.

Nell Flanders had described him as trapped between two worlds—his Native American culture and the modern world. Cade kind of thought he was trapped between asshole and violent asshole.

"You going to make love to that beer now that you've played with it?" Even over the loud rock and roll thumping through the dive, Cade could hear Sawyer's low growl.

And if Sawyer wanted to mess with him, he might take that beating. It wasn't like he had anything better to do. "You going to try to throw me out now that you have what you want?"

Sawyer snorted and slid his body into the other side of the booth. "You sound like a whiny asshole. And I didn't exactly get what I wanted. I wanted to pay five thousand less."

"I'm not running a fucking charity, Sawyer. You're getting a damn good deal as it is. That car is in mint condition."

"Why now?" Sawyer leaned over, sliding a bag to Cade's side of the table.

Cade stared down at it. "I need the money. It's only a car."

"That's not what I've heard."

Cade opened that bag, his eyes going wide. "Cash? You're giving me thirty thousand in cash?"

Sawyer's frown deepened. "Well, you won't keep it for long if you keep shouting out that you have it. Do you want to get knifed on the way out of here?"

Cade looked around the bar. Yeah, it was the kind of place where a knifing would be considered an everyday activity. The crowd was rough, the owner even rougher. "It's not like I can't handle myself."

Sawyer stared.

"I know how to handle myself."

"Yeah, well, you'll excuse me if I escort you to your bike. I don't need more trouble with the sheriff. He doesn't care that the place is under new management. He only cares that his wife almost died here."

"Died?"

Sawyer shrugged. "She wouldn't have been the first. Won't be the last. But I try to keep the murders outside. Less cleanup that way."

Yeah, he needed to find Lucy a new second job. "If Lucy gets raped or killed, I swear you're going to answer to me."

Sawyer's eyes got infinitely dark. "Yeah, you give a shit about Luce. I bet you do. You think I haven't seen a hundred of your kind come and go? You give a shit about her until something better comes along. I grew up with Luce. She's like my sister. She was supposed to marry my brother."

Lucy had been engaged? "What happened?"

A bitter smile crossed Sawyer's face. "What happens to most of my people. Prison. Got two brothers. One's in prison. The other's serving time in the US Army. I don't see the difference, if you ask me. Someone had to keep our mother going, so I came home. And if you ever accuse me of hurting Luce again, I'll break both your arms, and then we'll see how well you work."

"I'm trying to look out for her," Cade argued.

"Yeah, I see how you look out for her." Sawyer stared at him. "You looked out for her right up to the moment that rich blonde walked into town."

It was Cade's turn to laugh. "I should tell you to fuck off, but it's obvious you care about Lucy, and she's my friend. My friend. There's never been anything between us. And Gemma is broke. Who do you think this money is for? I'm not after her cash, dude." Her breasts.

Her hips. That sassy mouth that spit bile half the time and sucked his dick the other half. Those were the things he was after.

Sawyer sat back. "She said she was crazy about some new guy in town. She wouldn't give me his name. I kind of thought it was you or the other one."

"Nope. Me and Jesse are just friends with her. Ty from the ski lodge likes the hell out of her, but she won't give him the time of day."

A shudder went through the big guy. "Good. He's a walking venereal disease. Besides, we all grew up together. When you have that long a history, getting out of the friend zone can be impossible. So who is it? I don't know many new people in town."

"Lucy likes to go for broke." He gestured to where Novack was sitting in a booth across the bar. "You know who Michael Novack is?"

Sawyer's skin flushed, and his jaw became a rigid line as he looked at the other man. "I know him."

"So you can start worrying about him and stop threatening me."

Sawyer's fingers drummed along the surface of the table. "Good to know. Look, man, I don't get into town much. How about we help each other out? You tell me if Luce is getting into trouble, and I'll let you know some information about that tourist you and Jesse have been looking for."

A cold chill swept through Cade. "If you know something, you better tell me right fucking now."

"You love this girl?"

"Yeah." It wasn't like his love meant much, but his heart was hers and it would be until the day he died.

Sawyer looked like he didn't want to go into it, but he finally sighed and gave it up. "Fine. We had an asshole tourist with a New York accent walk into the bar yesterday."

Now Cade was interested. They'd scoured the local motels for Patrick. He never would have thought the urbane dickhead would dare to enter a place like Hell on Wheels. "About six foot, skinny dude?"

"He was wearing a fucking tie."

Sounded like their guy. "Yeah, that's him. Did you talk to him?"

"At length. He was asking around. Tell me something, what did

253

he do?"

His blood started to boil every time he thought about what had happened in the diner. "He tried to kill my woman."

Sawyer sat back. "Fuck. That makes sense. He came in late last night talking about needing to find a guy. I thought he was asking about drugs."

"What exactly did he say?"

"Well, first he wanted to know what kind of wine I had," Sawyer explained. "Fucking tourists. Red and white. He complained about the lack of a Sauvignon Blanc and then he proceeded to ask where a guy could hook up. I told him if he was looking for a buddy for the night, he should go to Trio."

Yeah, Sawyer didn't like the sheriff, and that seemed to include his partner, Zane. "Just get to the point, man."

"Fine. He asked about everything in a real roundabout way. It was obnoxious. I kept thinking if you want drugs, say it so I can punch you in the face and kick you out of my bar. I hate dealing with addicts."

Cade could do one better. "He's a lawyer."

Sawyer made a gagging sound. "Fucking lawyers. He walked around the bar talking to the regulars. I overheard him asking where he could find a man who needed a little cash. Again, a suit walks in, I start thinking drugs. He said he needed it real bad. So, I'm thinking well-dressed junkie."

Cade wanted to throw up because he knew what Patrick was looking for and it wasn't drugs. "He's looking to hire a hit man."

Sawyer nodded slowly. "Yeah. I get that now. He's serious about killing your woman. And he talked to one man in particular for a real long time. They sat in a booth together for over an hour. It was why I was upset about Luce being involved with him. I thought he was making a drug deal. It wouldn't be the first time former law enforcement went bad. Now I know it's darker than that."

Cade picked up the cash and shoved it Sawyer's way. "Put that back in the safe. I'm going to take care of a problem."

Novack thought he could make some quick cash by killing Gemma? Cade was going to beat that notion out of him. He would lay fists into the asshole until Novack told him exactly where Patrick was.

"Hey, think about this for a second." Sawyer tried to stop him.

He strode across the bar, his boots thudding on the floor. Out of the corner of his eye, he heard the door open. More witnesses to the crime he was about to commit. Novack's head came up, looking at the entrance. He muttered something Cade couldn't hear. Now the jerk was talking to himself.

That freaking tic above his eye started up again. His blood threatened to boil over. "Hey, Novack. You got something to say to me?"

There was a loud bang as the door closed, but Cade's eyes were on Novack.

Novack scowled as he looked up. "You motherfucker." He turned his face down. "He's in the wind. Asshole decided to have a conversation at the least opportune time."

A big body rushed past Cade, slamming out the front door. Cam?

Nate Wright walked up, pulling his hat off. "Goddamn it. Why didn't we see him?"

Novack slid off his seat. "He was hiding. People do that when they're committing crimes. Or hiring people to commit worse crimes."

What the hell was going on? He pointed to Novack. "Sheriff, I think Patrick Welch hired this jerk to kill Gemma."

The sheriff's eyes narrowed in irritation, but they weren't focused on Novack. "I know. Why do you think he's wired right fucking now?"

Sawyer walked up behind Cade. "What the hell is going on, Sheriff? I don't know if you recall, but this is unincorporated territory. Don't you think you owe me the courtesy of informing me you're working in my business?"

"Oh, yeah, because you would be cooperative." The sheriff squared off with the bar owner. "And you know this is perfectly well within my jurisdiction. When you stop catering to criminals, I'll let you in on my operations. This isn't your fucking kingdom."

"Damn straight it is. You watch me, Wright," Sawyer practically snarled.

"No. You watch me. You think I will ever forgive you for what happened to Logan here? Never. I'll shut this place down if it's the last thing I do." Wright got up in the big guy's face.

Sawyer stared down at him, rage plain on his features. "That is between me and Logan. You get the fuck out of my bar. I see you working in here and I'll sue the whole damn town."

Cam ran back in, shaking his head. "He's gone, Nate. I'm sorry."

"Damn it." Wright shot Cade a nasty look. "You, come on. Mike, let's get out of here. Let's hope he calls again. Damn it."

"I better not see any of you in my bar again." Sawyer shoved the bag toward Cade, who took it. "Except you. I want that car and the pink slip here tomorrow, and it better be in perfect shape. You know what the sheriff says about me. I don't know why Welch came after Novack when everyone knows I'm a killer."

Cade looked back at Sawyer, who shouted at someone on his staff. Nate pulled him along. "What the hell is going on?"

"You just fucked everything up."

Yeah, he got that a lot.

Chapter Eighteen

Henry Flanders opened the door with a smile that faded when he caught sight of Gemma. "Miss Wells, this is a surprise." He shut the door behind him a little as though trying to keep whoever was inside from seeing out. "If Nell has done something to upset you, you should get over it. I'll make sure she doesn't bother you, but I'm not letting you hurt her feelings."

God, she really did have a crappy reputation. "I'm not going to hurt her feelings."

"She came here to talk to Nell about a case. She's not some monster." Jesse stepped in front of her.

Nice. The Neanderthal hormones were taking over.

Henry frowned her way. "I've read up on Gemma and her former career. I know the kinds of cases she handled. I know women like my wife tend to annoy lawyers because she tries to keep them honest."

She rolled her eyes because she could feel Jesse getting brutally pissed off. If she was going to keep Henry's head in one piece, she needed to bring in the big guns. "Nell! Nell, I'm trying to join the good fight and Henry's standing in the way!"

Henry Flanders's face went tight as the door opened and Nell smiled.

"Gemma! How lovely. Please come in. Henry, why didn't you tell me we had guests?" Nell's blouse wasn't buttoned properly. She'd missed one right in the middle, and Gemma caught the hint of a scarlet red bra.

Not what she would have thought Nell would wear because that was shiny material. No cotton on that thing. That bra wasn't humanely sourced—or at least that wasn't its purpose. That bra was meant for nasty sex.

Henry wasn't trying to protect his wife's feelings. He was trying to keep from getting cock blocked. Unfortunately, she couldn't worry about that this second. She needed answers, and Nell was the only one who might be able to help.

Jesse frowned, obviously figuring out what Gemma had. "Sorry, man."

"Yeah." Henry's frown disappeared, and an evil glint appeared in his usually peaceful eyes. "It's okay. Come on in. Nell made some lovely tofu burgers. I will make sure you get one while your woman is talking to mine."

Gemma nearly laughed at the look on Jesse's face. The meaning was clear. Jesse would be enjoying fake meat for as long as she kept Nell talking. Well, unfortunately, Jesse was going to have to take one for the team.

Henry led Jesse away as Nell led Gemma into the house. Nell's house was everything Gemma would have thought it would be. The roof was covered in solar panels and there was a small windmill in the yard. Inside, the cabin was neat and sported a huge wall of bookshelves and all kinds of activist stuff. She had three working petitions laid out, and a bunch of stickers and T-shirts for her upcoming protest at Tremon Industries.

"It's nice to see you, Gemma," Nell said. "How can I help you? I was glad to hear you're okay. What a terrible thing to be allergic to. Strawberries are a gift."

"They're certainly a gift to the hospital," she replied. "The bill they sent me should keep them going for a while."

Nell's eyes flared, righteous indignation making them sparkle. "Health care is something I'm working on. I will protest that hospital.

You did not ask to be allergic to strawberries. Health care is a right, not a privilege."

If she didn't take control, Nell might start singing again.

"How many letters have you written to Tremon?" Gemma looked around the pretty living room. No TV. Was that the handle of a flogger poking out of the very sweet-looking flowered couch?

Nell used her ankle to shove the item in question out of the way. She didn't even blush. "Probably a hundred or so. Please sit down."

Yep, she caught sight of a ball gag. Nell was a freak. It made her way more comfortable. Nell always seemed perfect. But then honestly, why would getting freaky in the sack make her less perfect? It merely meant they had something in common. She took a seat across from Nell. "Have you ever written a firm called Giles and Knoxbury?"

"Oh, yes. Many times. I've been writing them for years, asking them to rethink their corporate politics. I've asked them to review many cases and rethink taking them. It's a horrible firm. It's number five on my hit list. I have several hit lists."

Gemma bet she did. Nell Flanders looked to be in her thirties, but there was a perpetual air of innocence about her that made her seem younger when she talked. "So they know who you are."

"Absolutely," Nell agreed. "I've actually protested against the firm before in person. They were defending a corporation against a group of farmers who had their organic farms bought out under false pretenses. They were supposed to continue organic practices, but the company immediately started using pesticides."

Recognition sparked through her brain. "Holy shit. You're the one who sent four hundred pounds of rotten lettuce to Mr. Giles. That was legendary at the firm." No one who worked there could possibly forget that day. Or that smell.

Nell smiled. "I was trying to make a point."

"So they definitely know you. Tell me what you think is wrong about the Calvin Township case. And do you have any more of those pictures?" She was looking for anything to jog her memory.

Nell retrieved the photos and handed them over. "They're mostly family photos. I use them to humanize the victims. It's too easy to see them as names and dates on a report. It's harder when you see that they're actual people."

She had to agree. Nell was smart when it came to running her particular business. And apparently she had quite a reputation. It struck Gemma that she and Nell weren't so unlike. They were both chasing something. Gemma had chased her career, and Nell chased justice. At least at the end of the day, Nell would have done something good.

Maybe it was time to chase something bigger, something more, something that if she caught it might do the world some good.

She looked over the photos as Nell explained how she became involved with the case. So many families hurt. The children were the hardest. They should have a lifetime of health, but they'd been unlucky. They'd been born in a place where the water they drank made them sick.

Except it didn't according to the EPA.

"What did the outside sources say about the water supply?" Gemma asked as she glanced at a photo that had been taken at some kind of party. The people in the picture were all milling around with drinks in hand, neon signs flashing behind their heads.

"We were only able to pay for one report. Our testing found the reservoir was plainly unfit for human consumption. I have a copy. Unfortunately, your firm has five separate reports that claim it's fine. It's going to be a hard sell. Juries don't like scientific data as it is."

She was right. Juries tended to sleep through lengthy scientific testimony. Getting an expert who could tell them in simple terms whether or not the water was fine would be the key. She kept flipping through party pictures. The man in the shot smiled gamely, as though he didn't particularly want to celebrate his birthday but wouldn't disappoint anyone.

Everyone in the picture looked happy. Even the men in the background.

She caught on the familiar sight of a man with well-cut blond hair and a perfect suit. Everyone else was wearing some form of Western wear, but not Patrick Welch. No. He would wear his Italian custom-cut suits even in the middle of the sticks.

Gemma turned the photo around. She pointed to the man sitting across from Patrick, though she suspected she knew the answer.

"Who is this?"

It would have been easy to pay four of the experts. When Giles and Knoxbury took on a case like this, they hired at least four experts to run tests. But in this case, they were dependent on the EPA's report as well. The EPA should have been the untouchable voice of truth.

Nell studied the photo. "Oh, that's the man from the EPA. Kevin something. Michaels. I have it all written down. I protested him, too. I think his report was lazy."

It all fell into place. "His report was paid for by Giles and Knoxbury. Or rather the firm negotiated the bribe for Tremon. See that jerk-faced, son-of-a-bitch asswipe next to him? That's Patrick Welch."

Nell went stark white for a moment and then jumped up, her fist pumping in the air. "I knew it! Yes." She stopped, her dance ceasing in an instant. "Are you sure?"

Gemma shrugged. "Nope, but why else would he be trying to kill me?"

And it wasn't merely Patrick. If she'd gone back to New York, she would have been brought into the fold, maybe, but she kind of thought she would have met a convenient mugger one night going home. He would have been paid by Giles and Knoxbury, too. And then the difficult Ice Princess wouldn't be a threat anymore.

Nell frowned. "He tried to kill you?"

"Yep. With strawberries."

"I don't like that man. Strawberries are a gift. They shouldn't be perverted."

Gemma kind of thought they were more like her curse, but she didn't mention that to Nell. "You understand what this means? All we have to do is prove the EPA was bribed, get new, clean reports on Calvin Township, and you'll win your case."

"How do we prove it?"

Gemma already had a plan. "We follow the cash, baby. The cash always leads the way."

And it would lead the way this time. She just knew it.

Henry emerged, a grin on his face as Jesse followed him. "Jesse and I have had a talk and a snack. How are you girls doing?" He glanced down at the pictures. "Calvin Township? Gemma, were you serious about the whole 'good fight' thing?"

At least she could still surprise someone. "Yes. Although I have to admit, I'm also happy I get to send my ex-fiancé to prison. My old firm and Tremon Industries bribed public officials to fake the reports on Calvin Township. I can't exactly prove it, yet."

"You need to follow the money." Henry's eyes suddenly became deeply shrewd. "Start with the EPA guy's accounts. We can even tap his credit cards. See if he's paid anything off recently. He'll almost certainly have been paid from a front account."

How the hell did sweet Henry Flanders know about front accounts? It was why the corporate structure was important. Accounting practices in large corporations could be labyrinthine, with smaller companies paying into larger ones, and even tinier ones taking the losses so the main front looked good to shareholders.

Nell smiled up at her handsome husband, hugging him. "He's incredibly smart."

Yes, he was. "You ever hacked a system, Henry?"

He laughed, an "aw shucks" kind of sound. "Of course not. I barely know my way around a computer. You need to talk to Cameron. I'm sure he'll be glad to help."

Nell practically gleamed up at him. Henry Flanders was roughly forty years old, but there wasn't a hint of middle-aged paunch to him. He was good looking, with a lean strength and an almost Superman-like handsomeness behind his glasses. And Gemma thought he was full of shit. If he didn't know how to work a computer, she would eat one of those tofu burgers that seemed to have turned Jesse a nice shade of green. She'd read jurors before, and she'd put Henry Flanders firmly in the no category. He would be a harsh judge.

But he was on her side. And she was kind of glad. She wasn't sure she wanted to be on Henry's bad side.

"Can you call Nate for me?" She reached for Jesse's hand. He'd had a rough night, what with all the fake meat. "We have to go to Hell on Wheels and haul Cade home."

Henry nodded. "Sure thing. We'll explain it to him and give Cam the name to start looking for. You be careful at that bar. It can be a dangerous place."

"I'll keep her safe." Jesse wrapped an arm around her.

They walked out the door and into the star-filled night. There was a brisk chill to the air, and she wondered what this place would look like blanketed in snow. She would find out. She was going to spend her life here. Now she realized her mother had come here for more than one reason. Beyond wanting to come home, she'd come here for Gemma, to reinforce the lesson her father had tried to teach her as he lay dying. Live. She'd existed before, but now far from everything she'd thought she wanted, she was finally alive.

"Did you get what you need?" Jesse asked.

He and Cade were what she needed, but she answered his question. She settled her bag on her shoulder, crossing it over her chest to rest on the opposite hip. "Oh, yes. And more. With a little help from my friends, I can put Patrick in jail." Where they wouldn't let him wear suits. Orange. He would look good in orange. It really was his color. And he could be someone's bitch in jail. "All I need is Cam's magic fingers. If he can get into the EPA guy's bank account, we should be able to trace the money. And I have a whole corporate map of Tremon. I put it together. I know that company down to the last piddly ass storefront. I can find the money trail."

Jesse gave her a grin. "This is the happiest I've seen you."

She frowned back. "Not true. I seem to remember being much happier that I'm getting married. I am getting married, right?"

He leaned over and kissed her. "Damn straight you are. Now, tell me why you're happy about this. Besides the fact that you get to dream about Patrick and his new prison friends."

He was going to make her admit it. Damn it. "I get to help those kids."

"And that's what my Gemma can be." He kissed her again, slower this time. "I love you." He stopped, his eyes squinting in the darkness. "What's wrong with my bike?"

She was about to give him his words back when there was a muffled sound and Jesse staggered. He touched his stomach, and even in the moonlight, Gemma could see blood.

"Don't scream or I'll shoot him again." Patrick stood in the middle of the dirt road, his hand shaking. "I didn't want to do this. Damn it. I didn't want to do this at all."

* * * *

Jesse fell to his knees, his strength fading.

"Jesse!" Gemma tried to get her arms around him. "Oh, god. Don't do this. Don't you die."

She put a hand on his abdomen as though she could stop the blood flowing out of his body.

Fuck, getting shot hurt. "Get out of here."

Her tears sparkled in the moonlight. "I won't leave you."

"Get up, Gemma." Patrick. Patrick was here and he'd shot him. Patrick was going to kill Gemma. "Unless you want me to finish off your boyfriend, you're going to get up and get me in that house. You found the evidence, didn't you? That idiot activist has it."

"Don't stay." Jesse whispered. "He'll still kill me. Run, darlin'."

She stared down at him, leaned over and kissed his forehead. "Can't."

"Gemma, if I see your hand move an inch toward that wretched bag of yours, I'll put one through his brain. You don't think I remember you carry a gun?" Patrick moved closer but was still out of reach.

"The sheriff took my gun," she admitted. "He hasn't given it back to me, yet. Nate Wright and I are going to have such a talk about that. The best I can give you is pepper spray."

If he came closer, Jesse might be able to get his damn limbs to function long enough to pull the fucker down to the ground. Gemma could run.

"Get up now, Gemma," Patrick ordered, his voice a bit shaky.

Jesse felt her kiss him one more time before getting to her feet.

"You did it. You bribed that official." Gemma wasn't shaky at all. There was a ton of judgement in her tone.

Patrick didn't move. "Of course I did. They were never going to promote you. I always knew you couldn't handle getting your hands dirty. This is business, and business is always war. I didn't like this part either, but I can't get out and I'm sure as hell not going to let some backwoods idiot's morality cost me my life."

Gemma's head swung toward the house. "They're nice people."

"Nice? God, what's happened to you?" He looked down at Jesse, a sneer on his face. "This guy? Or the other idiot you're shacked up with? What? You get a little cock and go soft?"

"I had a little cock, Patrick, or did you forget the years I spent with you?"

That was his girl. Sass to the end. He watched Patrick. Just a bit closer. His hands twitched.

Patrick took a step toward her. "Yeah, well, you were an ice princess, sweetheart. You know what happens to cocks in the cold."

Jesse grabbed his ankle and pulled with all his might, adrenaline rushing through his system. "Run, Gemma. Now!"

The gun went off again. Jesse felt something burn against his left side. He reached out to get the gun. It had fallen. Metal glinted in the moonlight, but all the air left his body as Patrick planted a knee in his gut. Agony filled his world. Unimaginable pain overtook him. He grunted, trying to breathe.

He heard a knocking and a shout and then Patrick was on his feet again, gun in hand.

"Catch me if you can, asshole. Let's see if you can get me before I get to the sheriff." Gemma's voice trailed off.

Patrick took off after her.

He tried to get up, to stop Patrick from following her. His limbs wouldn't move. Useless. He was so useless.

It was only a second later that Henry Flanders's face came into view. "How many?"

His voice was a flat monotone, not the light and sympathetic tone Henry almost always used. And the look in his eyes. Henry's eyes, always so filled with amusement at the world around him, those eyes were flat obsidian stones. It was like someone else had taken over Henry's body. Someone dangerous.

"I think I got hit twice." His gut was on fire. "You have to help Gemma. Call the sheriff. Call Cade."

Cade would come. No matter how broken they seemed, Cade would come to help them.

"How many guns?" Henry corrected.

His head was starting to spin, but he concentrated. "Just one."

"Excellent." Henry looked over Jesse. "Nell's coming. She'll take care of you. Do not allow her to come after me. I don't want her to see this."

Henry was gone in a flash, but Nell's soft hands were suddenly smoothing back his hair. "I called 911. They'll be here soon. I am sorry, but I have to cover this." A wave of nausea hit as she pressed a hand towel to his wound. "It's organic cotton. And it's clean. Oh, Jesse, please hold on. Where did my husband go?"

He reached for her hand. Whatever Henry was going to do would be rough. He'd seen it in Henry's eyes. And he was also pretty sure Henry wouldn't do it if his wife was around. He had to keep Nell with him. "Please. Don't leave."

Her eyes turned round and sympathetic. "Of course not."

And then it didn't matter because the world began to narrow. He looked to the sky. The stars were endless.

* * * *

Cade practically tackled the sheriff in the parking lot.

"We can talk about this debacle back at the station house, Sinclair. Go and get Gemma and Jesse and we can all talk about how fucked up this whole situation is." Wright stared back at the neon lit bar, an angry look on his face.

Cade would love to know what had happened to make those two men hate each other, but he had other problems. "I want the story now. I want to know why no one bothered to mention this sting operation of yours. How long have you known where Patrick is?"

Nate sighed. "He talked to Mike last night. We thought this would be the best way to gather the evidence we need against him. I was certain he wouldn't make a move on Gemma. Rafe trailed her all day until she left with Jesse. She's safe in the valley. Everyone's watching out for her."

Novack tugged at his shirt, pulling out a small microphone that had been taped to his body. "Won't need this now."

"He might call back, try to arrange another meeting," Cam said.

"Doubt it. Even if he didn't see the law here, he got spooked easily. And he said he had a deadline. She had to be dead by tomorrow morning, or he would be the one in a casket. He was very specific. She had to be dead by dawn or I wouldn't get my money."

Novack ran a hand through his longish hair. "I'm done with this shit. I'm not coming off my mountain again."

Fuck, he had to get to Gemma. He would tell Jesse what was going on, and then they wouldn't take no for an answer. They would get the hell out of here and hide until this whole thing was sorted through. His fear didn't matter now. He was way more afraid of a world without Gemma in it than he was of anything else.

Cam cursed as he pulled out his cell phone. "Rafe says Jesse and Gemma left a half an hour ago on Jesse's bike. They were headed to Nell and Henry's. Do you want him to go up there with them?"

Nate scrubbed a hand across his head. "Damn it. No. I'll go do it. Maybe someone will off this little shit and then we won't have to worry about him." He sighed. "Then we can worry about whoever killed him."

It was bigger than Patrick. Cade's mind spun with the implications. Gemma was involved in something big, and she didn't even know it. "Where do Nell and Henry live?"

Jesse had been out to their place to help Henry fix their biodiesel car, but Cade hadn't been.

"I'll take you there." Nate started for the parking lot. He'd left the county Bronco behind. Cade recognized Zane's black truck.

Cade went along because he didn't have a place to stash thirty grand on his bike, and the sooner he got to Gemma, the better.

He slipped into the backseat as the radio squawked.

"Sheriff? We have a 911 call from Nell Flanders. She says someone's shooting outside her cabin, and we already have one down. I've dispatched the Creede boys out there, but if you're still at Hell on Wheels, you can get there faster." Laura's voice came over the radio. "Rafe's on his way, too. I've called for Caleb and Ty, so expect a bunch of sirens coming your way."

Nate already had the truck in gear and the gravel was flying.

"Who's down?" Cade asked from the backseat. *Don't be Gemma. Don't be Gemma.*

Nate handed the handset to Cam as he flew down the mountain.

"Laura, do we have an ID on the victim?" Cam's voice was perfectly steady.

Laura paused, sending Cade's stomach into knots. "Jesse

McCann. No word on his status. The situation is fluid and dangerous. Use all caution. I'll update you if I can."

Status. No word on Jesse's status. They didn't know if he was dead or alive. The situation was ongoing. Patrick had made his move, and Jesse had paid the price.

Guilt swamped him. He'd caused this. Like he'd caused everything else. Patrick would have been arrested if he hadn't fucked everything up. He'd made Patrick desperate. He was the reason Patrick had walked straight out the bar and gone to find Gemma.

"I should have told you," Nate said, his words tight. "If I'd been in your same position, I would have gone after the bastard, too."

Cam talked as he checked the clip on his gun. "We got the message from Mike this morning. He didn't give us a lot of time to make reasonable decisions. He basically walked into the station house and invited us along."

"As fucked up as Mike is, we should be glad he didn't kill the guy himself," Nate said.

"Can you go faster?" Cade asked, keeping his voice even when all he wanted to do was scream.

"Not if I don't want us to die," Nate replied. "When we get there, you stay in the car, Cade. You let us do our jobs."

Cade kept his mouth shut because he couldn't promise that. If he could save Gemma, he would. If he could save Jesse, he would. His love. His brother. And if he couldn't save them, then nothing mattered anyway.

Chapter Nineteen

Gemma clutched her purse as she ran, praying the crazed knocking she'd done would bring the Flanderses out to help Jesse. If they hadn't gone back to their kink fest. When she'd realized he was going to kill Jesse, she'd knocked on the door and then taken off, certain Patrick would follow. The one thing she couldn't do was let Patrick walk into their small cottage and slaughter everyone there because he wanted to move up in the firm.

Jesse. She couldn't even think of him lying there. She couldn't contemplate the fact that Patrick might have spared a second or two to finish him off. If that second bullet hadn't done the trick.

She ran, her sandals thunking against the ground. She could hear the river. The Rio Grande was deep here. It also cut her off. The road was to her right, but Patrick would be able to see her there. She was safer in the cluster of white trunked aspens and thick pines.

"Gemma? Gemma, we can work something out."

Yeah, like she was falling for that one. She caught her breath behind the trunk of a tree. As quietly as she could, she unzipped her purse, silently cursing Nate for keeping her gun after he'd found out she'd never actually taken a gun safety class. She had a place in

Alexei Markov's next workshop. Apparently being a mob hit man had also made him an expert in gun safety. She wasn't allowed to carry concealed until Alexei signed off on it. Nate had offered her a shotgun, and she'd flipped him off.

Damn, she wished she had that shotgun now.

"Come on, sweetheart. You know you don't belong here. These people are nut-job idealists. They don't understand how the world works." He was using his courtroom voice on her, laying the charm on thick.

She used to think he sounded smart and trustworthy, but now she saw him for what he'd been all along. A slimy slickster who wouldn't know the truth if it bit him in the ass. Jesse's gruff but honest rumble was music to her ears. Cade and his frustrating Atlas complex was so much more lovable and true than Patrick. She took a deep breath as her hand sank into her voluminous bag. Where was it?

Lipstick. Snack-sized bag of almonds. Notepad. God, why did she have all that crap? How many pens did one woman need?

"Do you know who owns Tremon? On paper it's Martin Tremon. But who is his biggest stockholder?"

Gemma stopped. Senator Allen Cameron was the largest stockholder. Senator Allen Cameron, who was about to run for president on a green energy platform. He was ahead in all the polls. He was the perfect blend of politician and forward-thinking businessman. She'd heard some interesting rumors about the senator's personal life. There were rumors of one son who didn't speak to him and another who he'd swept under the rug long before, but nothing that would cost him the election.

A company he was heavily invested in polluting a town to the point that children were dying—oh, yeah, that would do it. Cameron hid his investments under cloaks of anonymous corporations, but someone could untangle that web and likely would. If he wanted to win the election, Calvin Township had to be clean.

Patrick had to kill her. He had to. Then he had to kill Nell and Henry and anyone else who might know something about this.

"Sweetheart, you know he's going to win the election. And I'm going to end up working at the White House. You can come with me."

In a coffin.

"You know we can get out of this," Patrick continued. "All you have to do is tell that idiot sheriff about how your boyfriend out there was screwing around with the dipshit activist and how her husband killed them both and then turned the gun on himself."

So that was supposed to be his out. Nate would never believe it. But Patrick was arrogant. He thought he could get away with anything. Air horn. Why was she carrying that stupid air horn that, according to everyone, would just piss off the bears?

And there it was. Finally. Pepper spray. She flipped the safety button off and waited.

"We could rule Washington, babe," Patrick promised. "You and me. We'll leave Giles and Knoxbury behind and ride Cameron's coattails all the way to the Supreme Court."

She couldn't tell where he was. The sound seemed to bounce off the trees, making it seem like his voice came from everywhere all at once. And then there was the sound of her heartbeat. It threatened to pound out of her chest, an alert to anyone and anything close that she was here and waiting to be taken down. Despite the cool evening air, she'd broken into a sweat. Her hand shook as she clutched the vial of pepper spray. She'd never used it before. Even in New York, she'd felt fairly safe.

"Or I can kill you here and frame the dumbass myself." Patrick moved from behind the tree. The darkness couldn't mask the self-satisfied smile on his face. "Guess your smarts don't win over my ambition after all."

But her pepper spray beat his gun because she didn't hesitate. She did exactly what the instruction manual had said. She sprayed, moving her hand back and forth in a waving motion.

Patrick screamed and the gun went off, narrowly missing her.

She took off because he was firing blind now. She ran as fast and hard as she could, looking back to see if he was coming.

And then the world tilted on its axis. Or at least that was the way it felt. Her foot hit a rock and she fell, her hands going out to catch herself, but she didn't hit the ground. Water filled her world. Cold and rushing fast. She hit the water and started to go under.

So freaking cold. She'd never felt cold permeate her skin the way the waters of the Rio Grande did. She tried to kick up. Her hand broke the surface all the way to her elbow. She could feel the air.

But she couldn't get to it. Her left foot moved freely, but her right foot had jammed when she fell. She was caught on a fallen log, her foot tangling in its branches, holding her under.

Panic swamped her every sense. Jesse was dying and so was she. How would Cade survive?

She pulled and pulled and tried to get her foot free. The sandal was stuck. And no one would know where she was. She would drown so close to the surface.

Air horn. It might not scare the freaking bears, but it could do what it had been made to do—alert someone to where she was.

It might be Patrick. Or it might be Henry. He could have come looking for her.

A bullet or a savior. Anything was better than dying like this. Cold and alone.

Live. Her one new mandate. She wasn't going to break it now. She dug into her bag, items she no longer needed floating away with the river.

She grabbed the air horn and let the rest go.

With one final hope, she thrust her arm up and pressed the button.

* * * *

Cade shot out of the truck the minute Nate hit the brakes.

"Goddamn it, Cade!"

He could hear Nate yelling, but he didn't care. In the distance, he saw red and blue flashing signals. Either the night shift at the sheriff's or Ty. God, he hoped it was Ty.

"We're over here." Nell was on her knees over a prone figure.

Jesse. Oh, his heart nearly stopped as he saw Jesse lying there on the ground. His best friend. His brother. Why the fuck had he left? It had been easier than staying. Easier than trying to be a better man. And now Jesse's blood soaked the ground around him.

Someone plowed through, shoving him to the side. Caleb Burke. He set his kit on the ground. "Baby, I need some light. Alexei, you keep anyone who fucking comes close off me."

Holly Lang stood over Jesse's body and shined a flashlight down. Jesse was pale in the light, blood staining his clothes.

Alexei tugged on Cade's shirt. "Come and allow doctor to work on friend."

"He's unconscious. GSW to the abdomen. It looks like another one grazed him, but it's nothing more than a burn. I need an ambulance. He needs surgery." Caleb turned his eyes up to Cade. "He's strong. Nell stopped a lot of the bleeding. I need to dig the bullet out and make sure he didn't nick any vitals. Ty was five minutes behind me. Go find Gemma. I've got him."

With a deep sigh of relief, he turned to Nell, who was talking to Nate and Cam.

She pointed toward the rear of her house. "I think they went to the backwoods. By the river."

The river. Every muscle in his body stiffened and his brain threatened to stop functioning. The river. It would always come back to her. Flashes of the night hit his brain. The cold. The dank air that filled his lungs before the water had rushed in. His sister's eyes as she died.

And none of it mattered. All that mattered was Gemma.

He calmly worked his way around the building as Nate and Cam planned a strategy. His strategy was to find Gemma and take any bullet that came her way. And to keep her away from the freaking river.

In the distance, he heard a voice talking. He couldn't discern the words, but it didn't matter. He took off. Nate was suddenly on his heels, and Cam managed to get in front of him. Cam ran like a freaking running back, sprinting ahead, his gun in his hand. Nate grabbed at Cade, forcing him to stop.

"You will not get killed while I'm on duty."

He tried to pull away. "Please. God, Nate, I love her. What would you do if it was Callie out there?"

"If I wasn't trained? I would let me do my goddamn job. That man has a gun and he's using it." Nate's face was fierce. "You stay here or I'll use mine on you and I will put your ass in jail for impeding the police."

Cade stopped. What was he doing? Charging in when he didn't

even have a gun. Hadn't he fucked up enough? Did he have to keep on doing it?

Cade sank to his knees in the soft dirt. He could smell the river, hear it rushing by. He was miles from the river he'd nearly lost his life in, but he'd never truly left it. He'd pretended to walk around and to smile and party and play all of life's games, but the best part of him had died that day.

He was back there. Nine years old and pissed off at the world because Annie always got all the attention. Annie was on drill team and got to be in the homecoming court, and who gave a shit about that? He'd come up with a plan. Annie got everything and he got nothing, so he'd left. Packed up his Power Rangers backpack and walked out of the house.

He hadn't counted on the rain. He hadn't counted on the storms that seemed to shake the whole earth that night. And he hadn't counted on his parents and Annie rushing to get him even though the storm should have kept them at home.

God. He'd killed them all because he was a brat who couldn't handle his sister's success. And she had nothing but a grave because he'd walked out.

He put his hands over his eyes. If Gemma died, nothing would matter. He should have been with her. He should have taken the bullet Jesse had taken. Jesse was the good one.

It was a weak sound that penetrated his ear. Like a shout from a muffled horn.

Cade brought his head up. Maybe he'd imagined it.

Nate walked out of the woods, his walkie-talkie in his hands. "Yeah, I'm going to need another bus. Don't hurry. He's a corpse. Henry Flanders says he tripped. No. I don't have eyes on Gemma. It looks like she ran. No blood trail."

Gemma got away?

There it was again. That weird sound. It was coming from his left. From the river.

"Cade, why don't you head home and check to see if Gemma ran back there," Nate said. "Patrick Welch is dead. He didn't have time to hide a body, and Henry says this whole episode lasted less than five minutes. She's gotta be hoofing it home."

Home. Gemma wouldn't go home. Gemma might lead a killer away from Jesse, but she would never run home when he was dying.

A third strangled sound was heard.

"Is that an air horn?" Nate asked. "Do we have kayakers in trouble? Who the hell gets on the river this late in the year? It's damn cold."

Cade took off running because he knew who it was. Gemma. Gemma, his always prepared, had-a-purse-bigger-than-a-damn-drugstore woman, was in the river and she was calling for help. For him.

He'd lost his life in a river in Florida. He'd clung to a tree limb, survival his only goal. He'd gone into the river a bratty kid and what they pulled out had been a zombie, a body that moved through life but didn't feel it.

Nancy cracked his shell, but he'd betrayed her.

Jesse wormed his way in.

Gemma. Gemma made him want to live again.

He saw it. A little white horn shining in the moonlight. She was under the water, her arm in the air, begging for help.

Without a second thought, he dove in. He hadn't swum in years, his fear of the water so strong it kept him away, but his parents had forced him to learn before and that training didn't go away.

His parents. His sister. Nancy, his not-mom who had loved him. They weren't ghosts who weighed him down. They'd loved him. He'd screwed up, but he hadn't meant to. He'd been a child. But a man went into the water this time. A man who loved a woman. A man who wouldn't come out again unless she was in his arms, whole and alive.

The water hit his system like an out-of-control freight train coming straight from the arctic. His skin burned where the water touched it, but the moon was high in the sky and the water was clear. He could see her.

She was caught and failing. Her foot had slipped between the branches of a log. She'd twisted and turned until she couldn't move, trapped in a deadly puzzle.

Her head came up, her eyes flaring with panic. She reached for him. He grabbed her arm and tried to pull, but she was well stuck. He pulled harder. And then again. Nothing. He was ready to pull her foot off. He didn't give a shit. He'd carry her around, but she had to get out of here. She was panicking. She refused to let go of his hand.

His lungs were burning so she had to be drowning. He braced himself against the log and pulled again with every ounce of strength he had. If she stayed here, he would, too. He would hold on and drown with her. He tugged until his lungs felt like they would explode and then finally Gemma moved, her body pulling free.

Another body entered the water, white washing all around. There was a great whoosh, the sound filling his ears. He clutched her, trying to get to the surface. Big hands came out, pulling at Gemma's body.

Cam. Cam was an athlete. Cam would take her. Cam could get her out.

Cade's job was done. He let her go. Cam immediately started swimming her to the surface.

Cade tried to follow, but he was stuck. The whole river was alive with things that pulled a person under. The river was hungry. Wanting.

And it was all right. Gemma was okay. Jesse would live. Cade could give in.

Or he could finally fucking fight. He'd spent too many years waiting for this. Longing for this. He'd waited for the water to take him. So easy. He wouldn't have to fight. Wouldn't have to hurt.

And he wouldn't be able to love.

Cade pulled, struggling. His pants were caught. Gemma was above. He should be above, too. He needed to be with Gemma. With Jesse. With his family.

His lungs were depleted. He couldn't breathe, but he wasn't done. He wanted Gemma. He wanted that family they could have. He wouldn't leave her alone. He would have his future. He would live.

There was another great white rush. Cam. His hand came out, reaching for him. Cade grabbed his hand and together they pulled. His jeans tore and he was free.

He broke the surface, the cold washing over him. Life rushed at him as he crawled up the banks of the river.

"We have her back. Breath sounds are good." Ty's voice broke through the quiet. There was the beautiful sound of coughing. "Let's move her. Get her to the hospital."

Cade let his head rest back. He was half frozen but it didn't matter. Gemma was good. Jesse was being taken care of. And he was alive.

Cam stared down at him. "Are you all right, man?"

Cade nodded. He was all right. He was fine. They were alive. His family was safe.

* * * *

Hours later, Cade sat by Gemma's bed, dreaming.

This time was different. He was in the river. He was nine, but there was none of the panic he always felt when he found himself trapped in this dream. The water surrounded him, but he knew. He would survive.

His sister wouldn't. He turned in his seat, no longer nine years old, but a man who could look at her with mature eyes. He'd made a child's mistake, and he missed his sister. He wished she'd lived, but she would have hated the way he'd stumbled through life. Annie would have taken it in both hands and not stopped until she'd drained it dry. Like Gemma. Annie would have adored Gemma.

He turned his head, the moonlight illuminating Annie's face. Where always she'd been panicked, now there was a small smile on her lips. Her light brown hair floated around her, giving her a halo. His sweet sister. His angel. Why had he ever thought she would want him to stay down here with her?

She reached for him, not to drag him down, but to touch him one last time. His parents were there, reaching for him, too, a final goodbye. And Nancy with her gentle smile. She'd taught him how to cook. She'd brought him together with his best friend.

He stayed there for a moment, the river now not such a terrible place to be. His former family was here. But he couldn't stay because all his tomorrows were above, in the air with Gemma and Jesse.

He held Annie's hand. Just for a moment because other hands reached for him, pulling him up, to the surface.

Where he belonged.

Chapter Twenty

"Holy shitballs, Nate. Think about it. Atlanto-occipital dislocation. Do you have any idea how few physicians see that in a lifetime? It's insanely rare. And who sees it? This guy. Right here in Bliss, Colorado. I know I complain about the autopsies, but this makes them all worthwhile."

Caleb's voice roused Gemma from her dreams. Her dreams where Jesse was alive and Cade didn't run. She kept her eyes shut, hoping to go back there.

"Caleb, I don't even know what that Atlanto thing is. Henry said the guy fell."

Caleb huffed. "You think the dude fell and internally decapitated himself? Seriously? Henry is lying. This is the kind of thing that happens when man meets bus or man meets ridiculously well-trained killer. I don't think Henry qualifies as mass transit."

Patrick was dead. Patrick hadn't gotten away. Apparently Henry had come after her and he'd taken out Patrick. She'd known deep down he hadn't always been a pacifist.

"Leave him be, man."

"Don't you want to know?" Caleb asked. "I could call my

brother. He's got serious connections. Henry isn't some professor. He's trained. He's either mafia, or more likely CIA. Henry fucking Flanders is ex-CIA. Come on. Don't you want to know?"

Gemma forced her eyes open. Henry had helped her, probably risking his relationship with his wife. She seriously doubted if Henry had a violent past that Nell knew about it. And it should stay that way. Bliss was a place for second chances. She should know. "Let him be. Henry has his secrets. Let him keep them."

Caleb frowned, striding to her, checking all the monitors hooked up to her body. "Gemma, you're in the hospital."

Yeah, the stark white all around her and the fact that the temperature was twenty degrees below comfortable told her that. She groaned. "I can't afford the hospital."

Caleb smiled, a rarity. "Oh, this particular stay is all paid up, Gemma. Look around."

Her head throbbed, but she forced herself to sit up. The room was filled with flowers. Lilies and roses and gardenias and pansies and daisies. It was like someone had bought out a florist. "What the hell?"

The door to her hospital room opened and two unfamiliar men entered. One was a tall, muscular man wearing a Western shirt and jeans. Well-worn cowboy boots were on his feet and a Stetson clung to his head. He was probably in his early forties, and most certainly a man in his prime. The other man was a younger version of the first, though he wore slacks and a collared shirt. She would guess they were brothers since they seemed too close in age to be anything else.

"Gemma Wells," the first man said, a warm smile on his face. "It is a pleasure to meet you. I'm Jack Barnes."

The big cowboy held a hand out and she shook it, trying to figure out why the man was acting like she was a rock star or something.

The younger of the two men took his brother's place, offering his own hand. "And I'm this one's brother. Lucas O'Malley. Damn, it's good to meet you. We heard the news and hopped on a plane as quickly as we could. It helps when you've got a billionaire friend who has planes waiting around."

"I'm confused." Suddenly there were billionaires? Maybe she wasn't awake yet.

Nate moved to the side of her bed. "Nell figured it all out. She's

279

been on the news networks explaining to everyone that Senator Allen Cameron bribed an EPA official and then paid to have you killed."

"It's all over the news," Caleb continued. "Cameron's had to pull out of the race. There's going to be an inquest, and everyone is talking about jail time for the senator and several members of his team."

He sounded like an asshole, but then she was pretty sure asshole was part of the job description for politician.

"Good for Nell. It does not explain why two men I've never met before are here in my room, a room I might add that they're going to be charging me way more than a motel for." Gemma shook her head. "This is from the networks?"

"No," the man named Jack Barnes replied. "This is from me and my brother. Don't worry at all about the hospital bill. I'm going to take care of it."

Lucas stood beside his brother. "Senator Cameron was our father. Not that he was much of a father. Jack here was born out of wedlock and quickly abandoned. I was not so lucky. The old goat raised me, if the definition of raising a child is sending him to boarding school after boarding school and only paying attention to him when he acts out."

Jack grimaced. "You'll have to forgive my brother. He's still got issues."

"Many of which are solved by watching the old man get his ass burned." Lucas's smile lit up the room. "He was going to run for president and I was worried he was going to win. He's polling well in the primaries. Or rather he was. He has to drop out now. I'm so happy. I'm actually a little dizzy with it."

Jack shook his head, though there was great affection for his brother in that expression. "We're all thrilled someone finally caught dear old dad with his hands in the cookie jar. We've always known how corrupt he was and I was not looking forward to four to eight years of having his face on my television during every news broadcast."

"They're grateful," Nate said. "And, Gemma, Barnes paid your hospital bills, all of them. And Jesse's."

Jesse was alive? Tears pricked her eyes. "Jesse?"

Caleb gave her hand a reassuring squeeze. Apparently getting to view and catalog an internal decapitation helped with his bedside manner. "It looked worse than it was. He was lucky. No serious damage. I'm keeping the both of you here strictly for observation. And because Barnes has a big wallet."

Jack smiled. "Hospital stays for everyone, and I will tell them to give you double the lime Jell-O."

He was okay. She took a deep breath, tears threatening to overtake her. Jesse was alive.

Nate pointed to the bed next to hers. "He's been here the whole time. Your mom and Naomi took him out for some fresh air. He wouldn't leave until Caleb promised him you would be alive when he came back. He's a little paranoid."

The door opened and Jesse's smiling face came into view. He was in a wheelchair being pushed by her mom.

"You're awake. Baby, you have no idea how happy I am to see you." He motioned for her mom to stop and got to his feet.

Her heart soared. He was alive and here. "Should you be walking?"

Caleb gave her a smile. "He's good. After a week or so he won't even notice he was injured. He lost some blood and a tiny section of his liver. But don't worry. That grows back. Seriously, as bullets go, he took a good one. He won't even have a big scar. I was able to use the robot."

Jesse shuffled her way, his eyes gleaming. "I wouldn't miss my wedding day."

Jack reached a hand out. "I will be sending you and your fiancé a very nice gift. Thank you both for helping bring this to light."

Jesse shook his hand and then Lucas's.

"I think the whole country is going to thank you because now we can focus all our attention on that senator from New York." Jack put a hand on his brother's shoulder and started for the door.

Lucas nodded. "Hayes. I like him. And hey, he never disinherited me so there's that." When he got to the door he turned around. "And Ms. Wells, I would love to talk to you about taking a place in my firm. We're in Dallas. We're a boutique firm representing some wealthy clientele. I think you would be an excellent fit and our compensation packages are amazing. Think about it. And again, thank you."

She watched the door close, turning her attention back to the people who had stayed in the room.

Her mom and Jesse and Naomi surrounded her with love. She accepted it all. But something was missing. She looked up at Jesse. "Is Cade gone?"

He sighed and sat down on the bed beside her. "Baby, he saved you. I'll tell you the whole story, but as to whether or not he's staying, I don't know."

Her mom smoothed back her hair. "He came in with you. He stayed here all night long, sitting right there and holding your hand."

Naomi frowned. "But this morning after Caleb assured him you were both okay, he had me take him to that bar. He said he had something to do. I haven't seen him since."

Jesse put an arm around her. "It's going to be okay. If he leaves, that's on him. We'll be fine. And someone named Knoxbury from your old firm called. From what we can tell, Patrick was working alone and without their knowledge. Apparently they do want you back. So this Lucas guy offered you a job. Does that mean we're moving to Dallas?"

She couldn't even conceive of moving. This was her home. Patrick was wrong. She did belong here. "Nope. I don't want to move. And I heard a rumor that in a month or so, my health benefits should kick in and I won't need rich guys to rush in and save me."

Nate smiled. "Uhm, I wouldn't say that. Those benefits are not that great. But I'm happy to hear I don't need another office manager. You don't have any other crazy stalker person in your past, do you?"

She couldn't say that with any real promise. "Hopefully not. And I might have to go part time because I'm getting my license to practice in Colorado and then I'm going to challenge the county ordinance."

"Thereby giving the mayor a heart attack. Nice, Gemma," Caleb said.

One by one they all left and others took their places. The whole town came out to say hello.

She was surrounded by friends and loved ones. But the one she needed to see didn't walk through her door.

Late that night, she carefully cuddled against Jesse and slept and dreamed of a world where Cade didn't leave.

* * * *

Cade stood outside the door and wondered why he was so damn nervous. They were just beyond the door. He'd spent two days getting everything ready, and now the fact that he'd only talked to Gemma on the phone hit him.

He'd known she was okay. He'd even talked to the doc to make sure everything would be fine.

He'd wanted everything to be perfect when he saw Gemma again. But now he wondered if he hadn't screwed up. What if she didn't like what he'd done? What if she was pissed that he hadn't stayed here in the hospital with her?

Just for a second he hesitated, falling back into old habits. But he was done with that. If she was pissed, she could yell at him and he would take it. The one thing he wouldn't do was let her go.

He pushed through the door, and his heart swelled as he saw Gemma buttoning up Jesse's shirt. He was grumbling something about being able to do it himself, but Cade noticed he wasn't trying too hard.

Gemma's eyes came up. "Cade."

Jesse turned, too, his eyes infinitely harder than hers. "You came back."

"I never left," he admitted.

Jesse stood. "She's been in the hospital for two days and you've only been to see her once."

Yep. He'd fucked up. And he'd been evasive about why he wasn't around. He'd wanted to make it a surprise.

"That's not true." Gemma turned to him. "He's come in the middle of the night. My mom told me he came that first night, but left before I woke up, and then I seem to remember having a dream about him last night. It wasn't a dream was it?"

She'd woken up, groggy and so tired she couldn't stay awake for long. He'd been sitting there watching her. He'd tucked her back in and cuddled her back to sleep. He was kind of glad she remembered.

He'd had to leave early. He'd had to go all the way to Colorado Springs to do what he needed to do.

"Where the hell have you been?" Jesse didn't seem impressed. He got to his feet with no trouble.

Cade hoped that was the case because he'd already talked to Doc Burke, and Gemma was in the clear for some playtime. Turned out the doctor had kept her in the hospital more for Jesse's sake than her own.

But Gemma still looked fragile. Maybe he should simply take her home and put her in bed.

"Are you going to answer me?" Jesse asked.

"Stop." Gemma got between the two of them, but not the way Cade wanted her. "He's here. Let him be."

"I don't know that's going to work for me." Jesse's eyes were lasers threatening to take Cade out. "I wanted a partner, not someone who shows up for sex every now and then."

He deserved that so he didn't put a fist through Jesse's face. "I've been in Colorado Springs taking out a couple of loans. And you might have only wanted one partner, but now you have two."

Jesse's brows rose in obvious surprise. "What?"

This was the part that hopefully didn't get him killed. He was making a lot of decisions that he probably shouldn't be making, but he needed them to know he was in. "We're buying into Long-Haired Roger's shop. He's agreed. It's going to be Roger and Sons from now on. I know we're not really his sons, but he says he thinks of us that way and he can't leave the business to Princess Two. Though he tried. If he outlives that dog, you should know she becomes our legal property, and there's a whole list of crap that animal needs including something about expressing some sort of sac that sounds god-awful. Let's keep Roger alive."

"How did you do that?" Jesse stared at him, his mouth slightly open in shock.

"Well, first off, I sold the Camaro."

Jesse gasped. "Your dad's car? But you've kept that for years. You spent so much time rebuilding it. Why would you do that?"

"To pay off Gemma's medical bills before I left town for good," he explained.

They both started talking at once, Jesse promising a good ass kicking and Gemma trying to give him logic.

"Stop. I'm not leaving. I'm not going anywhere. But once I figured out Gemma's bills had been paid, I thought I should put the money to better use. So I talked to Roger, and we'll go full time and he's going to start taking more jobs, including restoration jobs and custom bikes. We're buying the new equipment we need. Roger gives us the space to work. And"—he took a deep breath—"I also bought Holly Lang's old cabin. Doc Burke bought a big place on the mountain as an engagement present and they moved in yesterday. We still owe a lot on it, but it's ours and it came fully furnished."

They both stared, and Cade sincerely hoped they weren't going to walk out on him. He talked as quickly as he could, praying they would listen. "Look, if you don't like it we can always talk to Doc, and he'll probably give us the down payment back, but I like the valley and I think it's a great place. The cabin is small, but when we're ready, we can add on. We have river access and the views are spectacular, and Gemma's mom is right down the road and it's normally fairly safe and it's not far from work."

"Shut up." Gemma stared at him intently.

He closed his mouth, looking at Jesse, whose frown had been replaced with a big smile. But Gemma kept staring at him.

"You really bought us a cabin of our own?" she asked.

"Yeah. I know I should have talked about it, but someone else was interested and I had to move fast and…"

"Shut up."

He stopped.

Gemma walked up to him, her lips curving in a smile. "Well, then, Cade Sinclair. I suspect you should take us home."

One more damn confession. This was the worst of all. "I traded the bike for a car. A piece of crap, probably will break down in a heartbeat Jeep."

She gasped. "You traded your Harley?"

It hadn't been hard to part with it. "I bought that bike as a symbol. I was going to be free. But I don't want to be free and you can't put a baby seat on the back of a bike. And the three of us can't ride together on a bike, so I traded it in. Got a horrible deal."

Her smile nearly lit up his world. "Well, you'll have to let me do the negotiating from now on. Won't you?"

He would give it all up to her. "Damn straight."

"Speaking of negotiations, so let me see, you come with a tiny cabin, a half-baked business idea, a shitty Jeep, and a ton of debt," she pointed out.

Yeah, put that way he didn't sound like a premier catch. Still. "Marry me."

She tilted her head up. "You know I never turn down a good deal. Yes."

He kissed her soundly as Jesse slapped him on the back and joined in.

Chapter Twenty-One

Gemma sighed as Cade carried her over the threshold of their brand-new, slightly ragged and all theirs cabin. This place was hers. A place to build on. A place to raise their family.

"I get to carry her next time," Jesse groused as he followed behind, but there was a smile on his face that belied his words.

"I'm only carrying her this time because I'm not the one who got shot," Cade explained.

Jesse merely shrugged. "Fine, next time you get to be shot."

God, she hoped there wasn't a next time. "Stop talking about the very scary past and kiss me."

Cade set her on her feet, and his lips brushed hers. "Love you, G."

Just like that her world went dreamy and everything seemed more beautiful than it had been before. "Love you, too."

Jesse rested his head against hers, his front cradling her back. "I love you so much. We both do."

He and Cade exchanged a long look. It was a look between partners, one she couldn't ever hope to fully understand, but she appreciated it. It meant they would love her and take care of her and share the burdens and joys that came with being a family.

She looked around, and Cade had been busy with more than the bank. "You moved everything in here." Her pictures were already up. She had no doubt all their clothes had been brought in and put away. Instant home from her side, but for Cade it had been hours and hours of work. For her. For them.

"I wanted us to be able to get to the good part right away." Cade lifted her up again, cradling her in his arms.

"Damn straight, partner. I haven't been inside her for days. I couldn't get her to do it in the hospital." Jesse followed behind as Cade made his way to the bedroom.

Jesse had tried. As soon as he could walk freely, he'd been in her bed, kissing and teasing and nearly tearing his tiny stitches. "You were shot a couple of days ago."

"In the gut, baby. Not in the cock. The cock is perfectly fine and ready to go." Jesse had the biggest grin on that handsome face. He hadn't seen a razor in days, and it looked so hot on him.

"Gemma, are you in charge in the bedroom?" Cade asked, his voice harder than she could remember. His jaw was a gorgeous hard line.

She didn't want to be in charge in the bedroom. Everywhere else, yeah. She was that kind of girl. But not here. Here she wanted her men to be in control. Both of them. "No, I'm not."

Cade kicked open the door to their bedroom. He'd been hard at work here, too. She nearly cried at the sight of the bed. It was covered with a pretty quilt and strewn with wildflowers. Purple blossoms made a lovely pattern across the bed. She'd been given beautiful flowers before, but these had been picked by his hand especially for her. These were the loveliest thing she'd ever seen.

"You're not in charge. And you would do well to remember that, baby." He set her on her feet. "And I wouldn't do anything to jeopardize Jesse's health. I talked to Doc, who is way too comfortable discussing this shit. I'm serious. He will throw down some sex talk, man. Unfortunately, being on the bottom would be rough on him."

Jesse fist pumped. "I have always wanted to fuck that pretty ass. Yes."

Cade sighed. "Yep, Doc suggested you take the anal. In those words."

Gemma's whole face went up in flames. Caleb Burke knew way too much about her sex life and that was okay. Anything was okay as long as she got what she needed, and what she needed was to be between her men.

Jesse's eyes went dark, his voice a deep, sensual temptation. "Take off those clothes. Now."

She wasn't about to refuse him. Or Cade. They were her heroes. Her future. Her husbands. She slowly pulled off her T-shirt, revealing the utilitarian lines of her bra. She would have been self-conscious before, believing she needed to think and act a certain way to be sexy, but they had taught her all she needed to be was herself. That was the way it worked when people were in love.

She dropped the shirt and unhooked the bra, reveling in the way they looked at her. Hungry, loving predators waiting to eat her up.

"Fuck, I can't wait." Jesse moved in, his hand going to her breasts.

Cade started shedding his clothes, too. "And I want to start going to Mountain and Valley every now and then. I like being naked. I really like being naked with Gemma."

Jesse got to his knees, his mouth closing over a nipple. He sucked it in hard, tonguing her.

Cade moved that gorgeous body of his around to her back, his fingers catching on the waist of her jeans. "Time for these to go, baby. You won't need clothes tonight."

"Maybe for a while," Jesse agreed.

Cade dragged her jeans down her hips, his palms molding every inch of her. "We are going to fuck you so hard, G. You've never been fucked quite like we're going to fuck you tonight."

One in her pussy. One in her ass. All of her surrounded by her men. Her pussy responded to the idea, pulsing and aching, getting slippery wet.

Cade forced the jeans off, helping her balance before shoving them to the side. He came back up, gently turning her head to the side and taking her mouth in a ravenous kiss. His tongue plunged in, rubbing against hers as Jesse bit her nipple, an erotic pain.

When Cade came up for air, he looked down at his partner. "How should we get this woman of ours ready for taking us?"

A slow, slightly sadistic, completely sexy smile crossed Jesse's lips. "Oh, we need to warm her up."

Cade's hand slid to her backside, cupping the cheeks of her ass and squeezing. "You heard the man, Gemma. On the floor. Hands and knees."

A little shiver went through her as she dropped down in front of Jesse. When she was on her knees, Jesse tangled his hand in her hair, forcing her head back. "You're mine. Say it. Say you belong to Jesse McCann."

Such a damn Neanderthal. And she wouldn't have it any other way. She was done with polite, passionless partnerships. She wanted this. She wanted everything they could give her. "I belong to Jesse McCann."

There was a sharp slap to her backside as Cade growled a little. "You left something out, baby."

Well, of course she had. "And Cade. I belong to Cade Sinclair."

She didn't need to ask who they belonged to. She knew. They'd been hers before she'd thought to ask. They had given her so much, taught her how to love, what was really worth fighting for. They had brought her back to life.

"Damn straight," Cade replied. "Now get that pretty ass in the air."

Jesse moved, drawing off his clothes. She turned her eyes up, not wanting to miss a moment of the show. Jesse's body was all lean muscle and tight flesh. Her eyes caught on the small wound a few inches below his ribs on the right side. It was neatly bandaged, but she knew how close he'd come. He'd almost died.

Jesse looked down at her, his eyes softening for a moment. "I'm all right now, darlin'. I'm here and I'm not going anywhere. I'm going to be right here with you for the rest of our lives. That's a promise."

Jesse McCann kept his promises.

And he'd been right about his dick. It showed absolutely no evidence of any damage to that part of his body. His cock stood straight up, long and thick and proud. All of that was for her.

"Eyes front, darling."

But she was happy looking at his cock.

"Cade?"

Smack. She nearly screamed at the nice slap Cade gave her ass. Heat flushed through her system, lighting up her every nerve. She moved her eyes to the front, focusing on the wall of the bedroom. Cade had moved her bookshelf over, carefully placing all her law books back in the exact way she'd had them.

"Now that's better. Cade, have you ever seen a more perfect ass than this?"

"Never in all my travels. This is absolutely the prettiest ass I've seen. Spread your knees, G. I want to be able to see your pussy, too."

She widened her stance, cool air brushing against her hot pink parts. Her pussy wanted, waiting for the moment when they would fill her up.

"There it is." Jesse's voice washed over her. He was close. She couldn't see him, but it felt like he was on his knees behind her, so close to her skin. She gasped as his fingertips brushed her pussy, causing her to wiggle. "Cade."

Smack. He slapped her other cheek, his hand sending heat through her. The initial feel was shocking, painful, and then it sank in like a dark temptation. Cade smacked her ass twice more, moving around, spreading the heat. "Don't move. This is our playtime."

Hers, too. She needed this after all the days of worry and the horror of that night. She needed to float away to a nice, safe place. She was still when all she wanted to do was force Jesse's fingers deep inside.

"That's better. This is what we want, darlin'. We love our hell-raising Gemma, but here, we want our sweet plaything." Jesse's fingers made soft patterns across her exposed pussy. "And you like it like this. At least your pussy does. Look at all that juice."

Her pussy was wet. So wet. It had been since the minute she'd realized they could make love. And Jesse was right. She'd missed this side of herself, longed for it. She'd always wanted this but hadn't found anyone to share it with.

"See what a good girl gets," Cade said before she felt the heat of a mouth closing over her pussy.

It took everything she had not to scream and thrust back, but all she would have gotten was another smack and then that deeply talented tongue would be gone. She wouldn't do anything to make that tongue go away.

Cade's tongue. She knew that because Jesse spoke. "I hope you brought everything we needed."

"Nightstand," Cade said briefly, before plunging back in.

He licked at her labia, dragging his tongue from her clit to the bottom of her pussy before plundering inside. He fucked her with his tongue, taking her higher and higher.

"Come for me. Come on, G. Give it to me." He thrust his tongue back in, fucking her in smooth strokes while he fingered her clit.

Gemma let go. The orgasm rushed along her skin.

"That's what I wanted." The warmth of Cade's tongue fled. "Now it's time to get this pretty ass ready."

She shivered as one of her men held her cheeks open while the other dribbled cool lubricant right onto her asshole.

"You're going to grip me so good, darlin'. I can't wait to fuck this ass." Jesse's fingers slipped over her tight hole.

Cade got to his knees in front of her. "I'm going to give you something to focus on while Jesse gets you ready. Come on, baby. Suck me down."

His cock came into view, decadent and delicious with a nice drop of cream on top. Jesse rimmed her asshole, the sensation so dark she had to force herself to breathe. She leaned over and licked Cade's cockhead. She was rewarded with a long groan of pleasure.

"I love the way you suck cock, G."

She did it like she did everything else. She gave it her all. She lapped at the head and then concentrated on sucking him down. Over and over she whirled her tongue around as she sucked down and then up, glorying in the sounds he made.

All the while, Jesse pressed his fingers in, opening her wider and wider. She was stretched by his fingers, forcing her open.

His finger finally slipped in and Jesse fucked her ass, readying her.

Cade gripped her hair as she brought him to the back of her throat, ready to taste him.

Cade pulled back, his breath sawing in and out of his chest. "Not tonight. Tonight, I'm coming in your pussy. Come on."

Cade pulled her up, drawing her close as she heard Jesse retreat to the bathroom. "You're everything to me. I love you. You're it for me."

She wrapped her arms around his hard chest. It was all she could have hoped for. "I love you, too. You and Jesse are my whole world."

He smiled, his face glowing with happiness. "We're getting married."

He lifted her and turned, falling onto the bed and carrying her with him. Jesse was back, two condoms in hand. He tossed one to Cade. "Just until we're ready."

Cade had the condom on his cock in no time. "Come on, baby. Fuck me. Ride my cock."

She moved into place, astride him, lining his cock up and sliding home. He felt so good, filling her up.

"Just a little more, darlin'." Jesse's hand pressed against her back, pushing her on top of Cade. Their chests nestled together as Jesse lubed up his cock. "This is what we want. All of us together."

She nearly forgot to breathe as Jesse's cock pressed against her asshole. He was so much bigger than the fingers he'd used before. But it had to work. She wouldn't let it not work. "Tell me what to do."

"Press back against me. Help me slide in." His fingers squeezed her hips, rotating as he tried to gently move inside.

Gemma took a deep breath and then pressed back, glorying in the burn as his cock pressed past the tight ring of her ass. A fullness like nothing she'd ever felt encompassed her world. It wasn't pain alone or pleasure, but a jangly mixture of both.

Jesse groaned. "Damn, that's perfect."

Cade had the sweetest grin on his face. "You're perfect, G."

She knew she wasn't, but these men made her feel like she was. That was all a woman could ask. They were perfect for her. She tested out this new connection, pressing back against Jesse, taking his cock deep in her ass.

And that was all it took. She'd made a monster. Two in fact. They were off. Cade fucked upward, his cock burying itself in her pussy while Jesse lit up every inch of her ass as he pulled out almost to the rim. Over and over they pushed and pulled and plied her this way and that.

She was exactly what they'd claimed she would be—a sweet doll passed between them. But she was a woman and she was loved, so loved. Her heart swelled as they made love to her. This was what she'd needed all along. To live. To love.

The orgasm seemed to come from all sides. Every way she turned she found pleasure. She clenched down, tightening as the orgasm took her, and both of her men fell. Jesse shouted out her name as he filled her ass. Cade pulled her down for a kiss, his hips jerking, giving up everything he had.

She sank down, happy exhaustion threatening to take over as they landed in a heap, a joyous tangle of arms and legs.

And then someone knocked on her door.

"Hey!" Callie's voice drifted through the house. "We thought we'd have a little dinner party to welcome you all to the valley since it seems like Jesse and Cade are moving in!"

Jesse groaned. Cade cursed under his breath, but Gemma smiled because they were being welcomed to the valley.

And the valley was her home.

Nell and Henry return in a special prequel novel *Once Upon a Time in Bliss*, now available.

Author's Note

I'm often asked by generous readers how they can help get the word out about a book they enjoyed. There are so many ways to help an author you like. Leave a review. If your e-reader allows you to lend a book to a friend, please share it. Go to Goodreads and connect with others. Recommend the books you love because stories are meant to be shared. Thank you so much for reading this book and for supporting all the authors you love!

Sign up for Lexi Blake's newsletter
and be entered to win a $25 gift certificate
to the bookseller of your choice.

Join us for news, fun, and exclusive content
including free short stories.

There's a new contest every month!

Go to www.LexiBlake.net to subscribe.

Siren Unleashed

Texas Sirens Book 7
By Lexi Blake writing as Sophie Oak

Detectives Ben and Chase Dawson have been sent to investigate an unusual murder at an exclusive resort owned by Julian Lodge. The prime suspect is a young woman who was the last person to see the victim alive. Julian wants them to ensure her safety while also conducting the investigation. The job seems simple enough, until Ben and Chase discover that the beautiful woman they have both come to desire has dark secrets.

Natalie Buchanan came to the Willow Fork Tranquility Spa seeking sanctuary after escaping the clutches of a twisted sadist. Working as a massage therapist at the resort has given her a chance to heal. It also offers her an opportunity to reconnect to the lifestyle she thought she would never be comfortable in again. But when one of her regular clients ends up dead on her table, Natalie fears that the monster she once escaped has come back to claim her.

As Natalie rediscovers her own power, all three will be forced to confront her past.

About Lexi Blake

Lexi Blake is the author of contemporary and urban fantasy romance. She started publishing in 2011 and has gone on to sell over two million copies of her books. Her books have appeared twenty-six times on the *USA Today*, *New York Times*, and *Wall Street Journal* bestseller lists. She lives in North Texas with her husband, kids, and two rescue dogs.

Connect with Lexi online:

Facebook: www.facebook.com/lexi.blake.39
Website: www.LexiBlake.net
Instagram: www.instagram.com/Lexi4714
Twitter: twitter.com/authorlexiblake
Pinterest: www.pinterest.com/lexiblake39/

Sign up for Lexi's free newsletter at www.LexiBlake.net.

CPSIA information can be obtained
at www.ICGtesting.com
Printed in the USA
LVHW09203627 1120
672855LV00001B/25